A TRIO ... TREASUR ... SILVERBERG

*One of the most notable contributers to Ace Books' science fiction double novel series of the 1950s and 1960s was Science Fiction Grand Master **Robert Silverberg,** who graced Ace's pages with a dozen novels over a seven-year period, 1957-1964. In this, the second of two Armchair Fiction "Masters of Science Fiction" volumes covering these works, you'll be treated to three more of Bob's rousing, thought-provoking Ace novels: **"The Planet Killers," "The Plot Against Earth,"** and **"One of Our Asteroids is Missing."** All three are wonderful tales that kept sci-fi enthusiasts of the day on the edge of their seats. Not surprisingly, these stories still stand up today.*

*Also included in this volume is a **Silverberg Ace Cover Gallery,** showing the wonderful artwork that accompanied many of Bob's Ace novels. Featured are two of the best science fiction artists of the day, Ed Emshwiller and Ed Valigursky.*

*And finally, as we did in our first volume, we've thrown in two more Silverberg bonus tales, **"Death's Planet"** and **"The Assassin,"** both not seen in print in decades. Both tales come with their original illustrations.*

ABOUT ROBERT SILVERBERG...

While he was still in college in the mid-1950s, Robert Silverberg (1935–) began writing stories for sci-fi magazines like *Amazing Stories, Astounding Science Fiction, Fantastic, Science Fiction Adventures, Super-Science Fiction,* and many others. Soon he was issuing novels to the sci-fi publishers of the day: Ace Books, Avalon Books, Gnome Press, etc. He has gone on to author over a hundred science fiction and fantasy novels, including "A Time of Changes," "Roma Eterna," "The Last Song of Orpheus," and the bestselling Majipoor cycle, and is widely regarded today as one of the all-time greatest science fiction and fantasy writers. He is also author of more than sixty nonfiction works, in addition to editing or co-editing sixty-plus anthologies. He has won five Nebula Awards, four Hugo Awards, and the Prix Tour-Apollo Award. In 1999, Robert Silverberg was inducted into the Science Fiction Hall of Fame, and in 2004, the Science Fiction and Fantasy Writers of America presented him with the prestigious Damon Knight Memorial Grand Master Award.

TABLE OF CONTENTS:

MASTERS OF SCIENCE FICTION

Volume 12

ROBERT SILVERBERG:
The Ace Years, Part Two

ARMCHAIR FICTION
PO Box 4369, Medford, Oregon 97504

The original texts of these stories were first published by Ace Books, Headline Productions for *Super-Science Fiction,* and Greenleaf Publishing for *Imaginative Tales.*

All copyrights renewed by Robert Silverberg

Armchair Edition, Copyright 2017 by Gregory J. Luce
All Rights Reserved

For more information about Armchair Books and products, visit our website at…

www.armchairfiction.com

Or email us at…

armchairfiction@yahoo.com

The Planet Killers

CHAPTER ONE

Roy Gardner paused for a moment outside Security Chief Karnes' office, making sure his uniform was straight. Karnes had sent for him with only an hour's notice. That was fairly little time to get spruced up for an audience with your superior officer.

Besides which, Gardner had no idea why he was wanted. You never did, when you worked for Security. They sent you a message, or they buzzed you on the phone and said, "Karnes wants to see you," and you hopped to it. Security Chief Karnes was not a man who enjoyed being kept waiting.

Gardner stepped into the scanning field outside Karnes' office. The green glow bathed him for a moment, simultaneously checking his face against the master files and examining him for concealed weapons. Then the door rolled silently back.

Security Chief Karnes sat in the curve of a kidney-shaped desk, smiling pleasantly. He was a man still in his prime, no more than fifty-five. He had held his dreaded post as Chief of the Terran Security Service for fifteen years, and probably would hold it for three decades yet to come. Karnes was thin-faced and youthful-looking, with a bristly crop of copper-colored hair, and black eyes like little marbles.

"Come in, Roy," he said with warmth.

Gardner stood stiffly at attention in front of Karnes' desk. A quick gesture from Karnes relaxed his posture. Karnes did not insist on strict military bearing, provided nobody took it upon himself to deviate from the rules until receiving the Chief's permission.

"Sit down, Roy. I hate to have a man stand like a ramrod while I'm trying to talk to him."

"Thank you, sir."

Gardner lowered himself into a webchair to the left of Karnes' desk. The Security Chief riffled through some sheets of paper, found the one he wanted, and swung round to face Gardner.

"Roy, how much do you know about the planet named Lurion?"

"Very little, sir," Gardner admitted. It didn't pay to bluff knowledge with the Chief. "It's the fourth world of the Betelgeuse system, isn't it? Inhabited by humanoids. That's about all I can tell you, sir."

Karnes nodded. "The galaxy is full of worlds. You aren't expected to know everyone of them in detail. And you've given the essential information here. However, there's one additional fact about Lurion that you ought to know; and that's why you're here." Karnes tapped the sheet of paper in his hand. "We've been studying Lurion very closely. We've run some probability checks with the master computer. In sixty-seven years, plus or minus eight months," Karnes said, frowning heavily, "Lurion will launch an all-out war against the Solar System. During this war, Earth will be totally destroyed and heavy losses will be inflicted on Mars, Venus, and the other planets of this system."

Gardner started. "Earth *...destroyed?*"

"So the computer says."

"That's a nasty idea, the destruction of Earth. If the machine's telling the truth, that is."

"Truth? Truth is a concept that has meaning only when you talk about time past, and sometimes not even then. We're talking about the future. The computer says the attack *will* happen—if we allow it to take place. Do you think we dare risk it?"

"Oh," Gardner said softly. He leaned back in the firm webchair, watching Karnes very carefully. Around him, the computer system of Earth Central clicked and murmured. A bright bank of cryotronic tubes glared at Gardner from the wall.

Gardner crossed one uniformed leg over the other and waited. It didn't take a million-cryotron calculator to guess what Karnes was aiming at, but Gardner had long since learned to let Earth's Chief of Security have his own way in presenting a situation.

Karnes rubbed his cheekbones, a gesture that accented his gaunt angularity. He said, "According to the best figures we have, there are some three billion people living on Lurion."

"Half Earth's current population," Gardner said.

Karnes smiled coldly. "Ah, yes. Now, you realize that among Lurion's three billion people there are some who will be the parents of those who will aid in Earth's destruction sixty-seven years from now. The seeds of the conflict have already been planted. Probability says that if we sit back and do nothing, we will be destroyed. Therefore, naturally, we'll have to take preventive measures against Lurion."

Sweat started to roll down Gardner's face. "What sort of preventive measures are planned, sir?"

"Total destruction of Lurion, of course."

Gardner had seen it coming almost from the beginning of the conversation, but still the naked bluntness of the statement rocked him.

He studied his superior closely. Karnes didn't look much like the sort of man who could order the death of a planet, Gardner thought. Karnes didn't seem to have the necessary inner hardness, despite the precise angularity of his face and bearing. But you could never tell about people, it seemed.

Besides, Karnes wouldn't have to do the job himself; it was merely his decision to make. He would aim the gun, but someone else would have to pull the trigger.

Gardner said, "And suppose the computer is wrong?"

Karnes shrugged. "Worlds have died unjustly before, you know. The universe is unsentimental. A minor readjustment in the metabolism of a solar furnace, a flare of energy, and a totally innocent world dies."

"Of novas, yes. Natural causes. But this is entirely different. It's murder, isn't it?"

"In self-defense."

"Self-defense *before* a hostile blow has been struck?" Gardner asked.

Karnes looked displeased. "Thanks to modern computer science, it's no longer necessary to wait for the first blow to be struck. But you're forcing me to rationalize, Roy, and I don't want to have to do that. Let me make the situation absolutely clear: *we will never know* if the computer was wrong. If we destroy Lurion, there will be no war two generations hence. Therefore, we'll have to assume for the sake of our souls that the computer is telling us the truth."

"A tremendous assumption."

"I know that," Karnes said.

The Security Chief sighed. For a moment his professional guard was down, and Gardner saw beyond the mask to the inner man, burdened with guilt for the dreadful deed he had resolved to do. Pulling the trigger, Gardner thought, was perhaps not the worst of it. The man who aimed, who chose the victim, perhaps had more to justify to his soul.

"So Lurion will be destroyed."

"Lurion *must* be destroyed; otherwise Earth will be. We can't consider any alternatives to that set of statements. Either them or us, and we have to pray that we're more worthy of surviving than they are. From what I know of Lurion," Karnes said, "I think we are." He smiled grimly. "All right. By now you know why I've called you in here. You've been picked for the job."

Gardner said nothing. He stared at the thick red carpeting on the floor of the Chief's office.

Karnes added, "I might as well tell you that I don't think you're the man for the job; the computer does, though."

Coming so quickly, the snapper nearly threw Gardner.

"Sir?"

"I didn't think you could handle it," Karnes said. "You think too much. You're liable to get bogged down in conceptual syllogisms when an ethical choice is handed to you. But on the other hand, you're capable and you know how to handle yourself. I thought that your intellectual side would weigh down your active side and make you worthless for this job. But I fed your tape to the machine anyway. The machine says you're the best man we have. Well, I defer to its judgment."

Gardner blinked. He knew he was on the spot. He could beg off, on moral and ethical grounds, but that would accomplish nothing but the shattering of his career. Lurion had to be destroyed, in the opinion of Security Chief Karnes, and Lurion *would* be destroyed—if not by Gardner then by someone else.

He examined himself, wondering if he actually could do the job. He decided that he *could* if he sincerely felt that the future of Earth depended on it. So the computer was right, and Karnes wrong.

God help me, Gardner thought.

Out loud he said hoarsely, "All right. I accept the assignment."

"Thanks, Gardner."

"No thanks necessary, sir. You're asking me to do a job. I'll do it. Let it end there."

"As you wish."

Glowering across the desk at the Security Chief, Gardner asked, "How's it going to be done, and when do I leave?"

"You'll be in charge of a team of five," Karnes said. "You'll leave practically at once. Come with me and I'll see that you get briefed on the full picture."

In an office somewhere in the depths of the Security building, they gave Gardner the details of the project. The planet would be destroyed by a resonating circuit. It needed five separate co-ordinates. When all five co-ordinates meshed, that would be the end of Lurion.

"We ought to tell you, I guess, that there's already been one unsuccessful attempt at the job," Karnes said. "You represent our second try."

"What happened to the first team?"

Karnes frowned. "We sent them out to Lurion six months ago. They were carefully-chosen, hand-picked men, of course. Only three out of the five even managed to get to Lurion alive. One man got waylaid by pirates even before he could get out of the Solar System. Another one made a slight miscalculation of his orbit. He piloted his ship square into Betelgeuse."

"And the other three?" Gardner asked.

"They didn't do too well either," said Karnes. "The leader of the group was a man named Davis. He developed an addiction to *khall*."

"Which is?"

"Lurioni vegetable-mash wine. I've tasted some. It's potent stuff. Chalk Davis off. Then the second man contracted a Lurioni disease, went to hospital, and either died or was murdered there.

We never got the full story. As for the final man of the team, he got there safely, established himself, and is waiting now for replacements. He can't do the job alone. His name, by the way, is Jolland Smee. He'll be your contact when you get there."

"One man out of five. That isn't a very good score, is it?"

"We had hoped for a better one."

"How many teams will have to be sent out before a full complement of men reaches Lurion?"

Karnes pursed his lips together. "We try to profit by past mistakes. We hope that all four of the men we're sending this time will make it."

Gardner nodded. The fate of Davis interested him. Why, Gardner wondered, should a presumably sober, serious-minded Security man abruptly turn into a wino the moment he made planetfall on Lurion? An unbearable attack of conscience, maybe? That was the answer that suggested itself to Gardner, and he didn't like it one bit.

A subaltern presented Gardner with a metal band that fit round his wrist.

"Your indicator," Karnes said. "An ingenious bit of microminiaturization. There's a microscopic electroencephalograph tucked inside there, tuned to five particular mental wavelengths."

Gardner studied it. There were five little colored panels, unlit and quiescent.

"Your color is white," Karnes said. "The moment you land on Lurion, that white panel will light up. The red panel will light, too. It's the color of Jolland Smee. The other three panels will light up, one by one, as the other members of your team arrive."

Gardner nodded. The wristband looked innocuous, just a bit of ornament, dull and dark now. But when all of its five panels were lit, a world would be doomed.

The room darkened. A screen was lowered in front. A projector hummed.

"These are the other members of your team," Karnes said. "Study their faces carefully."

The first face was that of Deever Weegan. His color on the indicator band was green. Weegan looked hard-eyed, fleshless, a man of stoic reserve and forbearance. His face wore a grim, mirthless smile.

"After you've seen their faces," Karnes said, "we'll let you look at their psych-files and hear records of their voices. You'll have to be able to recognize these men with your eyes closed if necessary."

Jolland Smee was shown next. He was about forty and balding, but his face reflected a wiry toughness that did plenty to explain why he had been able to survive when the other four members of his team hadn't.

Kully Leopold was flashed on the screen after Smee. Leopold was a round-faced, round-eyed little man with a short, stiff red beard and twinkling eyes. He was the sort of deceptively mild-looking person that Security liked to save for the most ruthless of missions. His color on the indicator was blue.

Damon Archer completed the quintet. Yellow was his color on the indicator, but his color as a person, Gardner thought from a first look, was probably a sort of bland gray. Archer's face showed no outstanding characteristics, no peaks on the graph at all. It was the sort of face that could be forgotten in a moment.

Well, Gardner thought, Karnes probably knows what he's doing, or else the computer does. Archer probably had an overall competence that made up for his lack of specialties. A man who could easily be forgotten had an enormous asset on such an assignment.

"There's your team," Karnes said. "You're in charge of them."

"Why not Smee? He's there already."

"You're in charge," Karnes repeated. "If I wanted Smee to be the leader, I would have chosen him."

"Sorry, sir."

"The next step will be to brief you on the personalities of your colleagues. After that, we'll have some final instructions for you. Will you be able to leave for Lurion by tomorrow night?"

A Security agent is always at his chief's disposal. Gardner took care that there were never any entangling circumstances. "I'll be ready, sir."

"You have until tomorrow night, then, to think all this through, and have all your second and third and fourth thoughts. We're not forcing you to take on this assignment, Gardner."

"I understand, sir."

"You can back out any time you want until tomorrow night. Once you blast off for Lurion, though, you'll be committing high treason against Earth if you decide to change your mind."

Gardner moistened his lips. "I think I'll be going through with it, sir."

The briefing continued. Gardner hunched forward, committing everything that was said to memory. His life and the life of his planet would depend on how well he did his job.

Five men to destroy a world. Gardner wondered whether this mission would meet the fate of its predecessor.

Maybe. Maybe not.

Well, Earth had sixty-seven years to get the job done. Any number of teams could be sent out in that time. And there still would be time, in all those sixty-seven years. If the computer were right, Gardner thought.

But that was a very big *if*.

CHAPTER TWO

Gardner blasted off at midnight the following night. He left inconspicuously from a small spaceport maintained by Security; there was no need to go through normal channels in clearing him for departure. Security had its own means.

The ship was a medium-sized one, with room for five passengers. It was slated to be the getaway craft after the job was done. The other members of his team were under instruction to derrick their ships and land on Lurion by dropsuits.

As he traveled, Gardner went over the plan again and again, getting used to it. The murder of an entire world was not an easy thing to assimilate. But he had been shown the computations; he had seen the data. Earth's existence was threatened. A deadly configuration was taking shape on Lurion: the beginning of a power-lust that would lead inevitably to world-smashing war.

Lurion was the fourth "and only inhabited" world of the Betelgeuse system, a smallish planet swinging on a somewhat eccentric orbit half a billion miles from its brilliant sun. At the end of his lonely journey, Gardner came out of warp-drive a few million miles outside Lurion's atmosphere, shifted to planetary ion-drive, and coasted down.

It was important that the landing be a good one. He didn't dare crumple the ship into uselessness as he landed it. If anything happened to the ship, the five Security men might well find themselves stranded on the planet they had booby-trapped.

As the craft dropped Lurionward, Gardner retraced the plan once again in his mind, reviewed the names of his team members, brought their faces to mind, re-examined the thumbnail sketches of each that Karnes had given him. Gardner had never met any of the other four in the course of his previous Security work. Security was a big outfit, and its agents didn't go out of their way to identify themselves even to each other.

Gardner jockeyed his ship through Lurion's thick, turbulent atmosphere. He pulled out of a dizzying landing-spin when he was still a hundred miles up, got the ship pointing in the right direction at the right moment, shifted over to automatic, and let the cybernetic brain bring him down right on the button.

At the moment of landing, the indicator on his wrist flashed white. An instant later, as soon as Jolland Smee was able to signal contact, the red panel adjoining it lit as well.

So far, so good, Gardner thought.

He peered through his fore viewscreen and saw that his ship had landed on a broad brown dirt apron at the edge of a big, bustling spacefield. The field was bright in the yellowish-red sunlight. Spaceship hulls stuck up skyward here and there over the field in seeming random distribution. Maintenance crews toiled busily over some; others looked as though they had endured decades of neglect.

Unstrapping himself from the protective cradle, Gardner made his way aft to the cargo rack. His suitcase was stored there, the all-important suitcase. Gardner pulled it down delicately. Inside it were the jewels and loupe that went with the false identity Security had provided him with. The sonic generator was also in the suitcase. The jewels were worth at least a million, but Earth Central hadn't minded the expense; the budget could stand such things. It was the sonic generator that counted. It was more important than any quantity of bright-colored baubles.

Grasping the handle firmly, Gardner carried the suitcase down the catwalk. The Lurioni air was warm and mild, with a faintly pungent ozone tinge. Gardner made his way across the field, suitcase in hand, and toward the customs shed.

They had given him a hypnosleep training course in the chief Lurioni language. As was true of most planets that had reached the cultural stage of interstellar traffic, there were a number of languages spoken, relicts of an earlier day of nationalistic factionalism; but one generally-accepted tongue was spoken everywhere on the planet as a second language. Outsiders had only to learn the planetary language, which served as *lingua franca* everywhere, and which, on most worlds, was well on its way to supplanting the older languages.

The sign atop the customs shed was, therefore, written in planetary Lurioni, whose alphabet consisted of broad sweeping strokes vaguely reminiscent of Terran Arabic. Beneath the main lettering, in tiny cursives, a translation was inscribed in one of the lesser Lurioni tongues.

Gardner joined the line entering the customs shed. An eagle-faced Lurioni, swarthy and with bright gleaming eyes, pounced on him as he entered.

"Over here, please."

"I obey," Gardner replied in the formal Lurioni phrase.

The aliens were humanoid; that is nearly human in form. They were bipeds, mammalian, with swarthy skins capable of insulating them against the fierce radiations of distant Betelgeuse. They were a lean race; adipose tissue was at a premium on Lurion. With their seven many-jointed fingers, their long limbs, and streamlined thin bodies, they had a somewhat spidery appearance.

The Lurioni customs man looked down at Gardner from his height of nearly seven feet.

"Name, please?"

"Roy Gardner, of Earth—Sol III." There was little point in adopting an alias. The Lurioni made jottings on a form, scribbling busily away.

"Occupation?"

"Jewel merchant."

At that, the Lurioni's glittering eyes narrowed speculatively. "Hmm. So interesting. May I have your papers, please?"

It was important that the landing be a good one. He didn't dare crumple the ship into uselessness as he landed it. If anything happened to the ship, the five Security men might well find themselves stranded on the planet they had booby-trapped.

Obligingly, Gardner handed over the little leather-bound booklet that contained his Terran passport and the Lurioni jewel peddler's permit that Security had obtained for him.

The alien opened the booklet and scrutinized the documents carefully. It was all a formality, of course. Finally the customs official said, "I'll have to examine your baggage, of course. It's the government regulation, you understand."

"Of course," Gardner said mildly.

"Please step through with me."

The Lurioni led him to an inner room, bare and dank. What looked like religious icons were mounted on each of the damp, green-painted walls. The alien indicated that Gardner should place his lone suitcase on a wobbly bench in the middle of the room. Gardner complied.

"Open the suitcase, please."

Gardner thumbed the clasps and the suitcase popped open. The alien brushed methodically through Gardner's personal effects in a bored, matter-of-fact way, without showing any great curiosity. Finally he gestured to the little pouch of jewels.

"These?"

"My merchandise," Gardner said.

He undid the drawstring and let a few gems roll out onto his palm: three uncut blue-white diamonds, a tri-colored tourmaline, a large pale star sapphire, a glittering opal. The assortment Security had provided for him was a curious mixture of the precious and the semiprecious. Reaching deeper into the pouch, Gardner produced three garnets, a large emerald, a ruby.

The same jewels were usually found in the crusts of all Earth, but each planet's gems had a special characteristic of their own that made them desirable to connoisseurs; hence the interstellar jewel trade.

The customs man checked each stone off against the list on Gardner's invoices, nodded, and pointed to the generator that lay inconspicuously wrapped in the corner of the suitcase.

"And what's this?"

Gardner stiffened, trying to conceal his momentary discomfort. The generator was harmless-looking enough; that was why no attempt had been made to conceal it from the Lurioni.

"That ...that's a sonic generator," he said. "I use it to test gems to see ...ah ...if ...if they're genuine."

And, he thought, *it happens to be a vital link in a chain of generators that will split this planet into so much sand.*

"An interesting device," the alien said casually, tossing the wrapper over it.

"And very useful," Gardner said.

"No doubt."

The Lurioni made a fluttering motion with his seven-fingered hands, indicating dismissal.

"All right, jewel merchant. Your papers seem to be in order. Put your pebbles away. You may pass through."

The alien's eyes glittered meaningfully. Gardner caught the hint. He scooped up the gems to replace them in the pouch, and carefully allowed one of the diamonds to slip through his fingers.

It bounced loudly on the smooth floor.

"You seemed to have dropped one of your stones," the Lurioni remarked dryly.

Gardner shook his head emphatically. "Are you sure?" he asked, grinning. "I didn't hear anything drop." He did not look toward the floor.

The alien matched the grin, but there was nothing warm about it. "I guess I was mistaken, then," the Lurioni said. "Nothing dropped. Nothing at all."

As Gardner left, he glanced back warily and saw the Lurioni stoop and hastily snatch the diamond up. Gardner smiled. He had acted perfectly in his assumed character. *Rule One,* he thought. *A smart jewel merchant will always bribe the customs men when he arrives in a strange place. They expect it as their due.*

Suitcase in hand, documents carefully stored in his inner breast pocket, Gardner made his way out of the customs enclosure and into the crowded spaceport terminal. Ignoring the beckoning hands of salesmen and hustlers and pushers, Gardner went straight forward, heading toward the taxi stand.

Security had arranged through the consular service to have a room available for him in a mediocre Lurioni hotel. It was a small room in a crowded section of the metropolis, because they did not want him to attract undue attention. Jewel merchants were traditionally secretive; they did not rent majestic suites.

A low, snub-nosed taxi was idling at the stand. Gardner signaled to the driver, who opened the door for him with grudging courtesy.

"Where to?"

"Nichantor Hotel," Gardner said.

The cab left the curb and purred smoothly along the wide road that led from the spaceport to the city. Gardner sat back, relaxing.

"Earthman, aren't you?" the cabbie asked.

"That's right."

"Haven't seen many of your kind coming through this way lately. You're the first Earthman in weeks, you know. You take a liner?"

"Private ship," Gardner said.

It wasn't surprising that few Earthmen landed on Lurion nowadays, he thought. For the past year, ever since the computer's projected data had revealed that Lurion would destroy Earth if it were not first destroyed itself, Earth Central had kept a careful, if subtle, check on passports issued for travel to Lurion. No Earthman whose death would be a major loss was allowed to go there: the passport applications in such cases were politely refused, with the explanation that "current conditions" did not permit large-scale travel to Lurion. But there were few such cases.

On the other hand, it was necessary to have a goodly number of Earthmen on Lurion to provide protective camouflage for the Security team. If all the Earthmen on Lurion were suddenly to leave en masse, it would be extremely awkward for the five members of the destroying team.

According to present figures, there were some three thousand Terrans on Lurion, all of them private citizens there of their own accord. Diplomatic relations had not yet been established between

Earth and Lurion, which saved Karnes from the additional guilt of knowing that he had destroyed fellow members of the civil service.

The three thousand included students, tourists, writers, and more than a hundred jewel merchants. The Lurioni were eager purchasers of almost every sort of bauble. Choosing that as his profession would help to make Gardner that much less conspicuous as he waited for the arrival of the other members of his team.

The entire project had been planned very carefully. Of course, the *first* team had had the benefit of careful planning too. And where were they? Gardner knew he would have to be sure to avoid their mistakes.

The three remaining members of his team, Leopold, Weegan, and Archer, were scheduled to arrive on Lurion at intervals of approximately one week, each at a different spaceport on a different continent. Gardner had the arrival times of each man etched carefully into his memory. He didn't dare entrust any detail of the project to paper. So far as history was concerned, Lurion's violent death was going to be attributed to natural causes, and woe betide Gardner if the Lurioni, the Terran people themselves, or any other race of the galaxy got wind of exactly what was taking place.

The murder of a planet was the most damning crime a race could commit. No matter that the murder was being committed solely to rid the galaxy of a potential plague spot. The act itself was infamous. Discovery of it would mean the end of Earth's dominion in the universe. More than that, it might mean the end of Earth itself if the other planets of the galaxy chose to mete out to Earth what Earth had taken upon itself to mete out to Lurion.

Five generators were to be set up at specified spatial intervals to resonate with the same deadly note. The moment those five generators were attuned to each other, Lurion would crumble in on itself and would be no more.

It was simpler, Gardner thought, to declare all-out war. But a war required a real, not merely a potential provocation, and Terra preferred not to let itself be cast in the role of the aggressor.

Or Lurion might be disposed of subtly by dropping a fission bomb into Betelgeuse to trigger a nova. But Betelgeuse was far too huge a star to toy with so casually. The consequences might not be so easy to deal with.

No, Gardner thought. This was the only way.

The cab came to a halt in front of a dark, gloomy-looking building designed very much in the ponderous style of Terran twenty-first century architecture.

"Here we are," the cabbie said. "That'll be half a unit for the trip."

Pulling out a fistful of shiny Lurioni coins, Gardner counted out half a unit, added a ten-segment piece to it by way of tip, and climbed out of the cab. Gripping the handle of his suitcase tightly, he entered the lobby of the hotel.

It had the atmosphere of a first-rate, second-class hotel. The lobby chairs looked old and comfortably overstuffed: the Lurioni on duty at the desk wore the eternally frozen mask of hotel desk-clerks all over the civilized galaxy.

"You have a reservation for me," Gardner said. "Roy Gardner, Earthman."

"A moment, Earthman."

The clerk scowled over his reservation forms. At last he looked up. "Yes. Your room is ready. The boy will show you to it."

It was on the fifth floor, a curious three-sided room, with the entrance at the base of the triangle. Lurioni architecture seemed to utilize the layout of triangular rooms, back-to-back to form larger squares. The room was small, not very well lit, and its air smelled stale.

When the bellboy had left, Gardner sat down tiredly in the chair next to the bed. He glanced at the indicator on his wrist. The red panel and the white were lit. Next week Weegan would arrive, then Leopold the week after, and finally Archer three weeks hence. That would complete the team. That would seal Lurion's doom.

Until Archer's arrival, there was nothing to do but wait.

CHAPTER THREE

After refreshing himself with a quick vibrobath, Gardner donned a fresh tunic, checked his room for spy devices and left, carefully locking and sealing his door. The seal insured that nobody would be able to enter and prowl through his belongings while he was gone, a natural precaution for a jewel merchant, and a sensible one for someone carrying the sonic generator. Harmless though the device looked to a layman, there were those on Lurion who might conceivably be able to guess its dread purpose.

The room sealed, Gardner rode down in the ancient lift-shaft, getting off at the second floor, where, a sign told him, the hotel dining room was located. It was after the normal Lurioni dinner hour, and the restaurant was practically deserted. An elderly Lurioni, surprisingly potbellied for one of his race, sat in one corner sleepily shoving yellowish noodles into his mouth. At another table, a bleak-faced Trigonian sipped juice. Two waiters lounged in the back, obviously waiting for the last customers to clear out so they might go off duty.

One came shambling over to Gardner and dropped a grease-specked menu in front of him. The dishes were listed by their Lurioni names, with no attempt at an explanation of their contents.

Gardner picked one out at random and said, "What do they make this Varr Kinash out of?"

The waiter shrugged. "It is good. You will like it."

"Yes, but what's it made of?"

"Meat with vegetables."

Scowling, Gardner realized he wasn't going to get any specific details from the Lurioni. "All right, let's have some," he said.

Service was abysmally slow. When the food finally came, Varr Kinash turned out to be a sort of stew; chunks of pale-looking meat and gobbets of fat were afloat on a glutinous mass of vegetables and sticky sauce. The actual flavor was much less repugnant than the appearance of the dish had promised, but Gardner was hardly pleased by his first encounter with Lurioni cuisine. Grimly, he ate his way through three-quarters of the stuff, out of sheer hunger if nothing else. But he told himself that if this were a fair sample of the local cooking, the gourmets of the universe would be losing very little through the destruction of Lurion.

When the waiter finally brought Gardner his check, the Earthman signed it, covered it with what he hoped was an adequate tip, and left. The waiters returned to lounging in the back. The plump Lurioni was still gravely devouring noodles.

It was still fairly early in the evening, with several hours yet to go before midnight. But Gardner was tired; he had already had a very active day, and there was nothing he could accomplish now that would serve him better than getting some rest.

He undressed, darkened his lights, and got into bed. But hardly had he shut his eyes and begun to doze than he was awakened almost immediately by the annoying buzz of his door-announcer.

He sat up and blinked irritably.

"Yes?"

A high-pitched Lurioni voice said, "There's a call for you, *ser* Gardner. You'll have to take it at the main phone downstairs."

"Thanks," Gardner said wearily. He felt tension quicken his pulse. There was only one person on Lurion who would try to get in touch with him this evening. "I'll be there right away," he said, struggling out of bed and switching on the light again.

It took him several minutes to dress. When he finally opened the door, he saw a grinning Lurioni boy waiting in the hall with long arms folded in an improbable knot. He was obviously still waiting for a tip.

Persistent devil, Gardner thought. He gave the boy a coin.

The youngster took it grudgingly and stepped aside while Gardner once again locked and sealed his door. The boy was studying the mechanics of the seal with great interest.

"Will you show me where the phone is?"

"Maybe."

Gardner scowled and surrendered another coin, muttering a few unprintable words of Terran under his breath.

"This way," the boy said.

The Earthman followed him down the narrow corridor to the lift-shaft, and they rode down to the main lobby. There, Gardner was led to a tiny alcove in a corner near the registration desk. The boy drew aside a moth-eaten cloth curtain, bowed mockingly, and departed.

The phone was of the public-communicator type that had been obsolete on Earth for more than fifty years. It lacked a visiscreen. Gardner thumbed the switch and said, "Hello?"

"Am I talking to Mr. *White*?"

"No—that is, yes! Yes; this is white," Gardner said hastily, realizing that the reference was to his color on the indicator band. "Who am I talking to, please?" he asked.

"I'm a friend of yours from the old country, Mr. White. Perhaps you don't remember me, but I'd like very much to get to see you. If we could meet, you'd realize that I had *red* blood in my veins."

He accented *red.* Red was Smee's color on the indicator band. So that was the confirmation.

"That would be a very good idea," Gardner said, coming awake rapidly. "But isn't it too late tonight? I'll abide by yours wishes, of course."

"Tonight would be best," Smee said. "It's been so long since the last time I heard a fellow countryman's voice that I don't think I care to wait. Would that be terribly inconvenient for you?"

"I don't think so," Gardner said. "I can always relax some other time. Where can we get together?"

"There's a bar that I'm very fond of on One Thousand Six and the Lane of Light," Smee said. "Any cab driver will be able to get you there. It's in North City. Would you care to meet me there in ...say, an hour?"

"Fine," Gardner said. "I'll be there."

"How are you enjoying your stay on Lurion so far, Mr. White?"

"It's been very instructive. Thanks ever so much for getting in touch with me tonight. I'll be seeing you soon."

Gardner hung up. He hadn't bothered to arrange any identification signals with Smee. The other agent was smart enough to find some way of identifying himself, and, since the phone might, very well be tapped, the less there was between them by way of signals and other cloak-and dagger hocus-pocus, the less suspicious the Lurioni authorities were likely to be.

He went back upstairs and, before entering his room, checked the seal on his door to satisfy his curiosity. Sure enough, it had been approached, probably by the same houseboy who had brought him the message.

But the seal hadn't been tampered with; it had merely been pressed and prodded and investigated a little. There was absolutely no way to get that single giant molecule off the door without the key, and since the key happened to be Gardner's breath he wasn't particularly worried about being robbed. Thumbprints could be imitated, but it was a little harder to match a man's breath. And he doubted that anyone wanted to get into his room desperately enough to pull the wall apart.

Gardner exhaled, and the patch of seal that prevented entry slid together into a globe no bigger than his fist. Putting his thumb to the conventional doorplate lock underneath, he opened it and went in.

The room was as he had left it. The Earthman checked briefly, examining the sonic generator and his wallet and the jewels. All were intact. He slipped a few bills out of his wallet and put the rest away. Then, popping an anti-fatigue tablet in his mouth to keep him going the rest of the evening, he left, locking up again and sealing the door.

"Where can I get a taxi?" he asked at the desk.

"We will have to summon one."

Gardner waited. At length, a cab appeared in front of the hotel. It was an old model, scarred and paint-patched, but the Earthman had no choice. Wearily tipping the desk clerk, Gardner got in.

"One Thousand Six and the Lane of Light," Gardner told the driver.

"Ten-segment extra for crossing into North City, *ser* Earthman."

"All right," Gardner said. He slouched irritatedly back in his seat. These Lurioni could bleed a man white with their endless demands for tips and bonuses and special charges.

The cab ride was jouncy and uncomfortable. They wound northward through desolate slums, then through more imposing residential areas, and finally across a massive bridge that arched across a dark, sluggish little river.

The neighborhood brightened considerably on the north side of the stream. The cab came to a halt finally in a neighborhood studded with brilliant glow-signs; the boulevard stretched brightly off into the distance as far as Gardner could see. The Lane of Light had been well named.

Paying the cabbie, Gardner dismounted and found himself at a triangular wedge of streets all intersecting at the Lane of Light. He chose the one that bore the number-sign One Thousand Six, turned left, and was confronted immediately with the leaded glass windows of a bar.

Gardner entered and stood for a moment just within the doorway, letting his eyes grow accustomed to the dim light. He plucked the image of Smee out of his memory and searched for someone here who matched that picture of a short, tough-faced, balding man.

On his second sweep around, Gardner saw him. The register in the back of his mind clicked and instinctively said, *There he is.*

Smee was sitting by himself in the back corner of the bar, sipping a greenish drink. He was not looking at Gardner.

Gardner walked toward him and stood to one side of the table.

"Mind if I join you?" he asked.

Smee looked up casually from his drink, evidencing neither surprise nor warmth. "Suit yourself, friend. There's plenty of room for both of us at this table."

Gardner wondered whether he had been recognized. Terran espionage channels had been able to get his name to Smee, and the place where he was staying, but not necessarily a physical description. He sat down and said, "Mighty white of you, Mister."

The other grinned. "Hello, Gardner. Glad you're here."

"Smee?"

"Of course."

A Lurioni bartender appeared, fawned servilely, and inquired elaborately after the state of Gardner's health. But behind the courteous facade was an easily visible barrier of scorn, hatred, and contempt.

"Would the noble Earthman care for a drink?"

"The Earthman would," Gardner said. "Suppose you give me ...ah ..." He fumbled, not knowing what to order, and finished up lamely, "Suppose you give me the same thing my friend here is having."

"Certainly. One *khall*, at once. Do you drink it cool or warm?"

A quick glance at Smee provided no helpful hint. "Cool," Gardner bluffed.

"Your taste is excellent, *ser* Earthman. The drink is at its finest when cool."

After the waiter had gone to place the order, Smee muttered, "He's a lying scoundrel. If you had ordered it warm, he would have told you the same thing."

"Professional courtesy?"

"Just a love of lying," Smee said. "You're a prince among humanoids so long as there's a segment in your pocket; then he'll flatter you from here to Orion. But once you run out of cash, your existence ceases to matter here."

The drink arrived. It was served in a tall colorless glass, topped with a sprinkling of spice. Some sort of sliced fruit dangled limply over the rim. The drink itself was deep green in color.

Gardner stared at the glass reflectively before sipping. He had read Smee's report on the unhappy fate of his predecessor Davis. Davis had sampled *khall* on *his* first night on Lurion, too, and it had been his immediate undoing. He had even pawned his sonic generator eventually to buy more *khall*. Smee had redeemed the pawn at once, but by that time it was obvious that the first destruction team was doomed to failure.

Smee was watching him curiously.

"An unfortunate predilection for drinking *khall* was the downfall of a friend of ours," Smee remarked in a detached, ironic way.

"I know," Gardner said. "I was just thinking about the same thing. But I'm curious to see what stuff the vintners sell, etc. It must have been pretty potent to ruin Davis like that."

Gardner touched the glass hesitantly to his lips and let a small amount of the beverage enter his mouth. He frowned, swirled it around critically on his tongue, finally swallowed it.

The *khall* was sweet on first taste, he thought, with an immediate aftertaste of sourness. It was a subtle sort of drink, but not one that Gardner would care to drink very often.

"Interesting," he said. "But I'd hardly feel the loss if I never had any again."

The short man smiled. "Each man has his own poison. The fondness for *khall* grows on you in direct proportion to the quanity you consume. Davis liked *khall* to a fault. It ...it made him forget things."

"I see you're drinking it," Gardner said. "Do you want to forget things too?"

"I've been here six months," Smee said. "For six months I've been in the position of a jailer who lives right in the cell with the condemned man. I won't get forgetfulness out of a bottle that easily." He took a deep draught of his drink, none the less, and said, "When are your friends due here?"

"One, two, and three weeks, respectively. It'll be good to have the whole gang of us together, won't it?" Gardner said.

"Downright jolly." Smee ventured a funereal grin, but replaced it immediately with a cold frown. "Have you had any trouble yet?"

"Trouble?"

"Inside, I mean." He tapped his chest. "Inflammation of the conscience. Swollen guilt glands. That sort of trouble." Gardner saw what Smee meant, and shook his head.

"No. I haven't had that sort of trouble yet. But there's three weeks, yet, isn't there?"

"Yes. Three weeks. At least." Smee sipped again at his drink, and ran thick, stubby, powerful fingers through the comic fringe of fuzz on his scalp. In a muzzy voice Smee said, "Long time, three weeks, Gardner. Very long time. And maybe something will go wrong. Maybe we both stay here another six months. Or six years. Or sixty years. Or six hundred sixty ..."

Gardner suddenly made the discovery that Smee was drunk. It was a quiet sort of drunk, that didn't show from without.

Well, who wouldn't be? Gardner asked himself. *Living for six months on a planet you've been told to blow up. It's amazing that he's as stable as he is.*

Gardner wondered what *he* would be like if it took another six months or more before a full destruction team could be assembled. He began to hope fervently that Leopold and Archer and Weegan would get here on time, without delays that might necessitate replacement of personnel.

"Are you planning to stay on this continent?" Smee asked suddenly.

"Yes. Why?"

"Oh, nothing, I guess. Except that in the original setup, this was my area. And we can't all be in the same place, of course. We have to be separated by the proper distances."

"Naturally," Gardner said. "One of us will have to move elsewhere."

"You're the boss. Do you want to stay here, or should I?'

Gardner puckered his lip indecisively. Smee obviously did not want to be shifted. But Gardner knew that that was unhealthy; perhaps Smee, in his six months, had developed fixed habits, had involved himself with drinking cronies and the like. For the good of the mission, Smee would have to be pried loose from any such impairers of efficiency.

"I'll stay here," Gardner said. "You know this planet better than I do, so it's easier for you to move around. Take Continent East as your position."

Smee sighed. "Very well. I'll be there when the time comes."

CHAPTER FOUR

A very special geographical distribution was necessary if the generator were to produce its desired effect. Lines of force had to be drawn through the planet, pole to pole, hemisphere to hemisphere. The Five would be together only at the very end, after the generators had been activated, when they fled to safety in Gardner's ship.

Gardner began to regret having decided to meet Smee personally. The plan was so established that there was no real need for the five conspirators to have actual personal contact. When the indicator band would glow on all five wrists in all five colors, the time would have come, and each man would know where he was to be and what he was to do.

Gardner looked at the rings under Smee's deep-set, sad eyes and shivered. Six months of waiting, and Smee was still here; but how much damage had this hellishly prolonged assignment done to his soul?

"I think I'll be going," Gardner said. "You woke me up. I haven't slept in a while. And we've covered all the ground we need to cover."

Smee's hand shot out and caught Gardner's wrist with a surprisingly powerful grip.

"Why not wait? I asked you to come here for a specific reason. There's a floor show starting in ten minutes. You may find it interesting."

"I'd rather—"

"*Please* wait," Smee said strangely. He was half cajoling, half commanding. "The floor show here is quite unique. I ...find it healthy to watch it."

"Healthy?"

"You'll understand. I'm sure that watching it will benefit you as it does me."

"What kind of benefit?"

"Remain and watch."

Gardner shrugged. Smee seemed almost desperately insistent. And he was wide awake now anyway. "All right," he said. "I'll stay."

Leaning back, he took another sip of the *khall.* He could see how Davis had grown so fond of it. Its taste was insidious, growing in intensity as one kept on drinking it, and it could easily become compulsive. Probably, Gardner thought, it even had mild narcotic qualities. All in all, it was a good drink to stay away from, except when being sociable.

A few minutes passed, and then three burly-looking Lurioni appeared and began to clear to one side the tables in the front of the room. At the touch of a button, the streetfront windows were opaqued, to keep outsiders from getting free looks.

"It's starting," Smee murmured. "Be prepared for something nasty."

Gardner waited tensely. A sphincter in the wall just to his right irised open. There was a silent hush in the bar.

A beam of blue light wriggled through the opening in the wall, spun dizzingly across the opposite wall in wild circles, and came to rest finally in sharp focus. A bolt of bright yellow followed, spearing into the blue. The colors twined, moved snakily along the wall, suddenly blanked out.

Then two Lurioni stepped through.

They came to the center of the floor and stood there, bathed in light, unmoving, while from the regular patrons there arose a rhythmic stamping of the feet that was the local variety of applause. Gardner noticed that Smee, too, was pounding the floor.

The Lurioni were a man and a woman wearing only the briefest of loincloths. A harsh red light shot down from the ceiling and illuminated their thin, knobby-jointed bodies. Gardner studied them with interest.

They were particularly lean specimens of their race, thin and bony, extremely tall. The man was near seven feet in height, Gardner estimated, while the woman was at least a six-footer. They stood quite still, moving not a muscle, until the stamping of feet died away.

Then the two in the center of the floor began to dance to the accompaniment of grave music that came piping from a grille set high on one wall near the ceiling. Their motions were stiff, precise, jerky. Gardner winced a little at the music; he had a delicate sense of pitch, and the excruciating quarter-tone intervals and the jarring, totally unpredictable discordancies affected him strongly.

The music accelerated, and so did the dancers. The off-stage instruments struck a clashing chord so oddly tonal that it seemed wildly misplaced in that symphony of dissonances, and the female dancer went into an awkward pirouette.

She spun for a moment, spidery arms akimbo, one long leg drawn up so her foot touched her other knee. Then, breaking the pose, she fumbled at the belt of her loincloth. Long arms whirled. A knife flashed in the red spotlight, and red line of blood traced itself down the golden chest of the male dancer.

Gardner caught his breath sharply. "What sort of unholy dance is this?"

Smee smiled mellowly, sitting back with his thumbs hooked into his belt. "Entertainment here runs to the morbid side," he said. "If we're lucky, maybe the management was able to afford to hire a kill tonight. There hasn't been one here in weeks." Smee took another drink, grinning complacently.

Gardner felt cold. It seemed to him that Smee relished the weird dance taking place, that he had insisted on Gardner's seeing it only because he wanted the company of his own kind.

The dance continued, unwinding inexorably. The unseen musicians spun out their mercilessly complicated nonmelodies, and the dancers kept pace with the tempo, moving now at a frenzied pace. Their dark bodies were glistening with sweat.

The male dancer had a knife, too, Gardner saw; it flickered momentarily in the seven-fingered hands as he struck, and a line of blood appeared between the girl's breasts. Another tonal chord echoed in the room! The dancers separated, gliding, as if on bearings to opposite ends of the area. Polarized there, they spun in tight circles and glided back, coming together again under the red spotlight.

They passed by each other on tiptoe, taking little mincing steps, and the girl's knife slit the man's arm from elbow to shoulder. Each of the knife-strokes was precise, delicate, not a crude butcher-swing; Gardner guessed that none of the cuts penetrated very much deeper than the outer layers of the skin.

But even skin cuts are painful, and by now the bodies of both dancers were crisscrossed and streaked with slashes. And, as Gardner looked around, he saw the patrons—Lurioni, chiefly, with a thin sprinkling of outworlders—staring eagerly at the pair, waiting eagerly for the climax of the dance.

An invisible drum began beating a numbing tattoo. A flute wailed atonally.

Blood mingled with sweat. The dancers closed, danced lightly apart, rejoined. Each time they passed one another, a cut was inflicted. They seemed to be outdoing each other in the attempt to make the delivery and placing of the wound as artistic as possible. Their faces remained as rigidly emotionless as those of masks in a museum cabinet. Gardner wondered if the dancers saw the knife coming before the moment of pain, and whether the kiss of the blade had any effect at all.

"Don't they feel the cuts?" he asked.

"Of course not," Smee said. "It would ruin the dance. They're doped to the eyebrows and hardly know what's going on. It's the customers who feel it vicariously."

Looking around, Gardner saw that Smee had told the truth. Total empathy had been achieved. The Lurioni patrons sat stiffly, rocking back and forth, grunting a little each time a wound was inflicted, grinning fiercely, swaying and murmuring. They seemed to be participating in some blasphemous rite. Gardner found himself falling into the wild, chaotic rhythm of the music, and nervously checked himself lest some dark impulse take hold of him.

The dancers were moving jerkily and lamely now, their former angular grace utterly transformed into a marionette-like parody. The male dancer was soaked with blood and perspiration, and he gleamed under the lights. The female had come off slightly better. Gardner suddenly realized that there *was* going to be a kill tonight, and that it would be the male who would die. The girl had been setting him up, taking wounds herself as a matter of ritual, but inflicting more than she took, and maintaining control at all times.

The music swung deafeningly upward. The girl, eyes agleam, moved inward, coming to life, dancing bouncily on the outer edges of her feet, lifting the knife, bending to circle and display it to the watchers, letting it sparkle in the dimmed spotlight. The hapless victim danced too, but it was the death-dance of a cocooned fly twitching at the end of his silken cord while waiting for the spider who had snared him to suck him dry.

Gardner clenched his teeth. He had seen death before, but never death administered so casually, so brutally.

The killing of an individual, he thought, *is tragic murder. But the killing of a planet ...*

The girl came forward, knife held high, preparing now for the final moment, the climax, the moment of truth—

Then the lights went on.

Gardner felt the wrench back into reality with a painful, jarring tug. It was like being abruptly awakened, and even awakening from a nightmare can be a wrench. He knew that the impact on the others, who had been so closely bound up in the bloody little drama, must have been even more violent.

The dancers were frozen in midfloor, looking merely naked and no longer nude. Their eyes were vacant, their arms dangled limply, their shoulders slumped. Blood trickled in little runnels down their skin. They seemed totally bewildered at all around them, as though they had been transported here in the twinkling of an eye from some far-off cosmos where only the two of them had existed.

After the first frozen moment, Gardner reacted, glancing toward the door.

Four uniformed Lurioni stood there.

It's a raid, he thought wildly. He was right. Once the immediate instant of surprise was over, the patrons of the bar came to life, jumping up, making a scrambling dash for the rear doors, the windows, any available exit they could find.

"Don't panic," Smee said quietly. "Come with me and we'll get out of here."

Gardner felt Smee's powerful hand gripping his wrist once again, this time not holding him down but lifting him up, pulling him bodily from his seat. Gardner looked back and saw the four policemen marching into the bar, laying about them in vicious glee with heavy wooden truncheons. Half a dozen of the bar's Lurioni patrons lay sprawled unconscious on the floor, blood welling from their scalps. The two dancers stood grotesquely together in the dance area, covered with their own blood. They were holding hands, joining forces in their mute, bewildered way against the sudden and violent encroachment of the outer world.

Then Gardner felt a sharp, socket-wrenching tug on his arm.

"Come on," Smee whispered harshly. "Don't stand around gawking. I know the way out."

They darted toward the rear of the bar, and Smee put his shoulder to a door that led to the kitchen. Someone had bolted the door from within, but it gave way, with a great splintering of wood, after the fourth blow from the burly little man's shoulder. Smee rushed through, beckoning behind him for Gardner to follow.

Breathless, Gardner raced along at Smee's heels. He heard shouting behind him, but did not stop to see who was protesting.

They passed through a small, incredibly dirty kitchen, made a sharp turn, then thundered down a dark flight of stairs.

Another locked door confronted them. Smee grabbed the handle, wrenched, pushed inward. The door gave way. He yanked it open and they stepped outside.

They found themselves in a deserted-looking alley. From behind them came the sounds of shouted pain, and rising above that the keen, piercing shrieks of Lurioni laughter.

For a moment they stood still, catching their breaths. Gardner felt himself trembling from the exertion, and impatiently stiffened in a half successful attempt to regain control.

"We're safe here," Smee said. "But we can't stay here. Someone from one of the adjoining buildings might see us down here and telephone the police."

"How do we get out?"

"Just follow me."

Smee led him along the alleyway in a direction that traveled away from the raided building. As they walked, Gardner demanded angrily, "Why didn't you tell me that you were taking me to an illegal place? What would have happened if the police had caught us and given us some kind of truth-check? You could have wrecked the whole project."

Smee turned around and stared at him blandly. "I assure you I had no idea we were going to be raided."

"But you took the chance."

"I did not. The place isn't illegal. Besides the police never arrest anyone."

"Huh? But why did they come busting in there, then? It looked like a raid to me."

The short man snickered. "The police must have been bored tonight," Smee said. "They felt like having a raid, so they had one. The place was breaking no law. Those knife-dancers are perfectly permissible."

"What was the excuse for the raid, then?"

"Preventive discipline, I think they call it here. It means that a pack of policemen break into a place and bang people around with truncheons just to show them that there is *some* law on Lurion, and that they enforce it strictly."

"That's a lovely law enforcement system."

"It's the way *this* planet works," Smee said. "That was why I wanted you to stay for the show."

"You knew it was going to be raided?"

"No. I knew there was a *chance* of a raid. There always is, wherever you go on Lurion. I simply wanted you to see the dance, to see the forms of entertainment that pass for good clean fun on this world. You were lucky enough to see how they keep the law here, too."

"It was risky. Suppose one of us got beaten to death by the police?"

Smee shrugged. "You risk your life every time you step outside your room. What do you want to do, hibernate until the team is complete?"

Gardner shook his head. "No, no, you're right. It's good to see what sort of a world this is."

"I keep going," Smee said. "I need constant reassurance. But every day I prove to myself again that this planet is *evil*; that nothing worthwhile will be destroyed when this planet is destroyed.'" He shouldered his way out of the alley and into the street. "I wish I didn't have to keep thinking about it. But you don't snuff out a world as calmly as you'd cap a candle."

"I know," Gardner said hollowly. "I'm learning that a hundred times a day."

A light late-evening drizzle was falling, now; the air was warm and muggy, and his clothing clung stickily to his skin. But, inside, Gardner felt chilled. Smee looked completely sober now.

"We'd better not see each other again," Smee said. "Not until the time comes. We'll only depress each other otherwise."

"All right. Not until the time comes."

"I'll leave for Continent East at the end of the week."

"Don't rush about it," Gardner said. "Good night, Smee. And thanks for letting me see that show tonight. It makes me feel easier about what we have to do."

"Good night," Smee said.

CHAPTER FIVE

They parted, going in separate directions. Smee trudged off wearily to the left and Gardner headed the other way. After a while he paused, standing alone in the rainy Lurioni night. The night was moonless, and the mugginess even hid the stars behind a purplish haze.

Oddly, the strange exhibition of sadism and vicarious cruelty that he had just witnessed had calmed and soothed, rather than upset him. It was the kind of unmitigatedly evil entertainment that he had hoped to find flourishing on Lurion.

Gardner knew he was groping for rationalizations, for reasons that would justify the destruction of Lurion. Actually, it was sheer softheadedness, of course; no reason was necessary, said Karnes, beyond that of mere-common-sense precaution. The computer said that Lurion, if left unchecked, would destroy Earth in the course of time. Therefore Earth was acting out of the most basic law of self-preservation in reaching out to destroy Lurion. It was simple precaution.

But precaution was an abstraction, and Gardner operated best from concretes. He wanted to be able to see himself as an executioner, not as a cold-blooded amoral murderer.

Okay, he thought. *A world that thrives on this sort of senseless cruelty deserves everything that it's going to get.*

But the answer was dissatisfying. *False piety,* a mocking voice within him said.

He kept walking, stiff-legged, stiff-minded, trying not to think.

The city's name was City, a surprising bluntness for the usually devious Lurioni. Gardner's hotel was situated in South City. He was in North City, now.

He realized that the night was not moonless after all, but that the three tiny, splinter-sized moons had merely been obscured by the haze. Now he could make them out, dotted in vaguely equilateral triangle in the sky, looking like stray teeth that someone had hurled up into the heavens. They cast a feeble and confusing light, as Gardner made his way through the untidy streets. He wanted to walk, to keep walking in this stiff, mechanical, unthinking way, to walk the tension and fear completely out of his system. Only then, when he was calm once again, could he find a cab and return to his hotel on the other side of the city.

He had no idea which way he was going. The streets were silent now, completely empty. It was nearly two hours past midnight. The anti-fatigue tablet he had taken before coming out to meet Smee was wearing off now, and Gardner was beginning to feel tired. But he kept on walking.

He turned into a street lined on both sides with grubby little residential dwellings, illuminated only by dim glow-lights across the street, and abruptly someone hit him from behind.

It was a light, glancing blow, and Gardner had spent a hundred hours learning how to recover almost instantly from a surprise attack. He let his left knee go limp, dissipating the force of the blow, but before he could turn, another blow descended, and this one nearly knocked him sprawling. Only his special training saved him. He took two wild staggering steps forward, halted as if about to pitch forward face-first, and managed to recover his balance. He danced two or three more steps, then turned around.

A pair of young ugly-looking Lurioni stood behind him, their long arms folded. They were grinning in happy amusement.

"Hello, Earthman," one of them said.

They seemed to be boys, though it was hard to tell the age of a Lurioni without long practice. Gardner sized them up immediately as the local equivalent of juvenile delinquents. They were wearing open jackets flamboyantly ornamented with strips of silk. The rain had soaked them to the skin; evidently they had been prowling in search of strangers for hours. Gardner noticed little metal needles puncturing the skin of their cheeks—a symbol of their toughness, he figured. He decided to find out exactly how tough they really were.

"W-what do you want with me?" he asked in a timid, stammering voice.

"Got any money, Earthman?"

Gardner let an expression of abject fear and utter capitulation crawl across his face. "I don't understand. You want to *rob* me?"

The Lurioni boys laughed contemptuously. "Rob you? Hah! Who ever said anything about robbing you, Earthman? We wouldn't do a cruel thing like thatl"

"Oh, well, then ..."

"We just want your money!"

Gardner blinked bewilderedly. He hoped that he had successfully put over an appearance of complete futility.

"Hit him," one of the boys whispered to the other. The smaller of the two advanced boldly toward Gardner, grinned cheerfully at him, and struck him in the stomach. Gardner tightened his stomach-muscles and rode with the blow, following the Security-taught techniques, but he allowed an agonized grunt to escape, and his face became a crumpled mask of pain.

"Please," he whimpered. "Please, don't hit me again."

"Hand over your cash, or we'll give you a lot more, Earthman."

"Sure," Gardner wheezed. "You can have my money. Just don't hit me again, that's all I ask."

He started to reach into his right-hand pocket, but the taller boy said quickly, "Uh-uh, friend. Keep your hands out of your pockets. Tell us which one the money's in, and *we'll* take it out for you."

"It's in the right-hand one," Gardner said.

"Get the money," the tall boy commanded.

Gardner poised tensely, plotting out the precise pattern of muscle stress and counter-stress that he was going to bring into play. The younger boy was slipping a hand into the Earthman's pocket. The spidery hand closed on Gardner's billfold and started to draw it out. Gardner counted silently; this maneuver called for perfect timing, or else he might find himself lying in the gutter with his head kicked in.

Thousand one ...thousand two ...thousand three ...now!

Gardner turned suddenly at a right angle. The motion pulled the flap of his pocket tight shut, trapping the boy's hand at the wrist. Gardner grabbed the imprisoned wrist, ripped the hand from the pocket, arched his back, bent his knees, and flipped.

The lightweight Lurioni went catapulting into the air heels first, described a short arc, and crashed into his companion somewhere amidships. Gardner launched himself forward and was on them the next second, taking advantage of their astonishment.

His powerful arms straddled their shoulders and he pushed them to the ground. Instantly, he had one hand clamped on each throat. He tightened his grip until they began to have trouble with their breathing. The glared up at him, a mixture of hate and terror in their cold eyes.

"I think I'll strangle you," Gardner remarked casually. "One with each hand."

He increased the force of his grip on the throats, kneeling at the same time on their chests. They kicked and flailed their arms, clawing at his face desperately, but to no avail. By the dim light of the streetglows he could see their faces growing mottled. The urge to throttle them to death was strong, but Gardner resisted the easy temptation.

After a moment he released his hold on their throats. They had stopped resisting now. He rose from them; they remained on the ground, making hoarse gasping sounds. Gardner backed a step or two away from them.

"Stay right where you are until I've turned the corner," Gardner ordered brusquely. "You understand me? If either of you gets up, I'll let you both have it with my blaster."

He patted his pocket meaningfully. The blaster was pure bluff, but they had no way of knowing that. They made no sign of moving.

He edged away, facing them, only once stealing a glance behind him to make sure that no new adversary might be sneaking up on him. The vanquished pair remained flattened against the wet pavement until Gardner had reached the end of the street.

"All right," Gardner called to them. "You can get up now. Start running in the other direction, fast as you can."

They rose. Gardner heard them interchange hot words; they were angry at each other for the failure of their little prank, obviously.

Suddenly the older boy produced a bright curved knife from somewhere in his jacket. The younger boy sprang backward, but not quickly enough; the tall one thrust the knife into his companion's belly and ripped upward with a killer's practiced hand. Gardner gasped as the tall boy coolly watched his companion crumple; then the killer turned and trotted away.

A pleasant planet, Gardner thought.

He did not go to the assistance of the boy who had been knifed. There was never any percentage in helping thine enemy to wax strong and smite you. For all he knew, an attempt at help would only bring him a knife-thrust for his troubles. All things considered, he was lucky to have come out of the encounter in one piece.

His earlier qualms were almost completely dissipated now. This *was* an ugly, brutish world. For the first time, Gardner actually found himself impatient for the completion of the mission.

He began to walk rapidly toward a wide boulevard several blocks distant. He had no further desire to stroll aimlessly in this deserted neighborhood, and perhaps to have to fight for his life every block or two.

He had lost all sense of his direction. He had no idea where he was now in relation to the Lane of Lights, although he could not be more than half a mile from it. Reaching the boulevard, he found it described as Admiral Knairr Parkway; it was more brightly lit than the other streets, and there was still some vehicular traffic. Frowning, Gardner peered into the street, hoping to catch sight of a passing taxi.

Then he saw a box much like a fire-alarm box near him. Translating the Lurioni inscription, he read *To Summon Hired Vehicle, Press This Key.*

Gardner pressed it. An acknowledging red light went on. He waited.

Some fifteen minutes passed. The light rain continued to drizzle down, and he was getting thoroughly soaked, but there was no help for it. Grimly he stood guard by the taxi call-box, and finally a cab pulled up.

A Lurioni stuck his head out of the front window. "You rang for me?"

"Yes."

Gardner started to enter the cab, but the door remained locked. The cabbie said, "Stand fast there, you! Let me scan you first!"

A hand-scanner buzzed, and only after the taxi driver was satisfied did he allow Gardner to enter. Sinking back in the cushioned interior, Gardner said, "What was that for?"

"The scanning?" The cabbie laughed. "After midnight I'm not required to give a ride to anyone carrying a weapon, Earthman. It's the law."

"And if I *had* been carrying a weapon?"

"I would have driven on. I've been in this business twenty years, and I'm not minded towards suicide. Where to, Earthman?"

"Nichantor Hotel, South City."

The cabbie swore. "That's a long trip for such an hour."

"I can't help it. That's where I'm staying."

For one uneasy moment, Gardner thought that the cabbie was going to dump him out and leave him to his own devices, but, to the Earthman's great relief, the cab began to move.

They traveled in silence. When, nearly an hour later, the cab came to a halt in front of the hotel, the cabbie turned round and said, "Four units-twenty, *ser* Earthman."

"It only cost me three and ten to make the trip in the other direction," Gardner muttered, suspecting he was being fleeced.

"Double charge after midnight," the cabbie retorted. The door was locked, and would remain locked until Gardner paid. Reluctantly, Gardner surrendered a five-unit piece and the door opened.

"May you sleep well, *ser* Earthman."

"Thanks," Gardner growled.

He entered the hotel, going past a drowsy-looking night clerk, and went up to his room. He stripped off his soggy clothes and spread them out to dry. Then, for the second time that evening, he climbed into bed and closed his eyes.

But sleep, which had taken him so quickly that first time hours before, now refused to come. Gardner lay awake, staring up at the ceiling, listening to the distant trickle of water in the pipes, hearing the creak of a bed on the floor above him, the faint cough of his neighbor on the other side of the thin wall.

The night's events remained with him: the meeting with Smee, the dance, the raid, the encounter in the streets, the interchange of words with the taxi driver. It had been a very long evening, and an instructive one. He felt he understood Lurion. It was a world in which all of Earth's faults had been carried to an extreme of brutality, selfishness, and evil, and where the virtues of Terran civilization did not appear to have taken root. So far, in his brief time here, Gardner had seen no indication of a flourishing, healthy art or religion or ethical structure. The architecture was chaotic and hodge-podge, the music harsh and ugly, the people coarse, brutish.

Finally Gardner slept. But he was awakened early by the sound of people moving about, of chambermaids singing ribaldly as they thumped their way down the halls, of other tenants slamming their doors as they went down to breakfast. Gardner looked at his watch and saw that he had slept only five hours.

He rose nevertheless, showered and shaved, and was out of his room within three quarters of an hour. As he affixed the seal to his door, the chambermaid wandered by and said, "What are *you* doing?"

"Locking my room."

"How am I supposed to get in and clean?"

"You aren't," Gardner said. "I'll be responsible for cleaning my own room. You don't mind that, do you?"

"Just so long as you okay it with the management, I don't. But when they come to me and ask how come I haven't cleaned your room, and you say nothing about locking me out—"

"Don't worry. I'll defend you."

"How do I know? Maybe you just want to trick me out of my job?"

Gardner sighed. He handed the girl a two-unit piece as a token of his honesty, and headed for the lift-shaft. *Doesn't anyone trust anybody on this accursed world?* he wondered.

It didn't look that way. He rode down to the hotel dining room and breakfasted on an uneasy collection of mangled vegetables floating in a thin, vinegary oil. It was all he could do to get the stuff down, but he managed to eat it all. He was not developing any love for Lurioni cooking. He wondered how Smee had been able to stand it for six months.

CHAPTER SIX

After breakfast, Gardner set out to peddle his wares. If he had ostensibly come to Lurion as a jewel-merchant, he would have to work at his trade, unless he wanted to risk getting into trouble. The Lurioni authorities might just be checking on all newcomers, for unspecified reasons, and he wanted to cover himself.

The local jewel merchants' exchange was some five or six blocks from his hotel, which is why that hotel had been chosen for him. As in all cities on all humanoid worlds, jewel traders tended to concentrate in one crowded district, hawking their wares at each other out on the street, exposing palmsful of pearls and rubies and emeralds to the highest bidder. Gardner carried his little pouch of merchandise in his bosom.

The jewels, he knew, would have to be very carefully managed. He had to spin his supply out to last at least the three weeks, and possibly a good deal more. He had the usual six-month visa, but he dreaded the thought of spending an indefinite amount of time with no occupation to keep his mind away from the project.

He entered the bourse, which lined both sides of a narrow street for several blocks. Stern-looking Lurioni police, no doubt well paid by the jewel merchants' association here, stood guard.

The first step was to find an Earthman. Again, it was protective camouflage; a newly-arrived Terran would be expected to seek out a professional comrade from his home world.

In Gardner's case, though, it hurt. In three weeks or so, he knew, he would be on his way safely back to Earth, while the people he might meet and befriend now would have to perish with all of Lurion. Those Earthmen now on Lurion were considered expendable according to the harsh mathematics that governed this entire operation. Three thousand souls, more or less, could not be considered important when the lives of untold generations of Earthmen hung in the balance.

Gardner found himself suddenly face-to-face with an Earthman, a man in his sixties, short, stout, prosperous-looking, who smiled genially at him.

"You're an unfamiliar face. Welcome to Lurion. I'm Tom Steeves."

"Roy Gardner," Gardner said, extending a hand to take the plump, slightly clammy one of the older man.

"Just arrived?" Steeves asked.

"Yesterday."

"For how long?"

"Six months. Or until I've sold what I've brought. I represent a private trader."

Steeves chuckled. "You've got to be careful here, Gardner. These Lurioni will rob you blind if you don't watch out. Look at these."

The older man opened his palm, revealing three flawless-looking sapphires. Gardner bent close over them, uncomfortably aware that he was being asked to pronounce a professional opinion.

"Lovely," he said finally. "Of course, I'd have to study them closely."

"Of course they're lovely," Steeves said. "Full-blooded beauties. And phony, every one of them."

"No!"

Steeves smiled benignly. "They're products of the furnace of Guair bin Netali, and if I hadn't seen them manufactured myself I wouldn't believe they were paste. Netali is only one of the professionals here. Watch out for his work." Steeves restored the sapphires to his pocket, and patted his capacious stomach. "I've been here twenty years, Gardner. I know all the tricks of Lurioni jewel-trading. If you're unsure, check with me first. You'll always find me on this corner, every day of the week."

"Thanks," Gardner said. "I appreciate your offer. I may need some help until I know the ropes."

He chatted with Steeves a while longer, then moved on through the bourse. He spent most of the morning investigating, chatting with the other Earthmen, learning the angles, finding out who was trustworthy and who was not. By noon, Gardner had met and exchanged greetings with several dozen fellow Earthmen. He had had a hurry-up hypno-course in the technique of jewel trading, but now he was getting a practical course in professional argot and mannerisms.

At half past noon, he found himself in the company of two Earthmen and an Ariagonid who invited him to join them for lunch. Gardner accepted; they ate at a small Ariagonid-operated restaurant a block from the exchange, where the food was downright splendid compared with the usual Lurioni slops. During the course of dinner, Gardner consummated his first deal, unloading a ruby for a good price.

"Payable in Terran currency," he specified.

The Ariagonid, who was the purchaser, hemmed and hawed and stroked his purple wattles; the conversion rate would favor him if payment were made in his own currency. But Gardner remained adamant, whittling the purchase price down a little to ease the pressure on the Ariagonid, and the deal was closed.

"I will register the currency this afternoon," the Ariagonid promised. "By tonight you will deliver my gem?"

"Fair enough," Gardner said.

Glancing quickly at his two fellow Earthmen, Gardner knew he had struck a good deal. He was pleased at his bargaining success, though he knew all too well that he was simply playing out a game against time; the price he got for the jewels was an irrelevancy. All that mattered was the need to have some sort of gainful employ until the time came to leave Lurion.

At the end of the day, Gardner returned to his hotel, foot-sore and hoarse, but secure in the knowledge that he had firmly established his new identity. He had haggled and bought and sold most convincingly, he thought. If any observers had been trailing him, they could not fail to believe that he was a legitimate merchant of precious and semiprecious stones, nothing more.

When evening came, he remained in the vicinity of his hotel, taking special care to get indoors before the hour grew late. His life was far too precious to the project to chance it on the streets in so dangerous a city at night,

There was a *bistro* opposite the hotel; he spent the hours after dinner there, as he might be expected to do, sipping judicious quantities of *khall* and eyeing the passing crowd. Later at night, when the streets began to empty out and the neighborhood became more dangerous, Gardner would stroll back to the hotel. For a twenty-segment piece he could buy admission to the orthicon room, where a gay kaleidoscope whirled endlessly to the stupified delight of an eager audience. It was a harmless enough diversion, especially if you kept your eyes off the screen and watched with interest the efficient tactics of the numerous pickpockets moving through the room. Around eleven each night, Gardner would retire to his own room, read for a while, and go to sleep.

It was a lonely life.

On the third day, when Gardner was beginning to get bored with the routine, there was a call, late one night, from Smee.

"I just wanted to let you know that I'm leaving for Continent East tomorrow," Smee said.

"Fine. Drop me a postcard or something when you get there."

"How has it been, so far?"

"No complaints," Gardner said.

"You like Lurion?"

"It has its points of interest."

"Drinking much?" Smee asked next.

"A nip or two of *khall* before bedtime. It helps to relax me."

"I'm sure it does," Smee said thoughtfully. "Well, be seeing you in a few weeks."

"Yes. A few weeks."

Gardner hung up the phone and emerged from the curtained alcove. One of the ubiquitous Lurioni houseboys was staring at him quizzically. There was no privacy to be had at the telephone, of course. But Gardner was certain he had said nothing to Smee that might arouse the anxiety of a spy.

He was pleased that Smee was leaving, at any rate. He had been worried that so long as he stayed here, the little man might grow increasingly reckless. Just because he had survived six months in this city, he wouldn't necessarily be immune to a policeman's truncheon or the knife of a Lurioni delinquent.

The trouble with the project, Gardner thought, was that every man was indispensable. Five generators was the minimum, and one member of the team put out of commission would snarl the entire enterprise. Perhaps three or four or a dozen five-man teams would have to be sent out before the entire necessary complement could be assembled on Lurion at the same time.

The first four days had gone along smoothly enough for Gardner: up early, out to the exchange, mingle with the jewel traders, buy and sell; then back to the hotel, kill the evening in loneliness, get to sleep. It was not an exciting routine, or even a pleasant one, but it was one that he could endure. He resisted any attempt of the Earther jewel traders to form after-hours friendships with him. They were all men condemned to die at his hand, and he knew he could not allow himself to become intimate with any of them. The job was hard enough to shoulder as it was.

As he saw it, he would go along, living this way for a while. In a few days Weegan would arrive, and then Leopold, and finally Damon Archer. Then, if all were still going well, they would perform their dreadful task and leave.

But on the morning of the fourth day he saw the girl, and from then on he knew that there *would* be complications, much as he wanted to avoid them.

She was going out, just as Gardner arrived in the lobby. She was an Earthgirl, and she walked with a cheerful, determined stride. Gardner froze, watching her skip down the steps of the hotel and lose herself in the rapidly-moving crowd.

He thought about her all day. And, when he returned to the hotel at nightfall, after his day at the jewel exchange, he was pleasantly surprised to find her standing at the desk in the hotel lobby, tearing open an envelope she had just picked up at the mail rack.

He walked to the mail rack and made a conspicuous thing out of searching his own box for a letter. Inwardly he told himself not to be a damned fool; he had nothing to gain by this escapade but trouble. Still, he rummaged in the box, and shrugged his shoulders when he found the expected emptiness.

"Nothing for me, I guess," he said softly, and turned as though to leave. But the girl had noticed him, and she looked up, smiling.

"Hello, Earthman," she said lightly. "Do you live here? Oh, of course, you must, if you're looking for your mail!"

"I live here," Gardner said.

He studied her with care. She was tall, five-seven at least, with hair dyed green and an open, wide-eyed face with cheekbones just a shade too broad. She looked very attractive. She was well dressed, in an informal way, and a notebook was slung in a little harness over her left shouldtsr. Gardner guessed that she was in her middle, or perhaps late twenties. There were no rings on her slim, tapering fingers.

He realized the dangers inherent in any such encounter as this, and tried to wrench himself free. But his eyes had met hers, and he stood where he was, unable to move away from her.

"I live here too," she said, laughing prettily. "A few days ago they told me at the desk that another Terran had moved in, but I didn't know if you were the one."

"I've been here four days."

"Then you're the one they told me about. It's good to see a friendly face again."

"Yes," Gardner said vaguely. He knew that this was a crisis point. He had to succeed in breaking this relationship before it began, or all might be jeopardized foolishly. He said, "It was good to meet you, but I really ought to run along now. I—"

She was pouting. "You don't have to run away from me so fast, you know. I'm not going to bite you. Honest, that's a promise."

Gardner forced a good imitation of a chuckle. He told himself that he was getting into trouble, very serious trouble. But perhaps he might still work his way out of it without having to seem impolite.

"Okay, then. I appreciate your subtlety. Would you care to be bought a drink?"

"I would indeed. You're most kind to make the offer," she said impishly.

"There's a little cafe across the street."

She wrinkled her nose. She was lightly sprinkled with freckles, Gardner noticed. "That place is so terribly vulgar," she said. "Why don't we just go into the hotel casino?"

Gardner shrugged. Drinks in the casino were twice as expensive as across the street, for one thing. But he was bound by the rules of chivalry, now. "The casino it is, then."

They went to the rear of the lobby and through the automatically-operated doors into the dimly-lit room. A Lurioni clad in the local equivalent of a tuxedo-and-tails came gliding unctuously up to them to ask if they were interested in gambling.

"Not at the moment," Gardner said. "We'd just like a table in the back, and something to drink."

"Of course, *ser* Earthman. Come with me."

They were led to a nook at the rear, behind the gaming tables. It might have been romantic, secluded as it was, but the lighting in the ceiling was defective, and buzzed annoyingly; besides, the place had the sour reek of the foul Lurioni beer. They settled into the alcove facing each other.

"Do you drink *khall*?" he asked.

She nodded. "I've sampled a little. But you have to understand that I haven't had the opportunity to do much social drinking on Lurion. That's why I practically shanghaied you just now."

Gardner grinned and ordered two *khalls*. While they waited for the liquor to arrive, he said, "Now tell me what such a handsome piece of womanflesh is doing all by herself on a nasty world like this."

"I'm a graduate anthropology student, working on my doctoral thesis," she said.

"I never would have guessed it! What's your field of special interest?"

She said, as the waiter deposited the drinks on the table, "My thesis is called *Abnormal Cruelty on Civilized Worlds*."

"You've certainly come to the right place for that. How long have you been here?"

"Four months." She chuckled. "Here we are getting into a complicated discussion, and we don't even know each other's names. I'm Lori Marks."

"Roy Gardner."

"North American?"

"Yes. So are you."

"*Very* north," she said. "I'm Canadian. Born in Ottawa. And you're from the northeastern part of the United States, or else you're trying to fool me with a phony accent."

"I'm not. I'm a Massachusetts boy."

She giggled. "Massachusetts seems so insignificant when you're umpteen light-years away. So does Ottawa, for that matter. Or the whole hemisphere. They all seem to blur into one." Sipping her drink, she said, "And what do *you* do, Roy? Don't tell me you're an anthropologist working on the same thing I am, or I'll absolutely have a fit."

Gardner smiled gently. "No chance. I'm a dealer in precious gems."

"Really?" Her eyes went wide with disbelief.

"Really," he said. "Is it so improbable?"

"It's just ...well, funny, that's all."

"How so, funny?"

"Funny because I always pictured a jewel merchant as a little shrunken sort of man with a squint in his eyes from peering through his loupe. You just don't look the part, dammit! You look more like ...well, an adventurer, or a spy, or something romantic. Anything but a trader in precious gems."

Gardner tried to keep from wincing. "I'm sorry," he said. "Remind me to shrink next time I see you. And some day remind me to tell you what I think anthropologists ought to look like."

She giggled delightedly. *"Touche."*

The conversation, which had become almost giddy, slackened for a moment. Gardner looked at the girl thoughtfully. She was young, pretty, intelligent, lively, unmarried.

And she was condemned to death.

Gardner felt his throat grow dry. He lifted the glass to his lips and took a long, deep pull of the fiery *khall.* He looked away, suddenly, so she would not see the pain on his face.

CHAPTER SEVEN

An hour later, and two additional rounds of *khall*, and Gardner had his hand across the table, holding hers. He was forcing himself to take the *khall* one sip at a time, letting his body metabolize it before he allowed any more into his system. Otherwise he ran the risk of becoming maudlin, sentimental, and, perhaps, overly talkative. The combination might be fatal.

He eyed the girl closely, thinking of her and her thesis. It was a promising enough topic for research, and there was no doubt that she had come to the perfect world for studying cruelty. And then the thought returned that in three weeks—no, now only two weeks and a couple of days, now—he was going to kill this girl and the three billion Lurioni she was so assiduously studying.

"How long are you planning to stay on Lurion?" he asked, trying to sound merely formally curious, with no deeper motive.

"Oh, another month or so, I guess."

Gardner winced. A whole month!

She went on, "My visa's up in two months, you see, but I've observed about all the cruelty I want to observe on any one planet. These people have perfected it astonishingly well. You'd be surprised how many happy marriages there are on Lurion with one partner a sadist and the other a masochist."

"That sounds like a pretty sensible arrangement," Gardner said. Then, returning to the earlier subject, "So you're leaving in a month, eh? Guess I'll be on Terra afore ye, in that case. I'll be going back in two, two and a half weeks."

Her eyes brightened. "You can't imagine how much I envy you. Frankly, I'm sick of this place. If I could get passage back, I'd leave with you, or even earlier. But all the ships out are booked solid for a month. I've been checking."

"And no luck, huh?"

She shook her head. "There isn't a berth to be had on any ship."

Gardner felt the dull thudding of his heart beneath his breastbone. *She could leave with me,* he thought, but the hopeful thought died at once. There was no room for more than five on his little ship, and members of his team had to have priority. Besides, it would be a flat violation of security to take her with him. Terran civilians were not to be evacuated.

She's expendable, Gardner told himself savagely. *Earth Central would never have approved her passport if she had any value to anybody. The fact that she's young and full of life and wants to live doesn't matter to the computer. She's here, and so she'll have to die with the rest of them.*

He gripped the glass he was holding tightly, then released it for fear he would smash it. Getting involved with her was a monstrous mistake; he had known that at the start, and yet he had allowed himself to glide into this *tete-a-tete.* And now he would have to contend with sticky emotions all the way from here to the end. It made a difficult job practically impossible.

She noticed his mood. "You look pale, Roy. Is something the matter?"

"No, nothing," he said quickly. "There just isn't enough alcohol in me yet, that's all."

He took a hefty slug of *khall* and stared broodingly at the swirling greenish liquor that remained in the glass. *Khall* was cheap. Gordon wondered if his predecessor, Davis, who was probably still wandering some foul back alley of Lurion in a drunkard's rags, had also met a girl on Lurion. The *khall* helped to numb the guilt, all right. Not much, but enough.

"You really can't be feeling all right," Lori insisted. "You keep staring into your glass that way, or else off into space. Why don't you tell old Aunt Lori the trouble? Maybe I can help."

Her hand touched his and, irritably, he snatched it away.

"There isn't any trouble!" he snapped. "Don't start meddling with—"

He stopped, seeing the shocked, hurt expression on her face, and realized the depth of his boorishness. "I'm sorry, Lori," he said softly. "That was a miserable thing to say. You were just trying to help me, and I almost yelled your head off."

"It's all right, Roy. We all lose our tempers sometimes. Especially when strangers try to butt into our personal problems. Forgive me?"

"I'm the one who needs to be forgiven," he said.

They patched it up, but Gardner knew he had stung her deeply. He forced himself to look cheerful, to prevent any further inquiries. But, within, he told himself, *She's just a lonely kid on an ugly world, and I had to go and be nasty to her.*

"You are a strange one," she said.

He grinned. "I'm still sober, that's the real trouble. And so are you. Let's see if we can't do something about the situation."

He called the waiter over and ordered yet another round of *khall*, and another one when they had finished that. He realized that neither of them had as much as mentioned the thought of dinner, and now it was past the dinner hour. Another insidious effect of *khall*, he thought with curious clarity. It's a high-calorie drink, the kind that bamboozles you out of your appetite, but doesn't nourish you in place of the food you're skipping.

He got very carefully and meticulously crocked during the next hour, maintaining an iron control over himself all the while. His face felt fuzzy, his hearing was not as acute as it was when he was sober, and he knew that if he stood up he would have some difficulty co-ordinating his movements. But yet he was still his own master. He had had just enough *khall* to numb the burgeoning guilt growing within him, but not enough to cause him to say or do anything indiscreet.

Lori was considerably less careful. By the time the hour had passed, she was volubly prattling about her oedipus complex; her very real fear of becoming a spinster school-teacher in some small college's anthropology department; her feeling of loathing and repugnance for Lurion and all that happened there. In short, she tossed at Gardner her entire self.

"So you see, I figured it was better to come here first and get a good stiff dose of ugliness, and then I could use Lurion as a sort of yardstick when I moved on to other planets, on my list."

Gardner nodded gravely. Had he been a little more sober, he would have cut the conversation short before it was too late, before she had given so much of herself that it would be impossible for him ever to make the cold decision that would kill her.

He sat quietly, listening, until she talked herself out. Perhaps the *khall* was losing its hold on her, for she smiled suddenly, reddened, and said, "I've been talking an awful lot of drivel, haven't I?"

"On the contrary. It's all been most fascinating, Lori."

"But I've been hogging the conversation. I've hardly let you say a thing. And now you know every little thing I've done since I was seven, and I really don't know anything more about you than your name, your trade, and where you're from!"

Gardner smiled lightly. "Perhaps that's just as well. I've had a horribly dull life. It would only bore you if I went into all the dreary details."

She seemed to accept that as being reasonably sincere. They finished their drinks. Lori looked at the time and said, with a little gasp, "Oh, dear, its getting terribly late!"

"For both of us. In this place you just can't sleep past daybreak."

Gardner took her back upstairs; her room was two floors below his own. They stood for a moment outside her door.

"Goodnight, Roy. And thanks for spending the evening with me. It did me good to see a Terran face again."

"The pleasure was mine, Lori. Goodnight."

He was standing so close to her that a kiss seemed to be in order. But it was a light one, a delicate grazing of lips and no more, a gentle thank-you-for-an-evening's-company. She opened the door, staggered inside, nearly toppled on the bed, waved to him somewhat giddily, and closed the door. She hadn't invited him in, and Gardner hadn't been looking for an invitation. He smiled at her through the closed door, and went up the winding stairs to his own room.

As usual, the seal had been tinkered with. No surprise, that; the management and all the hotel employees knew that he was a jewel merchant, and they were dead set on robbing him before he left the hotel. But, unfortunately for them, there just wasn't any way for them to penetrate that seal.

Gardner broke it with a quick blast of air—the signal was unaffected by the quantity of alcohol fumes on his breath—entered, and sealed the door carefully from inside.

He slept soundly, waking just after dawn with a ferocious hangover. Triphammers kept exploding behind his forehead, as he made his way muzzily to the washstand and gobbled down a pill. The pill eased the throbbing considerably, but his head continued to ache. Lori was not in the hotel dining room for breakfast when he arrived. Gardner wondered if she were sleeping late, and debated going up to her room to pay her a visit. But he decided against that, and went straight to the jewel exchange from the dining room.

That evening, when he returned from his day's commerce, she was in the lobby again. She smiled graciously at him as he entered.

"Hello, Roy. Sleep well last night?"

"I slept fine. It was waking up that hurt."

She grinned. "I know what you mean."

"I missed you at breakfast," Gardner said. "You sleep through all the racket the chambermaids make?"

"It's easier to juggle hot coals," she said. "No, I was up and out early at the crack of dawn. I went down to the produce markets at sunup to watch the cockfights they stage down there."

Gardner's eyebrows rose. "I'm impressed. You couldn't have had more than four hours' sleep."

"It's the natural resiliency of youth," she said lightly. "But I'm starting to feel it now. I'm crumbling around the edges, if you know what I mean."

Gardner invited her into the casino for a drink; this time, they limited themselves to one apiece, then went on into the dining-room for dinner, and spent the rest of the evening in the hotel lounge talking to each other.

The next day, when Gardner arrived at the jewel exchange for his day's trading session, he saw Tom Steeves heading toward him. Steeves, the veteran of twenty years of jewel trading on Lurion, had made several attempts to get friendly with Gardner, but the Security man had warded Steeves off as politely as possible, not wanting to get entangled in a friendship with a man he had to kill.

But this morning Steeves would not be shaken off. "Are you free for lunch today, Roy?"

"Yes, I am ...uh ...*why?*" Gardner asked, wishing he had had the good sense to offer a defensive excuse.

Steeves smiled jovially. "I'm having lunch with a couple of interesting fellows, and I'm looking around for company. I'd very much like you to join us, Roy. I think it would be well worth your while."

There was something almost cajoling in Steeves' tone, as if the stout, middle-aged jewel merchant were pleading with Gardner to say yes.

Frowning, Gardner asked, "What sort of fellows do you mean? Are they in the jewel line?"

"Not exactly. They're ...well, philosophers, for lack of a better word. Two young Lurioni."

The idea of Lurioni philosophers seemed unlikely to Gardner, unless it was a philosophy of evil that Steeves' friends expounded. But the Security man felt strangely moved by Steeves' insistence. Wondering whether he were making another major tactical error, he accepted Steeves' invitation and agreed to meet the older man at noon.

It was a hectic morning. Gardner threw himself into his trading with such energy that he surprised himself; it was almost as if this really *were* his life's focus, this trading of stones and amassing of money. At noon, he found Steeves waiting at the prearranged street corner.

"The restaurant is a few blocks from here," Steeves said. "It's quickest to walk. My friends will meet us there."

As they made their way through the narrow, crowded streets, Steeves said, "Well, Gardner, you've been on Lurion close to a week now. What do you think of the place, eh?"

"You want me to be blunt?"

"I want you to be honest."

Gardner shrugged. "It's a hellhole, the most unmitigatedly evil planet I've ever seen; a world where the prime commandment seems to be *Hate thy neighbor.*"

"You seem to have sized the place up pretty quickly," Steeves said. "It doesn't take long, does it?"

"Not at all."

"Yet I've been here twenty years," the older man remarked. "I'm almost used to it. And you know something, Gardner? It doesn't bother me any more. My first couple of months on Lurion, I kept thinking that this planet was the pinnacle of savagery. I hated it here. But gradually I began to understand why Lurion was the way it was, and I stopped hating." He laughed self-consciously. "You think I'm a fat old fool, eh, Gardner?"

"I didn't say—"

"Of course not. But you're new here, and you can't possibly believe that anyone could learn to tolerate Lurioni ways. And maybe I *am* a fat old fool. Maybe living here so long has dissolved my brain. Here's the restaurant."

They turned in the doorway of a small, dimly-lit place with only a scattering of patrons. Two Lurioni were sitting at a table to the left of the door, and they rose the moment Steeves and Gardner entered. They looked young, and there was something about their eyes—a gentleness, a sadness, that Gardner had not observed before on this planet. He felt uneasy and troubled, and told himself that once again his curiosity had led him into risks. Meeting Lurioni socially was unwise, considering the nature of his assignment.

Steeves said, "Roy Gardner, meet Elau Kinrad and Irin Damiroj." As they all sat, Steeves said to the two Lurioni, "Mr. Gardner is new to Lurion. He's only been here a few days, and he told me just now that he despises Lurion."

Before Gardner could say something that would take the sting from Steeves' truthful remark, Damiroj said softly, "Your attitude is quite understandable, *ser* Gardner. We despise our culture ourselves."

The conversation was interrupted by the arrival of the waiter. After they had ordered, Steeves said to Gardner, "Kinrad and Damiroj are what you'd call progressive Lurioni. They're active in philosophical circles here."

"I wasn't aware that there *were* philosophical circles on Lurion," Gardner said.

Kinrad smiled. "It is a recent development, say, of the past three years. That is, our organization dates only from three years past. Previously there were always a few of us, isolated, generally unaware of the existence of any others like themselves. Usually their fate was suicide. Damiroj and I hope to counteract this."

Gardner was silent while they explained, speaking alternately, with Steeves bridging the occasional linguistic gaps. They began with a brief history of Lurion, a poor planet to begin with, badly cheated by nature; its soil was barren and devoid of many useful heavy elements, and its climate was treacherous and unstable from pole to pole. Dank hot seasons were succeeded by blood-freezing cold ones.

There was only one race of Lurioni, but there had been many nations, each toiling along at a bare subsistence level. Marginal life had given rise to a counsel of despair; on a world like Lurion, it was each man for himself. War had been frequent, usually for the basest imperialistic motives.

Some fifteen hundred years ago, the scattered nations of Lurion had finally begun to amalgamate. First came the alliances and ententes; then, the beginning of linkage between the alliances. Until finally Lurion had attained its present confederate form of government, with one central authority, one main language; but with considerable autonomy in the confederated nations. With such a shaky union, Lurion entered the era of interstellar space travel and established communications with most of the other planets.

But the old ways of fear and greed had remained. A planet-wide religion, conceived in ancient pre-technological days, still survived, though transformed and secularized; it was a free-enterprise kind of religion which counseled each man to do evil lest evil be done to him first.

"Our world is not an attractive one," Kinrad admitted. "Our laws are archaic, our ethics brutish, our art debased, our commerce rapacious. There are those on Lurion who even agitate for war with other worlds."

"No!" Gardner said.

"Alas, yes," Damiroj replied mournfully. "We hope this will not come to pass. But in the meantime we work quietly, privately, in hopes of influencing our countrymen. And Earthmen like *ser* Steeves are invaluable to us."

Steeves grinned. "I've become sort of father-confessor to the outfit, you might say. I try to show them how they can work for the betterment of life here. And I help out with cash. We're trying to get men into the government, you see, and that takes money, for we have to bribe bigger and better than the politicos if we ever hope to abolish the bribe system at all. So I contribute. Maybe now you can see what I'm driving at, Gardner."

"I see it; this is a pitch for funds."

"Exactly."

"But what makes you think I've got loose cash? And anyway, why should I give a damn about the Lurioni way of life?" Gardner asked.

Steeves did not flinch. "Even if you gave a couple of coppers, it would help. And I *know* you give a damn about Lurion, Gardner. Just in these few days, I've been able to size you up as a man who's got social conscience. You aren't just a money-grubber like most of our colleagues. You're intelligent. You understand that we've got to help the Lurioni to help themselves, or else civilization is going to stay on the backstabbing level here forever. Which makes Lurion undesirable for us. And which might lead to war, for all we know. So that's why I brought you along to meet these friends of mine. I thought—"

"No," Gardner said hoarsely. He rose from the table, though his meal was only half-finished. "You've got the wrong man. I'm not interested in contributing to anything. Let Lurion solve its own problems."

Pale, shaky, he bolted from the restaurant, while the others gaped in astonishment. Out in the street, Gardner stopped, wiping the sweat from his forehead. He was weak and shaky. The meeting had been a fiasco. Nothing could be more dangerous to his mission than getting mixed up with a bunch of Lurioni radicals.

He made his way to a sidewalk pub.

"Khall," he muttered.

He gripped the drink tightly and gulped it down. It was essential that he blot this luncheon from his mind, as soon as possible.

CHAPTER EIGHT

That day and the next, Gardner saw a good deal of Lori—*too* much, he admitted bitterly. He was a deeply troubled man. The smiling, gentle faces of Kinrad and Damiroj haunted him, carrying along the damning knowledge that Lurion was not wholly black, that there were those sincerely determined to help the world outgrow its ruthless past. And the involvement with Lori left him equally worried.

They spent most of their time in the hotel casino or in the lobby, since Gardner steadfastly refused to try to lure her to his room, and carefully avoided any opportunity of entering hers.

As they sat together at the casino table, Gardner wondered just what she thought of him. That he was a queer one, certainly; either that or a man of an unbreakably puritan frame of mind, someone who simply didn't care for the joys of the flesh. What other reason could there be for his failure to attempt the establishment of an intimate liaison with her?

She was wrong on both counts, Gardner thought, but he didn't dare let her find that out. There was no way of avoiding her company, but he was aware of the mortal dangers of letting their relationship get any more intense than mere friendship.

On the last night of the week, Gardner suggested that she let him take her on a field trip. "You probably haven't been to this place," he said, "and you ought to take it in before you leave Lurion. It's way out in North City, but it's worth the trip."

"You've got my curiosity aroused."

"Does that mean you'll go?"

It did. After dinner that night, Gardner summoned a cab, and they traveled into North City, to the bar on One Thousand Six and the Lane of Lights, the place where he had met Smee.

Gardner uneasily half-expected to meet Smee there again, despite the definite instruction Smee had received to leave the city and go to his action post. But, to Gardner's relief, Smee did not seem to be in the bar. He hoped Smee had actually moved on without a hitch to his permanent locale.

"You'll see cruelty at its most refined tonight," he promised her, as they entered.

Inwardly, Gardner hoped that there would again be a raid, with all the ruthless violence of the last one. He hoped the knife-dancers would be out in full glory. He wanted another reassuring demonstration of the foulness of this world.

They took a table at the back, where he had sat with Smee. Gardner looked around, checking on the location of that door through which he and Smee had made their escape the last time.

"What time does the show start?" Lori asked.

"About an hour after midnight, I guess. We've got lots of time yet."

They ordered *khall* from the scornfully obsequious waiter. In the past few days Gardner and Lori had sampled a few of the other Lurioni drinks, but had found them all equally unpalatable.

As they sipped their drinks, Lori said, "Can I have a preview of what I'm going to see? It always helps when I'm prepared to evaluate what's taking place."

Gardner told her, in detail. She listened in silence, her eyes wide and startled. When he had finished, she coughed a little and said sarcastically, "That sounds very lovely. I'm going to have the most lurid doctoral thesis ever written when I get back to Earth. I guess I could fill a whole book with the sins of Lurion."

When I get back to Earth, she had said. Gardner felt a pang, but shrugged it off. "It ought to make for exciting reading," he said. "Provided your examiners like exciting reading, that is."

"They don't. It's not the number of instances of cruelty I cite that measures how thorough a job I've done; it's my evaluation that matters."

"Quality, not quantity, of observation."

"Exactly."

The evening passed slowly. Gardner fought a rousing inner battle to keep sober. He won, but it was far from easy. It was so simple to bathe the brain in *khall* and cease to think, cease to brood. But the thought of Davis kept him temperate—Davis, the sober Security man who had turned into a shambling rummy in less than two weeks on Lurion.

Shortly after midnight the familiar hush fell over the place. The tables were cleared away, the front windows opaqued. The wall sphinctered open.

"It's beginning," Gardner murmured.

The dancers appeared. They were different from last time's, and this time there were three of them instead of a pair: two men and a woman. Sharp, harshly dissonant music began to grind in the background, piped in from the hidden rooms elsewhere in the building, and the dance started.

Gardner took a quick glance at Lori. She was watching, fascinated, leaning forward on the edge of her seat, as the dancers began their stylized motions.

Back and forth, up and down, now rapidly, now slowly, with a slash of the knife at each pass, until blood trickled down oiled skins, the dance went on. Fifteen minutes passed, twenty, thirty. Gardner split his attention between the dancers and Lori and the front door, knowing that he would have to move fast in the event of another raid.

But there was no raid. The dance, this time, was permitted to wind through to its conclusion. Feeling a curious chill, Gardner watched detachedly as the two male dancers advanced stiffly on the female, swung round her in a grotesque goose step, raised their knife-hands at the same time and, suddenly, simultaneously, transfixed her with both their blades.

Lori was taking notes at a fantastic rate. "Sexual symbolism?" he heard her mutter, as she scribbled.

Gardner gasped. The female was crumpling daintily to the floor, and the hypnotized audience was drumming its heels in lusty applause, yet Lori had not lost her composure. Gardner was astonished. It was a remarkable display of scientific zeal, not to mention sheer toughness of mind.

A riot of light bathed the floor as attendants dragged off the corpse of the female dancer. Suddenly, a new light struck Gardner's eyes, a sharp, insistent flash of green.

He glanced down at the indicator band on his wrist. The green panel was pulsating brightly.

Deever Weegan had just arrived on Lurion.

"Is there something wrong, Roy?" Lori asked. "You look so pale all of a sudden."

"I'm not used to public bloodshed, that's all," he said in a hoarse voice. "After all, I'm not an anthropologist, you know."

His fingers were quivering. He looked at the firm green light again.

Three fifths of the chain that would destroy Lurion had been forged.

CHAPTER NINE

They left the bar without incident, hailed a cab, and returned to the hotel. As ever, Gardner made his goodnights as quick as possible.

In his room, he stared for a long while at the green band on the indicator. Weegan was here, somewhere. So now only Kully Leopold and Damon Archer remained to complete the link.

The days of the next week passed smoothly. Gardner had developed into a skilled trader of jewels by this time; he kept his stock moving around, buying some jewels, selling others, appearing active at all times. He rented a visi-screen and had it installed in his hotel room, ostensibly for the benefit of customers who might have some need to get in touch with him.

At least, that was the reason he gave to the management in answer to their persistent inquiries. But in truth he had no interest in receiving calls from clients. He anticipated calls from the newly-arriving members of his team and, aside from finding it awkward and incovenient to do his communicating in an open alcove in the hotel lobby, he preferred to see their faces as he spoke. He was something more than a figurehead leader; it was part of his job to see that each of the other four was alert, stable, and ready to do his share of the job when the time came.

Gardner wondered what might happen if one of them *weren't* ready. Himself, for instance. Doubt loomed large in his mind. But he told himself that he would find the strength he needed, *when* he needed it.

He saw Lori frequently during that week, too. She gallantly insisted on paying her share of their entertainment costs, as if tacitly acknowledging the fact that Gardner was not getting full measure from her. Gardner made the proper protests, but allowed her finally to win the argument.

And at the end of the second week, the blue panel on his indicator flashed into glowing life. Kully Leopold had arrived, one day prematurely. The pattern was taking shape. Four out of five were present, scattered over the planet. Only Damon Archer, the anchor man on the team, was yet to be heard from, and he would be arriving in another week.

It was necessary that the team members spaced their arrivals. There was a regular pattern of coming and going between Lurion and Earth, just as there was between Earth and every other world of the civilized galaxy. The five team members would not be noticed if they entered Lurion one at a time.

And, since their landings were scheduled for five different spaceports on five different continents, it was unlikely that the sonic generator each one was carrying would cause much excitement, unless the customs officials at such widely separated points bothered to compare notes on strange devices.

Smee had arrived with a tourist group six months earlier. His generator had been accounted for as a souped-up camera, which it had been redesigned to resemble. Gardner's generator had gone through customs as a jeweler's apparatus. The others each had their alibis too. The Security planning had been excellent. Only the human factor in the plan was variable.

The day after Kully Leopold had landed, Deever Weegan called Gardner. The hotel management gave Weegan the number of Gardner's private room visi-screen, and the call reached him there.

Gardner, stared at the image in the screen, comparing the flinty face he saw with the photo of Weegan he had been shown back on Earth in Karnes' office.

"You're Gardner, aren't you?"

"Right. Weegan?"

The man in the screen nodded. "Of course."

Weegan had an ascetic look about him, Gardner thought. The man's eyes were so stony they seemed almost to glitter; his cheekbones jutted sharply beneath each ear, and his thin, bloodless lips were set in an austere line. Gardner wondered if the inner man were as coldly bleak as the exterior.

Gardner said, "What's on your mind, Weegan? You're set up all right where you are, aren't you?"

"Yes."

"Well, then?"

"I'm simply checking."

Gardner blinked. "Checking on *me*?"

"Checking on the project in general," Weegan said blandly. "I'm anxious for its success."

Gardner gasped and went pale. He scowled into the visual pickup. Was Weegan out of his mind, talking of "the project" so loosely over a public communicator?

"The sale of gems is going well," Gardner said icily, stressing each word. "I imagine we'll all return to Earth as rich men."

Weegan hesitated momentarily. He seemed to recognize the mistake he had made.

"Oh, of course," he said. "Are the other members of the corporation prospering?"

"I believe so," Gardner said. "Dudley and I were in contact the other day, and he said that vegetables were getting set for a rise. Also mining shares. Better check with your stockbroker about it. And Oscar told me his wife is better." He glared tightly at Weegan. *Catch wise, you idiot,* he implored silently. *Don't ask a foolish question now.*

"I'm glad to hear it," Weegan said. Gardner let out his breath in relief. The other went on, "Well, we'll be in touch again soon, won't we?"

"In about a week, I think. Is that soon enough?"

"No, but it'll have to do," Weegan said. "I'll be looking forward to it."

"Right."

Weegan broke the contact.

Gardner sat back and stared at the dying swirl of color on the screen for a moment, letting some of the blood seep back into his face, letting the butterflies in his stomach settle down into place.

The idiot, he thought.

Weegan had nearly collapsed the whole show. If Gardner hadn't managed to shut the thin-faced man up in time, Weegan might easily have gone prattling right on, inquiring after Smee and Leopold and the not-yet arrived Archer, linking the five of them neatly in one breath. Weegan's blunder might not have wrecked the project, but anything that tended to link the team was dangerous.

The deaths of five Security agents could be important to nobody but those agents. But if the Lurioni discovered what the generators were capable of doing, they wouldn't be content merely to devise unpleasant deaths for the five plotters. They would plaster news of the conspiracy all over the known universe. Earth's name would soon become something to spit at, a curse.

Naturally, Earth would deny that there was any official connection with the Five, but who would be naive enough to believe that? Five men don't decide on their own initiative to destroy a planet.

Shuddering, Gardner cursed Weegan, cursed Karnes, cursed the computer whose inexorably clicking relays had gotten them into this unholy business in the first place. And a new thought occurred to him.

The computer, presumably, had had a hand in choosing the first, the unsuccessful team. Well, Gardner thought, the computer had been eighty percent wrong that time; only Smee, out of the five men who were sent out, had the stuff to survive.

So now another team had been despatched, of whom at least one—Weegan—had the possibly fatal flaw of failing to reason out the consequences of his words. And one other, at least—Gardner—was given to serious interior misgivings about the validity of the whole project.

That made at least two of the computer's four new selections who weren't perfectly fitted for the job; and Gardner hadn't even met the other two, yet.

It wasn't a very good score.

Suppose, Gardner asked himself, suppose the computer's accuracy in making long-range predictions was equally miserable?

Suppose the computer was all cockeyed about the anticipated Lurioni invasion of Earth?

Suppose he was actually murdering a world that meant no harm? Or that could be redeemed by less violent means?

Sudden perspiration popped out all over him. He shivered for one dreadful moment, and then, just as suddenly, he was past the conflict-point and secure in his belief.

Lurion *was* an abysmal world. It was a hateful, cold-blooded, nasty place.

It was the sort of world on which you didn't turn your back on anyone. And even then, rear-view vision was a useful precaution.

Unquestionably, the planet was beyond any redemption.

For the first time in an uncomfortably large number of days, Gardner was able to smile, confident that the computer was right, that he was right, and that the job he was doing was right.

And then he heard Lori Marks' voice outside in the corridor, calling to him, and his newly-found complacency was shattered in an instant.

She knocked softly. "Roy? Roy, do you mind if I come in?"

"Just a minute, Lori. I'll have to unseal the door." Sweat started to course down Gardner's body again. This was going to be the test of his resolve, coming up now. This was the first time she had ever come to his room.

He breathed on the door seal and it curled into a ball. A moment later he was smiling at Lori, and she was smiling back.

"I hope I'm not disturbing you."

"Not at all. I was just wondering if I ought to go down and find out if you were around."

She was holding some typewritten sheets in her hand. Gardner glanced inquiringly at them. She held them forward and said, "I've been typing up my notes on that horrid dance we saw, and I've just finished. I wondered if you would care to check them through for accuracy."

"Be happy to," Gardner said. What else could he have told her?

But he could see easily that she hadn't come up to his room simply for the purpose of letting him verify her anthropological observations. She was wearing a clinging, low-cut synthilk blouse that seemed more calculated toward a session of biology, not anthropology. There was something keenly expectant about her manner. And, for the first time since he had known her, she was wearing perfume. It was a subtle, musky flavor that had an alien scent about it.

He closed the door behind her. She made herself at home immediately, sitting down in the chair next to the bed. She looked around the room with evident interest, and flushed guiltily when Gardner let her know by a glance that he was watching her.

She said apologetically as she handed him the typed sheaf of notes, "I hope you won't have too much trouble with the spelling. My machine is out of kilter, and I had to rent one of the local voice-writers. It's good and efficient, but phonetically it's a nightmare."

"I'll manage," Gardner said.

The first page was headed, *Notes Toward an Analysis of the Sadistic Element in Lurioni Entertainment Forms.* Gardner skimmed through the first paragraph or two of her notes, and allowed himself to appear to be reading the rest. Actually, his mind was occupied with the making of decisions and the formulating of a plan.

This relationship had to be brought to a crux at once. She had made the overt gesture, with this flimsy and transparent maneuver to get inside his room. The display of cleavage, the dab of perfume—all these, he knew, were calculated to force him to a point of commitment toward her.

Well, the time had come to settle the matter. If he delayed any further, he would be knowingly jeopardizing the success of the mission.

By the time he had finished his cursory scanning of the notes, he had made up his mind. The break would have to be complete and absolute.

"Well?" she asked. "No comment?"

Jolted back to consideration of the notes, he smiled weakly and said, "Ah ...hmm. Nice and accurate, I'd say." His eyes leaped over the blocks of words and paragraphs, searching for something he could seize on and criticize. "I think it's a bit lacking in real sparkle," he went on. "You don't fully convey the nastiness of the situation. Get me?"

She nodded. "I thought so too, when I read them back. Got any suggestions?"

"Focus it more sharply on the people watching the thing. Not us, but the others, the Lurioni patrons, the ones busy empathizing with the dancers. There's practically a psychic bond there. The killing, when it comes, is participated in vicariously by the whole audience. *That's* the really nasty part of the business."

"You're right," she said. "I'll add that when I'm preparing my submission."

Rising, she wandered around the room, and paused to peer curiously at the sonic generator, which Gardner had never bothered to hide, since the total effectiveness of a doorseal made furtiveness unnecessary.

"What's this gadget?" she asked.

Gardner sucked in his breath sharply. "That's ...that's a thing I use in testing jewels. It enables me to make sure they're genuine."

"Oh? Would you show me how it works?" she asked innocently. "I'd be terribly interested."

Gardner's face drooped. "It uses up a lot of power," he said. "Anyway, it's after working hours I'd just as soon not bother, unless you insist."

She shrugged. "I guess it isn't all that important, if it would mean a bother."

"I'll let you see how it works some other time," Gardner said, relieved. It was not for a moment that he realized the grim double-meaning of his words.

But Lori had already lost interest in the sonic generator. She crossed the room and boldly sat down on the bed next to him.

Gardner no longer had any doubt. Her intention in coming up here was almost embarrassingly obvious. Gardner felt a fleeting sense of guilt about what he was going to do, but banished the sensation. There was to be no more guilt about this.

As she snuggled close to him he edged away, forcing himself to ignore her warmth and softness.

"Roy, don't always keep running away from me," she murmured.

Gardner moved away still further, then stood up and said in a brittle voice, "Would it be too melodramatic, Lori, if I said I had something very important to tell you?"

"No, of course not, Roy. Tell me anything you want." Her eyes were half-closed and a little dreamy. Gardner took a deep breath.

"I'm married," he said.

It was a flat lie.

"I have a wife and family back on Terra," he continued, "and it happens that I'm very devoted to them. And before our relation gets any more awkward than it's already become, Lori, I feel you ought to know that I'm very much in love with my wife."

The girl looked steamrollered. The blow had fallen on her with crushing impact. The dreaminess vanished from her eyes, to be replaced with a catlike look of insult and injury.

"I'm sorry to hear that," she said softly. "For my sake, not yours."

"I understand. If ...if circumstances had been otherwise, Lori, well ...maybe ...you know what I'm trying to say. But as it is ..."

Go on, he thought savagely, *sound fumbling and shame-faced and sincere. If you're going to lie to this kid, at least do a convincing job of it.*

She stood up, facing him steadily, making the task easier for him. Impulsively, he gripped her hand tightly. He had never felt like such a heel in his life.

He told her, "I don't think we ought to see each other any more. I'm only going to be on Lurion another week, and it would be easier for both of us."

"Of course, Roy." Her eyes had the glitter that told of tears just barely being held in check, but there was a surprising curtness in her voice that both pleased and puzzled him. He had feared that she might go to pieces completely at the news that he was "married" but he hadn't expected her to come up with this sudden reserve of strength.

"Good-by," he said.

"So long, Roy. And, I'm sorry if I misunderstood things."

She picked up her notes, smiled bleakly at him, and left. She closed the door quietly behind her. Moving mechanically, Gardner replaced the doorseal, then stared unseeingly at the dirty black streaks against the dingy green of the walls.

It was easier now, he thought. There had been a clean break. When the time came to act, he wouldn't be entangled in the bands of a personal relationship.

If he could only manage to keep out of her way for the next week.

Suddenly the yellow panel of his indicator band pinged into brightness. Gardner looked at it dazedly for a moment, not understanding.

The yellow could mean only one thing. Damon Archer was on Lurion, the fifth man in the chain. And he was a week ahead of schedule.

Tensely, Gardner took down the *khall* bottle he now kept on his dresser, and poured himself a drink with quivering hands. If Archer were here, and the indicator band testified that he was, then Lurion's remaining time could be numbered in hours, not in days.

But why was Archer here so early?

CHAPTER TEN

Drink in hand, Gardner walked to the window. He had a fairly good view. He stared out over the city. A garish kaleidoscope of lights and colors greeted his eye, so brilliant that it quite obscured the light of the three tiny moons above.

The instructions engraved on his memory now sprang vividly to life. He could practically hear Karnes intoning, *"When all five members of the team have made their duly scheduled arrivals, you shall proceed at once to place the destruction plan into operation. Any delay at this point may result in failure."*

Gardner frowned. "*...their duly scheduled arrivals.*" But Archer was a week ahead of schedule. It implied some alteration in the plan. He could not act until ...

The visi-screen chimed three times, interrupting his stream of thought. It was the signal for a long-distance communication.

Gardner set his drink down carefully out of the range of the visual pickup and, pulling himself hurriedly together, activated the set.

Colors swirled aimlessly for a moment, a random stream of reds and yellows and blues. Quickly, they coalesced into a face.

It was Smee.

"Yes?" Gardner asked.

The balding operative smiled apologetically. The smile was a little lopsided, as though Smee had been drinking heavily and lost control of his facial muscles.

"I hope I'm not disturbing you, Mr. Gardner."

"No ...no. What's on your mind?"

Smee's eyes were little dark beads. "I suppose you're aware," he said, "that your friend has arrived on Lurion?"

"Yes, I know that," Gardner snapped impatiently. "He got here early. What of it?"

The impatience in Smee's face was suddenly mirrored by the sharpness of his tones. "Six months is a long time, *Mister* Gardner. Now that your friend is here, when do we—"

"Soon, Smee. You'll get the word."

"When?"

"I'm not sure," Gardner said. "There may be some last-minute instructions from the home company, and I don't want to close the deal in haste. Got that?"

Smee sighed heavily. "You're the boss. But I can't take much more of this."

"I know exactly what you mean."

"Okay, then," Smee said. "Let's see that the deal *does* get closed, Gardner. And let's not have to wait too long, either."

He broke the contact.

Nerves jangled, Gardner snatched at his drink and took a healthy gulp. Then he turned away, wincing as the fiery drink hit his stomach.

He couldn't blame Smee at all for being impatient. The little man had been living on Lurion for six months, which was a hellishly long time for anyone, particularly if you were someone waiting patiently for a chance to destroy the planet. Smee's only thought at this moment had to be that the team was now complete.

It was an understandable attitude. But Gardner couldn't work that way. For one reason or another, Archer had arrived on Lurion early; and, until Gardner knew the reason for the change in schedule, he couldn't give the blowup order. For all he knew, Archer was carrying a stay of execution for Lurion. He had to wait till he heard from him.

And then what do I do? Gardner wondered.

If there were no reprieve, it would be up to him at last to give the order to activate the sonic generators.

Gardner finished the drink and set the glass down. Then, acting with methodical precision, he corked the half-full bottle on the table, carried it to the disposal chute, sighed regretfully, and let it drop.

Whatever happened now, he wanted to make sure that he would be sober.

He paced round the room, hands tightly clenched into fists, feeling the frustration of knowing that there was absolutely nothing he could do now but wait. Archer was somewhere on Lurion; Archer knew the name of the hotel where Gardner was registered.

Gardner could not contact Archer, it had to be the other way around. Gardner waited.

Fifteen minutes later, the visi-screen emitted a double buzz. Gardner sprang toward it, yanking down the activating switch. He felt coldly apprehensive as he watched the swirling colors take on form and coherence.

The face that appeared was bland, mild, undistinguished and unmemorable in any way. Weak, watery-looking eyes stared outward, not attempting to look straight forward but shying diffidently off to one side. It was Damon Archer. He was smiling uncertainly. His chin was weak, his hair a mousy brown, his lips thin.

"Hello," he said in a voice that matched his physical appearance. "I'm Damon Archer."

"I know."

"You're Gardner."

"That's right," Gardner said. "I knew you were here, of course. I suppose you're getting in touch with me about the matter of your early arrival."

"Yes, that's it."

Gardner frowned suspiciously. The plan called for Archer to be on the planet's northernmost continent, a good thousand miles from here, but he had made a *local* call. Something must be very wrong.

"Where are you now?" Gardner asked.

"I'm at the spaceport. I've just checked through customs, and—"

"What? But your assignment from the Company specified that—"

"I know, Mr. Gardner," Archer cut in with uncharacteristic sharpness. "But there's been a slight alteration in schedule. I'll have to see you immediately. I want to talk privately with you before we go ahead with anything that's been planned."

Gardner tensed. He said, "All right, I suppose. How soon can you be here?"

"Within the hour."

"I'll be expecting you," Gardner said.

About forty-five minutes later, Gardner opened his door in response to a sharp triple knock, and admitted Archer. Archer was taller and a little leaner than Gardner had anticipated, but otherwise the man had a curiously nondescript quality that Gardner found morbidly fascinating. Archer was a blank, a cipher, a nothing.

Once inside the door, Archer looked quickly all around the room, noting the sonic generator in its place on the dresser, the pouch of jewels, the drinking-glass with its murky little residue of *khall.* Then he gestured to the doorseal that Gardner had replaced on the inside of the door.

"Do we need that here?"

"It protects us," Gardner said. "I keep it up all the time."

"I'd appreciate it if you'd remove it while I'm here," Archer said. He shivered lightly and looked shame-faced. "It's ...ah a sort of phobia of mine. Modified claustro, you see."

Gardner shrugged. "I guess we'll be safe enough in here without it."

He hid the generator and the jewel pouch carefully in the closet, then removed the seal from the room door and affixed it over the closet door. Archer's request struck him as curious; the man seemed too ordinary, too washed-out, to have any phobias. But it was his right as a guest to ask for the seal's removal, and Gardner saw no point in insisting on keeping it there.

"I'd offer you a drink," Gardner said, "but there isn't any left."

Archer flicked a glance at the drinking glass on the table. He said softly, "You needn't worry. I never touch alcohol."

"You're a wise man," Gardner said. He leaned forward, "Now, then. You've arrived a week early. May I ask how come? Also why you're here, instead of at your assigned post?"

"May I speak freely in here about the nature of ...ah ...the project?" Archer asked, eyeing the dirty walls furtively.

"If you must," said Gardner. "I've checked for spy devices. This room's safe, unless there are some ears in the hallway. Wait."

He rose and rapidly crossed the room, yanking the door open. The corridor outside was deserted. And there had not been time for any eavesdroppers outside the door to have hidden themselves.

Gardner closed the door. "It looks clear. Say what you want to say."

Archer folded his legs and tapped the suitcase he had carried with him.

"My generator is in here. Yours, I think, is in that closet. Are all five members of the team here on Lurion now?"

"Look at your indicator band!" Gardner said, surprised at the question.

"Of course." Archer laughed hollowly. "All five *are* here, aren't they? Now, my instructions from Earth Central require me to have a full recapitulation of the nature of our mission from your lips before we can act."

"What the hell for?" Gardner asked, bristling. "Just to give my mouth some exercise?"

Archer smiled apologetically, holding up one hand to stay Gardner's outburst. "As, pardon me, a check on your stability."

"What?"

"Karnes has had some misgivings about *you.* The computer has been called into use again. It revealed that your attitude was likely to deteriorate progressively, and that if we waited the allotted three weeks of the project, the probability was high that you would no longer be capable of carrying out your part."

Gardner's jaws tightened. What Archer was saying cut deep. "So you were sent early because they wanted to get the project taken care of before I blow my trolley completely, eh?"

Archer shrugged. "It was thought advisable to speed up the schedule. And now I must have a complete verification of your comprehension of the project."

Still simmering, although everything Archer had said so far had the ring of truth, Gardner muttered, "What do you want me to tell you?"

"A recapitulation of the nature of our mission," Archer said.

"Okay. Here's your summary: we've been sent here as a team with the assignment..." Gardner lowered his voice, "...of destroying Lurion. It takes five of us to do it, each equipped with a sonic generator that will set up a resonating vibratory pattern when tuned in at the proper geographic locality. I'm in charge."

"Who picked you for the job?"

"Karnes. Chief of Security at Earth Central. I was picked with the aid of the computer, of course."

Archer nodded. As if rehearsing a catechism, he asked, "And why is it considered necessary to destroy Lurion?"

"Computer prognostics have it that militaristic forces on Lurion will organize and launch a destructive attack on Earth some time within the next two generations or so. We have to strike first."

Archer sat back, smiling quietly. "All right. You've got it all down well enough. Just one thing remains to be settled."

"Which is?"

"Are you willing to carry out your share of the assignment?"

Gardner was silent a moment, staring at the bland face opposite him. He moistened his lips.

"Yes," he said finally. "I'm ready and willing."

"Okay, then. I guess we can proceed."

"I've passed the test?"

"You have. And now you're in charge again. When's the event due to take place?"

"As soon as you get up north where you belong," Gardner said. "There's no other reason for delay, now. Give me a call when you reach your assigned position, and I'll transmit the initiating signal." Gardner realized now that he had no more doubts, no hesitation whatever about bringing the project to its culmination.

"Very well, then. Now that we've got everything cleared up, I'll leave at once," Archer said. He rose, tugging his jacket-snaps together and sealing them. Gardner watched him, brows furrowed.

The visi-screen chimed again, the long-distance chime this time.

Gardner activated it and a round, bearded face appeared; it was that of Kully Leopold, the only member of the team Gardner had yet to hear from.

"I guess I'll be going now," Archer said, a little hurriedly.

"Stick around," Gardner told him. "Let's both hear what our friend Leopold has to say." He returned his attention to the visi-screen. "You *are* Kully Leopold, aren't you?"

"That's right. And I wanted to find out whether there's been any change in—Hey! He's leaving!"

Gardner whirled and was surprised to see Damon Archer, suitcase in hand, fumbling annoyedly with the intricate Lurioni doorlatch. A number of seemingly irrelevant but actually interrelated facts suddenly fit themselves together in Gardner's mind.

"Where are you going, Archer?" he demanded.

"I'm—" Archer got the door open at last and, without bothering to finish the sentence, started to slip out.

CHAPTER ELEVEN

Gardner moved rapidly. He jumped forward, getting between the door and its jamb before Archer could slam it in his face. Reaching out into the hallway, he grabbed the fleeing Archer by the shoulder and spun him back into the room; the door slammed shut.

"What's your hurry?" Gardner demanded. "I told you to stick around."

Instead of answering, Archer crashed a fist into Gardner's midsection. Gardner gasped and doubled up, but as Archer confidently brought his fist round for another blow, Gardner grabbed it suddenly, pivoted, and flipped Archer over his shoulder.

The thin man shot backward, landing heavily against the wall with a sharp crack. He scrabbled to his feet, but by that time Gardner was on top of him. Archer's eyes were glaring desperately; his mild face had come to life in a startling way. He strained to roll over, clawed at Gardner's arms, tried to force the weight of the heavier man off him.

He succeeded. Archer was thin, but he seemed to have the tensile strength of beryllium steel. He forced Gardner off him, and then sprang up. Archer was quick on his feet. He ducked back and lunged at Gardner. Gardner left his guard open, rolled with a soft punch under the heart, and sent Archer rocking backward toward the wall with a stiff jolt to the chin.

Gardner followed it up with a barrage of light punches and a swift crack across Archer's exposed throat. It was dirty fighting, no denying it, but such niceties didn't matter now.

Archer gagged and started to topple. Gardner caught him, slapped him twice, just to loosen him up, then thumped his skull hard against the wall. Archer's eyes glazed and closed.

Puffing for breath, Gardner turned back to face the visi-screen. Leopold, who had watched the entire encounter, peered out of the screen, eyes wide in the puzzled oval face.

"That was Archer, wasn't it?" Leopold asked. "What in blazes is happening?"

"I don't know," said Gardner, nursing bruised knuckles. He glanced at the unconscious Archer. "But he made me take the doorseal down, and then he maneuvered me into dictating what amounted to a full confession of ...of the Company's trade secrets. And then when you called he tried a quick getaway. I'm going to look through his suitcase. Suppose you call me back in about ten minutes, eh?"

Gardner broke the contact. He didn't think it would be very wise to have the contents of Archer's suitcase sent out over public beam.

Archer was still unconscious. Good, Gardner thought. Working hastily, he slit the suitcase open with a penknife and looked inside.

Much clothing. A small package containing the sonic generator. And ...

Gardner dragged a little device out from where it nestled between two layers of shirts, and peered grimly at it. A pocket recorder! One of those devilish little subminiaturized devices that could record for an hour on a single reel, one that picked up a good clear signal even when hidden in a suitcase.

Gardner depressed a stud and heard a tinny simulacrum of his own voice say, *"Okay. Here's your summary: we've been sent here as a team of five with the assignment of destroying Lurion. It takes five of us to do it, each equipped with a sonic generator that ..."*

Smiling coldly, he set the tape back to its beginning and pressed the *erase* stud. Checking again, he found that the tape was now blank. He tossed the little recorder down on the bed.

Then he drew a glass of cold water and tossed it in Archer's face. The man on the floor shook his head, sputtered, coughed, and opened his eyes.

Gardner knelt next to him. "I've just played back that tape you made," he said. "Who are you working for, Archer?"

Archer looked dazed. His head lolled to one side. "I don't know what you're talking about, Gardner."

"Don't bluster your way clear. It won't do you any good. Who paid you to wiggle a confession out of me?"

"Don't be crazy. First you attack me like a wild man, then you insinuate—"

Gardner slapped him. The big man's eyes blazed. "I suppose you were making that tape for yourself as a souvenir of this mission!"

Archer made no reply. After a moment's silence, Gardner said, "If you're really a Security man, you know that we don't draw the line at torture if we think the means is justified by the end. I'd hate to have to act uncivilized, Archer, but—"

Archer grinned confidently. "You wouldn't torture me. I've seen your psych report. You're soft inside, Gardner. You try to talk tough, but your mind is just a mass of doubts and contradictions and softbellied evasions—"

Gardner slapped him again, to shut him up. "Who's paying you?"

"No one, yet," Archer said quietly. "But I imagine the Confederacy of Rim Stars will be interested in the way Earth lives up to its high ethical pronouncements. Don't you think so?"

And Archer rose abruptly from his sitting position. His foot lashed out at the squatting Gardner. The heavy boot caught Gardner square in the chest and he toppled over, more stunned with surprise than injured. The attack had been wholly unexpected.

As Gardner came dizzily to a half-sitting position, he saw the other man open the door—this time Archer had no trouble with the latch—and race out into the hallway. Gardner gasped for breath, feeling a dull throbbing under his breastbone where Archer had kicked him. He forced himself up.

Gardner made his way into the corridor, pausing only to lock his door. Even in emergency, it was wrong to leave the room open to any plunderer who might choose this moment to come along.

By the time Gardner had finished locking up, Archer had disappeared into the lift-shaft. Cursing, Gardner streaked down the hallway just in time to see the lift begin to lower itself groundward. Gardner pounded impotently on the door, to no avail.

Other residents of the hotel, their early-evening slumbers disturbed by the fighting and chasing about, now began to open their doors and give vent to their complaints, loudly and in a variety of languages. Gardner ignored their protests. There was still a chance he might catch the fugitive Archer, after all.

Remembering how slowly the lift-shaft operated, Gardner made for the stairs. The staircase was poorly lit, a deepening spiral illuminated only by a sputtering glowlamp near each landing. Gripping the bannister tightly, Gardner sprang down two and three steps at a bound, half expecting to come fetching up against the curved Lurioni blade of some lurking looter crouching spiderlike on the staircase, waiting for just such an occurrence.

But he reached the lobby unhindered. The desk clerk looked up, blinking.

"Did an Earthman just leave the lift-shaft?" Gardner demanded.

"Why ...yes ...that is ..."

Gardner did not pause for details. Negotiating the steps of the hotel in one sprawling leap, he landed upright on the street and looked around.

It was late, only an hour till midnight, and the streets were far from crowded. That made it that much harder for Archer to escape. Gardner caught sight of the fleeing spy, half a block away, and gave pursuit.

Archer moved swiftly, but Gardner had the benefit of the same kind of training, and kept pace. That was all, though; the half-block gap between them remained constant, and no expense of effort on Gardner's part seemed to close it. Archer turned down a twisting side street; Gardner followed. But at any moment the fugitive might think to duck into one of the numerous doorways, and then he could lose himself forever.

Obviously Archer was panicking, or he would have evaded Gardner minutes ago. Gardner pressed forward dodging round the few passersby.

But there seemed no hope of catching him—unless there were help.

On a sudden impulse, Gardner shouted, "That man's a thief! Stop him! Stop that thief!"

A massive Lurioni, rounding the corner in front of Archer, heard the outcry and looked quizzically at the approaching man.

Gardner waved frantically and called, "Yes, that's him! Catch the thief!"

The Lurioni extended one broad hand and Archer ran squarely into it. The Earthman rebounded, turned, saw Gardner gaining on him.

Gardner watched Archer fumble in his pocket, as if hoping to bluff the Lurioni with a weapon. The alien's reaction was swift and decisive. Producing the short, wickedly curved Lurioni blade that no free citizen seemed to be without, the tall being stepped forward, passed the knife with blinding rapidity from one hand to the other several times, and deftly plunged it into Archer's breast.

Gardner stopped short, ten feet away; panting for breath. The Lurioni was smiling benignly.

"The thief has been stopped."

"You killed him!"

"What better way to stop a thief?"

Archer was on his knees, now, writhing in his last agonies. His face was a blank mask of pain; his hands clutched at the hilt of the blade, but his efforts to remove it only drove it in deeper. He had been slashed from belly to breastbone. Great gouts of blood welled out, trickling across the pavement into the gutter. Already, smelling the blood, inquisitive dog-like creatures were beginning to gather.

The dying man muttered something incoherent, stretched his limbs taut, held the spreadeagle for a moment, and went limp.

"He is dead," the Lurioni said calmly. "I have undertaken blood-guilt for you, Earthman."

"I didn't ask you to kill him, only to stop him from getting away."

"You said he was a thief. A thief's life is forfeit, is it not? I have saved the government money."

On this planet all lives are forfeit, Gardner thought. He stared down at the grotesquely twisted form lying sprawled on the pavement. Several strollers had paused on the far side of the street to watch. There was no sign of a Lurioni policeman anywhere.

The killer stooped and casually wrenched his blade free from the body. Looking down at Gardner from his enormous height, the Lurioni said, "This was no affair of mine. You must buy me free of it."

"How much do you want?"

"A thousand units," the Lurioni replied immediately. "It is the usual price."

Gardner scowled, wondering if he ought to try to haggle. He decided against it. The money meant nothing to him, and the sooner he extricated himself from this nightmarish incident, the better. He took out his wallet and surrendered ten hundred-unit notes.

"Is that all?" he asked.

"You must pronounce the formula. Say, 'I take upon myself the blood-guilt for the man slain at my request by Binnachar dur Sliquein.'"

"I take upon myself the blood-guilt for the man slain at my request by Binnachar dur Sliquein," Gardner repeated. "Is that all?"

"That is all. I am absolved."

"What about me, though? What happens to the body, now?"

Binnachar shrugged elaborately. "What concern is that of yours or mine? The man was a thief; you said so yourself. Since he is an Earther, he probably will not have relatives here to seek for his body. Leave him for the carrion-pickers."

"But the police?"

"The death of thieves does not interest the police." Binnachar knelt again and wiped his blade clean on Archer's jacket after which he replaced the knife in his own tunic. "I am grateful to have been of service to you, *ser* Earthman. A pleasant night to you."

Gardner remained where he was for a moment, still shaken by the swiftness, the brutality of the incident.

And no one seemed to care. Perhaps that was the worst of it. The knot of watchers was gone; Binnachar dur Sliquein, having received his blood-fee and having been absolved of blood-guilt, had probably already begun to forget the incident; the police had never even shown up on the scene. The only ones at all interested were the animals that clustered in the gutter, sipping the warm blood that runneled from the gash in Archer's breast. No doubt when they tired of drinking the blood, they would devour the body. Gardner shuddered.

The longer he remained here, he knew, the greater was his chance of finding trouble. Turning, leaving the body where it lay, he retraced his steps until he reached the hotel.

The desk clerk woke once again from his slumber to ask, "Did you find him?"

"Yes," Gardner said.

He rode upstairs.

To his relief, he saw that no one had attempted to enter his room during his brief absence. He sank down wearily on the bed, bitterly regretting the fact that he had thrown away the *khall* bottle. He needed a drink badly. He was shaken to his core.

The computer had failed again, he thought. And this time it had failed in a way that threw doubt on the validity of any of its predictions. Somehow it had managed to send out one who was rotten within, who had chosen to betray Earth instead of work for Earth's safety. How could such a thing happen? Security agents went through fine screening. Those chosen for this particular assignment were screened even more thoroughly. And yet Archer had passed through the net, a traitor.

The computer, Gardner thought, is only a machine. It takes the facts as given to it, weaves in a dollop of random variables, and produces a prediction. But it can't see into the human brain. It had proved unable to peer behind the bland exterior of Damon Archer and detect the traitor lurking within. Archer had fooled the computer; or, rather, the computer had failed to predict his behavior accurately. It had similarly bungled the first expedition to Lurion.

There was no escaping the fact now, Gardner thought. The computer's judgment could not be trusted. It had failed on a short-range prediction, the reliability of one man; how could its word be accepted for such a mighty extrapolation as the coming galactic war?

Gardner realized dully that he was on the edge of turning traitor himself: traitor to Security, traitor to Earth, traitor to the computer; all this, but, perhaps, not a traitor to himself.

Very carefully, Gardner took the dead man's recorder and touched the playback stud. The reel had been completely erased. But there were ways, he had heard, of compelling an erased tape to yield some of its secrets. Just to be absolutely certain, Gardner opened the mechanism, worried out the tiny reel of tape, and shredded it between thumb and forefinger. Then he stuffed it thoughtfully in the disposal chute, following it a moment later with the crushed casing of the recorder itself.

So much for Archer's spying, he thought.

The visi-screen bleeped. It was Leopold, calling back, no doubt. Gardner still felt shaky. He was on the threshold of an important decision, and he didn't want to talk to anyone till the decision was complete. But he couldn't very well ignore the screen.

Gardner activated the set. Yes, it was Leopold. The bearded man looked agitated.

"What happened?"

"He was making a tape of our conversation," Gardner said. "I guess he was planning to peddle it to some third party after the project was complete."

"The little worm," Leopold muttered. "Where did he go?"

"He woke up, knocked me over, and made a break for it. About three blocks from here he ran into a Lurioni with a long knife."

"Dead?"

Gardner nodded. "I left him in the street. He won't be making any little deals."

"But what about—?"

"The project?" Gardner's face darkened. "I don't know. I don't know at all, right now. Just stay in touch with me, and I'll keep you posted on the developments."

"Will do."

The screen went blank. Gardner pounded one fist into the palm of his other hand.

Assuming he still wanted to go through with the project, there would have to be a replacement for Archer. And perhaps a second replacement would be needed. Smee, cracking slowly under the psychological strain of the assignment, was obviously on the verge of a complete burn-out. He might not last out the time it would take to get Archer's replacement to Lurion.

Gardner put his head in his hands. Killing a planet was no matter for weak men.

He wondered about Archer. No doubt Archer had had some grand idea of collecting damning and unchallengeable evidence and peddling it. "The Confederacy of Rim Stars," Archer had said. Yes, that loose linkage of second-rate worlds would pay well for anything that might tear down Earth's interstellar prestige.

But Archer had panicked guiltily, and now he would do no betraying. His act might yet save a world, Gardner thought.

Weary, his head throbbing, Gardner rose and pushed Archer's suitcase into the closet, slapping the seal on the closet door. They'd have to rip up the walls before they found it.

What to do now? Send back to Earth for replacements? Continue as scheduled? No, Gardner thought.

He remembered Steeves and his two earnest young Lurioni "philosophers." He had to have another talk with Steeves. Then, perhaps, he could frame his decision. Meanwhile, he would have to stall off Smee, Leopold, and Weegan on the matter of asking for a replacement for Archer.

Gardner restored the room to a semblance of order. Then, knowing that the best thing he could do now was to get some sleep, he began to undress.

CHAPTER TWELVE

There were calls from Smee and Weegan in the morning, wanting explanations of the delay. As clearly as he dared, Gardner told them the story: that Archer was dead, and that they would all have to hang fire until a replacement arrived. He let them infer that he had already sent the coded distress signal to Earth that would get a replacement on his way.

Weegan took the news philosophically enough. He hadn't been on Lurion long enough for the assignment to have gotten under his skin.

But Smee was expectably agitated. "I can't take much more of this, Gardner. Any day now I'm going to blow my stack. If there's any more delay ..."

Gardner calmed him, avoiding Smee's eyes as he assured him soothingly that everything would proceed on schedule, that in a very short time the project would be completed. Smee seemed to accept the balm, although reluctantly. Gardner realized that Smee could not be counted on much longer.

There was no sign of Lori in the dining room when Gardner finally got off the screen and could go down for breakfast. After eating, Gardner repaired to the jewel exchange and looked around for Steeves.

Since the abortive luncheon date, Steeves and Gardner had seemed to avoid each other by unspoken mutual consent. The abrupt end of the little meeting had been too embarrassing. Gardner reddened now in memory as he approached Steeves' trading area.

"Steeves, can I talk to you for a moment. Not on business."

The older man frowned. "What is it?" he said impatiently.

"It's about that lunch we had, I want to say I'm sorry for charging out that way. I was ...upset."

"Well? What of it?"

"I've been thinking things over, Steeves. I'd like a chance to meet those two again."

"Why? Planning to peddle them to the government?"

"You know I'm not an informer," Gardner said sharply. "I want to talk to them again. I think I might be able to make them an offer of support. A considerably larger offer than you might expect me capable of."

Steeves was thoughtfully silent. At length he said, "All right, Gardner. Tonight, at my place. The address is 623 Thuurin Square. But I warn you, if this is some kind of trick—"

"I'll see you tonight. And thanks for giving me the second chance."

Gardner walked rapidly away.

The day passed slowly. Gardner made, broke, remade his decisions a hundred times. He remembered how Karnes had said, *"I might as well tell you that I don't think you're the man for the job. But the computer does, though."* Chalk up another error for the computer. Karnes, with his merely human abilities, had been a shrewder judge of character.

He left the exchange early and returned to the hotel. A close, dank fog hung low over the city, blanketing the streets; and a warm, muggy rain was starting to fall. It was the kind of weather, Gardner thought, that caused rot—of clothing and of men's souls.

The visi-screen was bleeping when he walked in. Quickly Gardner activated it.

It was Smee again.

This time Smee looked more upset than ever. His face was pale and shiny with sweat, and the few strands of his hair seemed glued to his scalp by perspiration. His hands, just visible in the lower corner of the screen, were quivering visibly.

"What is it?" Gardner asked. "Are you going to keep calling me every couple of hours?"

Smee's face was piteous. "Listen, Gardner," he said in a hoarse whisper, "I'm coming apart at the seams. I can't take it any more."

"You've lasted this long, Smee. Can't you hang on a little while longer?"

"It's been six months of hell. I ...I nearly killed myself half an hour ago."

"Smee!"

Gardner wanted to reach out into the screen, seize the other man by his thick shoulders, and shake him back into sanity. Smee's head was bowed, his eyes downcast and weary-looking.

"I'm fighting it, Gardner. I want to do my part in the project. But, dammit, can't you understand what this sort of life is doing to me?"

"Look, Smee, the replacement for Archer will be here soon," Gardner lied. "A few days ..."

"Weeks!"

But the man is *coming*. Take hold of yourself, Smee. Don't wreck everything for the rest of us. Try to hang on a little while longer."

"It's hard, Gardner."

"Try."

"I'll ...try."

Gardner smiled. "Good man. Ease up, now. Call me again, if you have to. Remember, it'll all be over soon."

"I hope so," Smee said. His voice was a harsh, doleful croak.

After the screen had cleared, Gardner sat back, anxiously knotting his hands together. He was dripping wet, as much from his own state of tension as from the mugginess of the weather.

Tonight, he thought, would see the tale told. Either he would throw up the project entirely, or he would proceed as ordered. In the latter instance, he would have to ask for replacements: a replacement for Archer and probably one for Smee. The man might possibly hold together for the weeks it would take for a new agent to arrive, but it was doubtful. Smee was going to pieces in a hurry. He would be no good for anything except a pension, whenever he did get off Lurion. No executioner, Gardner thought, should be required to hold the gun at his victim's head for six, almost seven, solid months before pulling the trigger.

Someone knocked unexpectedly at the door.

Gardner glanced up, startled. "Who is it?"

"Lori. I want to talk to you, Roy."

He opened the door. The girl looked tense and distraught. She was dressed in prim, unseductively severe clothes, in sharp contrast to the way she had looked the last time she had knocked on his door.

"Aren't you going to invite me in, Roy?"

"I ...suppose so." He held the door open uncertainly. "But ...I thought we had agreed not to see each other any more after last night, Lori."

"That was our agreement. And maybe I shouldn't have broken it. But, I think you owe me some explanations, Roy. That's why I'm here."

He remained standing, and so did she. "What sort of explanations?"

Her eyes did not meet his. "It was the wrong thing for me to do, I know," she said in a hollow voice. "Call it schoolgirl jealousy, call it whatever you want. But I went to the Customs Office this morning and checked your immigration records."

Gardner felt as though he had been butted in the stomach. But he said nothing.

Lori went on, in the same remote tone, "I told them I wanted to know if you were married. They didn't like the idea of showing me your papers, but when I told them how you ...you had ..." She paused. "When I told them, and gave them some money besides, they were willing to let me look. Your entrance papers say you're not married. Why did you tell me you were, Roy? Did you want that badly to get rid of me?"

Gardner was dumbfounded. He said lamely, "I never thought you'd check the records, Lori."

"It's terrible of me to come in here and accuse you like this. The ladylike thing to do would be to swallow my pride and forget the whole affair. But, Roy, how could you lie to me that way?"

"I had to."

"To preserve your precious bachelorhood? I wasn't going to entrap you forever," she said bitterly. "You didn't have to think I would spin a web around you and suck your blood."

"It wasn't anything like that," Gardner said thickly. "I have ...*had* ...professional reasons for not wanting to get emotionally involved with anybody on Lurion."

"*Professional* reasons?"

He nodded helplessly. The girl stared strangely at him. Quietly she said, "I wonder just what your profession is."

"I'm a jewel-trader. You know that."

"I'm not so sure. The hotel people whisper a lot about you, you know. They say you have strange friends, that you get visi-screen calls from distant continents. And last night there was a fight in your room."

"How do you know that?"

"I came up here late last night just to tell you how sorry I was to have caused you trouble, you know. I still thought you were a married man. I heard the sound of a struggle going on in here. There was another man, and he said something about the Confederacy of Rim Stars paying highly for information he could give them, and you were talking about torture, and Security, and then there was the sound of furniture breaking ..." She stared at the floor. "I was frightened. I ran away. And then, did you know, this morning they found the dead body of an Earthman named Archer a few blocks from here? He had been knifed. He was the man you were fighting with in your room, wasn't he? *Roy, what are you?*"

Gardner felt a knot of tension tightening in his belly. The girl's face, frightened, accusing, hovered before him. He knew that what he was about to do violated all precepts of Security. Yet he had to do it. He had to unburden his soul of the massive weight it bore.

"You want the truth?" he said. "All right. I'll give you the truth. But you'll have to keep it locked up in your own skull. No one will believe you if you blab it, anyway."

"Roy, I don't understand."

"Quiet, and listen to me." Gardner's face was set in a stern mask. "Archer, the dead man, was part of a team of five men sent out by Earth Central to do a job here on Lurion. Then Archer sold out, or was planning to as soon as he had a confession from my lips. He didn't get it."

"What kind of job?" Lori asked.

"We were sent here to destroy Lurion."

The girl's eyes widened for a moment, then focused on him in a bewildered glare.

"What?"

He told her. Speaking slowly, dragging each word out from where he had hidden it so long, Gardner told her about Karnes and about the assignment. And why he had felt it necessary to pretend he was married. His heart felt lighter with each word of the bizarre confession.

When he was finished, she forced a little lopsided smile and said, "And I was studying cruelty on Lurion! I could have stayed at home and done a better job."

He shook his head. "Look at it through the computer's eyes. From the data given, the computer determined that there would be nothing cruel about what Earth would do to Lurion. We would be killing three billion people, destroying an entire culture. But we would be removing a filthy plague spot from the universe. We would be saving Earth and we would be protecting the rest of the civilized galaxy."

"It would be murder in cold blood," she said numbly.

"Yes. To save Earth the agony and destruction involved in acting in hot blood when Lurion springs its war on us."

"But are you God? Once you take this power on yourself, to destroy whole worlds, where does it stop? Suppose you decide that Argonav is evil next, and then Simulor, and then Hannim? Do you go around blasting one planet after another, in the name of saving Earth and civilization?"

"Look at it from the viewpoint of the computed data. Lurion is rotten through and through. Eventually some of that rottenness is going to flare up into a galactic war. Fifty billion people may die—*fifty* billion, not just three billion. The economies of hundreds of worlds may be disrupted. A dozen future generations will have their birthrights mortgaged to pay for the havoc Lurion will cause. And, the computer says, the probability is extremely high that Earth herself will be destroyed in a surprise attack, as the opening salvo in the war. To avoid all this, I was sent here ...to destroy Lurion."

"But *I* would have died too!" Lori exclaimed, realizing the fact all at once.

Gardner nodded. "That's why I've been trying to keep away from you. It was a mistake for me ever to get entangled with you. You couldn't have been saved if the project had gone off as scheduled."

"But now there'll be a delay, you say, because this man Archer is dead. You'll have to send for a replacement, and by the time he gets here my ship will have left. But then Lurion will be destroyed when that fifth man gets here."

"I have another man going, breaking down under the strain. He's been here too long, you see. So I would have to replace *him.* More delay. And by the time the replacements finally did get here, most likely it would be my turn to have a breakdown, and then ..." Gardner clenched his fists. "But all this doesn't matter. There isn't going to be any project. Lurion *won't* be destroyed."

"Lurion won't—"

"At least, not by me." Gardner smiled, feeling the strength of his decision now. "The computer has made some big mistakes already. It let Archer get past, and Archer was a traitor. It approved me, even though I wasn't really the right kind of person to act as executioner. It bungled the whole first batch it sent out. I can't trust the computer's judgments any more. Certainly I can't give the order to destroy a world on the basis of them."

"But, what *are* you going to do, Roy?"

"I'm not sure. But I've found a group, an underground organization of Lurioni, who are working to change the ways of society here. I'm seeing some of them tonight, to find out just what their program is. Then I've got to return to Earth, I've got to find out whether the existence of that group was known, whether it was fed into the computer with the original data on Lurion."

"What difference will that make?"

Gardner leaned forward anxiously, "If the group didn't get computed in, it meant that the extrapolation of Lurions future is faulty. I'll demand a new computation before any drastic steps are taken. On the other hand, if the computer *did* know about these people, and extrapolated that they would have no effect on the general trend ..." Gardner shrugged. "In that case, I guess Lurion will have to die."

CHAPTER THIRTEEN

Steeves' house was a tall old building, one of a group of identical tall, narrow buildings that bordered a tiny grassy square in a quiet part of the city. Steeves lived on the top floor. Lori and Gardner rode up in a creaking lift-shaft.

They were slightly early, but the two Lurioni, Kinrad and Damiroj, had already arrived. They rose politely as Gardner and Lori entered.

"Miss Lori Marks," Gardner said. "An anthropologist from Terra. A very close friend of mine."

"Pleased," Kinrad said.

"A pleasure," said Damiroj.

Their manners, thought Gardner, were very refined. He was willing to bet that these two had been off Lurion, had picked up their cultured ways on some more genteel world.

There was a frosty little moment of uncertainty. The two Lurioni, doubtless remembering the peculiar behavior of Gardner at their last meeting, were slow to begin a conversation. Steeves broke up the rigidity by offering drinks; he served, instead of the ubiquitous *khall*, a sort of local brandy that Gardner found interesting. The apartment was small but well furnished, with objects from a number of worlds arranged tastefully. Steeves had prospered in his twenty years on Lurion, no doubt of that.

Gardner smiled disarmingly and said, "I guess I ought to begin with apologies for my queer behavior the last time we met."

They tried to shrug the incident off, but Gardner insisted. "I was very upset, that day. I wasn't thinking clearly. I'll have to ask you to forgive me, and to forget all that took place."

Steeves said, "Then you really *are* interested in our group, Gardner?"

"Yes. But I've got to have more information. And there's some information I'd better give you. It's time to drop some of the masks. I'm not really a jewel merchant. I'm a secret agent of the Terran Security Corps."

The Lurioni looked startled. Steeves reared back and exclaimed, "What?"

"Yes. Lurion is under very close observation by Earth, and I'm one of the observers. You understand that this is absolutely secret, not to go beyond this room."

"Of course."

"Very well, then. Let's put it that Earth is extremely disturbed by the probable course of events on Lurion. Bluntly, Earth thinks the pattern is pointing toward war. But we hope to avoid this war by sponsoring groups such as yours that can alter the course of events on Lurion. Have I begun to make myself clear?"

Kinrad, Damiroj, and Steeves looked utterly floored by Gardner's announcement. Steeves muttered, "We had no idea. I thought you were a private merchant."

"Has anyone of an official capacity ever approached you as I'm doing now? Anyone from Earth, I mean."

"No." Steeves said. "We've only mentioned the matter to a couple of other Earthmen, close friends of mine. You were the first outsider I chose."

"A lucky choice," Kinrad said.

Gardner nodded. His hopes rose. If this group were really unknown, then it couldn't have been taken into account when the computer had worked up its Lurioni extrapolation. Which meant there might still be a chance to avert the holocaust of total destruction.

Gardner said, "I'll be returning to Earth soon, reporting to my superiors. Can you give me some idea of your program of action? How big is your group anyway?"

"We have five hundred members on three continents," Damiroj said. "The number is growing, slowly but constantly.

"And just what are your aims?"

It was Kinrad, the more articulate of the two, who leaned forward to speak. "Lurion is in, shall we say, a primitive stage of culture, speaking not technologically but in term of interpersonal relationships. Our plan is to infiltrate positions of responsibility here, and gradually to bring about change."

"We have several men in local legislatures," Damiroj said. "Others have received judgeships. Soon we shall elect delegates to the central congress. Perhaps before long we wil have a few men on the High Committee."

"Several religious leaders have joined us," Kinrad went on. "As we progress, we hope to gather support from influential men of business. Enlightenment is spreading. Perhaps it will take us two or three generations before our influence is felt. But it *will* be felt if we have support! And Lurion will change! We will break up the power blocs, the hate-mongering ones who lead us. We will reduce the competition of everyday life, the competition that turns us into beasts. We will bring the long-overdue cultural change that will transform this world!"

Eyes bright with the fervor of crusaders, Kinrad and Damiroj paused in their outburst. Gardner felt his own heart pounding. This was what could save Lurion, this upsurge from within, so unsuspected by the computer who had ordered this planet's destruction!

This time Gardner did not rush out abruptly, as he had before. But he knew that he could leave at once. He had heard what he had hoped to hear.

He stayed on for an hour more, listening to the grandiose plans unfolding. Finally, when the time came to leave, he assured the two Lurioni that he would do everything in his power to aid their cause, and thanked Steeves profusely for having arranged the meeting.

"You'll never know what you've done." Gardner said.

And indeed Steeves would not. But he had saved one world from destruction and another from a monstrous load of guilt if, Gardner thought, he could succeed in getting Security to order a recomputation of the probabilities. That might not prove so easy.

"Well?" Lori asked, outside in the square. "What do you think of them?"

"They've got a lot of enthusiasm, Lori. They know what needs to be done, and they're going to do their damndest to do it."

"Do you think they'll succeed?"

Gardner shrugged. "The culture pattern of Lurion is thousands of years old. You can't eradicate that much viciousness overnight. But the important thing is that someone will be trying to do it."

He hailed a cab. Lori said, "What are you going to do now?"

He shrugged. "Return to Earth and put the case before my superiors."

"Will you go alone?"

"I'll take Smee," he said. "He'll never hold out here. No sense having him wait any longer. And ..."

"Yes?"

"What about you, Lori? Will you go back to Earth with me? Or do you want to stay out of this whole thing? You've got your research to finish."

"It can wait."

"I might get in trouble on Earth. They might put me away for safekeeping. I know too much. So do you. It's risky to go with me."

"I'll go."

"And afterward?"

She gestured ambiguously. "I might finish my thesis. Or I might not. Let's not worry about that now."

In the morning, he put through a call to Smee. The conversation was brief; Gardner said that he had received word from Earth to hold the project up indefinitely, pending new considerations. "I'm going back to Earth at once. I thought you might like to come with me. It may be months before the go-ahead comes through."

"What will you do with Weegan and Leopold?"

"They'll stay here," Gardner said. "They can wait a while. I know you can't."

"When will you pick me up?"

"Later today. I'll land at Norivad Spaceport and have you paged."

Gardner called Weegan and Leopold next, and informed them of the change in plans. They were both surprised and more than a little troubled by the prospect of a delay, but they agreed to stay on.

Packing was quick. Gardner unsealed the closet and took out Archer's generator. It had been modified somewhat, to the form of a twin-turreted microscope. He stuffed it into his own luggage, sealed everything up, and went down to Lori's room to see how she was progressing. Shortly after noon, they checked out of the hotel and took a cab to the spaceport.

There was a brief delay while he identified himself, passed through Customs, and claimed his ship. Thankfully, his papers were all in order, though it took a small bribe to squeeze through the Customs shed without a full-scale inspection.

He and Lori trooped out onto the field. He found his ship, thumbed open the hatch, and they entered. He radioed the control tower, got blastoff clearance, pressed down on the blasting key. The ship rose, bobbed for a moment on its jetstream, and soared into the stratosphere. Gardner navigated along a tight arc, never more than two hundred miles from the ground, as he shot along toward Norivad, the city where Smee was stationed.

"Request landing clearance," he called, giving his identification data.

The spaceport at Norivad was very much like the one Gardner had left behind. He brought the ship down smoothly on an outjutting flange of the spacefield and asked the control tower to page his passenger for him. Ten minutes later Smee appeared, riding out from the terminal in a small truck. A porter unloaded his two pieces of baggage. Smee came aboard, looking like an old man, bent, roundshouldered, his face withered, his eyes dreary.

"I don't understand," Smee muttered, as he settled down inside the ship. "They let me rot here for seven months, and then they call the whole thing off. As if I was a robot. As if I didn't have feelings."

Gardner did not look. Smee was shattered, crushed under the toll of his assignment. And the shattering had been for nothing ...*maybe.*

"Why did they change their minds?" Smee asked.

"Some new information came to light. New information that made Lurion out to be a better place than it looks on first glance."

"Lurion is hell," Smee said thickly. "It should be destroyed."

"So the computer says. But there's new data to be considered. We can't go blowing up worlds that might be salvaged."

But Smee had lived with the thought of destruction for too long. It had seared channels into his brain. Now he could only shake his head and repeat, "It should be destroyed."

Gardner felt a surge of pity, and he did not dare tell the other man that it was on his account that the project had been postponed. Smee would have only asked why the planet had not been blown up first, with the recomputation to come later. Gardner wondered whether the efficient medicos of Security would be able to repair this empty hulk of a man who had been sacrificed for nothing.

He concentrated on his piloting. Some hours later, the tiny vessel hung three quarters of a billion miles from Betelgeuse and three hundred million miles from Lurion. It was the conversion-point. Gardner jabbed down hard on the controls and the ship flicked out of normal space and into warp.

He wondered what kind of reception would be waiting for him on Earth.

CHAPTER FOURTEEN

Gardner stood at the entrance to the concentric series of offices that led inward to Security Chief Karnes' office. He felt uncertain and tired. It was only hours since he had landed on Earth; Lori had gone to a hotel, Smee to the Security medical department. Gardner had not warned anyone of his return.

He was not in uniform, and he was conscious of his shabby, travelworn appearance as he presented himself at the front reception desk. The clerk, a recruit Security man, glanced up suspiciously.

"Yes?"

"I'd like to see Chief Karnes."

"The Chief is in conference, sir. Do you have an appointment? I could ring him if—"

"No, I don't have an appointment," Gardner said wearily. "But he'll see me if you tell him who I am. Ring him up and tell him Agent Gardner is here to see him and make a report."

The receptionist frowned quizzically. "Very well. He'll be free to take calls in half an hour. If you don't mind waiting ..."

"I do mind waiting," Gardner said icily. "Call him now."

"But—"

"Call him, you ninny, and don't sit there yammering nonsense at me!" Gardner snapped.

Cowed, the receptionist shrank back into his cubicle and began plugging in phone-jacks. Gardner heard him talking to one clerk after another; Karnes was not an easy man to approach without an appointment. But at last he heard the receptionist say, "Agent Gardner is out here. He says he has a report to make."

Karnes' reply was loud and anguished enough for Gardner to hear it clearly. The receptionist poked his neck out and said, "Excuse me, but is that Agent *Roy Gardner?*"

"Yes, it is. Just back from Lurion."

The receptionist relayed the information to Karnes. A moment later the youngster looked up dazedly at Gardner and said, "The Chief will see you immediately, Agent Gardner."

The double doors opened and Gardner strode through. He knew his way; he had only been in Karnes' office a handful of times, but the way to the Chief's office was something no Security man ever forgot.

He came finally to the end of the long series of interlocking hallways and made the sharp left turn that put him in the vestibule of Karnes' office. The scanning field bathed him for an instant; then the door rolled quickly back.

Karnes was *standing* at his desk when Gardner walked in: the first time in Gardner's memory, and perhaps in all of recorded history, that Karnes had not been seated when a subordinate entered the room. Karnes' thin face was frozen in an expression of shock and perplexity. His fleshless lips moved for a moment impotently before the Security Chief was able to get out the words:

"What the deuce are *you* doing here?"

"Reporting back to request a recomputation, sir," Gardner said evenly.

Karnes sank limply into his chair and fixed hard, narrow eyes on Gardner. "Without orders? Without asking permission? Gardner, have you gone insane? What about the project?"

"Perhaps the project is better canceled, sir. I couldn't give the order to proceed. There's some additional information about Lurion that has to be figured into the computation before we can act."

"This is incredible, Gardner," Karnes said darkly. "You stand there to tell me that you abandoned your post and returned to Earth merely to let me know that you don't think the computer was right? I—"

Gardner recklessly interrupted him. "Sir, I've been in the Corps long enough to know the consequences of what I've done. But I had to. The computer is wrong!"

"The computer spent three years formulating its decision, Gardner! We scoured Lurion for data, fed every relevant fact we could find into the programming."

Gardner's jaws clenched. "The computer was capable of sending out a traitor to take part in the project, though. It's far from infallible."

"What are you saying?"

"Your man Damon Archer. He showed up at my hotel with a hidden recorder and took down a full discussion of the project. Then he bolted. Luckily, he was stopped. But he was planning to sell that tape to the Confederacy of Rim Stars. Doesn't speak well for the computer, does it, to pick such a man?"

Karnes' face clouded even more. "Archer was screened as thoroughly as anybody we've ever selected for an assignment."

"Exactly, sir. And still the computer made a mistake about him!"

The point should have been a telling one, but Karnes shrugged it off. "You should have requested a replacement for him. Under no condition should you have come all the way back to Earth."

"Archer wasn't the only lemon. Smee was rapidly going psycho. I brought him back with me too."

"In other words," said Karnes, holding himself in check with deadly calm, "you've smashed the entire project. Only Leopold and Weegan are still on Lurion. Or have you subverted them too?"

"They're still there, but I gave them orders to hold things up. You see, sir, while I was waiting for the group to assemble, I met some of the Lurioni. I became involved with a group that's dedicated to upsetting the present way of life there, to get into government and change things. There are over five hundred of them, and they're growing more influential every day. It would be wrong to destroy the planet while there's still hope for it, sir. If this group gets proper support—if we nurture it along—it ought to be possible to salvage Lurion without the need to blow it up. That is—"

"That's enough, Gardner," Karnes said in a low voice.

"But, sir—"

"Listen to me, Gardner. It's close to five years since we first began to realize we had to destroy Lurion. Ever since that moment every man in the top levels of government here has lived with a weight of responsibility on his back. We've checked and rechecked. There's no room for error. The war drive on Lurion is unstoppable. It's going to reach a head in sixty-seven years and the top will blow off unless we stop things *right now.*

"You say Smee cracked up after only six months. How about us, Gardner? We've been living with this thing for years! Wrecking a world isn't something you undertake lightly. We've checked, rechecked, doublechecked. We reached our decision.

"You were picked to implement this decision. If you remember, I didn't think you were the right man. The computer overruled me. And instead of carrying out your task, you've acted in a directly contrary way."

"Then you were right about me, and the computer was wrong!" Gardner shouted triumphantly. "If the computer can be wrong about me and wrong about Archer, what makes you so sure that it's right about Lurion?"

"That'll be enough," Karnes barked. "Our decision has been taken. The project will continue as—"

"But all I ask is that you run a recomputation with the new data! It can't take more than a year. Can't you spare a year when the life of a whole world is at stake? The recomputation may change everything. It—"

"The project will continue as scheduled," Karnes repeated inexorably. "Replacements will be sent to Lurion for Archer, Smee, and yourself. You are relieved of your position on this project, and your rank will be reduced to—"

"Reduced to nothing," Gardner said. "I resign my commission on the spot. You'll get the official notice by registered mail in the morning. I don't want any part of this filthy organization!"

Saluting ironically, he spun on his heel and stalked toward the door. The panels rolled back obediently as he approached them.

"Gardner! Come back here! That's an order, Gardner, do you hear me?"

"I don't have to obey orders any more, sir."

"Gardner!"

Without looking back, he stepped through the doorway, and it closed behind him. He began to walk rapidly down the long corridor. Voices sounded behind him, but he kept on going, through passageway after passageway, out to the front desk finally, past the goggle-eyed reception clerk, into the waiting lift-shaft.

Down. Out into the street.

Only when the fresh air reached him did he begin to think again. His mind had been numb all the way down, concentrating only on getting out of the building as quickly as possible.

Karnes had refused to listen. The project would continue as ordered. And he had resigned his commission. Like a string of firecrackers, the events had followed each other in explosive speed.

In no more than five minutes he had destroyed a career that had taken years to build.

He felt hollow and lost. But he knew he had done the right thing. That alone was a consolation.

In all conscience he could not have proceeded with the destruction project. Nor could he continue to associate himself with the organization that would be responsible for Lurion's murder.

He had cut himself adrift, but at least his hands were clean. Whatever happened now would be no guilt of his. He had tried.

A taxi glided up to the curb. Gardner stepped in and gave the driver the address of the hotel where he and Lori had registered earlier that day.

Lori was reading when he came in. She put away her book immediately and ran to him, eyes bright, smiling with anticipation. Her smile faded as she saw the expression on his face.

"What happened, Roy?"

He shook his head and dropped dispiritedly into a chair. "The damned obstinate fool," he muttered bitterly.

"Wouldn't Karnes see you?"

"Oh, he saw me all right. He damned near had a fit when he heard I was waiting outside. I bet nobody ever got shown into Karnes' office so fast. But then he wouldn't listen to me."

"What do you mean?"

Scowling, Gardner said, "I told him everything. About Archer, about Smee, about the Lurioni underground. And all he did was chew me out for having left my position without permission. The project is going to continue as scheduled. He won't even consider the idea of ordering a recomputation."

"No, Roy! That's horrible!"

"There's more," Gardner said. "He removed me from the project and started to demote me. So I resigned. I tossed in my commission."

"Of course. What else could you have done? You couldn't have remained attached to them after all this, could you?"

"No, but now I'm in a mess. I don't have any other livelihood, and it isn't easy for Security Agents to get jobs. People tend to distrust us. When I put down on the application, 'Former Security Agent,' they suddenly decide that the vacancy has been filled by a prior applicant due to apply at a later date. So Earth is closed to me. Besides, I'm walking around with a lot of top-secret classified information in my head. Karnes may decide that I'm too dangerous to stay at liberty. The safest thing for them to do is to lock me up until after the Lurioni blowup, or maybe even indefinitely. To keep me quiet, you see."

Lori pounded her fists against her thighs in anger. "But this is all outrageous! Aren't they human? Can't they at least order the recomputation instead of arresting you and blowing up a world? How can they dare to take such a responsibility?"

Gardner said quietly, "That's the attitude I had until a little while ago. But now I understand Karnes and his bunch better. They've been living with this thing for five years, now. They've already gotten numb to the guilt. Their minds are frozen in the thought that Lurion has to be destroyed. It's a dreadful thing to do, and they know it. But if they order the recomputation, and find out that they *don't* have to destroy the planet, then all their suffering and guilt of the last five years was wasted; don't you see? And they've reached the point where they'd rather blow Lurion up than admit that they were operating on insufficient data."

He stared dumbly at the textured pattern of red and green whorls in the carpet. Lori said, "Roy, what are we going to do now?"

"*We?* I'm going to become a victim of the Preventive Detention laws. You're going to finish your thesis and get your degree in anthropology."

"Don't be stupid. Are you just going to sit here and let them arrest you?"

"What else is there for me? The cleanest thing would be to go back to Lurion and wait there for the blowup. But I'm not cut out for suicide. So I'll rot in a jail instead. It's the price I'll pay for being an Earthman. We'll all share the guilt of this Lurion thing."

"No, Roy. Can't we escape altogether, go off to some distant planet, some colony-world where we can buy land and just live and farm and forget this whole nightmarish thing?"

Gardner looked up. "Why should you get yourself mixed up in this?"

"Maybe I love you," she said. "Or maybe I'm just an idiot. But I want to go with you wherever you go. And I don't want you to sit by and let yourself be locked up."

Gardner managed a faint smile. "Are you certain that this is what you want, Lori?"

"Yes."

"What about your thesis, your doctorate?"

"What do those things matter? A lot of typed paper, a diploma, a title. They're just substitutes for being alive, for being in love."

"Get your doctorate. Marry some rich banker, the owner of a spaceline, a jetpolo player. You've got looks, brains—"

"I don't want any rich bankers. I want you, Roy."

He was silent a long while, his eyes closed, his face bleak. At length he said, "I've got some money saved up. Security men get paid pretty well. It would be enough to take two people about nine hundred light-years on a one-way ticket and still leave a little over for living expenses."

"I have money too, Roy. Not much, but it's at least three thousand credits."

"How fast can you lay your hands on it?"

"Within an hour. I don't think the bank will make trouble about a withdrawal."

"Okay," he said. "I'll go down to the Bureau of Emigration and pick out a planet and get my passport validated while you're taking your money out. When I get back, you can go and do the same thing. We'll leave on the first available ship."

"Why can't we go to the Bureau together?"

Gardner shook his head. "There's time to start doing things together when we're safely off Earth. There might be some hitches in getting my emigration visa, and we'd be smartest to avoid linking ourselves publicly until I'm cleared."

"If you think that's best," Lori agreed.

They parted in front of the hotel, Lori heading for the bank, Gardner toward the towering headquarters of the Bureau of Emigration.

In the lobby of that great building, he found a private viewing booth and punched out his request for information. Data began to appear on the screen set in the wall. It was nearly half an hour before he had picked out the most attractive world.

It was called Herschel, and it was 383 light-years from Earth. Fourth planet of a warm G-type sun, gravity .96 Earthnorm, atmosphere Earthlike to four places. It had been settled three hundred years earlier by Terran colonists, had no native intelligent life, and had received full independence from Earth fifty years ago. The current population was only fifteen million, spread loosely over three fertile continents. New colonists were welcome, and received two hundred acres of land as a free homestead, with the option of buying more at low prices. Government was by representative legislature; taxes were at a minimum.

It sounded ideal. Gardner punched for a printed information form on Herschel to show to Lori. Then he began to fill out his application for an emigration permit. The Bureau would take care of the rest, notifying Herschel by ultrawave that a new colonist was on the way and securing a visa for him.

When he had completed the application, he joined a line. It inched along slowly. At any hour of the day or night, the Bureau hall was filled with Earthmen ready to try a change of luck on some distant, unspoiled world. Earth's sphere of influence covered nearly five hundred planets of the galaxy, and nearly all of them were under-populated and welcomed newcomers.

Finally he reached the front of the line. He slipped his application across the ledge to the smiling clerk. The clerk scanned it briefly, maintaining the glossy professional smile.

Then, just before stamping out the validation, the clerk reached to his left and consulted a long sheet of green paper with many numbers typed on it. The smile wavered for a moment, but held firm.

Gardner stiffened. He knew what that sheet of paper was. A knowledge of the interior workings of Security could be helpful at times.

The clerk said urbanely, "There seems to be a minor difficulty, Mr. Gardner. Would you mind waiting for just a moment to the side here while we ..."

Gardner did not choose to wait. Karnes, he thought, had acted swiftly. The pickup order had gone out, and every branch Emigration Bureau already had the number of his passport, with instructions to detain him if he made any attempt to leave Earth.

He reached out swiftly and snatched his application and passport back from the stunned clerk; then he turned and made his way quickly out of the crowded hall, before the clerk could recover and cry out for him to be seized.

CHAPTER FIFTEEN

"They've got me on the list," he told Lori in the safety of the hotel room. "That means that Karnes has already regretted letting me walk out of his office the way I did."

Lori's face was tight with anxiety. "Do you think they're searching the city for you?"

"I'm sure of it. I know all about how Security runs a manhunt. They'll have every means of transportation covered. Not even a flea will be able to get out of this city without being spotted. And they'll flash word to the city police, too. By the time twenty-four hours has passed, there'll be close to a million people looking for me in this city. And by the time forty-eight hours has passed, the probability is about ten to one that I'll be holed up in the Keep for an indefinite period of preventive detention."

"No, Roy! Isn't there some way?"

"To escape?" Gardner smiled. "Yes, one way. But only a Security man would know about it. How fond are you of my face, Lori?"

"You mean plastic surgery?"

He nodded. "It's the only way. I know a man, a good man. He'll give me a new face and a new identity while I wait. Also a new passport. He's an expert. The only trouble is, there won't be anyone on Herschel capable of giving me back my old face. The operation is a difficult one; there aren't likely to be skilled plastic surgeons on a frontier world. But you won't miss my face, will you? My nose is too sharp, my eyebrows too heavy. I could use a different mouth, too. I've gotten so used to the official Security scowl that my lips won't smile the right way any more."

"It's a good face, Roy. It's a strong face, an honest face. It's *your* face."

"I can keep my face and go to jail, or I can get a new face and settle on Herschel with you. Which do you want it to be?"

After a pause Lori said, "That's a silly question. But make it a face I can love, Roy. Don't let him make you unreal. Be different, but don't be false. Do you know what I mean?"

"I think so." Gardner scratched his chin reflectively. "Listen, get yourself down to the Bureau and make out an application for Herschel. Put yourself down as single and no prospects; colony-worlds are always happy to get good-looking unmarried women. When you've got your papers in order, find out when the next ship leaves and make a reservation for *one.* Don't give them any hint that you figure on having a traveling companion. When you've done all that, check out of the hotel room and get yourself another one somewhere else. I'll find a room near the spaceport until blastoff time. We won't have any contact with each other from today until the time that ship leaves for Herschel, and when we meet aboard the ship it's going to look strictly like an accident, love at first sight."

"Do we have to do it that way, Roy? The ship might not be leaving for a month!"

"Then we go our separate ways for a month," Gardner said. "There's no alternative. We have to avoid giving Security any connection between us. I know how they work, Lori."

"All right, then," she said hesitantly. "But I hope it won't be a month."

He smiled. "So do I"

They kissed and went their separate ways again, not looking back. The separation was going to be difficult, Gardner thought, but it was essential. Security would have ways of checking back on

Gardner and linking him with the girl. Smee could give them that much information. All they needed to do was check forward and discover that the girl was leaving for Herschel, and they could easily pick up her traveling companion and give him an overhauling in the Interrogation Chamber. But if she kept her own counsel, had no contact with him, then Security would be helpless.

It was late afternoon now. Twilight was descending on the city; shadows were long; and people were hurrying homeward. Gardner kept close to the buildings, moving on foot, his eyes lowered to avoid calling attention to himself. He knew he still had a little time. The pickup alarm was probably flashing all over, but Karnes would be too smart to sound a general alarm, complete with pictures in the telex and all. Because if he did that, it might prove the motive for Gardner to spill what he knew about the Lurion project. And, once Gardner spoke out, the project would be hopelessly shattered. If they went through with it, it would look strangely suspicious that Lurion should die in exactly the way the renegade Security man had predicted.

But, Gardner thought, Karnes had one ace in his sleeve: the knowledge that Gardner almost certainly would *not* expose the project. For, if he did that, it would be a heavy blow to Earth's prestige; it might damage forever Earth's reputation as an ethical world. And Gardner was still loyal to his native planet. Karnes knew that. No Security man could shuck off his loyalty overnight, however strong the provocation.

So Karnes could be sure that Gardner would not blab, at least not for a while. Soon, perhaps, the compulsion to speak out would outweigh the bonds of loyalty; but Karnes hoped to have Gardner in custody long before that.

An hour later, Gardner was halfway across the city, making his way through shabby, darkened streets that had not been repaved for generations. This was the poor quarter of the city, where the human refuse came to rest at tide's end.

The address was something Gardner never had forgotten. The store was where he remembered it to be: the windows were just as dingy, the neons just as noisy, the sidewalk in front just as filthy. Only the old man had changed. He was now even older.

Gardner let himself in and stood by the door. The old man peered at him out of eyes dulled and yellowed by years.

"Yes? Repair your shoes?"

Gardner grinned. "You mean you don't remember me, Hollis?"

"My name isn't Hollis! Why do you call me ...?" He paused. "Gardner?"

"The same."

The old man showed brittle stumps of teeth in a broad grin. "You young devil! What brings you around here?" The grin faded immediately. "You aren't going to turn me in, are you? Not after all these years?"

Gardner shook his head. "Far from it, Hollis. I need a new face and I need a new passport, all in a hurry; overnight, if you can manage it."

"Are you serious? Have you gotten in trouble?"

"Big trouble," Gardner confirmed. "I had a quarrel with Karnes over procedures, and resigned my commission. He didn't move fast enough to grab me while I was in his office, but he's got the word out now. I'm to be picked up and detained. I know too much."

The oldster hobbled out from behind his bench and peered up at Gardner. "Come in back," he said. "I'll lock up the store. You go straight through, turn right, open the door."

Gardner did as he was told and found himself in a tiny but well-equipped little office, hidden away in the rear of the shop. He smiled. Security could be troublesome, but a good Security Agent could always use some of his own knowledge to evade capture.

Hollis had been a Security Agent once, and a good one. He had been a plastic surgeon, specializing in disguising Agents for special missions. But he, too, had quarreled with Karnes over procedures, and had resigned from the Corps. Gardner had never known the exact circumstances of the quarrel, though Hollis had let it be known that it was a matter of ethics. Karnes had sent out an order for Hollis' pickup, but Hollis had slipped through the net, changed his appearance, and set up shop in a dismal part of the city, cobbling for a living but practicing plastic surgery for the benefit of the underworld.

Gardner had stumbled over the old man's refuge three years before. It was his duty to report Hollis to Karnes but the old man had pleaded desperately and had finally swayed Gardner into forgetting to turn him in.

Now it was time to let Hollis repay that favor.

"They've got my passport number on the list," Gardner said. "It's a top-priority search. I've got to get off Earth fast, or I'll never get another chance."

Hollis grinned. "You needn't worry. I'll have you fixed so well they'll never spot you. Overnight, you say?"

"It's best that way."

"Too bad. If I had a week, I could fix you so they'd never have a chance. Alter your bone structure, change your whole physique. But I suppose I can do enough tonight to get you through. How do you want to look?"

"The same, only different—get what I mean? I'm not handsome now. I don't want you to give me a handsome face, but don't disfigure me either."

"I could turn you into a godling, you know. No woman would resist you."

"I've got a woman already," Gardner said. "She likes me pretty much the way I am. See if you can make the alterations without changing the basic character of the face."

"Hmm. See what I can do."

Hollis took out a pad and stylus and began to sketch out a face, keeping the sheet away from Gardner's angle of vision. Gardner fidgeted. Fifteen minutes later, Hollis grunted his satisfaction.

"There. Take a look."

The face that looked up at the paper bore no resemblance to his own. The nose was flatter, rounder; the lips were wider and fuller. The chin protruded a little in a rugged, not unattractive way.

"It looks all right," Gardner said.

"I'll alter the color of your hair, of course, and of your eyes. And you'd better grow a mustache, too. How about identifying scars?"

"I've got a slash on my forearm."

"I'll cover it with synthoflesh," Hollis said. "Nobody will tell the difference. The synthoflesh will wither away in about a year.

It'll be gradual. Your lips and chin will return pretty much to what they are now. But the angle of your ears is going to stay different, and the shape of your nose. Unless you find someone who can put you back the way you were."

"I doubt that I will."

"All right, then. Lie down on the table. Get your shirt off while I'm preparing the anesthetic."

Gardner waited, tensely, while the old man bustled busily about, getting things ready. He wondered if it would be painful; he wondered if he would ever get used to a different face looking back at him from mirrors. Then the anesthetic cone descended over his face, and he ceased to wonder.

His next sensation was the sound of Hollis' voice saying warningly, "Don't move."

Gardner opened his eyes. His face ached, his head throbbed.

"Don't try to talk, either," Hollis said. "I finished an hour ago, but you've got to let things set. Here, take a peek."

Hollis held a mirror in front of his face. Gardner stared into the glass and saw blue eyes staring back. His eyes had been brown. Brown hair now was orange-red. His nose was different, his chin jutted, his mouth was broader. It was a stranger's face. Yet, somehow, he knew it was his own.

"It's ten o'clock in the morning," Hollis told him. "I've been working on you all night, snipping muscles, beaming you with quickheal, rearranging, grafting synthoflesh. Look at your arm."

Gardner picked up his arm. The long white scar along the inside of his forearm, a relic of an old sporting accident, was gone. Hollis had matched the old skin perfectly. Even the hair growing on his arm matched. It was all an even red now.

"I've treated your follicles so that your head and body hair will grow in red for about a year," Hollis said. "After that, it'll gradually return to its old color. You'll have to figure out some explanation for your neighbors, but you've got time to worry about that." Hollis reached behind him and picked up a sheaf of documents. "By the way here are your papers. Your name is Gregory Stone, now. I faked a complete background for you. Make sure you study it till you're letter-perfect. I guess it's safe for you to talk, now. The incisions ought to be healed by this time."

As cautiously as though made of sand, he rose to a sitting position and looked down at himself. "You've made me a lot heavier," he said.

"There's twenty pounds of synthoflesh around your middle," Hollis said. "You'll absorb it rapidly enough. But just for now it makes quite a difference in your physique."

"You're a magician, Hollis!"

"Just a craftsman," Hollis murmured. "I didn't do anything to you that any other plastic surgeon couldn't have done. I simply did it quicker and better, that's all."

"When will I be fully healed?"

"Go easy for a day or so. Don't shave and don't get into any horseplay. After that, you'll be fine. And the only way they can identify you is by your retinal index. I can't change that. But nobody's going to check your index unless you provoke them to. There's no reason for anyone to suspect you of being Roy Gardner."

"Unless Karnes decides to take eyeprints of everybody leaving Earth for the next couple of months."

Hollis shrugged. "If he does that, you'll be caught. But it would cost him practically his entire budget to do it. Are you worth it?"

"I might be," Gardner said grimly. "But there's no use worrying about it now. You can't get into my eyes to change things. How much do I owe you?"

"Seventy credits."

"Don't be silly. This job is worth at least a thousand, Hollis!"

The old man smiled. "Seventy credits represents my operating expenses. The rest of the fee would be recompense for skills. In your case, Gardner, the labor is on the house. You'll need your money, wherever it is you're going. I haven't forgotten that I was indebted to you when you walked in last night. Go, now. And remember—your name is now Gregory Stone."

By noon, Gregory Stone was on line at the branch office of the Bureau of Emigration. He had spent some time locked in a public washroom, studying the papers Hollis had forged while he slept. Gregory Stone was a year older than Roy Gardner, had been born not in Massachusetts but in Maine, and he had worked on a public-owned farm all his life. Hollis had supplied a convincing-looking employment certificate.

All of Roy Gardner's funds had been deposited in a new account, opened by Gregory Stone and made transferable to the Central Bank of Herschel. Roy Gardner no longer existed. The heavy-set redhaired man who had filled out the application was Gregory Stone.

Gregory Stone slid the papers across to the clerk, a different clerk in a different branch from the one where Gardner had tried to apply the day before. The clerk, smiling as fixedly as the other one had, went through the routine motions in a flurry of hands and elbows. The applicant underwent an uneasy moment as the clerk checked the passport number against a list by his side, but there were no difficulties. A clatter of rubber stamps finally validated the departure permit.

"We wish you success in your ventures, Mr. Stone. Your papers are in order."

"Thanks," Gardner-Stone said mechanically.

He wandered away, into the section where flight arrangements were made. The next voyage to Herschel, he learned, would depart in five days. It was a four-stop affair, with Herschel the end of the line. Travel time, six weeks one way. He filled out the form, requesting a single one-way passage, and waited while the robot brains checked to see if there still was room aboard. There was. He was assigned a compartment.

"You have three days to make final payment, Mr. Stone," the clerk informed him.

"I'll make it right now," he said.

He wrote out a check drawn against Gregory Stone's new bank account, countermarked it with Gregory Stone's new thumbprint, and handed it across. The check was validated. Five minutes later, Gardner walked out of the building with a set of cleared papers and a paid-in-full ticket to Herschel in his pocket.

CHAPTER SIXTEEN

The Seedlings were coming up. It was a wonderful feeling to stand there, with the full golden light of the sun splashing down, looking at the little greenish-yellow sprouts pushing their heads up.

Gardner and Lori had only cultivated enough acreage to support themselves this first year. Later, when there were five or six grown children to help out, they would cultivate all five hundred acres of his land, and perhaps buy more. There was plenty of room. Their nearest neighbor, here on Herschel, was twelve miles to the east.

"Smell the air," Lori said. "Clean, fresh."

"Like wine."

"Yes. Like wine."

Gardner smiled. They had been on Herschel ten months, but it seemed like only a few weeks. He thought back to those hectic last few days on Earth when he was holed up in that hotel, never going out for fear of Karnes, wondering where Lori was, waiting for those five endless days to come to their end.

They had, finally. And, as Gregory Stone, he had boarded the spaceship without incident. They had given him a bunk in the bachelor quarters, but on the third day out he had caught the eye of a handsome young single woman. He flirted with her for nearly half an hour before he identified himself. Lori was red with shame.

That would be a memory to cherish forever, Gardner thought: Lori blushing beet-red from forehead to ankles at the way he had trapped her.

They had formed a solid couple, and there had been a shipboard marriage, and Mr. and Mrs. Gregory Stone had moved into the married peoples' quarters as soon as a cabin became vacant after the ship's first stop. And then there had been the day when Herschel hung in the viewplates, all green and gold and blue and brown.

It was a good life, Gardner thought, full of fresh air, hard work, and love. Earth seemed like a bad dream, the interlude on Lurion a worse one. Gardner subscribed to the telex service and scanned every word every day, waiting for the day when he would read of the dreadful disaster that had befallen Lurion of the Betelgeuse system. But the news never came. Had he missed it, Gardner wondered? Or was Karnes still having trouble getting his team of five in position?

It wasn't easy. There had to be five, and they had to synchronize the activation of their generators. And if one of them had an attack of conscience at the critical moment, they would all have to begin again.

Gardner tried to forget about Lurion and what Earth planned to do to it. Earth and Lurion were both very far away, invisible, both of them, in the nightly glory of Herschel's sky. The only reality that mattered was right here.

Gardner stood with his arm around Lori, looking out over their land. It was midmorning, the sun still not yet at its zenith. The excitement of spring crackled in the air.

A helicopter droned overhead, suddenly.

"Looks like we're getting company," Gardner said.

Lori frowned. "I wonder who. We saw the Tompkinses last week, and we're supposed to go over the hill to the Vreelands on Fourday. So ..."

"Maybe it's a traveling salesman," Gardner suggested.

The helicopter hovered over an uncultivated clearing and began to descend. It bore, Gardner saw, the Herschel City crest, which meant that it was an official car being used to ferry some visitor out to the Gardner farm. It landed, and a short, stocky, balding man clambered out; then the copter took off again. Within a moment it was only a dot against the cloudless steel-blue sky.

The man began to walk toward the Gardner house. Gardner stiffened. "Good God," he muttered hoarsely. "It's Smee! Get the rifle, Lori!"

But before she had a chance to move, the newcomer waved cheerily and called out, "Hello, Lori! Hello, Gardner!"

"My name is Stone. Who are you?"

Smeee laughed. "I can recognize you behind the false face, Gardner. And Lori hasn't changed at all, except to get prettier."

Smee had changed, too. He was not the shattered hulk of a man who had come back from Lurion with them. He looked younger, stronger, more vibrant and tougher than ever. Gardner felt the chill in his belly begin to sweep upward to his heart. He had never expected to see anyone from the old life again.

"Aren't you going to invite me in?" Smee asked.

"What do you want with me?" Gardner asked tightly.

"A friendly visit and a little talk," Smee said. "For old time's sake."

"We'll talk out here. How did you find me?"

Smee grinned. "Seems that Security picked up an old crock name of Hollis. The name mean anything to you?"

"Go on," Gardner said. Lori, by his side, clung to him in terror.

"This Hollis used to be a Security medic, it seems. Gone into private practice. There was a tip that he was doing illegal surgery, and a couple of Agents picked him up. Under hypnosis he revealed a few of his recent clients. He told us he had changed you all around and given you the name of Gregory Stone."

Gardner's shoulders slumped. After eleven months, he still had not outrun Security and Karnes.

"What about you?" he asked. "You were a wreck when we left you, Smee."

"They took me apart and put me back together," Smee said. "Two months of round-the-clock therapy. It did wonders."

"I see."

"And when Karnes finally traced you down and found out you had emigrated to Herschel, he sent me out after you."

Gardner moistened his lips. "It's going to take more than you to bring me back, Smee. And you aren't even armed. You're underestimating me."

Smee folded his thick arms across his chest. "You aren't under arrest, Gardner. Karnes just wanted to know if you were interested in rejoining the Corps."

"Huh?"

"It's a trick, Roy," Lori murmured.

Smee shook his head. "No trick. You see, Karnes ran a recomputation on Lurion. He sent a dozen observers there to find out about this underground group of yours, and then he ran the new information into the computer. The computer said there wouldn't be any war if the underground got control. With help, it predicted, Lurion could be swung toward decency within twenty years."

"You're joking!" Gardner gasped.

"You think I am? Security is turned upside down about this business. Karnes is sending his best men into Lurion to work with this underground and help them, Gardner. It's the biggest project going."

"What's this matter to me?"

"Just this," Smee said. "Karnes sends his apologies via me. If it wasn't for you, he said, Lurion would have been blown up. But you planted the seed of doubt in him, that day when you stormed out of his office. He realized he had to make the recomputation before he did anything else. So he did. And plans were changed. And he sent me out here to ask you if you'll reconsider, come back to the Corps, and go to Lurion to head our unit there."

There was a long moment of silence. At length Gardner said softly, "But I'm pretty well established here. We've built this farm practically with our bare hands. We like it here. We were thinking of starting a family, next year. And you come along out of nowhere, asking us to move out of Eden and sign up for another tour of duty in hell."

"It won't be hell forever," Smee said. "Not if we all do our share. But you make up your own minds. I'll be staying in town two days, till the next ship leaves. I'm going straight to Lurion from here."

Gardner felt a lump growing in his throat. He looked out over the land, at the sprouting seedlings, at the dark hills in the distance, the trees, the rivers. He sucked a deep breath of air into his lungs.

"I don't know," he said slowly. "We'd be giving up a lot."

"You were once a Security man, Gardner. You took an oath. You had a loyalty."

Gardner nodded dreamily. He turned, looking at Lori. Her eyes were moist. She was clinging tight to paradise, too. It would be so easy to shrug shoulders, to tell Smee that Earth and Lurion could solve their problems without Roy Gardner. And then live with the shame of knowing that you had failed your world.

Lori managed a smile. Gardner saw the look in her eyes, and he knew what it meant.

"Lori ..."

She nodded gently. "We can always come back here later, when you've done your job."

"All right," Gardner said. He turned to Smee. "Stay here with us tonight. Tomorrow we'll fly into town and arrange the sale of the farm. Lori, call the spaceport and book two reservations on that flight to Lurion."

"You sure this is what you want to do?" Smee asked. "You've got a pretty nice place here. Maybe you don't really want to give it up."

"It can wait," Gardner said. "Lurion can't. I've got a job to do there. Only this time the job isn't murder."

THE END

The Plot Against Earth

CHAPTER ONE

The morning was bright, clear, and crisp. The sun, a blazing yellow-white ball, climbed toward its noonday height, casting long shadows in the streets of the city of Dyelleran. This was the hot season on the main continent of Morilar. Those beings whose business forced them out into the open moved rapidly toward their destinations. Only a few stopped to peer at the Earthman.

Lloyd Catton was his name. He was tall, tall as any of the elongated natives of Morilar, but unlike them he was solidly and powerfully built, with none of their spindly flimsiness. He was built to stand up to punishment—even the punishment of a noontime walk in 115-degree heat. One didn't go to an alien world expecting to find comfort and convenience.

Catton was dressed in the accepted style of a Terran diplomat: a light-weight sleeveless red doublet, gloves of green velvet trimmed with orange, a golden sash. His dark brown hair was cropped close to his skull. The gleaming blaster fastened to his sash was purely for ceremonial purposes: it neither could be fired nor was intended to be fired. A local law prevented non-residents from carrying any sort of functional weapons, but Catton's official position required him to be at least decoratively armed.

An attache case dangled from his left hand. In it was his identification plaque, as well as the credentials naming him for the post of Special Investigator for the Terran Work Government. Sweat beaded his broad back and shoulders, pasting the doublet to his skin. This assignment, he knew, might keep him on Morilar for a long time. He was simply going to have to get used to the heat.

He crossed a broad well-paved street and looked up at the name-label riveted to a building wall. Translating from the wedge-shaped Morilaru characters, he read: *Street of Government.* He nodded, satisfied. This was the place he had intended to reach. And he had found his way across the city from the Terran Embassy by himself, without the need of asking a single person for directions, on his first morning here. That was the sort of performance his job was going to require as a constant norm.

He had arrived late the night before, on a special liner non-stop from Earth. By arrangement, he was quartered at the Terran Embassy. Last night he had met the Ambassador and his attractive young daughter, Estil; this morning, he was due to present his credentials to the Interworld Commission on Crime, of which he was now a member. Catton had been well prepared for this mission. He had been chosen with care from the entire corps of Terra's Special Agents.

Standing at the head of the broad street, he looked to the west and saw imposing sleek-walled buildings rising on both sides. His eyes took in the unfamiliar Morilaru numbers, and he searched until he had the one he wanted. There it was—Number Eleven, Street of Government. The towering building with the gray-and-yellow decorative pattern along its flanks. Catton walked toward the main entrance.

There was no door, only a golden curtain of force. The Earthman stepped through, and his nostrils registered a faint tang of ozone as he passed through the field. He knew he had just been scanned for dangerous weapons. He knew he would never have passed successfully through the field if he were carrying anything more deadly than the plugged blaster. The Morilaru were an innately suspicious race.

A guard paced back and forth in the pleasantly cool, antiseptically austere lobby of the official building. He stared curiously at Catton for a moment; it was not every day that Earthmen came in here. Catton paused, wondering if the guard would hail him. But the guard made no sign of interference. The Earthman walked past him and into the open liftshaft that waited for him, as if by special appointment, in the rear of the lobby.

Once he was inside, the walls of the liftshaft closed instantly around him. Catton eyed the indicator dial and twisted it to the Morilaru equivalent of Sixteen. Purring smoothly, the liftshaft rose. The gravitic column that was pushing it upward halted at the building's sixteenth floor. Catton got out.

A frosted office door confronted him. The inscription, right-to-left after the manner of Morilaru writing, read:

INTERWORLD COMMISSION ON CRIME
Please enter.

Catton put his hand to the doorplate and the frosted door flicked open. He stood at the threshold, his hand tightening convulsively on the sweaty handle of his attache case.

A Morilaru receptionist smiled coolly up at him from her desk. It was impossible to tell her age; she might have been twenty, or just as easily seventy. She wore the green crest of an unmarried woman twined in her hair. Her skin was a soft purplish hue; her eyes, light crimson, stood out brilliantly against that background. The clinging blouse she wore left her shoulders bare, revealing the three little inch-high nubbins of bone on each shoulder that marked the chief external anatomical difference between Terran and Morilaru.

She said, using the local Morilaru dialect, "You have an appointment, sir?"

Catton nodded. "Pouin Beryaal is expecting me. My name is Lloyd Catton. From Earth." He spoke the language fluently; after a hundred hours of intensive hypnotraining in the three major Morilaru dialect variations, it was not surprising.

"Lloyd Catton," she repeated tonelessly, as if memorizing. "From Earth. To see Pouin Beryaal. Yes. Just one moment, Lloyd Catton. I will check."

Catton waited while she spoke briefly into an intercom grid. She used a somewhat different dialect, apparently not realizing that Catton would be aware of its implications. All she said was, "The Earthman is here to see you, Pouin Beryaal." But the inflected form of the dialect was an expression of contempt. Catton was not annoyed, merely interested. It was vital to him to know exactly how all of these outworlders, whether receptionists or potentates, regarded Earthmen.

He was unable to hear Pouin Beryaal's reply. A moment later an inner door opened and a male Morilaru appeared—a hulking purple-skinned spider of a man, with enormous elongated arms and legs. "I am the secretary to Pouin Beryaal," the Morilaru said in his own language. "You will come this way."

Catton followed him inside. The atmospheric pressure dropped considerably in the inner office. Evidently they had conditioners on in here. Catton's ears were discomforted by the change, but at least it was a relief to emerge from the steam-bath for a while. The humid climate of Morilar was hellish.

His guide kicked a doorstop and a wooden slat door folded up with a loud clap, admitting them to a circular office whose walls were an iridescent blue-green that flickered irregularly down to the violet end of the spectrum and back again.

A Morilaru sat at the head of a wide table, and his posture and demeanor left no doubt that he was Ponin Beryaal, chairman of the Interworld Commission on Crime. Seated to his right was an enormously fleshy orange-skinned being whom Catton recognized as a native of Arenadd, and to Beryaal's left was a gaunt, spectral gray creature from the Skorg system. All three outworlders were staring at Catton with undisguised curiosity.

The Morilaru said, "I am Pouin Beryaal. Do you speak Morilaru, Earthman?"

"The rules of interstellar contact," Catton said evenly, "require government personnel to be capable of speaking the language of the world to which they are assigned. I understand your language. My name is Lloyd Catton."

"Sit down, Lloyd Catton," Pouin Beryaal said, making no comment on Catton's acid reply. It was difficult to judge from the intonation, but it seemed to Catton that the Morilaru's tone in asking him to sit had been intentionally offensive.

The Earthman sat. He lifted his attache case, placed it on the table before him, and thumbed the release catch. There was a moment's halt while the scanner-band examined his thumbprint; then the case popped open. Catton drew forth a thin document bound in dark gray fabric.

"These are my credentials," he said, handing the document to Pouin Beryaal.

The Morilaru nodded and leafed through the booklet with no apparent change of expression. When he had reached the last page he nodded again, and casually handed the papers to the ponderous Arenaddin. The Arenaddin's eyes seemed to emerge from a welter of fat in order to scan the pages. The document was in all four of the major languages of the galaxy: Terran, Morilaru, Arenaddilak, and Skorg.

In a moment, the Arenaddin was finished. He passed Catton's document across the table to the Skorg, who leaned forward and perused it with awesome intensity for perhaps thirty seconds.

"Your papers are in order," Pouin Beryaal remarked. "Earth now has a delegate to this Commission. Your colleagues, beside myself, are Ennid Uruod of Arenadd, and Merikh eMerikh of Skorg. Do you find the atmosphere of this room offensive, Lloyd Catton?"

"I have no complaints."

"A stoic," said the Skorg in hollow, cavernous tones. "He would have no complaints even if we turned off the scent-conditioners, no doubt."

"I don't happen to be as sensitive to discomfort as some Earthmen are," Catton said, restraining himself. The smell of a Skorg was almost intolerable to an Earthman, he knew. But he also knew that Skorgs were tremendously less tolerant of Earthman-odor than Terrans of Skorgs; five minutes after the purifiers in the room were turned off, the Skorg would be groveling in a retching heap on the floor, while Catton would merely feel severe distaste. "I would have no objections if the scent-conditioners are turned off," Catton said.

"That will not be necessary," said Pouin Beryaal dryly. "We do not intentionally wish your discomfort, Earthman. You are, after all, a member of this Commission—a colleague."

Catton nodded. He sensed the undercurrent of tension and hostility in the room. It was only to be expected. These three outworlders were representatives of races—Morilaru, Arenaddin, Skorg—that had known and vied with each other for centuries. Into the group had come a fourth race, galactic newcomers. Small wonder that the old, well-established races would regard the fast-moving humanoids from Sol III with some suspicion. Not yet a century had passed since Earth's first contact with the other races of the galaxy. Hardly an instant, on the galactic timescale.

Pouin Beryaal said, "When we organized this Commission last year, we felt it was desirable to include an Earthman. Hence the invitation that resulted in your appointment and your presence here. Our problem is a problem that concerns every intelligent race in the galaxy."

"Hardly a new problem," rumbled the Arenaddin. "But one that has become more serious in recent years. It is time to take concerted action."

"Have you ever seen a hypnojewel, Earthman?" Pouin Beryaal asked.

Catton shook his head. "I've seen the documentary films on them, and I know what they can do. But I've never actually seen a hypnojewel itself."

The Morilaru's face creased in a faint smile. "You should understand the nature of your enemy, Earthman, before you begin to plot his destruction. Here. Look at this, closely and with concentration."

Pouin Beryaal drew a small glittering object from a green leather box on the table before him, and slid it down the burnished surface to Catton, who stopped it with his hand. He picked it up. It was a small cloudy gem, a good size for mounting in a ring. It was milk-white in color, and it had been cut with crude, irregular facets.

"This?" Catton said.

"Look at it," murmured the Skorg.

Uneasily, Catton concentrated on the surface of the stone. He had been warned, at the outset of this mission, to fear traps every step of the way. Perhaps it was better, he thought, not to look at the stone. These three outworlders might have prepared some unpleasant surprise for him. It was wisest to smile and decline the invitation, and hand the stone back. Yes, thought Catton. That was the wise thing to do. He would hand it back to Pouin Beryaal. He would—

He could not take his eyes from the stone.

It glowed, he saw now, with some inner light of its own. It was a warm radiant nimbus that swirled in patterns round the core of the gem, dancing and bobbing, weaving dizzyingly. Catton smiled. The tiny blaze of color was breathtakingly beautiful, an intertwining thicket of reds and greens and clashing blues. The stone appeared to have enlarged in size. It was tremendously relaxing to go on staring at it, watching the gay flame dance, while all tension ebbed away, all consciousness of self, all fears and torment vanished.

The edge of an alien hand chopped down numbingly on the upturned wrist of the Earthman. Catton cried out, and his fingers, suddenly robbed of strength, opened to let the stone fall. It went skittering across the glossy floor. Pouin Beryaal scooped it up with a quick motion and restored it to its box.

Catton sat transfixed, breathing deeply, while the vision of beauty faded. For almost half a minute, he could not speak.

"Half an hour more," said the Skorg, "and to take that stone away from you would have been to destroy your mind. As it is you probably feel withdrawal pangs now."

"I feel as if my brain's been drawn out through my forehead and embedded in that stone," Catton murmured.

"The effects are immediate and impressive," said the Arenaddin. "There isn't a humanoid race in the galaxy that can withstand them."

"Devilish," Catton said quietly. He was shaken to the core. Up till this moment, he had not really been interested in whether the hypnojewel trade flourished or not; his real purpose lay elsewhere. But now, as he measured the intensity of his yearning for the stone now hidden in the leather box, he realized that this matter was graver than he had suspected. "Where do these things come from?" he asked."

We don't know," Pouin Beryaal said. "They almost seem to enter the galaxy of their own accord."

"We have suspicions," the Skorg interjected. "There are races in the universe—non-humanoid races—which do not respond to the hypnotic effect of these jewels. One of those races might be manufacturing them and filtering them to the humanoid worlds. We do not know. But the trade in these jewels must be wiped out."

Catton nodded weakly. He was a strong man; yet a few seconds' exposure to the gem had left him limp. "Yes. Earth will do its best in fighting this trade," he said.

"The jewels are absolutely deadly," exclaimed the Arenaddin. "Men have been known to mail them to their enemies—who look at them and are immediately trapped. And there are others, voluntary addicts who escape this life by giving themselves up to the dreamworld the stones offer. Within an hour, the hold is unbreakable."

Caffon said, "You did well to invite an Earthman to join this Commission. This is a matter that threatens the well-being of all worlds. It transcends what little differences of thinking there may be between Earth and the other humanoid cultures of the galaxy."

"Well spoken!" Pouin Beryaal said. It seemed to Catton that there was more than a trace of cynicism in Beryaal's tone. The hypnotic jewels were dangerous, of course. But the unvoiced enmity between Earth and the Morilar-Arenadd-Skorg axis would not vanish overnight in response to this threat to universal well-being. Only a fool would think so, and neither Catton nor the people who had chosen him for this journey could lay claim to the title of fool.

"Have you any other—ah—*demonstrations* for me?" Catton asked.

"Just this," the Morilaru said. He drew a thick portfolio from a drawer in the table. "It is a file of our investigations and deliberations previous to your arrival. It may help you to read this, in order to bring yourself up to date. We will have it coded for your retinal patterns."

CHAPTER TWO

Catton was conducted to a laboratory elsewhere in the building, and there a technician took readings of his eyes with an elaborate measuring device. It was a familiar security measure among the Morilaru. From the retinal readings, a print of his retinal pattern—unique in the universe, as all were—was taken. The pattern was then embedded through a simple process on every page of the portfolio Beryaal had given him. As he turned each page, it would be necessary for Catton to stare at the sensitive patch for a few seconds, until the correspondence could be established. If he failed to perform the desensitization, or if any eyes but his scanned the page, the entire portfolio would char and burn beyond readability within half a minute.

When they had finished preparing the portfolio for him, there was no further reason for Catton to remain in the building. He could not function as a member of the Commission until he had familiarized himself with the situation and with their previous conclusions. So, locking the portfolio carefully into his attache case, Catton made polite but distant farewells to his three fellow Commissioners and stepped out once again into the blazing heat of Dyelleran, capital-city of the world Morilar.

It was early afternoon, now. The daily siesta-period was coming to its end. The temperature, Catton estimated, was still well over a hundred. He had been assured before he left Earth that there would be few days when the mercury dropped as low as ninety.

In a way, he realized, Pouin Beryaal had been discourteous in calling the meeting for noonday. The heat was at its worst then; it had been deliberately tactless to force him to travel from his lodgings at that time. But Catton was prepared for rudeness on Morilar. Earthmen were not excessively popular here.

He hailed a cab. It was android-operated, according to the sign on the door. The android, of course, was of the Morilaru type, with dark bluish-purple skin and the vestigial bony spikes on its shoulders. Each race created androids in its own image.

"Take me to the Terran Embassy," Catton said.

The cab pulled away. It was cool inside; he loosened the throatband of his doublet. Traffic was heavy at this hour, and the trip across town, which had taken less than fifteen minutes in the morning, now lasted nearly three times as long. At length, though, the cab drew up outside the high gates of the Embassy. Catton pulled a couple of Morilaru coins from his pocket and dropped them into the pay-slot. The android automatically released the door-catch and Catton stepped out.

Ten minutes later, he was in his room on the fifth floor of the Terran Embassy, climbing out of his sweat-soaked clothes and heading for the shower. After a quick freshening-up, he stretched out on the lounger and rang Service for something to eat.

He was tired. The Morilaru gravity was about 1.2 that of Earth, and the heat was never-ending. But no one had ever implied he was going on an easy mission.

There were rumors circulating in the galaxy that the three established humanoid races were planning some maneuver that would seriously damage the Terran economy. None of the talebearers could be very specific; no one had any concrete evidence. But the rumor persisted, and the Terran World Government was getting worried.

Coincident with the rumors about an alien plot against Earth had come the request from Morilar for a Terrestrial delegate to a Commission whose job it would be to investigate and control the illegal interstellar traffic in hypnojewels. Catton, specially trained for his job, had been chosen as the delegate—with the additional task of keeping his eyes open and trying to detect some substance behind the rumors of an anti-Terran conspiracy. What better way was there to camouflage a special investigator than as a special investigator—for something else? Catton would be only superficially interested in uncovering the sources of the hypnojewel trade; his real job was to find out what plans the Morilar-Arenadd-Skorg worlds might have for bedeviling Earth.

For they were troubled worlds, despite all their outward signs of calm. It was only ninety years before—2214, by Earth reckoning—that Earthmen had broken out into interstellar space. And now a dozen Terran colony-worlds hung in the sky; Terran traders operated with skill and efficiency on the planets of the older cultures; Terra had won a place as a ranking galactic power. All in ninety years.

Not surprising, then, that Morilar—whose interstellar era was more than a thousand years old—feared Earth. Or that Skorg, which once had been dominant in half the galaxy before the rise of Arenadd, viewed the newcomers with alarm. Nor, for that matter, that the fleshy people of Arenadd, themselves relatively late arrivals in the galactic scheme of things, with only a few hundred years of star travel behind them, should be worried about the rise of a new galactic power.

Perhaps the three worlds schemed some way of throttling the Terran expansion. Which was why Catton had been sent to the outworlds. He was an observer; he was to watch, and see, and possibly to discover what steps the threatened worlds meant to take to maintain their galactic supremacy.

After Catton had refreshed himself and eaten, he turned his attention to the portfolio Pouin Beryaal had given him.

He lifted the metal hasp and stared at the solemn warning on the first page:

NOTICE!

This book is for use by authorized persons only. It is coded to prevent unauthorized persons from obtaining access to its contents. Turning this page without taking the proper precautions will result in instantaneous destruction of the entire volume.

Catton turned the page to look at the words that were meant for his eyes alone. In the margin at the upper left-hand corner of the page was a small pinkish oval patch, about the size of a man's thumb. As he had been instructed to do, Catton stared at the patch, counting off five seconds. Then he began to read. The code had been keyed in; for the next ten minutes, he could leave that page of the portfolio open without fear of its destruction. A longer look would require him to desensitize the protective patch a second time.

He read with care, pausing each time he turned the page to desensitize the marginal patch. It developed from the reports that the Commission had already uncovered considerable data. Included in the papers he had been given were details on the number of hypnojewels in the galaxy—more than a thousand were known to exist, and many of these had already been located and confiscated. But each year a dozen or more new gems entered the galaxy. The problem was not so much to track down and confiscate those jewels that already were in circulation, as to cut off the pipeline at its beginning.

There were speculations that the jewels originated in the fringes of the galaxy, on one of the worlds populated by non-humanoid beings. Eleven different non-humanoid races had been found to suffer no ill effects as a result of handling the jewels. But any humanoid who stared at one for more than a few seconds found himself drawn inextricably into the hypnotic web.

Catton finished leafing through the collection of transcripts. The situation seemed a genuine one: the aliens were troubled about the spread of this hypnojewel thing, and they had decided to enlist the aid of Earth by inviting an Earthman to join the Commission. There was no actual state of hostility between Earth and the other three galactic powers, of course; there was only a chill incordiality that had led a Terran historian to revive an old term, and dub the present galactic situation a Cold War.

Cold War it was. Terra and her few colonies versus the seventy worlds controlled by the Morilar-Arenadd-Skorg axis. Diplomatic relationships still prevailed, and the worlds still engaged in friendly trade. But there was no telling when some crucial act of hostility might touch off an open war. And the advent of Earth onto the galactic scene had driven the other three worlds into their closest alliance in centuries.

Catton decided to test the effectiveness of the Morilar secrecy precautions. Leafing through the portfolio once again, he selected one page—it contained some unimportant data on budgetary appropriations for the Commission—and ripped it loose from the binding. Carefully, Catton closed the portfolio, and placed the loose page on the table before him, deliberately neglecting to key in the sensitized patch.

He got results in less than thirty seconds. The sheet of paper began to turn brown along the tear; then, almost instantaneously, its entire surface was swept with a wash of blue flame, and within moments nothing but crumpled ash lay on the table. Catton nodded and cleared up the mess. He was going to have trouble carrying on his investigation if *all* secret Morilaru documents were as proof to spying as this one obviously had been.

Rising, he locked the portfolio away in the privacy-cabinet in his closet, and proceeded to dress, formally, in a stiff tunic of green with gold trim, a wide orange sash, and high polished boots. This evening there would be a reception at the Embassy in his honor.

When he was dressed, Catton locked his room and strolled down the wide, carpet-cushioned corridor of the Embassy's floor. It was a spacious and attractive building.

The sound of music was in the air—tinkling alien music, played on a strange instrument that produced a plangent tone not unlike that of a harpsichord. Following the music, Catton rounded the bend in the corridor and found himself at the entrance to a drawing-room which was occupied by several people. The music came to an abrupt halt at his arrival.

Catton saw that the people in the room were not all human. There were five: two Morilaru, lean and angular in their tight clothing, and three Terrans. Catton recognized two of the Terrans—Estil, the Ambassador's eighteen-year-old daughter, and her tutor, an elderly woman named Mrs. Larch. The remaining person was a Terran of dignified aspect who wore formal business clothes.

It had been Estil who had been playing, it seemed. She was seated at a wide keyboard connected to a complex stringed instrument of alien design.

"Pardon me," Catton said. "I didn't mean to intrude. I simply heard music, and—"

"Please be welcome here," Estil said. She spoke well, but formally; she had the accents of a child who had been raised with care, by a too-devoted governess. Catton had formed that impression the night before, during their brief meeting when he had arrived at the Embassy from the spaceport.

The girl rose from the keyboard and, graciously taking Catton's hand, led him all the way into the room. "This is Mr. Lloyd Catton, of Earth," she announced. "He arrived on Morilar last night. He's—uh—a member of the new Interworld Commission on Crime. Am I right, Mr. Catton?"

"Precisely," he told her.

She made introductions. "This is Doveril Halligon," she said. "My music teacher. And his friend, Gonnimor Cleeren."

"How do you do," Catton said gravely to the two aliens. They bowed in return.

"I think you know Mrs. Larch," Estil said. "And this," she went on, pointing to the somber, middle-aged gentleman in business clothes, "is Mr. Bartlett, a friend of my father's from Earth."

Catton and Bartlett shook hands. Catton felt vaguely uncomfortable about the entire little scene. It was more convenient for him to stay at the Embassy than anywhere else on Morilar, but he was not easily at home in the milieu of drawing-room music recitals.

He said a trifle awkwardly, "The music sounded charming from a distance, Miss Seeman. I'd appreciate it if you'd continue playing."

Estil flushed prettily and returned to the keyboard. Her governess said, "The instrument is known as the gondran. Estil has been studying with Doveril Halligon for two years now. She has become quite proficient."

Catton stared at the alien music teacher for an instant. Doveril Halligon did not meet the glance. Instead he signaled to Estil, who began to play—falteringly, at first, but gaining in confidence after the first few measures. The piece seemed, to Catton's untutored ears, to be a difficult one; the keyboard technique was tricky, and the harmonies were strange. He joined politely in the applause when the last tinkling note had died away.

An Embassy android entered the drawing-room bearing a little tray of cool drinks, and a few minutes of sociability followed the end of Estil's recital. Catton, improvising desperately, managed to keep the conversation going as he discussed musical techniques with the two aliens, while Mrs. Larch and Estil exchanged sentences with Bartlett. Then the groupings broke up. Catton and Estil started across the room toward each other. Suddenly the girl stumbled and began to fall to her knees.

Catton moved forward rapidly, caught the girl, and steadied her on her feet before anyone else could move.

"Are you all right?"

"Perfectly," she said. "Thanks very kindly." In a lower voice she added, "I have to speak to you alone tonight. It's very important."

CHAPTER THREE

There were more than a hundred guests at the reception in Catton's honor that evening. The list included virtually every Terran of note in Dyelleran. A quartet of Morilaru musicians kept up an endless flow of melody; the punchbowl, spiked with a tawny alien liquor, was never allowed to be empty. Catton did not care much for this sort of formal pomp, but he knew it was essential to his role that he allow himself to be presented to the world as a typical Terran diplomat.

As guest of honor, it was his privilege to claim the first dance with the Ambassador's daughter. The alien musicians played a fair approximation of a waltz, interpolating just enough of their own chromatic harmonies to destroy any link the waltz tune might have had with ancient Vienna. Estil moved lightly in Catton's arms. She was a slim girl, gravely attractive, with serious violet-blue eyes and a soft cloud of dark hair.

"You said you wanted to talk to me alone tonight," Catton said softly as they swung round the floor.

"Yes. I'm in trouble, Mr. Catton. Maybe you can help me."

"Me? How can I help? I'm a stranger here?"

She nodded. "Perhaps that's how. Somehow I know I can trust you. I hope you don't mind listening to me go on like this."

"I'm always willing to help a damsel in distress. What's your difficulty, Miss Seeman?"

"I'll—I'll tell you about it later. We'll go out on the balcony to talk. Daddy will think it's so romantic of us!"

Catton smiled, but within himself he felt uneasy. He hoped the girl was not leading up to something along the line of telling him she had fallen for him at first sight. For one thing, charming though she was, she was only a child, half his age; for another, his profession made romantic entanglements of any sort unwise. But he realized he was probably flattering himself. Estil would not be likely to develop much romantic interest for a craggy-faced man who was almost forty. He wondered what kind of trouble she was in.

The dance came to its end, and Catton escorted the girl across the floor to the table at which her father sat. Ambassador Seeman was a great barrel of a man, immensely tall, hugely broad; his voice was a mellow bass boom. As the Terran World Government's Ambassador to Morilar, it was his task to keep diplomatic relations between the two worlds on an even keel despite the constant stresses that arose.

"Your daughter dances very well," Catton said.

Seeman chuckled. "She's had good tutors. I've spared no expense."

A man wearing the uniform of an officer in the Terran Space Navy approached, said something to Estil, and danced away with her. As soon as the girl was beyond ear-shot, the Ambassador remarked, "She's come along wonderfully well since her mother died. Become the very image of my wife."

"How long ago did she die?"

"Twelve years. Almost as soon as we arrived on Morilar. Estil was six, then. She hardly remembers Earth at all now, except as a vague blur."

"You haven't been back in all this time?"

"No," Seeman said. "She's never shown any interest in returning to Earth. Morilar is her home world, I'm afraid. After all, she's spent two-thirds of her life here."

Catton nodded. A woman came up to them; Catton had been introduced to her earlier in the evening, and he dimly recalled that she was the wife of one of the lesser Terran diplomats stationed on Morilar. They made conversation for a while, and then Catton completed the formalities by dancing with her. She chattered on and on about the complexities of life on an alien world—houseboy trouble, the heat, the strange food, all the rest.

The evening dragged along. Some time later, Catton found himself dancing with Estil again; and, at the end of the dance, they strolled out onto the open balcony at the far side of the ballroom. Catton noted with irritation that they were being stared at, and no doubt commented upon, as they left the dance floor.

The night was warm. The sky, speckled with the unfamiliar constellations, was partly veiled with murky clouds. The two bright moons of Morilar hung high overhead. Below them, the city sprawled out toward the horizon.

Estil said, "Will you promise to keep absolutely secret everything I'm going to tell you?"

"That's a pretty tall order. Suppose you tell me that the sun's going nova. Should 1 keep the news to myself?"

Catton regretted his facetiousness instantly. She said, "I mean it. *Please* be serious."

"All right. I'm sorry. What do you want to tell me, Estil?"

"I'm in love," she said simply.

Catton peered out over the balcony. A river wound like a glittering snake through the heart of the city. "Every girl your age should be in love," he said. "It's good for the spirit."

"You're patronizing me," she said crisply.

Catton smiled. "I guess I am. Again, I'm sorry. I mean it. I won't do it again."

"Will you hear me out?"

"Go on," he said.

"Very well. I'm in love with my music teacher. Doveril Halligon. You met him this afternoon in the drawing-room."

Her quiet words detonated like bombshells. Catton turned pale. He swung round to face her. "But—but he's a Morilaru! An alien!"

"He's a *person*," she replied. "A kind, warmhearted person. As good as any Earthman I've ever known. Why shouldn't I love him? He understands me. He loves me."

Catton moistened his lips. The implications of this thing were explosive. An ambassador's daughter, in love with an alien? The scandal would be enormous. "All right," he said calmly. "You're in love with him. Why tell this to me?"

"I want to go away from here with Doveril. Far away, where no one can find us and break us up. I know, it's a shocking thing, an Earthgirl falling in love with—with an alien. I can't help myself. It—just happened that way. I have a little money saved. So does Doveril."

"And how do I fit into this?" Catton asked.

"You're here to investigate the hypnojewel racket, aren't you?"

Catton's jaw dropped. "Yes. How did you find *that* out?"

The girl smiled. "Daddy told me. Daddy tells me almost everything I want him to tell me." She paused. "You're here to investigate trade in hypnojewels. Well, sometimes, I've heard Doveril talking about hypnojewels with his friends. Whispering. This afternoon, when he was here at the Embassy, giving me my music lesson, he brought that friend of his along, Connimor Cleeren. They said a few things. I guess they didn't think I understood. I heard them mention hypnojewels."

"Are you sure? But—"

"I'm afraid," the girl said, trying to keep an adolescent quiver out of her voice. "Doveril doesn't like to talk much about his past.

I'm afraid he may be mixed up in the hypnojewel business, or that he might have been involved in it some time in the past. So what I want you to do for me—if you can—is find out whether he's in the clear. Can you do that for me?"

"Tell you whether or not Doveril has ever been mixed up in hypnojewel trafficking?"

"Yes. Oh, you must have access to the police records, as a member of the Crime Commission, and—"

"And those records are supposed to be confidential."

"I know," she said. "But I love Doveril so much—and you wouldn't want me to run away with him if he were a *criminal*, would you?"

I wouldn't want you to run away with him for any reason, Catton thought. It would be suicidally foolish for her to elope with a penniless alien musician. But he kept his thoughts to himself.

He said, "I see your position. You must be terribly worried about him."

"I am."

"I hope for your sake that he's in the clear."

"I hope so too," she said. "You'll help me, then?"

"I can't promise anything. I'll do my best, though. I'll try to find out."

"You'll do it soon, won't you?"

"As soon as I can find anything, I'll let you know." He smiled. "We'd better go back inside now," he said. "We've been out here almost fifteen minutes. People are going to start whispering things about us."

They returned to the ballroom. The dance was still in full swing. Catton grinned at the girl and she went dancing off in the arms of one of the young Space Navy officers. Catton wandered toward the sidelines and poured himself a glass of the highly spiked punch.

Ambassador Seeman was deep in conversation with two Terran businessmen and their wives. Catton wondered whether the Ambassador had even the faintest notion of the sort of thing his little girl had become involved in, at her tender age. Probably, Catton thought, Seeman had no suspicion whatever. He shrugged.

About midnight, the reception ended. The guests departed, and Catton, wearily, returned to his own room two floors above the

Embassy ballroom. He flickered on the lightswitch. The visiphone blinker was on, telling him that there had been a call for him during the evening.

He activated the playback of the call-recorder, and the screen came to light.

The head and shoulders of a Morilaru woman appeared in the viewing area. Above her head, the time of her call was imprinted. She had called nearly two hours ago.

She said, "You don't know me, but I have some information that can be very useful to you. If you think you're interested, call me any time before midnight at K22-1055B."

Frowning, Catton looked at his watch. It was after midnight, but not much after. He decided to try the number.

Blanking the screen and wiping away the recording of her call, he punched out the number on the keyboard. A moment passed, while the screen remained cloudy. Then the murk cleared. The head and shoulders of the Morilaru woman appeared. She seemed to be young, as far as Catton could tell, but there was a cold hardness about her eyes and lips.

"Yes?" she said.

"This is Lloyd Catton. You left a message for me to call you.

"Oh. Yes. I'd like to meet you, Catton."

"Why?"

"It isn't something I could be happy talking about on a vision screen," she said.

"If you don't feel like telling me what you want to talk about," Catton said, "I might as well switch the screen off. It's too late at night for playing mysterious guessing-games."

"All right. I'll tell you this much: I have some information for you on a subject you're very interested in. A subject connected with jewelry."

Catton nodded slowly, concealing his confusion and surprise. Word certainly traveled quickly on this planet. He said, "Okay, I'm interested. I suppose you want to meet me?"

"Yes. Tomorrow."

"Where?"

"In the old quarter," she said. "There's a tavern where I could see you. It's on the Street of the Two Moons, just over the bridge. Think you can find it?"

"I'll manage. What's the name of the place?"

"The Five Planets," she said. "My name is Nuuri Gryain. Will you be there at noon sharp?"

"I'll be there," Catton said. The Morilaru woman grinned at him slyly and blanked the screen. Catton stared in puzzlement at the dying pattern of light for a moment, then shrugged and clicked the switch. The Five Planets, tomorrow at noon. It was a date.

CHAPTER FOUR

Dyelleran, capital city of Morilar, shared one characteristic with many other capital cities throughout the galaxy: the contrast between the district of official buildings and the slums was extreme. Dyelleran was divided by the River Mhorn, which pursued an east-to-west course through the city on its tortuous path to the sea. The river was bridged twenty times within the city proper, but there was no real bond between the two halves of Dyelleran. The contrast between the east bank, on which the government buildings and the best residential areas were situated, and the west bank, or Old Quarter, was extraordinary.

It was mid-morning when Catton crossed the bridge into the Old Quarter. The moment he stepped from his cab he knew this was a considerably different neighborhood from the serene and architecturally impressive governmental half of the city. The streets were crooked and paved with cobblestones; a nasty stink of rotting vegetables hung in the air, and sleeping Morilaru huddled in the doorways. The heat, which had been annoying on the other side of the river, was impossible here. Droning mosquito-like insects hovered in greedy clouds.

The Street of the Two Moons turned out to be one of the widest in the entire district: that is, vehicles could pass comfortably in both directions. The old houses that lined the street tilted crazily in all angles and directions. Some of them, Catton guessed, were more than a thousand years old, and still used as dwellings.

He had checked the city directory and discovered that the number of The Five Planets was 63, Street of the Two Moons, but the information did Catton little good; no house numbers were apparent on any of the buildings. But he had no difficulty finding the tavern. A huge grimy banner dangled out over the street, moving fitfully in the faint breeze, and emblazoned on the tattered cloth Catton saw five brightly-colored worlds arranged in a loose circle. He quickened his pace.

The tavern door was no fancy electronic affair; it was a simple slab of solid wood. Catton dragged it open and stepped inside.

The place was dark, according to the universal custom of taverns. Along the left wall was the bar, manned by a dour-looking bald old Morilaru; tables were scattered at irregular intervals throughout the dimly-lit, low-roofed room. Only four people, all Morilaru, were in the tavern as Catton entered. All four turned to stare at him.

The girl was sitting at the table closest to the door. A mug of wine was in her hand, and another was on the table, evidently having been poured for him. He walked over and looked down, trying to be certain she was the one he had spoken to the night before. It was often not easy to tell one Morilaru from another.

"Nuuri Gryain?" he asked.

She smiled at him, showing flashing white teeth. "Sit down, Catton. I've already ordered a drink for you. I hope you like our wine."

He pulled out the seat, lowered himself into it, and cradled the wine mug in his big hands. The mug was of yellow clay, and refreshingly cool to the touch in the hothouse atmosphere. He looked closely at her.

"Who are you?" he asked.

"Somebody with a grudge. That's all."

"What kind of grudge?"

"A grudge against a certain man," she said. "That doesn't concern you. Let's say I'm interested in seeing justice get done. My own kind of justice."

Calmly, Catton lifted the wine to his lips. The liquid was cool, faintly bitter. He allowed about half a spoonful to enter his mouth, and he held it there, without swallowing it, as he tasted it.

"Go on," she said. "It's safe to swallow. The wine isn't drugged or poisoned, Catton."

He swallowed the half spoonful. "Why should I trust you? The wine was on the table when I came in. You might easily have doctored it."

"Do you want me to drink the rest of your wine?" she asked. "Or wouldn't you trust that either?"

"There are drugs that effect a Terran metabolism but not a Morilaru one," he said, grinning. "But I'll take my chances. The first mouthful didn't kill me." He took a deeper sip: the wine was good. He set the mug down half empty. "Suppose you start telling me why you wanted to see me."

She locked her fingers together. Like most of her race, she was long and thin—spidery, that was the way most Morilaru looked to Catton. But there was a strange grace about her. Her red-hued eyes sparkled oddly, and her gaunt cheekbones had a way of highlighting the subtle colors of her skin. She wore the green crest of maidenhood in her lustrous black hair.

She said, "You're here to investigate the traffic in hypnojewels, Earthman." It was not a question but a flat declarative statement."

"How do you know that?" Catton asked.

Her spike-tipped shoulders lifted lightly in a shrug. "I've had access to the information. Let's leave it at that, shall we?"

"For the moment. All right: I'm investigating hypnojewel traffic. What do you want to tell me?"

"I can help you uncover a ring of hypnojewel smugglers, Catton. I'm volunteering my services as a go-between. Think you're interested?"

He tapped the table. "You've got a price. What is it?"

"No price. I just want to see this bunch put in jail, that's all."

"Simple as that, eh?"

"Yes. As simple as that."

"All right," Catton said. "I'll go along with you, maybe. How do you plan to work this uncovering?"

"I'll take you to the place where you can make contact with these people," she said. "We can fob you off as a would-be purchaser of a hypnojewel. I think we can do it convincingly. The transaction can take place, and then you can crack down, once you have the incriminating evidence. Does it sound okay?"

For a moment Catton made no answer. Then he said in a soft voice, "You're selling out some friends of yours, aren't you, Nuuri? Why?"

"What does that matter to you? You Earthmen are only interested in results. In smashing the illegal smuggling trade. Isn't that right?"

"Yes."

"Very well. I'm offering you a chance to uncover something big—and you're asking questions."

"I just want to know what you stand to gain personally out of this," Catton said.

The girl took a deep draught of her wine. "I'll spell it out for you simply. I was in love with one of the members of this group. He is not in love with me. He claims to be in love with another woman, and he also says now that he's going to run away with her as soon as the proceeds from the next hypnojewel deal come in. I'm just angry enough at him to want to turn the whole bunch in to the law. Now do you get it, Earthman? Now do you see the picture?"

"Jealousy. Pure green jealousy."

"Call it whatever you want. But Doveril thought he could grind me into the dirt, and I want him to find out he isn't going to get away with it."

Catton felt a pang of painful surprise. *"Doveril?"*

"Maybe I shouldn't have let that slip. But that's his name, as long as I've dropped it out. He's the head of the group. He earns his keep as a music teacher, right now. Maybe you've seen him around the Embassy. He teaches music to the Ambassador's brat."

Catton nodded, shutting his eyes for an instant. He was not ordinarily susceptible to emotional distress, but he felt deeply saddened now. Poor Estil was going to be in for the nastiest jolt of her young life.

"Tell me," Catton said. "This woman who's taken your place in his affections—you know who she is?"

"No. And it's a good thing, too. I'd scratch her eyes out!" There was snapping fire in Nuuri's voice. Catton thought he understood the alien girl completely, at that moment: sensual, highly emotional, eager for revenge. He felt relieved that she did not know the actual identity of her hated rival.

"I'm not sure I care for your motives in this business," Catton said. "But the end result is what matters, and I'm anxious to see the hypnojewel trade rooted out. When will you take me to these people?"

"Whenever you want. Tomorrow's a good day."

"Good enough," he said. "Tomorrow, then. Suppose I meet you here, at this time."

"Right. How about another drink, Earthman?"

Catton shook his head. "One's enough, thanks." He rose and dropped a coin on the table. "This ought to take care of the drink I had. I'll see you tomorrow, right here. Don't change your mind overnight."

"I won't," she said vehemently. "Don't worry about that." Catton stepped from the dimness of the tavern to the bright searing heat of the street in early afternoon. There was no cab in sight; he walked down to the foot of the Street of the Two Moons, breathing shallowly to keep from retching at the filth all about him.

He would have to tell Estil, of course. He wondered how she would take it. Badly, no doubt. She was in for an emotional wrench. But at least she had already had misgivings about Doveril, so it wouldn't be a total shock to her to learn of his criminal activities. And, in any event, finding out now would save her from making a mistake of life-shattering consequences. In a few months she would probably forget all about the impecunious, fast-talking music teacher.

Catton walked eastward toward the newer section of the city. He crossed the bridge on foot, stopping once to peer down at the sluggish, dirty water, coated with bright oil slicks, and at the men working on the barges that passed beneath the bridge. They worked stripped to the waist, tall fleshless purple beings who looked almost but not quite human, and they didn't seem to object to the killing heat. Probably, he thought, Morilaru who visit Earth are astonished at our ability to function in such a dread chill. It was all a matter of viewpoint.

There was a public communicator-booth at the eastern end of the bridge. It was time, Catton decided, to report to Pouin Beryaal.

He entered the booth and clicked the door shut behind him. Fishing an octagonal ten-unit coin from his change-purse, Catton placed it in the appropriate slot and punched the number of the Interworld Commission on Crime.

There was a moment's pause; then, on the tiny screen of the communicator, the blurred image of a Morilaru female appeared.

"Office of the Interworld Commission on Crime. Your party, please?"

"This is Lloyd Catton. I'd like to talk to Pouin Beryaal, if he's in."

"Just one moment, please."

Catton waited, reflecting on the universal similarity of receptionists and switchboard operators all over the galaxy. A few seconds later, the angular, austere face of the chairman of the Commission appeared.

"Catton?"

"Good afternoon, Pouin Beryaal. I'm calling from a public communicator just over the bridge from the Old Quarter."

"Are you out slumming today?" Beryaal asked sardonically.

"I've been conducting a little investigation."

"So soon? And without consulting us?"

"Someone phoned me last night and said she had some information that would interest me. We made a date today in a tavern over on the other side of the river. Seems she's had a love-spat with her boyfriend, who's a hypnojewel smuggler, and to get even with him she wants to expose the whole ring. I'm seeing her again tomorrow."

Pouin Beryaal chuckled. "You Earthmen certainly waste little time in beginning an investigation."

"I'm still not fully convinced she's going to go through with it. She says she means it, but maybe she'll kiss and make up with him tonight. I'll keep you posted on further developments."

"Very kind of you," Beryall said. "I'll tell our colleagues of your progress. We hope to see you again in our office soon—there is a room provided for your use now. Is there anything further you wish to report?"

"Not just now," Catton said. He broke contact and left the booth.

Catching a cab as it came thrumming across the bridge, he returned to the Embassy. There, he was surprised to find a cluster of the green vehicles of the local police parked outside the building. Morilaru police were everywhere, milling over the Embassy grounds like a swarm of buzzing insects.

Puzzled, Catton entered the Embassy gates. A policeman stopped him and said roughly: "Where are you going, Earth-man?"

"I'm residing at the Embassy. What's going on here?"

"We will ask the questions. Proceed within."

Catton obediently entered the building. Half a dozen members of the Embassy staff were clustered in an anxious little knot in the lobby. Catton approached them.

"Will someone please tell me what all the fuss is about?" he demanded.

It was the Ambassador's cook who answered. "It's Miss Estil—Ambassador Seeman's daughter."

Catton caught his breath sharply. Was he too late? Had the little fool decided to run off with her Morilaru lover anyway, without waiting for information about him?

"What about Miss Estil?" he asked.

"She's vanished," was the twittering reply. "Her bed wasn't slept in all night. She left her note with her father, saying she was running away—running away with the man she loved."

CHAPTER FIVE

The hubbub at the Embassy lasted well into the night. Catton stayed out of the foreground. He was interrogated briefly by Barnevelt, the head of the Embassy security staff, who looked flustered and chagrined, and then he was interviewed all over again by a Morilaru crime-prevention officer who seemed not too terribly interested in the disappearance at all.

Catton told the same story word-for-word to both of them. He had been on Morilar only a couple of days, had met the Ambassador's daughter twice, had had a brief conversation with her at the ball the night before. She had talked obliquely of being in love, but Catton could provide no details. After all, he had hardly known the girl.

The interrogation over, Catton made his way up to his room and settled down. He was puzzled and not happy over the girl's disappearance. Doveril was a criminal, as Estil had suspected—but yet she had run away with him the very day after she had asked Catton to check on Doveril's record. Perhaps she had had a sudden change of heart, and decided to elope before Catton could provide her with the information she did not want to have; or else there had been some coercion involved in her abrupt disappearance. Catton hoped not. But for the sake of his own investigations he decided to keep quiet about those aspects of the case he had data on.

The next day he kept his appointment with Nuuri Gryain, meeting her once again at The Five Planets shortly after noon. It was a swelteringly hot day. Catton was growing accustomed to the oven heat of Dyelleran.

The Morilaru woman was waiting for him at the table nearest the door. She was bent over a local news-sheet, puzzling out the wedge-shaped characters. As he came in she looked up, smiling coldly.

"Morning greetings, Catton."

"Hello, Nuuri. What's in the paper?"

"That's what I'm trying to figure out. My reading isn't so good, Earthman." She chuckled. "I find this item interesting. Can you read our language?"

"Well enough to decipher a newspaper," Catton said. She shoved the sheet over to him and tapped a front-page story meaningfully. Catton frowned. The headline said, clearly enough, *DAUGHTER OF TERRAN AMBASSADOR VANISHES.* It was an article about Estil Seeman. He read slowly though it. About all it said was that the Earthgirl had disappeared yesterday, leaving a note for her father—contents unspecified—and that a galaxy-wide search was being instituted for her.

"It seems Doveril has lost a pupil," Nuuri commented when Catton looked up.

The Earthman frowned. "It would seem that way. Think she'll be found?"

"Who knows? The galaxy is a big place; a young girl can lose herself easily enough. I doubt they'll ever find her."

"Enough talk of the girl," Catton said. "You know why I'm here today."

"Of course. I'll take you where you can buy what you're looking for. But first a disguise is in order. Come—let's leave."

Catton followed her out into the street, which was all but empty because of the mid-day heat. She strode purposefully along at a rapid pace, turning corners twice, and stopped finally in front of a shabby shop with darkened windows.

She threw open the door.

"In here," she muttered to Catton.

The Earthman stepped inside. An old Morilaru, so old his skin had faded from its one-time purple to a musty grayish-blue, sprawled dozing behind a counter. Nuuri slapped the flat of her hand down on the wood inches from his face. The Morilaru awoke with a start.

"Nuuri! What—"

"A job for you, you old fool." She indicated Catton. "Turn him into a Dargonid, and do a good job of it for your money."

"Right now?"

"This very moment," Nuuri snapped.

The ancient Morilaru elbowed himself wearily upward, beckoned to Catton, and shambled off into a back room partitioned from the front of the shop by a frayed and dilapidated curtain of glass beads. Nuuri followed, standing in the doorway with her arms knotted together across her chest, hands gripping shoulder-spikes in a typical Morilaru posture of relaxation.

Catton blinked uneasily. "Just how permanent is this transformation going to be?"

"It will take fifteen minutes to make the change, half that time to restore you," the old man said. "It is a simple enough process. Remove your clothes."

Catton eyed Nuuri questioningly, but she made no motion to leave. He shrugged and stripped off his clothing, tossing it carelessly in a corner. The Morilaru selected a spraysqueeze vial from a rack and advanced on Catton.

"Shut your eyes."

Catton did so. A moment later he smelled an acrid chemical odor and felt a faint coolness playing about his body. The application took several minutes. When it was complete, Catton opened his eyes again and saw that his body was now colored iron-gray from head to foot.

The rest of the disguise followed in short order. Catton was fitted for contact lenses that provided him with yellow pupils on a black background; another spray turned his hair from brown to blue; lovingly-applied strips of collodion accented his cheekbones, tripled the length of his earlobes, and gave a downward slant to his eyebrows. The final touch was the clothing; the Morilaru stored Catton's Earthman clothes in a locker and gave him the brief tunic of a Dargonid.

Nuuri came forward, jabbed a finger against the flesh of Catton's shoulder, and scrubbed it up and down to test the permanence of the color-spray. It held fast. She nodded in critical approval.

"A fine job. Catton, you look like a native-born of Dargon."

"Will it convince your friends?"

"I'm sure of it." She nodded at the old man. "Pay him, Catton."

"How much?"

"Five thrones?" the old man suggested hopefully.

Nuuri snorted. "Give him a hundred units now, and a hundred more when we return—for the safekeeping of your clothes. Two thrones is more than enough."

Disappointment was evident on the venerable Morilaru's seamed face. But Catton did not care to cross Nuuri. He took two fifty-unit pieces from his money belt and gave them to the Morilaru.

"Here's a throne for you," Catton said. "Another for you later in the day."

"My gratitude, good sir."

"Come on," Nuuri said. "Let's get out of here."

They left through a back exit and walked briskly through the crooked, vile-smelling streets. Catton was steaming beneath his layer of coloring, but he forced himself to keep pace with the girl.

"What's my name?" he asked. "And why am I here?"

Nuuri thought for a moment. "You're—ah—Zord Karlsrunig. I once knew a Dargonid of that name. You're a merchant here on business, leaving for Dargon at the end of the week. Don't worry about the other details. Hide behind your passion for anonymity. The purchaser has certain rights of silence too, you know."

"Zord Karlsrunig," Catton repeated. "All right. And the story is that I'm in the market for a hypnojewel, and am willing to pay cash down for it."

"Yes. We'll make all the necessary negotiations. Then you'll tell them you have to return to the bank to get the cash. Instead, of course, you notify the authorities."

Some minutes later, they paused in front of another saloon, this one emblazoned with the name, The Deeper Draught. It was smaller and, if anything, dingier-looking than the other bar, The Five Planets, where Catton had first met Nuuri.

"Wait here and don't get into trouble," Nuuri whispered. "I'll be back in a moment."

Catton nodded. The alien woman went inside. He waited at the door, trying to rehearse his lines, struggling to don the character of a Dargonid. He would have to introduce a slight guttural quality into his speech, and perhaps adopt some clumsy locutions of construction. He would have to remember never to display a characteristically Terran posture—crossing his legs was out, and steepling his fingertips. Dargonids—how the devil did Dargonids hold themselves, he wondered?—Dargonids customarily sat with one hand on their kneecap, the other gripping the first arm's elbow. It would be awkward for him, but he knew he had better perform the gesture as if he had been doing it all his life.

Nuuri returned a few moments later. She looked angry. "They're all there—except Doveril! Except the one I was most anxious to have apprehended!"

That was no surprise, Catton thought, in view of the fact that the Morilaru music teacher was by now many light-years away, bound outward for—where?—with his beloved. But he did not want Nuuri to know that.

"Take me inside anyway," he said. "We'll round up this batch whether Doveril's here or not."

"But I don't care if the others are arrested. I'm only interested in arranging Doveril's downfall."

Catton scowled. "I'll see to it that Doveril is implicated somehow." His hand darted out, seized her wrist. "You've taken me this far. Don't back out now. We'll catch these, and one of them will confess Doveril's complicity."

Sighing, she said, "Very well. Come inside with me."

They passed through a poorly lit, foul-smelling saloon whose only customers were two bedraggled Morilaru drabs, and he followed her up a creaking stairway to the upper floor of the tavern, where, inn-fashion, there were a few rooms available for lodging.

Nuuri paused in front of the furthermost of the rooms and knocked twice, then twice more. The door opened. A Morilaru head popped warily out, looked around, stared curiously at Catton.

"You may enter."

Catton followed Nuuri into the room. There were five male Morilaru there, of indeterminate ages. The Earthman realized with a sudden jolt of shock that one of the aliens was Gonnimor Cleeren, the friend of Doveril's who had been present at the music-lesson the afternoon of the Ambassador's ball. Cleeren was staring at Catton keenly, but gave no outward indication that he had penetrated the Earthman's disguise.

One of the other Morilaru said, "You speak our language, Dargonid?"

"Well enough," Catton answered, putting the accent on the wrong syllable in each of the two Morilaru words. "I understand you, and my money speaks even more well for me, Morilaru."

"The woman tells us you wish to buy."

Catton tipped his head to one side, a Dargonid affirmative gesture. Thank God, he thought, that he had once carried out an assignment on Dargon. It had been years ago, but he still remembered many behavior patterns of that predominantly mercantile world.

"I wish to buy, yes. And you, to sell. But can you give immediate delivery? I return to Dargon shortly."

"If you can pay, we can deliver."

"My account is large at the great bank," Catton said. "Though I will not be cheated on the price."

"The price," said another of the Morilaru, "is ten thousand thrones."

Catton inserted a finger in his mouth to show annoyance. After a brief silence he said, "It is much for a piece of polished stone. I will give you six thousand."

"Ten thousand," repeated the Morilaru, "and not a unit less."

Catton shook his head. "Six thousand is too high. But I will extend my price another few thousand units. I offer you six thousand five hundred thrones."

"Ten thousand," said the Morilaru inflexibly.

The Earthman was pensive. As a thrifty Dargonid, he was expected to haggle; as an investigator, he was interested only in making the incriminating purchase. But if he gave in too easily, they might suspect him.

He said, "You are stubborn men. Well, I stubborn can be with equality. Break your price or I go elsewhere. If need be I will go to the wholesale source for the stones."

Several of the Morilaru laughed at that. One said, "You'll need a strong nose, Dargonid!" Another scowled at the one who had spoken. Catton narrowed his eyes thoughtfully. That was a useful bit of information. The strong odor of Skorg was proverbial in the galaxy; were they implying that the hypnojewels came from there? Catton filed the information away.

He rose. "Business I will do, extortion no. I raise my offer to seven thousand two hundred thrones. Will you be inflexible?"

"The price is ten thousand."

Catton flicked his tongue back and forth in the Dargonid equivalent of a shrug. "I argue not. Your price is too high. Thank you for your courtesies," he said to Nuuri. "And to the rest of you, good day."

He edged toward the door, taking his time, wondering if his bluff would be called.

As his hand touched the doorknob a voice behind him said, "Wait."

Catton turned. "Why?"

"Nine thousand five hundred thrones."

"Eight thousand."

"You Dargonids would bargain for hours of your life!" the Morilaru spokesman exclaimed. "Nine thousand is our lowest price. You've peeled a thousand thrones off—be content with that."

Catton was silent a long moment. At length he said, "We are hardly more than ten percent apart. I offer you eight thousand five hundred as a meeting-ground."

The Morilaru eyed each other, debating silently. They nodded. "Done," the spokesman said. "When will you have the cash?"

"I'll leave you five hundred thrones as a binder. The rest will I obtain at my bank within the hour. When will I receive the stone?"

"Upon payment. Would you inspect it now?"

"I would indeed."

One of the Morilaru knelt, peeled up a loose floorboard, drew forth a small velvet pouch. He tossed it to Catton, who fumbled the catch deliberately, then snatched the falling pouch with his other hand in a desperate grab. The Dargonids had the reputation of clumsiness.

He snatched a glance at the Morilaru. They seemed to be holding their breaths.

"Be wary, Dargonid," the spokesman advised him. "You know the peril of the stone."

"That I do," Catton replied. He undid the catch at the mouth of the pouch and let the stone drop out onto the palm of his hand. He looked at it only long enough to verify its identity, then returned it to the pouch and tossed it back to the Morilaru.

"I am satisfied. Herewith the binder; I'll return with the rest within the hour. Remain you here."

Catton counted out ten golden fifty-throne pieces from his moneybelt and handed them across to the Morilaru. Then, bowing courteously, he withdrew from the room, leaving Nuuri there with the hypnojewel smugglers.

He made his way rapidly through the tangle of streets to the nearest bridge into the eastern half of the city. After making sure no one had followed him, he stepped into the first public communicator-booth he found, and dialed the number of Pouin Beryaal.

After the usual routine delays, Beryaal appeared on the tiny screen.

"Close your circuit," Catton ordered. "This is important material."

"The circuit is sealed. Speak away."

"I've encountered a ring of hypnojewel peddlers. They've agreed to sell me a stone for eighty-five hundred thrones. I left five hundred as a binder and I'm supposedly on my way to the bank to get the rest."

Beryaal's eyes widened. "Have you seen the stone?"

"Yes. It's the real item."

"I suppose this accounts for the alteration in your face," Beryaal commented. The screen, black-and-white, did not indicate Catton's color change. "Very well. Where can they be found?"

"A tavern called The Deeper Draught, across the river on the Street of Cutpurses. Upstairs, in the furthermost room from the stairs."

"I'll have men there in twenty minutes," Beryaal promised.

CHAPTER SIX

The arrest went off smoothly enough. Catton and Pouin Beryaal had agreed on the details before breaking the communicator contact. Catton was to be allowed to escape; Nuuri would be arrested and later freed.

The Earthman went on to the Grand Bank of Morilar and drew out eight thousand thrones from the special account placed there for his use. The clerk frowned in confusion at the inexplicable sight of a Dargonid drawing money from a Terran account, but the identification-placket matched, and the teller had no choice but to hand Catton eight crisp thousand-throne bills.

Catton took a cab across the bridge, left it at the Street of Two Moons, and covered the rest of the way to The Deeper Draught on foot. He was rapidly learning his way around the knotty maze of streets in Dyelleran's Old Quarter. His mnemonic training stood him, as always, in good stead in this city.

He had timed his excursion precisely. Unless Beryaal's crime-detection men missed their cue, he would have three or four minutes and no more before the arrest. He mounted the tavern stairs two at a time and knocked in the prescribed manner on the door.

"It is I, Karlsrunig, the Dargonid. Let me in!"

The door swung back. Catton nodded in satisfaction. All of the Morilaru were still there, a tense, narrow-eyed group. Nuuri looked particularly nervous. Catton said, "I have the cash. Take the stone from its hiding-place."

"Show us the money."

Catton riffled the eight bills in front of them. The stone was produced. Catton said slowly, "Seven thousand five hundred thrones?"

"The deal was closed at eighty-five hundred," the Morilaru reminded him. "Would you bargain now?"

Catton smiled. "Force of habit solely, friends. Let me have the stone."

"At the agreed sum?"

"Here is my money. Eight thousand, plus the five hundred you have already. The stone!"

Catton extended the eight bills, and at the same time reached out a hand for the pouch. The timing of the crime-detection men was extraordinary. Catton and the Morilaru were frozen for a moment in a little tableau, each with one hand on the money and one on the pouch, when the door exploded inward. A bright purple flash of light told Catton that the transaction was preserved on film, as indisputable evidence. A moment later, after an abortive exchange of shots, the arrest was concluded. One Morilaru lay dead, his body gone above the chest. The others, as well as Nuuri and Catton, held hands high in the air.

"I'll have that pouch," said the crime-detection group's leader. He snatched it, opened it wide enough to ascertain that it held a hypnojewel, and pocketed it. "All right, come along, all of you."

As they reached the street Catton felt the handcuffs that bound him suddenly loosen and drop away; they had been set, by prearrangement, for only three minutes. He squirmed out of the middle of the group of captives, cut sharply to his left, and streaked for a garbage-bordered alleyway. The crime-detection men shouted sharply; one dashed after him, firing a blaster burst that nearly seared Catton's shoulder. The Earthman ducked into a beckoning doorway and crouched there a few minutes. He peeped out, finally, and saw that the captives had been taken away. One of Beryaal's men had remained behind, ostensibly to search for the escaped Dargonid, for the sake of appearances.

Catton emerged from the alley, grinning wryly. "Your idea of pretense is a little grim, brother. That shot of yours nearly hit me."

"The aim was faulty. I apologize."

"Where are the others?"

"Taken to the Crime Office for interrogation. I am officially to report that you were killed attempting escape. The girl will be released after questioning."

"How about the others?"

"Intensive probing."

Catton nodded. "All right. Consider me killed attempting escape. I'm going to get this paint taken off me now."

He made his way through the back streets to the shop of the old Morilaru, which he found with a relatively small amount of difficulty. The old man was dozing again. Catton woke him and said, "Turn me into an Earthman again. The disguise has done its job."

Catton stripped and let the dye-remover be applied; in ten minutes he was once again himself. He gave the old man a one-throne piece, as promised, and then, grinning conspiratorially, said, "Here's another throne for you. But don't tell Nuuri I gave it to you."

"My deepest gratitude," murmured the Morilaru.

Catton was happy to be rid of the layer of coloring, the contact lenses, and all the rest. An Earthman again, he hurried to the Street of the Two Moons and hired a cab there to take him to the offices of the Interworld Commission on Crime.

En route, he had time to think about Estil Seeman. The girl had run away, or perhaps she had been abducted by Doveril—but where might they be? Catton thought he knew. The hint dropped by one of the hypnojewel smugglers seemed to indicate that the source of supply for the gems was somewhere on Skorg. It was possible that Doveril might have fled there with Estil. Perhaps, he thought, it would be profitable for him to go there as well—ostensibly investigating the hypnojewel trade, less ostensibly searching for the missing girl, and actually observing for Earth's purposes the second most important world in the Morilar-Skorg-Arenadd axis.

This time, when he arrived at Number Eleven in the Street of Government, he had no difficulty gaining entry to the offices of the Interworld Commission on Crime. He was, after all, a member of that Commission now himself. He went directly to Pouin Beryaal's office. Beryaal was not there, but Ennid Uruod, the flabby Arenaddin member of the Commission, was.

"Where's Beryaal?" Catton asked.

"Interrogating the prisoners. He and eMerikh enjoy such torments; my stomach is weaker."

"How about the girl?"

Uruod lifted a fat-encased arm and pointed to an adjoining office. "In there, waiting for you. They've finished questioning her."

Catton thanked the Arenaddin and passed through the doorway into the next office. Nuuri was there, looking tense and troubled. But she managed a smile as he entered.

"They've officially released me," she said.

"How about the others?"

She shrugged. "They'll get the usual fate. Interrogation until their minds crack. I pity them."

"You betrayed them," Catton reminded her bleakly.

She showed no sign of emotion. "I was betraying only Doveril. The rest were incidental. But Doveril is free, and they are downstairs in the interrogation chamber."

"They'll pick up Doveril eventually," Catton said.

"This is doubtful. By now he's probably hundreds of light-years from here."

"You think so?"

"I'm sure of it. Doveril frightens easily. And news moves rapidly here."

"Where would he be likely to run to?" the Earthman asked.

Nuuri said, "There are many worlds in the universe. He could be anywhere."

Catton frowned for a moment. "I'm planning to make a trip to Skorg shortly. Do you think there's any chance he might be there?"

"Skorg? Why do you go to Skorg?"

"The reason doesn't concern you, Nuuri. I'm going on official business."

"Hypnojewel business?" she asked curiously.

"Of course. And if I could find Doveril there—"

"Skorg is a crowded world. You'd have trouble finding anyone there."

Catton nodded. "I'm aware of that. But there are ways of finding people."

"I hope you find Doveril," she said with venom in her voice. "I want to see him on Pouin Beryaal's rack, coughing out his life as they comb his mind."

"You hated him enough to betray five of his friends," Catton said. "All because he crossed you in love. It's a strong revenge, Nuuri."

Her eyes fixed on him beadily. They were silent for a moment; then Nuuri said, "I have nothing further to say now. I will leave you."

"Will you keep in touch with me?" he asked.

"Why should I?"

"I'm interested in wiping out the hypnojewel traffic," Catton said. "You've helped me once. Possibly you can help me again."

She shook her head. "I'm not a professional informer. I did you a service to satisfy my own desires. But I feel no yearning to betray others to you."

"You realize that I could have you taken downstairs and put under deep probe?" he asked. "You've as much as admitted that you're concealing important information that could be useful to us."

She stared at him unwaveringly. "I realize that. Would you take me to interrogation after my service to you? Is this your reward?"

"You claimed you didn't want a reward."

"I want a safe-conduct out of this building as my reward. I've helped you once. Now let me go."

"In a moment," he said quietly. He glanced around the room, looking for traces of any hidden detector equipment. In a low voice he said, "I'm an Earthman, Nuuri. I'm interested in the safety and welfare of Earth."

"So?"

"There are stories circulating in the galaxy that imply that some worlds plan an attack on Earth. I'm trying to find out if anything lies behind those stories. Will you work for me?"

"In what way?"

"Help me investigate these rumors."

She smiled bitterly. "You aren't satisfied with my betrayal of friends. Now you'd have me betray my world as well."

"No betrayal is involved. I'm acting in the interests of galactic peace."

"What do I care about galactic peace?"

"What do you care about being hauled downstairs to the interrogation room?" Catton said levelly.

She laughed. "You'll never gain allies with threats, Catton. I won't work for you. I'm only interested in seeing Doveril Halligon punished. Nothing else matters to me."

"I'll look for him on Skorg. And I apologize for seeming to threaten you. It was a mistake."

"A man in your position isn't permitted many mistakes," Nuuri remarked. "But I'll condescend to bargain with you, anyway. Let me out of this building untouched and I'll promise to forget this entire conversation."

"Fair enough," Catton agreed. "You can go."

She rose without another word and left. Catton walked to the window of the office and stared out, frowning troubledly. He realized he had probably said too much. But the girl had proven herself to be useful, and he had hoped to win her services. He needed an ally to help him uncover the facts Earth had sent him here to find; there was little hope of his finding anything alone.

The trip to Skorg was his best bet at the moment, he thought. He wondered whether anything useful had been mined out of the hapless unfortunates in the interrogation chamber. A hint as to the whereabouts of Doveril Halligon, perhaps. Doveril's disappearance was bound to be linked to the vanishing of Ambassador Seeman's daughter before long.

Catton returned to Beryaal's office. The Arenaddin had now been joined by Merikh eMerikh, the Skorg delegate to the Commission. Catton and the Skorg nodded coldly at each other in formal greeting.

Catton said, "How's the interrogation going?"

"It is all but over. Two of the prisoners have unfortunately succumbed. Beryaal is questioning the remaining three right now."

"And what's been learned?"

"Beryaal will tell you when he returns from the interrogation. But one fact appears certain. It will not be necessary to place the prisoners on trial after the interrogation. It is too bad, but we do not expect them to live."

CHAPTER SEVEN

Catton said nothing. These were alien worlds, where alien ideas of justice prevailed. It was not proper for him to object if the Morilaru preferred questioning their prisoners to death rather than bothering to try them. But it did indicate the sort of beings Earth was dealing with. Shrugging, Catton sat back to await the arrival of Pouin Beryaal.

The Morilaru entered the Crime Commission's office ten minutes later. There was a glint of satisfaction in his eyes.

"The interrogation is over," Beryaal commented briskly as he took his seat at the head of the table.

"Were there any survivors?" Catton asked sardonically.

Beryaal took no notice of the Earthman's sarcasm. "I regret to say that the prisoners died during interrogation. But we obtained much useful information from them before they succumbed."

"I think," said the Arenaddin slowly, "that our new colleague from Earth has done a fine job in apprehending these five. I suggest a note of commendation be forwarded to the Terran World Government."

"The Earthman," said eMerikh of Skorg in his hollow voice, "has far exceeded the call of duty. Members of this Commission are not required to disguise themselves and search out the hypnojewel traders themselves."

"I wasn't *required* to do it, no," Catton agreed. "But it seemed a good way of getting something done. How long has this Commission been in existence—and how much has it accomplished?"

The Skorg glowered balefully at him. "We have been laying the groundwork for—"

"Please," Beryaal snapped. "We are wasting time in futile argument."

"Suppose you tell us, then," Catton said, "the results of the interrogation?"

"Transcripts are being prepared and will be made available to you shortly."

Catton shook his head. "Can't you summarize the findings without making us wait for the transcript? Was anything learned about sources of supply, ringleaders, methods of transportation, other smugglers?"

"You will see the transcript," Beryaal replied.

The door opened and a clerk entered, bearing a sheaf of vocotyped papers. The clerk moved obsequiously around the meeting-room, placing one booklet in front of each of the Commission members.

Catton picked his up. It consisted of three or four sheets stapled together. The front page bore the date and the heading, TRANSCRIPT OF INTERROGATION CONDUCTED BY THE INTERWORLD COMMISSION OF CRIME, *Pauin Beryaal, Chairman.*

The Earthman flipped rapidly through the document. It said remarkably little. The names of the five prisoners were given, and the text of a series of questions-and-answers with Beryaal as interrogator.

The questions-and-answers went like this:

Q. Do you admit attempting to sell a hypnojewel to a visiting Dargonid?

A. You have proof of that.

Q. Why do you sell hypnojewels?

A. To make money.

Q. Who is the leader of your group?

A. We were all equals.

Q. But wasn't there someone who served as contact man, as go-between, as spokesman?

A. We shared all responsibilities.

Q. And how did you obtain the jewels you sold?

A. We bought them.

Q. From whom?

A. From those who sell such things.

The entire transcript read that way. The five captives had played their torturers for fools; not once had a concrete fact been elicited. It was pathetic. The replies of the prisoners had been couched in evasions, half-truths, and truths that conveyed nothing. Nowhere in the document was there a hint as to the source of the hypnojewels, nor was there a mention of Doveril Halligon. Nuuri, Catton thought, would be fiercely angry if she ever found out that Doveril had not been implicated.

Because of his relative unfamiliarity with the printed Morilaru language, Catton was the last one to finish reading the transcript. When he had done with the final page, he looked up sharply at Beryaal.

"For *this* you killed five men?" Catton asked.

"They were stubborn. They would not answer."

Catton chuckled grimly. "It doesn't speak well for the skill of the Morilaru interrogators, in that case. Any idiot can kill a man under torture; skill is needed to extract information."

"The Earthman is right," protested the Arenaddin mildly. "There is remarkably little solid information in this transcript. It would seem that the prisoners led you a merry chase."

Catton sat back, frowning. The transcript was a little *too* devoid of fact to suit him. It was impossible to believe that the Morilaru interrogation system was as incompetent as this report indicated. Catton knew better than to take it at face value. Certainly truth serums and deep hypnosis might have been used to draw out the name of the group's supplier, the method used for getting the hypnojewels onto Morilar, the source from which they originated. What did they use in the interrogation, he wondered—the rack and the thumb-screw?

He could not believe that the interrogation had been as fruitless as this transcript implied. Which meant that the important data was being suppressed by Beryaal. But that made little sense. Why would the Crime Commission chairman be interested in holding back vital information from his fellow members, Catton wondered?

"It seems to me," Catton said, "that you've taken five choice sources of information and wasted them, Pouin Beryaal."

The Morilaru inclined his head amiably. "You are not satisfied with the results of our interrogation?"

"Satisfied with *this*?" Catton asked, tapping the skimpy transcript. "Of course I'm not satisfied. We've run ourselves right into a dead end. You yourself pointed out that our job is not to track down petty jewel-runners like the ones that died today, but to cut off the hypnojewel pipeline at its source. How does this set of questions-and-answers help us do that?"

"The Earthman is being unjust," said the Skorg, coming to Beryaal's defense. "I was present at the interrogation; you and our Arenaddin colleague were not. I can vouch for the fact that every attempt was made to elicit information from the prisoners."

Or else you and Beryaal are in cahoots, Catton thought. He shrugged and said, "All right. I'm not placing any charges of incompetence. I'm simply saying that I went out and got you five perfectly good sources of information, and you used them up and threw them away without getting a damned thing out of them."

Beryaal said, "Like most Earthmen, you are overly impatient. It's a characteristic of young and uncertain races."

"Maybe so. If it's a racial failing to want to get results, I plead guilty." Catton gestured with open hands. "The job of this Commission is to smash the hypnojewel racket. I'd like to get that job done as quickly and as directly as I can."

"Have you any immediate suggestions?" Beryaal inquired calmly.

"I have several," Catton said. "I've checked carefully through the record of your past deliberations, and so far as I can figure very little has been done by way of figuring out the planet of entry for the jewels. I'm not talking about the place of origin, now—I mean the planet that funnels hypnojewels into the main stem of the galaxy. I think I have a lead on that planet's identity."

"Oh?" Beryaal said.

"When I was engaged in the purchase of that hypnojewel, someone let drop a remark implying that the planet where hypnojewels might be obtained from the makers was—was a major planet in this galaxy," Catton finished, deciding at the last moment not to name the world.

"This is hearsay, is it not?" Beryaal said.

"What of it?" Catton retorted. "It's worth investigating. At this stage, any lead at all is worth following up. And I intend to follow this one up personally."

"We have a network of agents for this purpose," remarked the Skorg.

"I realize that. I still intend to visit this planet on my own."

"With typical Earthman energy," Beryaal noted. "Very well; what is this planet you suspect?"

"I'll file my report when I return," said Catton.

Beryaal leaned forward. "It would be safer if you told us now. That way we could arrange for your protection, you see."

"And in the event of an accident to you," added the Skorg coldly, "we would know which planet it was you suspected. It is not wise to withhold information of such importance, Catton."

"All right," the Earthman said. "Be it hereby read into our records, then. I'm requesting a leave of absence from my Commission duties in order to make a journey to Skorg."

Merikh eMerikh reacted as if he had been slapped. The thin, angular being jerked upright and goggled amazedly at Catton.

"*Skorg?* You claim the hypnojewel traffic originates on Skorg?"

"I make no claims," Catton said quietly to the outraged Skorg. "I simply want to check."

"This accusation is perhaps a trifle rash," Pouin Beryaal said slowly. "One must consider that crime prevention on Skorg is well organized, and that—"

"One must consider nothing," Catton snapped. "I'm leaving for Skorg immediately. If I find anything, I'll let you know."

Uruod, the Arenaddin, said in his gentle voice, "It is wrong for the delegate from Skorg to take the statement of the delegate from Earth as a personal insult. The honor of Skorg is not impugned."

Catton smiled thankfully at the blubbery Arenaddin. "I've made no accusations. For that matter, it might be wise to intensify investigation on Arenadd too—and on Morilar. There's no reason to assume that these hypnojewels necessarily come from outside the galactic core. I had hoped to get some information out of the men I brought in today, but—" He gestured expressively.

"Very well," Pouin Beryaal said with obvious reluctance. "The delegate from Earth is, of course, free to conduct investigations wherever he pleases. We'll manage to carry on by ourselves until your return, Catton."

"Glad to hear it," the Earthman snapped. The meeting was rapidly degenerating into a backbiting contest; and, though the Arenaddin had attempted to act as a kind of moderator, Catton was aware that the true alignment was Beryaal, eMerikh, and Uruod against him. These aliens obviously did not want an Earthman stealing their thunder. He was on the Commission solely for the sake of appearances, because it was felt to be a measure of loosening the tension that bound the galaxy since the emergence of Earth as a major power. But they had never expected the Earth delegate to go charging around investigating such worlds as Skorg.

Well, they had no choice, Catton thought. They had agreed to accept a delegate from Earth, and now they were stuck with him.

"Do you plan to make the trip alone?" Beryaal asked. "Or will you accept the use of the Commission staff?"

"I could use a few assistants," Catton said. "I'll need an interpreter, for one thing—I'm anything but fluent in the Skorg language. I'll also need an administrative adjutant, and a personal secretary. Three men; that ought to be sufficient."

"Will you make the necessary travel arrangements yourself?"

"I'll arrange for the passage, yes, out of my allotted expense fund," said the Earthman. "My passport isn't validated for Skorg, merely because I wasn't originally planning to go there, but I'm certain that my colleague eMerikh will help me make the necessary visa arrangements, and that there'll be no difficulties on that score."

Catton glanced inquisitively at the Skorg, who nodded stiffly. Catton was certain that the tortured Morilaru had let slip something about their source of supply being on Skorg, and that Beryaal and eMerikh had agreed between themselves to keep that fact from the records. No wonder they were annoyed at having Catton pop up with the same information, and, worse, embedding it inextricably in the Commission minutes. It was too late for Beryaal and eMerikh to do anything but acquiesce, now. Catton had successfully boxed them in.

Catton rose.

"Is there any further business to be discussed at this meeting?" he asked.

"No," Beryaal said. "I merely wished to present the results of the interrogation."

"Those results having duly been presented," Catton said, "I intend to leave now. You can reach me at the Terran Embassy, eMerikh, when you've obtained a visitor's permit for me."

"I will contact you then," the Skorg said.

Catton nodded to them, turned, and left the meeting room. It was late in the day, now. Some of the heat had left the air. He smiled as he thought of how discomforted his fellow Commission members had been. But their motives troubled him. Why hide information? Why object to his going to Skorg? It was a poor prognosis when he couldn't even trust the alleged forces of crime prevention on these worlds.

He decided to leave for Skorg on the first available flight. Perhaps, he thought, the trail might be less muddy there. But he doubted it. He realized that forces were operating on levels deeper than he suspected; the only thing certain was that Earth stood to lose in the coming maneuver for galactic power, if these worlds had their way.

CHAPTER EIGHT

Two days later, a Terran Embassy automobile deposited Catton at the passenger desk of the Dyelleran Spaceport. In the Earthman's pocket was a ticket for a first-class passage, round trip from Morilar to Skorg and back, aboard the Skorg Spacelines vessel, *Silver Spear.* Two days of feverish preparation had preceded Catton's arrival at the spaceport.

It had been necessary to obtain an entry visa for Skorg; some fast subradio communication had taken care of that matter, with the more or less willing cooperation of Merikh eMerikh and the local Skorg Ambassador. It had also been necessary, for Catton's own protection, for him to receive a neural block inhibiting his sense of smell; the planetary odor of Skorg was something to make strong men blanch. And, for the same reason and at the same time, he had received a metabolic booster shot designed to reduce production of the bodily secretions that made an Earthman's smell so intolerable to a Skorg.

Thus fortified, Catton was ready to go. Three Morilaru attaches accompanied him, as he requested. Untroubled by budget restrictions, Catton had lightheartedly purchased first-class passages for the four of them on the twelve-day voyage—a matter of some eight thousand thrones, or better than $10,000 Terran, for the four tickets. The *Silver Spear* was a luxury liner. It was virtually a spaceborne city, holding nearly eight hundred passengers.

Catton and his three men, with their diplomatic visas, passed through the emigration desks with no trouble, and boarded the ship two hours before blastoff. The three aides said little as they inspected their magnificent staterooms. Either they were not impressed, or else they were too overwhelmed by the luxury to be able to comment.

Alone, Catton surveyed his room with awe. It was twice the size of the cabin he had occupied on the Terran liner coming to Morilar, and that had been one of Earth's finest passenger vessels.

On the *Silver Spear* his room was carpeted with thick broadloom, hung with noise-cushioning drapes, furnished with a handsome record player, a supply of music tapes, a video set which could tap the ship's immense library of Skorg films, and other elegant appurtenances. He sprawled out on the oversized bed, clamped his learning-disk of Skorg to his ear, and settled down for a couple of hours of intensive study of the Skorg language before blastoff time came.

An hour later, his cabin door chimed; Catton nudged the remote-wave opener and the door slid into its oiled niche. A Skorg in the uniform of a crewman waited in the corridor outside his room.

The Skorg bowed obsequiously, a gesture that looked strange coming from a member of that austere-faced species. "I am your steward, Mr. Catton," the Skorg said, in Morilaru. "If you lack anything, be sure to call upon me."

"Thanks," Catton said, using the Skorg word.

"Blastoff is in thirty minutes. When the signal comes, please go to your bed and remain on it until we enter free nulldrive. Dinner will be served one hour after the entry into warp, sir."

The steward bowed again and moved off down the hall. Catton closed the door, resetting his learning-disk and focusing his concentration once again on the difficult inflections of the Skorg tongue.

Blastoff was right on schedule. A speaker grid in the ceiling of his stateroom came to sudden life and advised him purringly in Skorg, Morilaru, and Arenaddin to remain on his bed until further word. Catton wondered what happened if you didn't understand any of the languages the instructions had been delivered in. You didn't travel the Skorg lines, in that case, he decided.

There was a countdown, in Skorg numbers. When it got down toward the final numbers Catton tensed involuntarily, waiting for the thrust of blastoff to jam him down against the spun foam of his bed.

"*...drog ....*"

"*...halk-segan ...*"

"*...zhuur ...*"

"*...naal.*"

Naal. Zero! But there was no fist of acceleration on the final count. Catton felt a momentary pressure, flattening him gently against the bed, but it was so light a push that he could have remained upright through it without difficulty. Evidently on a Skorg luxury liner, one traveled in *luxury.* Blastoff had been so thoroughly cushioned, probably by contragrav, that it almost seemed like an inertialess drive was at work.

Ten minutes after blastoff, the voice from the speaker grid advised Catton that it was now safe to leave one's bed, as the ship was now in nulldrive and would remain there until reaching Skorg. Dinner, the voice added, would be served in one hour.

Catton went on an exploratory trip through the vessel in the hour before dinner. He attracted a great deal of attention, as might have been expected; there were still few Earthmen in this part of the galaxy, and one traveling on a Skorg luxury liner was an extreme curiosity.

The ship was lavish. There was a grand ballroom, a smaller auditorium, two great dining halls (one reserved exclusively for Skorgs, the other open to all comers—a bit of deservedly instituted discrimination, considering the distinctive Skorg odor). Catton also saw a library of book-tapes, mostly in Skorg, with a scattering of Morilaru and Arenaddin volumes, and a recreation room designed to serve the recreational needs of several different species.

He ate that evening in the unrestricted dining room, since he had no entry into the Skorg room nor much desire to enter it; the bulk of his companions in the room were Morilaru, though he noted a few Arenaddin and even another Earthman. Catton resolved to introduce himself to the Earthman after the meal.

The food was Skorg food, mostly yellow vegetables and stringy lean meat—probably it was superbly prepared, but the raw materials were nothing much. The main dish was preceded by a cocktail which tasted astonishingly like a Terran martini, though Catton knew the Terran liquor industry had not yet established trade channels through to Skorg. During the meal Skorg wine was served—a bitter but palatable green liquid.

Catton encountered the other Earthman in the lounge after the meal. It was more of a simultaneous coinciding of orbit than a one-sided pursuit; the other Earthman, it seemed, had been anxious to meet Catton, too.

"My name is Royce, H. Byron Royce. I don't suppose you remember me, Mr. Catton."

Catton didn't. The Earthman was in his sixties, tall and weatherbeaten, with blunt, open features and faded pale-blue eyes. He was dressed conventionally in a Terran business suit. Catton had no idea who H. Byron Royce might be, but he hazarded a guess. "You were at that reception given for me at the Embassy in Dyelleran, weren't you?"

Royce smiled. "That's right. We exchanged a couple of words then, if you remember—"

"I'm afraid I'll need my memory refreshed," Catton confessed. "There were so many strange faces that night, you realize—"

"Sure, I know how it is. A hundred people come up and shake your hand, you can't remember all of 'em. Well, I'm Byron Royce of Royce Brothers, Terra. Does that ring any bells now?"

Catton nodded. Royce Brothers was an enterprising export firm; through holding companies, it controlled most of Terran trade over a span of fifty light-years out from Earth, and now, no doubt, was looking to extend its sway to Morilar, Skorg, and Arenadd. Catton realized he was talking to a billionaire. It was a slightly unsettling thought.

"Bound for Skorg on diplomatic business, Mr. Catton?"

"Yes," Catton said. "I'm not at liberty to reveal anything, of course."

"Wouldn't think of prying," Royce said cheerily. "Naturally, if there's anything involved that might possibly have an effect on Royce Brothers, I'd greatly appreciate a leetle hint, but—"

"I'm afraid it's a matter of considerable secrecy," Catton said, perhaps a bit too brusquely. "But I can tell you that it's of no commercial interest to you."

Royce took the hint and changed the subject immediately. "Too bad about the Ambassador's daughter, wasn't it? Pretty little girl like that running away to nowhere. You think they're going to find her, Mr. Catton?"

Catton shrugged. "It's unlikely, unless she wants to be found. The galaxy's too big for an efficient search to be carried on."

"Funny, that note she left."

"Oh, you heard about it?"

"The Ambassador himself told me, with tears in his eyes. Ran away with the man she loved. He didn't have any idea who that might be. Damned if they didn't run a checkup on every Earthman who'd been on Morilar in the past six months, and there wasn't one of them missing."

"So there's no notion whom she ran off with, eh?" Catton asked.

"Not a touch. Mr. Seeman half figured she'd made the whole part up, about her lover. But he couldn't understand why she'd want to run away."

A Skorg steward passed, carrying a tray of drinks. He paused in front of Catton and Royce and inquired in Morilaru if they were interested. Catton helped himself to a highball which tasted vaguely peppery; Royce, protesting that he never drank, declined the tray.

Catton sipped his drink. The lounge was crowded; there were life-forms of a dozen kinds in it, including, Catton noted with some amusement, a Dargonid who might have been the twin of the one who had purchased the hypnojewel from Nuuri Gryain's unfortunate friends. Catton also noticed two of his attaches nearby—keeping an eye on him, no doubt.

Suddenly he heard a distant dull booming sound, reverberating as if far away. A moment later it was repeated, slightly louder but still muffled and faint. Conversation in the lounge was unaffected.

But H. Byron Royce was standing on tiptoes, head cocked to one side for better hearing. He looked worried.

"What's the matter?" Catton said. There was a third boom—still louder.

Muscles tightened suddenly in Royce's cheeks. "Come on," he said. "Let's get out of here, Catton."

"Out of here? Why?"

"Hurry up!"

Mystified, Catton followed the tall, old Earthman through the crowd of chatting passengers and out into the companionway that fronted the lounge. A fourth time the sound came—and, out here, Catton could hear it distinctly and clearly.

It sounded like an explosion.

"What's going on?" Catton asked.

"I don't know," Royce replied. "But every time I hear loud booms on a space-liner, I get out into the hall and start looking for a lifeship. I was aboard the *Star of the Night* when it blew up off Capella in '83."

A fifth boom came rippling up from the depths of the ship—and this time Catton fancied he could hear girders giving way, strutwork ripping loose, engines exploding, men dying. A drive-room explosion aboard a faster-than-light spaceliner was a dreadful thing. Even if the ship survived the blast, it would no longer have means of propulsion, and would drift helplessly, unlocatable, until its food supply ran out. There would be nightmarish frenzy before that time, culminating in cannibalism.

Royce began to run, and Catton followed him. Other people were coming out of the lounge, now. Footsteps echoed in the companionway.

A loudspeaker voice said, "There is no cause for alarm, ladies and gentlemen." The voice was speaking in Skorg, but it hastily repeated the words in Morilaru. "Please remain where you are. Members of the crew will aid you. Do not panic. Do not panic."

It might just as well have been an order to the tides to hold back. A mass of screaming people came sweeping out of the lounge, crowding desperately into the narrow companionway. The loudspeaker's shouted exhortations were drowned out by the cries of the crowd. Another explosion sounded, this one larger than the others.

"That was the central drive chamber blowing," Royce muttered. "This ship is done for."

He paused at a doorway, flung it open, and went racing down a ramp toward the lifeships. A ship the size of the *Silver Spear* was probably equipped with fifty or seventy-five tiny lifeships, each capable of holding a dozen passengers, fifteen or twenty in an emergency. The lifeships had miniature warp-drives and enough fuel to get them to a nearby planet.

Royce swung over the hatch of the nearest lifeship with the amazing self-preservation impulse of a man to whom life is very important indeed, and hurled himself in. Catton followed. A moment later five other people rushed into the small ship.

Catton was surprised to see that one of them was the Morilaru who had accompanied him as his administrative adjutant. Another was an enormous Arenaddin who was bleating like a frightened cow. Two others were Morilaru women clad in costly gowns—and, astonishingly, they had dragged aboard the ship a man in the uniform of a member of the crew. The Skorg was writhing and protesting, trying to free himself. "Crewmen must not board lifeships until all passengers are safe," he was insisting.

"Quiet, you idiot," one of the Morilaru women snapped. "You want to stay alive, and so do we. We need a skilled spaceman aboard this ship." They fastened their fingernails into the Skorg's shirt, and held him fast.

The lifeship hatch opened again, and a Morilaru entered, wild-eyed and frantic.

"The ship's blowing up," he gasped. "Let's blast off out of here before we get killed!"

Catton started to protest. There were only eight people in the lifeship—nine, giving the Arenaddin double credit for his bulk. There was room for three or four more passengers, as many as ten if need be. It was grossly unfair to blast off half full.

But as he moved forward, one of the Morilaru women stepped in front of him and blocked his path. The male Morilaru hastily dogged the hatch shut and yanked down on the red-handled lever that released the lifeship from its fastenings.

A hatch in the side of the wounded mother ship opened as the lifeship glided down its passageway and into space. Instants later, a gigantic explosion split the *Silver Spear* apart. The lifeship, with its eight occupants, rocked and tossed in the shock wave caused by the explosion—and then righted itself and sped off into space.

CHAPTER NINE

A lifeship has only rudimentary controls. There was a viewscreen, a plot-tank, a simplified course-computer, and a book of instructions, trilingual. As Catton thought back over it, half an hour after the explosion, he was grateful that a crewman had come along.

But the crewman was unhappy about it. His name was Nyaruik Sadhig, and he brooded loudly about his plight. "If I ever survive this, I'll be sacked," he muttered. "Think of it—a crewman entering a lifeship and letting passengers remain behind!"

"You were coerced," Catton pointed out. "They can't hold that against you."

"Yes," said one of the Morilaru women who had dragged him aboard. She produced a tiny woman-size blaster from her carryall. "I'll testify that I forced you into the ship at gunpoint," she said. "That ought to count in your favor, won't it?"

"No," said Sadhig bleakly. "According to the law, I'm supposed to resist such coercion—even at the cost of my life. I'm ruined, damn it! Why did you have to pull me aboard your accursed lifeship?"

"Because," remarked the other Morilaru female sweetly, "we wanted to live. And we weren't sure we could pilot this ship ourselves."

"How far are we from civilization?" Royce asked.

Sadhig shrugged. "It's impossible to tell until I've had a go with the computer."

"But we can't be very far," objected one of the Morilaru women. "It was still the first night of the trip. We should still be close to Morilar."

Sadhig shook his head. "I'm afraid you don't understand how the nulldrive works. The ship's generators thrust us into a fivespace continuum, and when the computer says so we return to normal space. But points in nullspace don't have a one-to-one correlation with points in normal space. There's no matching referent. We might be a billion light-years from Morilar—or we might be just next door."

The explanation flew over the heads of the women. They merely looked dazed.

Royce said, "Very well, young man. Suppose, as you seem to be the only spaceman among us, you find out just where we *are*, then."

The Morilaru rose and made his way through the crowded single cabin to the control section up front. Catton, sitting in the farthest corner of the cabin, scowled darkly at the floor. Lifeships were all well and good, but this business of traveling in nullspace did have its drawbacks. He had heard of lifeship survivors beached on the far shores of the universe, returning to civilization only in extreme old age.

Suddenly the problems of Skorg, Morilar, and Arenadd seemed very unimportant to him. If they emerged from the warp continuum far enough away, he would be stranded long enough so that the current crisis became so much galactic ancient history.

The cabin was silent while the Morilaru made his computations; the only sound was the steady rasping breathing of the Arenaddin. The bulky creature did not enjoy the artificially sustained gravity of the lifeship, which was set for Skorg-norm, or about 1.7 times the pull on Arenadd. Catton was mildly discomforted by the gravity—it was also 1.4 Earthnorm, too. The difference added some seventy pounds to his weight, better than two hundred to the Arenaddin's; small wonder the alien was uncomfortable.

At length the Skorg crewman returned from the computer, wearing an unreadable expression—Skorg facial expressions seemed morose at their most cheerful, and grew darker from there.

"Well?" Royce demanded. "What's the bad news?"

"It isn't as bad as it might have been," Sadhig said. "But it isn't very good, either."

"Where are we?" asked Catton.

"We're five hundred light-years from Morilar," said the crewman.

"Is that within the range of this ship?" Royce asked.

"Unfortunately, no. We have a limited range—about a hundred light-years in radius. And, also unfortunately, there seems to be only one planet within our immediate access."

"What's its name?" asked one of the Morilaru women.

The Skorg gestured unhappily. "It has none. It's listed on the charts as DX 19083. It's a small jungle world, claimed by Morilar but never settled. The chart says there's a rescue beacon erected there, so we can call for help once we land."

"Doesn't this ship have a radio?"

"Yes," the Skorg said. "An ordinary radio. It doesn't have a generator big enough to power a nulispace communicator. So we could send out a message, but it would take five hundred years for it to reach Morilar. We don't have quite that much time, I'm afraid."

"So we'll have to make a landing on this jungle planet," Catton said. "And use the rescue beacon communicator to get ourselves picked up."

"What if the rescue beacon is out of order?" asked Royce.

"There's small chance of that," said the Skorg crewman. "The beacons are built to last, and they are service-checked every ten years. The greater danger is that we will not be able to *find* the beacon, once we land. But we must risk it. I will begin immediately to compute a course taking us to DX 19083, unless there are objections."

There were none. Sadhig returned to the control cabin and busied himself with the relatively simple job of targeting the lifeship toward the uninhabited world.

Catton prowled uneasily around the cabin. It was crowded enough, even with less than capacity aboard. He opened a cabinet and found a considerable food supply and an elaborate medical kit. A second cabinet yielded tools—blasters, electrohatchets, bubbletents, a collapsible canoe no bigger than a bastketball when folded.

They were well provided for. But the delay would be a nuisance. And in case they had any kind of survival problems, most of the lifeship passengers would be drags on the group. The two Morilaru women, Catton thought, would be less than useless in any kind of situation of hardship. And the Arenaddin was obviously not accustomed to roughing it. Catton figured that Sadhig and Royce could be counted on to do their share of work. That left two Morilaru men—Woukidal, his adjutant, and the other man, the one who had released the lifeship from its parent vessel, and who had not spoken a word since.

Catton made his way forward. Sadhig was bent over the computer, tapping out course indications.

"Any difficulties?" Catton asked in Skorg.

Sadhig looked up. "Of course not. A child could operate this lifeship. But those women had to drag me aboard—"

"Still brooding about that?"

"I shall be in disgrace when I return to Skorg. My father will never forgive me. Do you know who my father is, Earthman?"

Catton shook his head.

The Skorg said, "My father is Thunimon eSadhig, Earthman. First Commander of the Skorg Navy. How will he feel when he learns that his eldest son escaped from a damaged ship in a lifeship?"

Sadhig's face was cold and tightly drawn. Catton realized that within the Skorg ethic, it was undoubtedly a humiliation for a crewman to escape alive while passengers died, no matter what the circumstances. He pitied the Skorg.

"What position did you hold on the *Silver Spear*?" Catton asked.

"Flight Consultant First Class. I was the eighth ranking officer—assistant to the astrogator."

"Those women sure picked the right man when they collared you, then!"

"They seized blindly," Sadhig said without looking up from his work. "For all they knew, they were snaring one of the cooks. But a cook could have piloted this craft as well as I do." Bitterly, Sadhig snapped down the courselock and rose from the controls. "There," he said. "It is done. We will make landing in two days absolute time, Earthman. And then we must find the rescue beacon, or we will die. I do not greatly care."

"If it's a disgrace to leave a ship and let passengers remain behind," Catton said, "it must be equally disgraceful to be cast away with passengers and not expend every effort to ensure their survival."

The Skorg nodded. "You are right. I intend to help all I can. Your lives are important to me; mine no longer matters."

Catton felt that the conversation was taking an uncomfortable turn. To change it he said, "Just what happened aboard the *Silver Spear*? There was some kind of explosion in the drive compartment, wasn't there?"

The Skorg's cold eyes glinted sardonically. "Yes, there was 'some kind of explosion,' all right."

"I thought such accidents were so rare as to be just about mathematically nonexistent."

"Statistically," said the Skorg, "you're correct. But this was not an accident. Nor, strictly speaking, was it an explosion."

"Not an accident? What do you mean?"

"I had little time to gather information before I was forced into this lifeship. But as I was told by my superior, five implosion bombs had been concealed in the drive compartment before the voyage. One would have been enough to disable the ship. Five destroyed it completely. Hundreds must have died."

Catton was taken sharply aback. "Implosion bombs—you mean, sabotage?"

"What else? The ship was deliberately destroyed. I have no idea who would do such a thing."

Shrugging, Catton returned to the rest of the group in the main segment of the ship. "We're landing in two days," he told Royce in Terran. "Everything's under control, according to the Skorg."

"I heard part of your conversation. What were you saying about implosion bombs?"

"Sadhig told me that the ship was blown up deliberately. Five bombs went off in the drive compartment."

"What? Eight hundred passengers, aboard, and—"

"Quiet," Catton said. "There's no point letting everyone know. There'll be enough hysteria if we have trouble finding that beacon."

Sadhig's words had greatly disturbed Catton. There were many reasons why someone would want to destroy a luxury liner in transit—to collect insurance, to gain notoriety, to dispose of some important figure, even to provoke a war. Catton's thoughts kept coming back to the assassination possibility. Suppose, he thought, it had been decided to get rid of him before his investigation proceeded further. Blowing up a ship to accomplish his murder was on the drastic side, he admitted. But these were alien beings. Their innermost reactions were not necessarily the same as a Terran's. Their values differed from Earth's at the most basic levels.

Of course, he realized he might be greatly exaggerating the situation. There had been other important people on the *Silver Spear*—Royce, for one, a major figure in interstellar commerce. No doubt the cream of Skorg society had been aboard. He had no right to assume that an act that killed hundreds of innocent people had been aimed directly at him. But it was something to consider, in any event, when and if he finally reached Skorg.

Life on the small ship was not pleasant in the two days that followed. Privacy was impossible, sanitation difficult. Tempers sharpened. Royce complained privately that he found the Skorg pilot's odor almost unbearable, but that he was struggling to ignore it. Catton was thankful for the sensory block that prevented him from undergoing such difficulties.

The Morilaru women seemed interested only in eating; Catton compelled them to abide by a rationing system, and unofficially established a watch rotation so that an eye would be kept on the food cabinet at all times; he, Sadhig, and Royce took turns at the job.

The Arenaddin was in considerable pain; the relatively high gravity was troubling him, and he was not concealing the fact. Catton and Sadhig spent some time trying to get at the mechanism that controlled the artificial gravity on the lifeship, but the box was hermetically sealed and welded too carefully for opening by amateurs. The idea was to keep passengers from tinkering with the lifeship's gravity and perhaps inadvertently squashing themselves flat under a twenty-gee pull. Since there was no other way of alleviating the Arenaddin's difficulties, Catton went prowling through the medical supplies for a sedative. He found one whose label was printed in Skorg, Morilaru, and Arenaddin, and which was presumably, therefore, suitable for use by members of all three species. Catton injected an entire ampoule into the Arenaddin's arm after considerable trouble locating the proper vein beneath the insulation of fat; the Arenaddin slept soundly for the rest of the trip.

At the end of the second day, Sadhig reported that the mass-detector showed them within reach of their destination. The landing would have to be made on manual deceleration, since there was no spaceport below to supply a landing-beam as guide. It was impossible to wake the Arenaddin, so he was strapped down securely, and the other passengers clambered into the deceleration cradles and waited for the landing.

There was an instant of transition as the lifeship left nullspace and re-entered the normal universe. A planet burst into view on the viewscreen, green except for the blueness of its seas. Up front, Sadhig caressed the controls of the manual-landing keyboard.

The landing itself took better than an hour. The tiny ship swung down on the uninhabited planet in ever-narrowing circles. Catton felt the jounce as the ship cracked into the thickening atmosphere. Gravity dragged at him; the ship began to drop.

It touched down gently. Catton glanced out the single port in the passenger cabin. The landscape that greeted him was profuse with vegetation. The scene had the fierce grandeur of prehistory.

CHAPTER TEN

They ran the usual tests before leaving the ship. The lifeship's instruments indicated an atmosphere of breathable oxygen-nitrogen-plus-inerts-and-carbon-dioxide constitution, though both the oxygen and the CO_2 were on the high side for Catton's tastes—34% oxygen, 1% carbon dioxide. It was a rich mixture for an Earthman to breathe, even more so for the hapless Arenaddin; the Skorg and the four Morilaru would not be bothered by the high oxygen content. Gravity, Catton was pleased to note, was .5 Skorg-norm, which was about three-quarters of a gee by Terran standards; the Arenaddin would enjoy the respite from Skorg gravitation, while Sadhig and the Morilaru, all accustomed to the fairly stiff gravitation of their native worlds, were apt to feel a bit light-footed and queasy-stomached for a while. Atmospheric pressure at sea-level was—as best as Catton could translate it from Skorg terms—18.5 psi, which was something on the soupy side.

One important fact remained to be determined before they left the ship.

"How far are we from the rescue beacon?" Catton asked.

Sadhig's lean face was puckered into one immense frown. "I'm still trying to get a fix," the Skorg said. "I'm picking up the carrier beam intermittently, but until I get the directional fix I can' t—ah—there!" Sadhig began to scribble computations in the involved squiggles that were Skorg script. He chewed on the stylus for a moment, added up a column, fed the results into the lifeship's miniature computer, and waited for confirmation. It came, a moment later.

"Well?" Catton asked.

"It's better than I hoped for, considering I didn't have any idea where that damned beacon was located. We hit the right continent—our luck's with us. We're only about five hundred miles due south of the beacon. It could have been a lot worse."

"Five hundred miles!" Catton exclaimed.

Sadhig nodded. "By forced marches, we ought to get there in a month's time. We don't have a month's food, of course, but we ought to be able to find something edible in the jungle."

Catton peered through the viewscreen. He saw close-packed vegetation, beady with moisture. This was a young planet, only seventy million miles from its Sol-type yellow sun. The temperature out there, according to the instruments, was about 310 degrees on the Skorg scale, which was reckoned up from Absolute Zero. Sadhig informed him that the mean temperature on Morilar was about 305 in Skorg degrees; juggling the figures hastily, Catton decided that the temperature outside was in the neighborhood of 110 Fahrenheit. Hiking for a month on a damp, humid, world like this wasn't going to be any Boy Scout jaunt.

When Catton returned to the rest of the group, he found them stirring uneasily; none of them had any basic scientific understanding of the problems involved in landing on an unexplored world, and they regarded Catton and Sadhig with some suspicion.

"Well?" Royce asked. "What have you two been figuring out?"

"The planet's livable," Catton said. "We can all breathe the air, the gravity is fairly low, and the temperature isn't much hotter than that of Morilar. We won't be comfortable, but we'll survive. The rescue beacon is five hundred miles north of here. If there aren't any large bodies of water in between to give us trouble, we ought to reach it in a month."

"A month?" gasped the older and more talkative of the two Morilaru women. "You mean we're going to walk for a *month* in that jungle?"

"You don't have to accompany us. You can stay behind," Catton said. He could just as well do without the women on the trek. "We'll leave you a blaster and your pro rata share of the food, and you can live in the ship. When the rescue ship arrives, we'll have him pick you up—if he can find you in this jungle."

"I don't like that idea. But why can't we fly this ship to the beacon?"

"Two reasons," said Sadhig crisply. "The first is that we have very little fuel, possibly not enough for a blastoff. The second is that this lifeship is not a precision vessel. It is virtually a toy. If we attempted a new blastoff and landing, there is no guarantee we will not come down even further from the beacon."

"Oh," she said faintly. "Well, in that case—I guess we walk!"

The trek began an hour later. The ship was stripped of everything that was portable and might have some conceivable use. Catton, who had taken charge of the group without any nomination or intention, parceled the food out equally for each to carry, for the reason (which he did not voice) that in case of the sudden disappearance of one member of the party he did not want the entire supply of a given item to be lost. Similarly, he distributed the blasters and other weapons and tools.

When the outfitting was done, they set out—Catton and Royce in the lead, followed by Woukidal and the other male Morilaru, then the two Morilaru women, with Sadhig and the Arenaddin bringing up the rear. Catton set a jaunty pace for the party. The air was thick and rich, invigorating almost to the point of intoxication; after a few hundred yards the Earthman realized that he would burn himself out quickly at this pace, and he slowed up. With air that was more than a third oxygen to breathe, it was easy to overlook the bothersome heat and humidity; between the low gravity and the richness of the air, Catton felt an exuberance he had never known before.

The vegetation consisted largely of gigantic trees, thirty or forty feet thick at the base, towering far into the sky. The trees had no limbs for at least their first hundred feet of height; far above the ground they branched heavily, and their crowns intermingled, with a thick mesh of vines to provide a virtual roof for the forest. Evidently the ceiling two hundred feet above blocked most of the rainfall from the jungle floor; it was sparsely vegetated except for occasional seedlings and man-high ferns. A soft red-brown carpet of dead leaves lay underfoot. Compass in hand, Catton doggedly led his little band on a steady northward path, pausing every ten minutes or so to make sure that no stragglers were falling behind.

It was difficult to tell when the day was actually ending, because the close-knit forest roof kept most sunlight from penetrating anyway. After three hours—Catton's watch was calibrated in Galactic Absolute Time, whose minute was arbitarily pegged to Morilaru time and whose day lasted twenty-six and a fraction Terran hours—Catton called a rest halt.

"And about time we stopped, too," sighed the younger of the Morilaru women. "We've been walking *forever*!"

"We've covered about seven miles," Catton said. "That's a pretty fair stint for people who aren't trained hikers. We'll rest for a while and then go on until nightfall hits us."

He distributed anti-fatigue tablets—the medical kit held a packet of five hundred tablets, which would be ample for the entire month if they were parceled out with prudence. After half an hour of resting, they continued on. Twilight overtook them within another hour.

They made camp by the side of a small stream that had accompanied them northward for more than a mile. Woukidal and Royce inflated four bubbletents—one to be shared by the two women, one to be used by the Morilaru who had ejected the ship and the Arenaddin, and a third to be shared by Catton, Royce, and Woukidal. The Skorg was permitted to sleep alone.

While Royce and Woukidal busied themselves with the tents, the women were sent out to gather wood for a fire, and Catton and Sadhig budgeted out food for the evening meal. The Arenaddin was still groggy from sedation, and Catton gave him no task.

Night fell quickly. The little planet had no moon, but through the breaks in the jungle roof could be seen the bright dots of unfamiliar constellations. The temperature dropped considerably during the night.

A watch system was instituted. Catton stood the first three hours himself, then woke Sadhig, who passed the duty along to Woukidal after three more hours. Night was nine hours long. The entire day, Catton discovered, was slightly more than one Galactic Absolute day in length—about thirty hours by Terran reckoning. His body was quick to adjust to variations in its schedule. Only the Arenaddin, accustomed to a day that was nearly twice that of a Terran une, would experience any particular disorientation, and before many days he would be fully adjusted to the new schedule of living.

Three days passed without significant incident. The local fauna made itself evident quickly enough, but nothing of an unpleasant size appeared: the animals that showed themselves were no bigger than Terran sheep, at best, and showed no hostile intentions. The animals were constructed on the standard four-limbed pattern of most oxygen-breathing life-forms; they appeared to be marsupial mammals, judging from those who came close enough to be studied. Several looked as though they might be useful when the regular food supply ran out, as it would probably do in another seven or eight days.

There were a few annoying flurries of rain; the castaways could hear the water pounding the jungle roof, and enough rainwater trickled down to make life uncomfortable below. The moist clothes began to mildew rapidly. Insects became a nuisance, too; they came big on this planet, some of them ugly beasts with wingspreads of a foot. The big ones did not seem to sting—Catton imagined it would be a nasty experience to be stung by one—but some of the smaller kinds did. Why is it, Catton wondered, that mosquitoes happened to evolve on 95 percent of the worlds of the universe?

At the mid-day break on the fourth day, however, when they had covered better than fifty miles since leaving the ship, the Arenaddin suddenly declared he could go no further.

The massive creature was seated on a tree stump. Rolls of fat sagged around his middle, and his breathing was rough and irregular. The Arenaddin's orange skin was wet with perspiration. He pointed to his swollen feet. The six splayed toes were designed to support three hundred pounds of bulk without collapsing, but they had never been intended to take their owner on extended hikes through a forest.

"Go on without me," the Arenaddin insisted. "I'm slowing you all up. And I can't last much longer—I'm not built for this kind of strain."

"We'll build a litter," Catton said. "We ought to be able to manage you."

The Arenaddin shook his great globe of a head sadly from side to side. "It is not worth your trouble. I consume too much food, and I do no work. Let me remain behind."

But Catton would not hear of it. While the others ate, he started to plan out the most efficient sort of litter to carry the Arenaddin. Two sturdy branches about six feet long, he decided, with one of the duriplast ponchos swung between them. The Arenaddin could ride in the poncho as if he were in a hammock. Two men between them should be able to support his weight for short stretches; Royce was a little old for that kind of a strain, but there were still four able-bodied men who could take turns at it.

Catton began to scout around for a tree whose branches were low enough for cutting down. It took a while; the adult trees were bare for a hundred feet, while most of the seedlings were too spindly. He found one at last—a young tree no more than thirty feet high, with forking branches thick enough to hold the Arenaddin's weight. Catton turned, meaning to call to Woukidal and Sadhig to help him with the logging operation.

He heard the swift sizzling sound made by a blaster fired on narrow beam.

As a matter of reflex, Catton flung himself to the jungle floor. But no second shot came. Deciding that it had not been aimed at him, Catton rose and returned to the group.

The Arenaddin was dead. He lay sprawled grotesquely in the middle of the clearing, a blaster still in his hand. He had fired one narrow-beam shot upward into his mouth; it was an instantaneous death.

Royce was staring in blank-faced horror. Neither the Skorg nor the four Morilaru seemed particularly moved by the suicide.

Catton glared at them. He, Royce, and Sadhig were the only ones armed with blasters.

Royce was pointing at the Skorg. "It—it was his gun!" Royce said in a shaky voice.

Catton wheeled on Sadhig. "Is this true? Did you let him take your gun away?"

"No," the Skorg said calmly. "I gave it to him."

"*Gave* it? Why'd you do a mad thing like that?"

"He asked me for it," Sadhig replied. "He saw that you refused to honor his request to be left behind, and he was determined to remove himself rather than become a burden to the group."

Catton goggled. "You knew he was going to commit suicide—and yet you gave him the blaster?"

"Of course," the Skorg said with some surprise. "It was the least I could do for him. He was in physical pain, and he felt a necessity to do away with himself. Would you refuse a fellow being the means of death?"

Catton could not answer. Once again it was a conflict of values; the Skorg saw nothing ethically wrong with handing a weapon to a declared suicide, and no amount of debate would ever produce agreement on the point. Catton turned away. The Arenaddin had, after all, acted in the best interests of the group. Carrying a cripple would have meant a delay of many days in reaching the beacon. But as an Earthman Catton held certain ideas about the sanctity of life that left him chilled by the matter-of-factness of the Arenaddin's decision.

In accordance with Arenadd traditions, they cremated the corpse and scattered the ashes. With that task out of the way, they donned their gear and moved on northward. Catton realized an hour later that they had never even known the dead Arenaddin's name.

CHAPTER ELEVEN

On the fourteenth day of the trek—Catton estimated they had journeyed better than two hundred miles northward, by virtue of unflagging discipline—Woukidal, the adjutant appointed by the Interworld Commission on Crime to aid Catton during his investigations on Skorg, fell ill of some jungle fever.

They had no choice but to pitch camp and treat him. A Morilaru would not commit suicide as lightheartedly as the Arenaddin had done, merely to ease the burden on the others; in any event, Woukidal was beyond consciousness, unable to make any such decisions.

They rigged a tent for the ailing Morilaru and decided to wait until the fever broke before moving on. Woukidal lay twisting and tossing in the tent, his eyes puffed shut, his face swollen, sweat-beaded, skin paled almost to a light ultramarine. He had alternate spells of chills and perspiration; half the time he was racked by shivers, the rest he lay drenched in sweat.

Catton found a drug in the medical kit which claimed to be an antipyretic; it was labelled in Skorg and Morilant, but not in any other language. Evidently Skorg metabolic systems and Morilaru ones were similar enough for the same drugs to be effective for both. Catton wondered bleakly what would happen if he or Royce came down with the fever. They would die, no doubt.

He injected an ampoule of the antipyretic into the big vein at the side of the Morilaru's throat, and within an hour the fever had dropped two degrees. Woukidal was reading five degrees above that figure, and unless the fever broke soon it would kill him.

That evening, after Catton had administered a second dose of the drug, he wandered off to his own tent and sprawled out on his back to rest. The jungle air, hot and moist, pressed down clammily. He thought back over the two weeks they had spent in the jungle.

First there had been the Arenaddin's suicide. Then, on the seventh day, the near-mutiny of the older Morilaru woman, who demanded to rest a full day—not for any reasons of sabbath, but simply because she was tired. Catton had granted her four hours during the hottest part of the day, and then had forced her to get up and begin walking.

On the ninth day they had come to the lake—better than a mile wide, and extending so far in either direction that it might as easily have been a slow-moving river. They had inflated the coracle and made it across, gear and all, in four trips. Catton shuddered as he remembered the clashing teeth of the water reptile that rose from the depths to spear the bottom of their coracle on the final trip. It had filled with water in minutes, and they had just made it across. If they encountered another body of water between here and the beacon, they were in trouble.

On the eleventh day, Catton thought, they had met the Monster. It had been fairly harmless, at that—an amiable dinosaur-type, ninety or a hundred feet long with half an ounce of brain. But it had damned near put one of its huge feet down squarely on Sadhig as it blundered across their path. The incident, at the time, had been funny to all but the Skorg—but it would not be very amusing if they chanced to encounter a carnivorous beast of the same size. Which they might very well do, with three hundred more miles of jungle between them and the rescue beacon, Catton thought darkly.

And now, on the fourteenth day, Woukidal was down with some nuisance of a fever. The Morilaru was rather a cold fish, obviously instructed by Pouin Beryaal to keep a close watch on his superior and probably told to report back if Catton stumbled over anything important on Skorg. Caton had doubts of the man's loyalty—but, dammit, the Morilaru was a sentient being, and Catton was going to do everything he could to help him recover.

The flickering campfire just outside the opening of Catton's tent revealed a tall figure standing at the tent mouth. It was Royce.

"What is it?" Catton asked. "Did Woukidal's condition change?"

"He's talking," Royce said.

"Rationally?"

"What do you mean?"

"Come listen," Royce replied.

Catton followed the older man across the clearing to the tent where Wouikdal lay. The Morilaru women were sprawled near the fire; Sadhig and the other Morilaru were asleep. Catton could hear low moaning and muttering coming from Woukidal's tent.

The sick Morilaru seemed to be a little better, but not very much; his face still had the flushed, moist look of fever. He was talking to himself deliriously. Catton leaned close, but failed to make any sense out what Woukidal was saying.

"It's just so much gibberish," Catton said.

"He was talking sense before. Ask him—ask him about matter duplicators," Royce said.

Catton looked up, startled. "Matter duplicators?"

"He was mumbling about them before. Ask him."

Catton bent low over the feverish face. "Woukidal! Can you hear me?"

The muttering continued with no apparent response to Catton's question.

Catton groped for the medicine kit on the ground near Woukidal's cot. He pulled out an antipyretic ampoule, knocked the safety cap off with his thumb, and pressed the syringe against Woukidal's throat vein. There was a faint hiss as the sonic spray drove the drug into the Morilaru's bloodstream. Catton waited a few moments; as the drug began to take effect, Woukidal's fever visibly abated.

"What's this about matter duplicators, Woukidal?" Catton asked quietly.

"Duplicators ...being built. Sent to Earth."

Catton's eyes widened. Matter duplicators had been discovered in the galaxy hundreds of years ago. They were long since under strict ban on every world; it was death to manufacture one or even own one, since a matter duplicator could wreck a world's economy overnight.

"Who's building matter duplicators?" Catton asked.

Evidently the Morilaru's tongue had been loosened by the fever and the drugs. He tossed restlessly, eyes still tight shut, and said, "We are. To finish off Earth. We'll send hundreds."

"Where are the duplicators coming from?"

"Beryaal can get them," Woukidal murmured. "Beryaal!"

"He's—he's in charge. And eMerikh, the Skorg. To crush Earth. Send hundreds of duplicators to Earth. I—I—"

Woukidal's words trailed off into meaningless nonsense. Despite the evening heat, Catton felt chilled. He glanced up at Royce.

"Do you think he's serious? Or is it just some kind of fantasy he was having because of the drugs?"

"It's a pretty improbable fantasy to have," Royce said. "I'm inclined to believe him. There've been stories drifting around that Morilar and Skorg are cooking up some kind of maneuver against Earth."

Catton nodded tightly. "I've heard the stories too. But matter duplicators—that violates every code these aliens have!" He bent over the Morilaru again. "Woukidal! Can you hear me?"

"It's no use," Royce said. "He won't be coherent any more. The drug's putting him to sleep."

They left the tent. Catton swatted at the insects that droned annoyingly around his head. Woukidal's unintentional revelation opened many corridors of possibility. Beryaal in charge of the plot! Beryaal, head of the Crime Commission, himself violating the most basic agreement of the galaxy, an agreement arrived at centuries before Earth ever sent a ship into space!

That explained many things. If Beryaal were the leading figure in the conspiracy against Earth, and Beryaal had somehow discovered that Catton's true purpose here in the outworlds was to uncover that conspiracy, then it was altogether likely that the *Silver Spear* had been blown up at Beryaal's orders, for the express purpose of disposing of Catton. Men who would dump matter duplicators on a civilized world would hardly draw any ethical line at destroying a space liner to kill one man.

But how would Beryaal have found out Catton's true purpose? Catton had told only one person of his real motive for visiting the outworlds.

He had told Nuuri Gryain.

Was the girl linked with Beryaal? It was hard to believe; but Beryaal had found out about Catton some way, and perhaps Nuuri had sold him the information for purposes of her own. Catton moistened his lips. He was caught up in a net of intrigue, and every alien seemed his enemy just now.

Catton swung round to face Royce.

"I'll have to place you under secrecy restrictions on this matter duplicator business," Catton told him. "If word ever got out that anyone knows about this plot, there'll be war in the galaxy overnight."

"Are you going to stand by and let Earth be ruined?" Royce demanded.

"I'm going to do my best to uncover the rest of the plot, once we get out of this damned jungle," Catton said. "But I don't want Earth flying off the handle, and I don't want Morilar or Skorg to realize the secret's out. Give me some time to work, Royce."

"I have important commercial interests at stake in this thing, Catton."

Catton took a deep breath. "I'm cognizant of that. But there's more at stake than your commercial interests, Royce. Will you give me a pledge of silence?"

"Suppose I don't?"

"I'd have to kill you, I guess," Catton said evenly. "But I don't want to have to do that. I don't like killing, and I especially don't like killing Earthmen. But unless I get a guarantee that you'll keep mum about what you've heard tonight, I'll have to make sure you keep mum."

Royce was silent for a long moment. Then he shrugged. "All right," he said finally. "I'll pretend I didn't hear a thing."

"Thanks," Catton said.

Roycee turned away and headed toward his tent. After a moment, Catton returned to the sick man's tent. Woukidal was knotted up in a fetal ball, groaning. Catton sat down to wait, in case the Morilaru's delirious ramblings became intelligible again. But they never did. Despite the drugs, Woukidal's fever mounted steadily during the next two hours, until his forehead felt blazing to the touch. He died shortly after midnight without speaking again, and Catton returned to his tent after waking Sadhig, who was scheduled for the first watch that night. He told the Skorg of Woukidal's death. Sadhig merely shrugged. "His pain ended," the Skorg said, and squatted down by the fire.

In the morning they held a brief interment ceremony; the three surviving Morilaru uttered the ritual prayer for the dead, and Royce and Catton lowered the body, shrouded in the fabric of a bubbletent, into the grave that had been prepared. They broke camp immediately afterward and moved on.

There were no further fever attacks on the trip northward. On the seventeenth day, Catton was stung by a tiny golden-green insect, and his left arm balooned grotesquely, swollen with fluid from shoulder to wrist. The pain kept him from doing any work for two days, but the swelling subsided rapidly and there were no aftereffects.

On the twenty-second day, the last of the lifeship food supplies ran out. But by that time nearly half the castaways' diets consisted of native fruits anyway; the fertile jungle yielded dozens of edible fruits, which were tested by the only method possible, the empirical one. The only casualty was Sadhig, who had a day's indigestion after sampling honey-colored berries from a creeping vine. On the twenty-fourth day Catton shot a gentle-eyed, bluish-skinned creature the size of a fawn, and that night they feasted on local venison with no serious digestive consequences.

A broad river blocked their northward route on the thirtieth day. Their boat was gone, and swimming the river was out of the question; instead, they sidetracked to the east for two days until the river became narrow and shallow enough to ford on foot. Royce slipped during the crossing, ruining one of the blasters but causing no damage to himself.

By now the troupe was a bedraggled one indeed. Clothing had long since rotted away to a bare minimum; Catton had sprouted a bushy, startlingly red beard, and Royce a straggly gray one. Sadhig and the Morilaru male, both coming from races which were not afflicted with facial hair, had no such adornments. The women, too, looked seedy and unkempt. They had no nudity taboo, but they were unhappy about the appearance of their uncoiled hair, and so wrapped the remnants of their clothing about their heads to conceal the lack of proper Morilaru hair grooming.

On the thirty-ninth day, Catton announced that they had covered the estimated five hundred miles, and that the beacon should be not too far. They set out to patrol the area. Sadhig built a detector out of equipment that had been taken from the ship, and a day later they came to the rescue beacon, a tower a hundred fifty feet high topped by a subspace communicator antenna whose spokes poked skyward for eighty feet more.

Instructions were posted plainly on the side of the beacon tower in several dozen tongues—not including Terran, of course, since the beacon had been erected long before Terra's entry into interstellar life. Catton read the Morilaru instructions. They were absurdly simple; all he need to do was trip a lever, and an instant-communication beam would go out to the Morilaru space-rescue service. It would be only a day or so before a pickup ship would arrive.

Catton prepared to trip the signal. He heard a sudden shout from Royce and one of the Morilaru women simultaneously, and turned to see what was happening.

Sadhig, a hundred yards away, was casually training his blaster on his temple. The Skorg was smiling. Catton took two steps forward, but there was no time to interrupt the act. Sadhig squeezed the trigger.

They held another funeral that night, while waiting for the rescue ship to arrive. Sadhig had kept faith; he had served well on the long trek to the beacon. But he had forfeited his right to live, in his own eyes, the moment he had entered the lifeship on the doomed *Silver Spear*. Now, with rescue in sight, he had paid his forfeit.

CHAPTER TWELVE

A Morilaru ship picked the five survivors up early the next morning. Royce and Catton both decided to continue on to Skorg; the others elected to return to Morilar, where they intended to bring legal action against the spaceliner's owners for negligence. All five were taken to a relay point, a Morilaru-colonized planet called Thyrinn, where Catton and Royce boarded a small passenger vessel bound for Skorg. The trip, which lasted nine days, was uneventful. It was pleasant to sleep in an air-conditioned cabin again, to shave, to eat regular meals.

Catton had managed to retain his passport and identification through all the vicissitudes of the jungle trek. He presented them now to the authorities at the vast spaceport at Skorgaar, capital city of the Skorg Confederation. The immigration officer, a wiry, basilisk-faced Skorg, examined Catton's papers and returned them with a dour smile.

"According to these you left Morilar more than a month ago. It must have been a slow trip."

"I came via the *Silver Spear*," Catton said.

The Skorg's eyes widened in surprise. "But—"

Catton nodded. "Yes. I spent forty days wandering around on some jungle planet five hundred light-years from Morilar. But I'm here, finally. My three Morilaru attaches—there's a notation about them on the visa, over here—didn't make it. Two died in the wreck, I imagine, unless they got away in time. The third died in the jungle."

"How long do you plan to stay on this world?"

"The visa won't expire for a year. I don't have any definite plans," Catton said.

A cab took him to the heart of Skorgaar, and he checked in at a large metropolitan hotel that catered to aliens. Skorgaar was a city of some twelve million people; there were always visitors from other worlds here on commercial trips. Skorg was a large, low-density planet; the gravity, 1.4 Earthnorm, was a bit strong for Catton's comfort, but the climate was cooler than that of Morilar, for which he was grateful. The worlds were generally similar culturally; it was a favorite Morilaru theory that the Skorgs were descended from a pioneer ship of Morilaru spacefarers, thousands of years in the past, and certainly there were enough biological evidences to support the notion. Skorgs were gray in color, in contrast to the Morilaru purple, and their bodies were more elongated, their flesh more sparse. Terran biologists suspected that they were the same common stock—perhaps both descended from some ancient race long since extinct, which had colonized the area in the unimaginable past.

Catton's first official stop on Skorg was at the office of the Terran Ambassador. He was a lean, short, hardbitten little professional diplomat named Bryan, who whooped with surprise when Catton presented his identification.

"They announced that you were lost on the *Silver Spear*!" Bryan exclaimed. "I got the cable from Morilar weeks ago, from Seeman."

Catton shrugged. "I got away in a lifeship, but I was missing until ten days ago. How many died in the wreck?"

"I think there were about forty survivors, not counting any who may have escaped with you. Three lifeships got away before the ship blew. Four, altogether. Including the crew, close to nine hundred died."

"Nine hundred," Catton repeated softly. Pouin Beryaal had been willing to kill nine hundred people in order to dispose of one Earthman. If they were that anxious to kill him, Catton realized, he was going to have to get about his business swiftly and efficiently.

"I've come to Skorg for official reasons," Catton said. "I'm investigating the hypnojewel traffic as a member of the Interworld Commission on Crime."

"You think you'll find anything here?"

"I don't know," Catton said. "There've been some hints. I mean to look. But I've got another motive for coming here, besides the official one. You know about Ambassador Seeman's daughter, of course?"

"The bulletin was spread through the entire galaxy," Bryan replied. "The Skorg police have been cooperating to some extent, but there's not much you can do by way of finding one girl in a galaxy of umpteen trillion people. Or even of finding her on a single world."

"I have an idea she may have come to Skorg," Catton said.

"To Skorg? I told you, we've checked. But with nineteen billion people here, it's hard to accomplish much. She could be right under our noses and we wouldn't necessarily find her."

"Maybe I'll be lucky," Catton said.

"Why are you so interested? It's nothing personal, is it? I don't mean to pry, but—"

Chuckling, Catton said, "It's nothing romantic, if that's what you mean. But I think her disappearance has something to do with the hypnojewel business. That's why I'm looking for her."

The next few days were fruitless ones for Catton. He had Bryan arrange interviews for him with the chiefs of the Skorg police authorities, but they told him nothing about the hypnojewel trade that he had not already learned by consulting the Commission's files. And, of course, no one knew anything about the whereabouts of the girl. They had searched; but Skorg was a crowded world. Catton got the impression they were not particularly interested in finding her. They seemed to scoff at the idea that she might be on Skorg at all, and suggested that she had fled back to Earth, where she could melt into the billions and never be found.

Catton chafed impatiently. He was getting nowhere. And, he suspected, time was running out.

He was sure that Doveril had abducted her. And Doveril was deeply involved in the hypnojewel trade. Find the girl, find Doveril. But how? Where?

And then there was the business blurted by the dying Morilaru in the jungle. If it were true, if it had not been merely a fever dream, then Earth lay in imminent danger. A few matter duplicators, parachuted down from the skies at random, could crumble a civilization in days. First money, then all material goods would cease to have value. A world might bring order out of the chaos eventually, but in how many centuries?

And Pouin Beryaal was at the heart of the plot, if truth had been told. That was very neat indeed, thought Catton. Pouin was a figure of major importance on Morilar. Merikh eMerikh was an influential Skorg noble. Whether Uruod, the Arenaddin, knew about the scheme or not hardly mattered. Enough strength was mustered against Earth as it was.

Where would they get matter duplicators? No one within the bounds of the accepted galaxy would manufacture them. But perhaps there was some other source, beyond the humanoid worlds. Where, Catton wondered? He needed an opening. Only luck would give it to him.

Luck did.

It was his sixth night in Skorgaar. He had been to see the local head of the Crime Commission that day, to find out if anything significant had been uncovered that might give him a wedge toward solution of the hypnojewel problem. No help was forthcoming.

Catton found himself far across Skorgaar, in a strange part of the city; it was dinner time, and he chose a restaurant at random.

It was a plush establishment. The waiters were not Skorgs but Chennirids, slim green humanoids from a world subservient to Skorg. The patrons of the restaurant seemed to be largely outworlders on expense accounts—about half Morilaru, with the rest chiefly Arenaddin and Dargonid.

Few native Skorgs were to be seen on the premises. And the menu, when it came, proved to be an exotic one, specializing in Morilaru cookery. Morilaru food ran to the salty side; Catton ordered a vegetable dish of Arenadd instead, and got a respectful bow from the Chennirid waiter.

While he waited for the food he looked around. The decor was Morilaru. Most of the patrons were. And there was even Morilaru music playing—tinkling, graceful music played on that instrument Estil Seeman had been playing that day in the Embassy. What was its name? Ah, yes—the gondran. He saw now that the player was seated at the far end of the restaurant, behind him, on a small dais. With some surprise he noticed that she was an Earthwoman. Then he gasped in shock and half rose out of his seat, nearly knocking a tray of soup from the waiter's hand.

The waiter apologized humbly for his clumsiness. Catton wasn't listening. Currents of amazement pounded in his mind. Talk about needles in haystacks, he thought! What luck! What blind luck!

He took a note pad and stylus from his pocket and printed a note in Morilaru characters, inviting the gondran player to his table when her stint was finished. He called the waiter over, handed him the folded note, and said in Skorg, "Take this to the girl playing in the back. I'd like the pleasure of her company." He gave the man a tip and watched him cross the room to the girl.

She played for ten minutes more, having read his note without breaking the thread of her improvisation. After the final cadence she rose, nodded gracefully in acknowledgment of the polite applause, and came to Catton's table.

It was Estil, all right.

But she was no longer the demure, blushing eighteen-year-old of a few months ago. Catton saw that the moment he saw her eyes.

They were woman's eyes. She looked as though she had found out what misery meant.

It was her turn to gasp as she recognized Catton. "You—the Crime Commission man!"

He rose, pulled out a chair for her. "Hello, Estil. I didn't expect to find you so easily."

She sat, staring at him wordlessly. She seemed unable to speak. Catton said after a moment, "Shall I order something for you?"

"No—no. Please. I ate before I went on."

"You played very well."

"I have to play very well. It's my livelihood."

Catton raised an eyebrow. "Doveril sends you out to work?"

"I'm—not with Doveril any more," she said in a barely audible voice.

Catton let the point go for a moment. He said, "You've caused quite a stir by your disappearance. There's been a galaxy-wide hunt for you. And you're sitting out in the open for anyone who has eyes to see!"

"They—they haven't seemed to be looking for me for weeks. The first few weeks we were here, Doveril made me stay out of sight. But now it doesn't seem to matter. The Skorg police have forgotten all about me."

Catton said, "You ran away quite suddenly. As I remember, you asked me to get you some information—about Doveril. Then, before I had a chance to see you again, you were gone."

Her eyes did not meet his. "Doveril found out what I had asked you to do. He came to me that night, late, and asked if I trusted him. He said he had two tickets for Skorg for a flight two hours after midnight. He—insisted I go with him."

"And you went."

"Yes," she said bitterly. "I went. I suppose you found out about Doveril?"

He nodded. "We rounded up a bunch of his accomplices in the hypnojewel business not long after you left. But Doveril was the kingpin, and Doveril was gone. You say you left him?"

She shook her head sadly. "No. He left me. Three weeks after we arrived on Skorg."

"He left *you*?"

"He lost interest, I guess," she said with a pale smile. "We were really strangers to each other, after all, despite everything. I found a note from him one morning when I woke. I haven't seen him since. But I know where he is."

"He isn't on Skorg any more?"

"He's—somewhere else. I don't want to talk about it here."

"Where are you living?"

"There's a hotel, not far from here. I'm registered under another name."

"And how long have you been working at this place?"

"Since Doveril left. It's a Morilaru-owned restaurant. Doveril took me here a couple of times. I asked for a job, and they gave it to me. Playing the gondran is about the only useful trade I picked up, being an ambassador's daughter. I'm afraid I wouldn't be much good at waiting on tables, or something like that." She smiled again—a pale, wan smile. She looked exhausted. "They don't pay me much, but it's enough to keep my rent up to date, and I get most of my meals here."

"Why don't you just notify the authorities? You don't need to work in a restaurant," Catton said. "You could be on your way back to Morilar tonight, if you let someone know you were here."

She shook her head. "I'm afraid to go back. I don't dare face my father, after what I did. Running away, giving myself to an alien—" She tightened her jaws, fighting back tears. "So I've been staying here, frightened of returning, frightened of living on a strange world all alone. I don't know what to do. I've been hoping someone would find me and turn me in—I don't have the strength to do it myself. And I know things. About the hypnojewels, about worse. Doveril talked. But I don't dare tell anyone the things I know."

She looked pitiful, Catton thought. Cast away by her sly lover, afraid to return home, probably living in fear every minute here on Skorg—it was not a pretty picture for a girl who had been raised in the splendor of an ambassadorial mansion.

He looked down at the food on his plate. He was not hungry any more.

"How much longer do you have to stay here tonight?" he asked.

"I have to do one more turn. I'll be through in about an hour."

"Do you trust me, Estil?"

"I—I think so," she said faintly. "It isn't easy to trust anyone, after—after—"

"Believe me, I'll help you. I'll wait for you to finish your stint here. Then I want you to leave here with me and tell me all the things you're afraid to tell me. Nothing's going to happen to you. The worst is over. Will you believe that?"

"I'll try."

"Good. Get up there and earn your pay, then. I'll be waiting for you back here."

She returned to the dais. There was a scattered trickle of applause. Catton watched her carefully. She adjusted the height of the seat and, back straight, fingers arched over the keyboard, began to play as if for all the world she were back in the Embassy drawing-room, with her tutor looking on and beaming with pride.

CHAPTER THIRTEEN

The hotel where Estil Seeman was living was almost incredibly dingy. Sputtering argon tubes gave the only illumination in the halls. Her room was nothing more than a cubicle with a bed, a dresser, and a mirror in it. There was a common lavatory at the end of the hall. The rank Skorg odor was everywhere.

Catton quelled his disgust. "How much do you pay for this place?"

"Five normits a week."

The Earthman scowled. His own room, halfway across the city, cost more than that by the day. "How much does the restaurant pay you?"

"Twelve normits a week, plus food at cost," she said tiredly. "I haven't been able to save very much since I've been here."

"I imagine you haven't," Catton said, sitting down in a creaky, deflated pneumochair. He swung around to face her. "All right, Estil. Let's talk. Let's talk about Doveril."

"If you want to."

"The night of your father's ball, when you spoke to me, you said you suspected Doveril was mixed up in hypnojewel trading. How soon was it before you found out definitely that he was?"

"As soon as we landed on Skorg," she said. "He—seemed to change. To grow cold, and hard, and self-confident. Before he seemed, well, almost shy. But all that left him. He started boasting to me."

"About what?"

"About how important he was in the hypnojewel racket, and how rich he was going to get. He told me all this as if he expected me to applaud him."

"Just what does he do to be so important?"

"He's—a courier. He helps distribute the hypnojewels."

Catton's eyes gleamed. "Did you ever learn where the jewels come from in the first place?"

She shook her head. "N-no. He kept that part very mysterious. I never found out."

Catton frowned; he had hoped Estil could give him that vital bit of information. "Will you tell me where Doveril is now?"

"He's on a planet named Vyorn," the girl said.

Catton had heard of Vyorn only several times; it was a remote world, hundreds of thousands of light-years from the central lens of the galaxy. And it was not an oxygen-breathing world; as he recalled, it had a chlorine atmosphere. The inhabitants were completely non-humanoid and had little dealing with that vast majority of peoples that breathed oxygen.

Catton grasped her arm. "Is that where the hypnojewels come from?"

"No." She dropped her eyes. "On Vyorn they make matter duplicators. Doveril went there to buy some."

"What?"

"I know. It sounds horrible. But one day there was a call from Morilar—from Pouin Beryaal. I listened in, but Doveril didn't know it. And Beryaal told Doveril to leave for Vyorn immediately, to arrange for the shipment of matter duplicators. I don't know what Beryaal is planning to do with a cargo of duplicators, but—"

"I know," Catton said darkly. "He's planning to dump them on Earth."

"No!"

"Beryaal's behind a plot to smash Earth before it gets too powerful in the galactic scheme of things. The way to do it is to drop matter duplicators." Catton's head was beginning to ache. Beryaal was like an octopus, with tentacles wandering everywhere. He ran the Crime Commission, he schemed to shatter Terran civilization, he employed Nuuri Gryain to spy on Catton, he employed Doveril Halligon to obtain the matter duplicators for him, not seeming to care that Doveril was also involved in an illegal traffic which Beryaal was supposedly trying to stamp out. Or was Beryaal bound up in the hypnojewel business too? It would hardly be surprising.

And Nuuri had tried to betray Doveril. Either the right hand knew not what the left was doing, or else the entire incident had been another scheme within a scheme. Catton tried to puzzle out the whole complex plan, without success.

"You look so troubled," Estil said. "What's wrong?"

"I'm trying to put the pieces of a puzzle together. But the puzzle keeps getting more complicated every day." Catton shook his head. "How long ago did Doveril go to Vyorn?"

"Four weeks ago."

Four weeks, Catton thought. He did not remember how long it took to reach Vyorn by nullspace drive, but it was certainly several weeks. So Doveril had just arrived there. Catton realized he would have to follow him.

He rose. "It's getting late, Estil. I shouldn't be in a young lady's hotel room at this hour without a chaperone."

She reddened. "I don't have much reputation left to lose," she said softly.

"If that's a proposition, consider it refused," Catton said, laughing. "I'd never be able to look your father in the eye again."

He walked toward the door. She followed him—a tired little girl who had grown up too fast, still wearing the tight, low-cut dress that was her costume as a restaurant perfonner.

"Are you going to go to Vyorn?" she asked.

"Maybe. I'll see you again before I leave Skorg, in any event. Good night, Estil."

"Good night."

The next morning, Catton paid a visit to the travel agency office in the lobby of his hotel. The agent at the desk was a female Skorg of forbidding height, who flashed a professional smile at him—a neat touch, since Skorgs used a hand gesture rather than a mouth gesture to indicate amiability, and it showed her familiarity with Terran customs of courtesy.

He said, "I want to book passage for Vyorn on the next ship."

She looked a little surprised. "I'm sorry, sir. There is no through service from Skorg to any planets in the Vyom region."

"You aren't going to tell me that I simply can't get there from here, are you?"

The old Terran joke was lost completely on her. She smiled again, gravely, and said, "Oh, certainly not, sir. I merely said that there was no *direct* route from Skorg to Vyorn, but that should not be taken to mean that no link exists between those worlds."

"I see," Catton said, choking back a grin. "Would you work out a route for me, then?"

She began thumbing through books, consulting timetables, examining maps. Finally she said, "There is a way, sir. But it is a complex one. You would have to take a liner to Tharrimar—a ten-day trip. There you would make connections with a ship bound for Dirlak, and at Dirlak you would get the passenger ship to Hennim, which is the closest world to Vyorn in its own solar system. A shuttle runs from Hennim to Vyorn."

"And how long will all this take?"

She jotted down figures. "Ten days from Skorg to Tharrimar ...then a two-day stopover waiting for the Dirlak trip ...five days more to Dirlak ...a one-day wait until the ship for Hennim leaves ...three days from Dirlak to Hennim ...one more day for the Hennim-Vyorn shuttle. A total of twenty-two days from departure to arrival. Will that be acceptable?"

Catton told her that it was, and she arranged a round trip for him which allowed him five days on Vyorn. He would depart from Skorg on the Tharrimar bound ship in three days; the agent subradioed ahead to reserve accommodations for him at the various stopover points, and within an hour the packet of tickets and reservations was completed. The cost of the trip was three thousand normits, or twenty-seven hundred thrones in Morilaru currency. He paid out of the funds he had drawn from the local office of the Interworld Commission on Crime.

The arrangements complete, Catton headed across the hotel lobby to the dining room, for lunch. A Skorg bellhop neatly stepped in front of him and said, "Are you the Earthman, Catton?"

"That's right."

"A woman from Morilar wishes to see you. She's waiting in the front of the lobby."

Frowning. Catton gave the boy a coin and went forward. A woman from Morilar? Who—

It was Nuuri Gryain.

She was sitting in the lounge chair nearest the lobby door. As he came into view she rose and walked toward him.

"Hello, Catton. I figured I'd find you here."

"Nuuri—what—how come you're on Skorg?"

She shrugged. "I took a little trip. There was a reward for the bit of informing I did, and I put my money into a round trip ticket to Skorg. But I'm hungry and thirsty now. Have you eaten?"

"No," Catton said. "I was just about to."

He escorted her toward the hotel dining room. They found an empty table for two.

Catton said, "How did you know I was here?"

"I knew you were on Skorg because it was splashed all over the news-sheets that you'd survived the *Silver Spear* explosion, had been rescued from a jungle world after weeks and weeks, and had come to Skorg. So I called a few hotels when I landed in Skorgaar, starting at the most expensive and working down. You were registered at the third one I called."

Catton smiled politely at her, but behind the smile was a more cautious expression. He did not know how far to trust the Morilaru girl. He still suspected that she betrayed him to Pouin Beryaal. And a girl who lived on the other side of the river in Dyelleran did not waste her money on pleasure jaunts to Skorg. There had to be a deeper motive for her trip.

A waiter hovered behind his shoulder. Nuuri said, "Order some wine first, yes?"

"All right. Get us a bottle of something good, waiter. Make it a six-normit bottle."

The waiter bowed low and glided away. A few moments later the wine steward appeared with a faceted green bottle. The sommelier showed the label to Catton for approval. It was in a language he did not know. "Where's it from?" he asked.

"Jammir," said the wine steward with faint supercilious undertones. "One of our finest light wines."

"Very well," Catton said. "We'll try it."

Following the ancient custom of his trade, the sommelier unstoppered the decanter, poured a bit of wine into Catton's glass, and waited for a verdict. Catton tasted it. The wine was dry, with a curious flavor of fresh wood smoking over a fire. He liked it. He nodded to the wine steward, who poured out a glass for each of them and restoppered the decanter.

Catton reached for his glass; at the same moment Nuuri, going for hers, knocked her purse to the floor. Automatically Catton bent and scooped it up. Then, cautiously, he thought of glancing at his wineglass. The clear surface of the wine seemed momentarily roiled and clouded; after an instant it returned to its transparent state.

Catton nodded. It was all very neat, very slick, he thought. The accidental knocking-over of the purse, giving her a moment to drop something in his wine while he bent.

"On Earth," he said in a quiet voice, "it's traditional that when a man and woman dine together, they exchange their wine glasses before drinking. The tradition goes back to the dim past of Terran civilization—it's a symbol of the trust that a man and a woman should have when they share food."

Nuuri's eyes glimmered uneasily. "I don't think it's a very sensible custom."

"But it's a touching one. Let me have your glass, Nuuri, and you take mine."

"Don't be foolish, Catton. Earthman customs don't interest me. Drink your wine."

"Please. It's a particular custom of mine."

"I didn't notice you asking me for my glass when we drank together at the Five Planets," she said.

"We didn't eat afterward," Catton improvised.

"Drink your wine and don't trouble me with your Earth-man customs." She raised her glass to her lips. Catton reached across the table, caught her slender wrist between his thumb and middle finger, and forced her hand back to the table. She let go of the wineglass. He did not release his grip on her wrist.

"What's the matter, Nuuri? Are you afraid to drink my wine?"

"You're being silly."

"Answer me. *Are you afraid to drink my wine?*"

"Of course not. Do you take me for a poisoner? Let go of my arm. I don't intend to sit here and let you accuse me of—"

"You don't think I'll let you storm out of here and escape, do you? Drink the wine. And don't try to spill the drink intentionally." He dug his middle finger into the network of blood vessels that lay just below the skin of her wrist. She gasped involuntarily as the pressure tightened.

"Let go. You're hurting me."

"Tell me why you won't drink my wine, Nuuri."

"You're making a scene. I could have the waiter throw you out."

He dug his finger deeper into her wrist. Her fingers were quivering from the pain. "Don't try to raise your voice, Nuuri, or I'll break your wrist," he warned in a level voice. "You put something in my drink while I bent over to pick up your purse."

"No! It isn't so!"

"It must be so. Otherwise you wouldn't have made a fuss about exchanging the drinks."

He tightened his grip. His own fingers were beginning to hurt from the constant pressure; her arm, he thought, was probably numb to the elbow by now. But still he intensified his grasp. She bit her lips to keep from crying out.

"Please ...let go of me."

"I want an answer. You came here to poison me, didn't you? Tell me the truth! Isn't that why you're here? Who sent you?"

"Please." Her voice was a strangled whisper. "My wrist—you're crushing it—"

From a distance, in the crowded dining room, they gave the appearance of an affectionate mixed couple, the man leaning forward and holding the woman's arm. Closer, the picture was different. Catton forced his fingers to contact even further.

"All right," Nuuri gasped finally. "Pouin Beryaal sent me. He was furious when he heard you had survived the ship explosion. He sent me to Skorg to kill you!"

CHAPTER FOURTEEN

Catton casually knocked the glass of poisoned wine to the floor. A moment later Skorg attendants came bustling up to mop the parquet, remove the broken glass, and to assure Catton that they were terribly sorry about the accident.

He and Nuuri finished the meal in silence, Catton never taking his eyes off her. After he signed the check he said quietly, "Okay. Let's go up to my room. We can talk there."

They rode up in the gravshaft together. Catton let her into the room first, locked the door, and said, "Give me your purse." He took it from her and tossed it into the closet, which opened only to the thumbprint of the room's occupant. "You can have it back when you leave," he told her. "I'm not taking any chances with whatever artillery you might have in there."

"How do you know I'm not concealing a blaster in my clothes?"

"I don't. Suppose you strip and let me search them."

She glared at him, more in annoyance than in outrage; Morilaru did not feel modesty about displaying their bodies. She peeled her clothes off sullenly. Her body was like that of the two Morilaru women he had been marooned with: lean, practically without fatty deposits anywhere. He examined her clothing, found no concealed weapons, and told her to dress.

"Are you satisfied?" she asked him.

"Satisfied that there's no way you can kill me right this moment, anyway." He sat down facing her. On Skorg there was no prohibition about non-residents carrying weapons, and he was armed with a small blaster in case she tried anything violent. "So you're working for Pouin Beryaal," he said reflectively. "And he sent you here to kill me, eh?"

She did not speak.

Catton said, "I suppose you were the one who told Beryaal that my real motive for coming to the outworlds had nothing to do with hypnojewels, too. You told him I was investigating the plot against Earth. And he saw to it that the spaceliner I was taking blew up. You informed on me, didn't you? You were in Beryaal's pay?"

"You're remarkably wise," she said acidly. "But I don't have to listen to you talk. Kill me and be done with it, Catton!"

"Kill you? Not till you've told me what I want to know, Nuuri. Perhaps, if you tell me enough, I'll release you."

"I'm not telling you anything."

He steepled his fingers. "One aspect of this tangle puzzles me. You worked for Beryaal. So did Doveril. But you offered to betray him to the crime-detection people, and only the fact that he had run away the night before kept him from being picked up with the others. How come one minion of Beryaal would try to sell another one out? Did the wires get crossed?"

Astonishment registered on Nuuri's face. After a frozen pause she said, "Doveril was working for *Beryaal*?"

"Does this come as news to you?"

"I never knew it. Beryaal must have been furious with me! I offered to betray his underling Doveril to you out of personal motives of revenge."

"Because Doveril jilted you?"

"We lived together for a while. We were planning to take out a permanent residence permit. Then, suddenly, he told me that it was all off, that there was someone else, that I would have to leave. I resolved to punish him for that. I was acting on my own, not Beryaal's designs, when I informed on Doveril."

Catton shook his head slowly. "Doveril was a kingpin, in the hypnojewel business, but he was also doing some very important—and illegal—work for Beryaal. And Beryaal was employing you to spy on me."

Nuuri's spiked shoulders slumped. "So it didn't matter that Doveril escaped capture. As head of the Commission, Beryaal would simply have freed him if he had been caught with the others."

"I'm afraid so," Catton said.

"But how do you know so much about Doveril? Where is he? Have you seen him?"

"No. But I've seen the girl he jilted you for. Doveril dumped her too."

"She is here? On Skorg?"

Catton nodded. "The night before I first met you, Doveril eloped with her to Skorg. But he dropped her after a few weeks. She's still living on Skorg, here in Skorgaar."

Anger glinted in Nuuri's eyes. "Who is this woman?"

"Estil Seeman. The daughter of the Terran Ambassador to Morilar. Doveril talked her into running away with him when he saw trouble shaping up for himself. She's living in a cheap hotel on the other side of town, and playing the gondran in a restaurant so she can pay her rent."

Nuwi laughed harshly. "Of course! He was her music teacher, and she disappeared the same night he ran away! But I was too stupid to connect them. He's left her, you say? Where is he? On Skorg, too?"

"No. He's out of the system, on some filthy business of Bervaal's."

"You know where he has gone? Tell me!"

"It doesn't concern you," Catton said.

"Anything about Doveril concerns me! Tell me! I'll go there with you, help you capture him—!"

"Hold on!" Catton said. "I'm going to turn you over to Skorg authorities before I leave."

"No! Let me go with you!"

"After you tried to murder me downstairs? You think I'm going to give you another chance?"

"I have no interest in killing you," she said. "Beryaal ordered me to come here and attempt it, and I obeyed him. But Beryaal means nothing to me. I'm interested only in engineering Doveril's downfall. Let me go to this world with you. We'll arrange a trap for him. Doveril may still trust me; I'll lure him to you."

"You'd sell anyone out. How can I trust you?"

"Trust me on faith. I want revenge on Doveril. Nothing else matters to me." She smiled craftily. "I'll make a deal with you,

Catton. Take me to wherever Doveril is—and when we find him, I'll tell you where the hypnojewels come from!"

"You know?"

"Doveril once let it slip. I've been saving the information until I could put it to good use. And now I can. Take me to Doveril, let me help capture him—and I'll give you the name of the world where the hypnojewels are made. Is it a deal?"

Catton was silent a long while. The girl was of shifty loyalties; no doubt about that. But how sincere was she now? She had sold out friends, attempted to murder him, lied and betrayed. By accepting the offer of her help, he might be clutching a viper to his bosom. But, on the other hand, catching the wily Doveril on Vyorn might not be easy. Using Nuuri as bait, it would be much simpler for him. And there was the additional handy factor of her offer to give him the hypnojewel information—unless, of course, she was bluffing there.

He decided to risk it. Her hatred for Doveril seemed unfeigned. She was an uncertain ally, but he would take his chances with her.

"All right," he said. "I'm going to Vyorn in three days. Can you leave then?"

"Of course."

"We'll travel together. I'll include you on my papers as a secretary. There shouldn't be any trouble."

Catton had his doubts about joining forces with a woman who had spied on him and attempted to murder him. But at this stage of the conflict he needed any ally he could get, even a risky one. He did not have much more time, now that Pouin Beryaal knew that he lived.

He phoned down to the travel agency and arranged for a second set of reservations, in Nuuri's name, along with accommodations—separate ones—for her during the stopovers.

That night he visited the restaurant where Estil Seeman played, and told the girl he was leaving soon for Vyorn, to apprehend Doveril, and that if he met with success he would stop off and pick her up on his return trip, to take her back to Morilar. He did not mention his meeting with Nuuri to Estil; it might only fan her jealousy.

During the next three days Catton remained in the hotel. He realized that Beryaal might easily have sent more than one agent to dispose of him. Since he had accomplished all he needed to on Skorg, there was no point needlessly exposing himself now. On the third day he and Nuuri journeyed to the spaceport outside Skorgaar, had their papers validated for emigration, and boarded a small 180-passenger ship of the Skorg Line, bound out non-stop to Tharrimar, fifth world of the Tharrim system.

The ten-day voyage dragged hopelessly. The small ship lacked the awesome splendor of the *Silver Spear*, and Catton spent his time reading, gaming in the lounge, or sleeping. Nuuri was poor company. Her only topic of conversation was the fierce hatred she bore for Doveril, and Catton soon tired of that.

Tharrimar was a medium-sized world populated by loose-skinned red humanoids governed by a Skorg administrator. The meager city near the spaceport held few attractions, and Catton was bothered by the heavy gravitational pull, nearly twice that of Earth. He was not sad when the two-day stopover ended and the ship for Dirlak blasted off.

This ship was even less imposing than the last—half passenger, half freight. But, blessedly, it was only a five-day journey to Dirlak, a bleak place two billion miles from its sun. The temperature never rose above zero on Dirlak. Frozen winds howled all the time, for the twenty Galactic hours Catton and Nuuri were compelled to wait before their ship to Hennim left. Dirlak was a trading outpost of the Skorg Confederation, thinly populated, rarely visited except by transient travelers.

Three days aboard a slow-moving transport ship got them to Hennim, sister world of Vyorn. Hennim was an oxygen world, not much larger than Earth but cursed by a fiercely capricious climate. Torrential rain was falling as Catton landed at the spaceport; within an hour, a searing blast of solar radiation was baking the mud that the fields had become.

The natives of Hennim were humanoids, squat and sturdy, who peered quizzically at Catton from oval eyes the color of little silver buttons. It developed that most of them had never seen a Terran before. A Skorg interpreter informed Catton that less than a hundred Earthmen had ever visited this system; it was too remote to attract Terran industry, and the tourist trade was put off by the difficulties in getting there from any major world of the galactic lens. Of course, there were no diplomatic relations between Earth and any world of this system. When Catton replied that he was going to Vyorn, exclamations of surprises were audible on all sides. No more than a handful of Terran travelers had ever gone to Vyorn.

The shuttle left Hennim the next day. Catton and Nuuri were in the oxygen-breathers' section of the vessel, along with several dozen Hennimese and a few Skorgs. Behind a partition, Catton learned, eight Vyorni were traveling, breathing their peculiarly poisonous chlorine atmosphere.

The trip took six hours. Near its conclusion, a Hennimese in crew uniform appeared in the passenger cabin to announce—first in his own language, then in Skorg—that landing would shortly take place. "All oxygen-breathing entities are required to wear breathing-suits for their own protection. Those who are without suits may rent them from the purser."

Catton and Nuuri rented suits, standard medium-size humanoid type, for small sums payable in Skorg currency. Catton adjusted his to the familiar chemical makeup of Earth's atmosphere; it was the first time he had breathed it since the assignment began.

Not long after, the planet they sought came into view. It was vaguely circular, swathed in a thick green shroud of chlorine. The shuttle-ship landed with minor difficulties. After the last jolt, the Hennimese purser reappeared to convey the oxygen-breathing passengers through the airlock to the waiting spaceport coach.

Outside, Catton got his first look at Vyorn. Flat, barren land stretched outward to the horizon. The greenish murk hung low overhead. The scenery was utterly alien, totally strange. Within his protective suit, he was comfortable enough—but the temperature outside, he knew, was no more than 250 degrees above Absolute. It was a cold, ugly, forbidding world, alien in every respect.

And here, Catton thought, are produced the matter duplicators designed for the destruction of Terran civilization.

CHAPTER FIFTEEN

Three of Catton's allotted five days on Vyorn slipped by before he got his first inkling of Doveril's whereabouts.

The Vyorni were of no help. They refused to give any information. They were remote, unpleasant creatures: the size of a Terran, but unhumanoid in form, with six jointed arms and three legs; their bodies were dead white, waxy in appearance, and their eyes glowered beadily out of protruding triangular sockets. Better than 90 percent of the life-bearing worlds of the universe produced oxygen-breathing creatures; Vyorn was different. Its inhabitants breathed an atmosphere of chlorine and gave off carbon tetrachloride as respiratory waste. The Vyorni plant life broke the carbon tet down into chlorine and complex hydrocarbons, and so the cycle of respiration went on. In every way these beings were different from all others in the galaxy.

The difference was psychological as well as physiological. The Vyorni seemed cosmically indifferent to the ways of the oxygen-breathers who came to their world. There was no organized government on Vyorn, nor any legal system. All Vyorni were free to do as they pleased, so long as they brought no harm to a fellow Vyorni.

Catton, via a Skorg interpreter, spoke with the Vyorni who was in charge of the residence compound for oxygen-breathing beings. "Tell him I'm here to find a Morilaru named Doveril Halligon. That it's important for the security and peace of the galaxy that I find him."

The interpreter reeled off a string of harsh, clicking, consonant-heavy words. After a moment the Vyorni replied: three clucking syllables.

The Skorg translated. "He says he doesn't care."

"Tell him it's vital—that I'll pay him for information."

Once again the Skorg spoke, and once again the Vyorni replied—this time with one snapped grunt.

"Well?" Catton said.

"He doesn't want to be paid. He just isn't interested in helping you."

"Tell him I'm a crime-prevention officer! I'm a member of the Interworld Commission."

Shrugging, the Skorg translated. The answer was curt. "This is Vyorn," he says. "Oxygen-breathers' law is no good here."

Catton sighed. "Okay. I see I'm not going to get anywhere with him. Maybe you can help me, then. Is there some central registry of immigrants here? Or a Morilaru consulate where I could ask about my man?"

"There's no central registry of *any* kind here. Nor any consulates. Vyorn doesn't enter into diplomatic relations with oxygen-breathing worlds."

Further investigation later got him more of the same. The Vyorni were not interested in cooperating. If oxygen-breathers wanted to come here to do business, they were welcome, but they would not necessarily be treated with warmth. Catton began to understand how this race could so casually manufacture things like matter duplicators. The Vyorni were not motivated by profit or any other typical oxygen-breather motivation. But they derived some sort of satisfaction from seeing their products go forth and harass and confuse the oxygen-breathers who occupied most of the universe's worlds.

Catton began asking questions. He went about it with care, for he did not want word to reach Doveril—if Doveril were still on Vyorn—that an Earthman was here, asking questions about him. Catton let Nuuri do most of the actual questioning. There were about twenty Morilaru in the compound, engaged in trade with the Vyorni. She approached them one by one, subtly leading the discussion around to Doveril.

On the third day they got some concrete information at last. Nuuri was talking to an abnormally plump Morilaru named Gudwan Quinak, who ostensibly was on Vyorn to deal in furs, but who, Catton privately suspected, was involved with some sort of drug trade. Catton had Nuuri approach him slyly, wheedlingly, and within ten minutes she had him talking.

"He's a drug man, all right," she reported later to Catton. "And he knows Doveril pretty well. He's at another Vyorni city, about two hundred miles from here. According to Quinak, Doveril landed here about a month ago, and let drop a couple of hints that he was involved in something *big*. Doveril could never resist boasting."

"How do we get to him?"

"We'll have to rent a jetsled. There's no public transport between here and there. Vyorni don't travel much, it seems."

They rented the jetsled at an extravagant cost from a knowledgeable, covertly smiling Skorg who had a local concession. The Skorg's beady eyes glinted as Catton paid over the stiff deposit, as if the Skorg itched to make some remark about the relationship between a Terran and a Morilaru woman who were renting a sled together. But the Skorg kept his own counsel, probably afraid of losing the sale.

The sled was well built, a compact bullet-shaped vehicle totally enclosed in duriplast, with keen snow-runners and a triple array of rocket tubes. Catton checked out the mechanical parts of the sled with great care before they left. He knew enough about the Vyorni by now to realize that if their sled broke down somewhere in the frozen wastes, they would be left to rot before anyone came out to rescue them.

They left the residence compound about mid-day, with Vyorn's small yellow sun directly overhead, dimly visible behind the thick atmospheric swath of chlorine. Catton kept the speed at fifty miles an hour; more might be dangerous. There was no road, just a well-worn track through the bleak tundra. Scattered Vyorni settlements lined the route: odd needle-shaped homes, thirty feet high and no more than twelve feet wide at the base, and farmland ploughed by weird swaybacked creatures whose bodies were segmented like crustaceans and whose eyes had a haunting wisdom about them, as if they were the eyes of intelligent beings who had been subjugated by the Vyorni.

The sun had nearly set—Vyorn's day lasted only some sixteen Galactic hours—when the sled reached the outskirts of the village that was Catton's destination. They pulled up outside a domed building much like the other residence compound.

"You so inside," Catton ordered. "Find out if Doveril's around. If he is, see if you can get him to come out here."

Nuuri slipped through the exit hatch of the jetsled and trotted toward the compound's airlock. Catton waited in the sled, cradling a small blaster in his hand. Five minutes passed; then Nuuri returned. She was alone.

"Well?"

"He's across town at the spaceport. Supervising a cargo loading."

"It looks like we got here just in time." Catton slapped down the starter switch on the sled, and it shot off down the road.

The spaceport was a small one, a few miles from the compound. Catton saw only three ships—two small shuttles bearing Hennimese insignia, and one larger, unmarked ship that stood by itself at the edge of the field, glinting dull gray in the gathering darkness. A dozen Vyorni were going back and forth between the ship and a nearby cargo shed. They were bearing wooden crates two feet square into the ship. A figure in a spacesuit stood near the open hatch, counting the crates as they entered the ship.

"Should I go over to him?" Nuuri asked anxiously.

"Wait. They've almost finished loading the ship."

The Vyorni made one last trip to the shed, then paused as if waiting for further orders. The figure in the spacesuit seemed to be dismissing them.

The hatch on the gray spaceship closed abruptly. The spacesuited figure started to walk off the field, toward the administration building at the edge of the blast area.

"Okay," Catton said. "Go over and talk to him. I'm tuned in on the wavelength of your suit radio."

Nuuri ran across the field. Crouching in the jetsled, Catton heard her cry out: "Doveril! Doveril!"

The spacesuited figure halted. "Nuuri? What are you doing here?"

"I—came to see you, Doveril."

"Followed me all the way to Vyorn? How did you know where I was?" Doveril demanded suspiciously. "Who sent you here?"

"Beryaal sent me," she said evenly. "I have a message for you.

"What dealings have *you* had with Beryaal?"

"He employs me," Nuuri said. "Come with me to that jet-sled. I have a message-disk from Beryaal for you, in it."

"I'll wait here," Doveril said cautiously. "Go get it."

"No—come with me."

"Go get it, I said!"

Catton, waiting hidden beneath the jetsled seat, caught his breath. Doveril suspected a trap. The former music teacher was a wary one.

Nuuri came to the jetsled alone. Bending over Catton, she cut her radio and touched her helmet to his to say, "Give me a weapon. He won't come."

Catton handed her his auxiliary blaster. "Here. But don't use it. I want him alive."

She took the weapon without replying, and returned to Doveril. Catton picked up the words over his suit radio.

"Here's the message, Doveril." She extended her space-gloved hand. The gun's nozzle protruded. "Your schemes are finished. I know about the Earthgirl, Estil. I know how you treated her, and how you treated me. This is the time for vengeance, Doveril."

"Nuuri? Are you crazy? You—"

A sudden purple spear of light flashed from the blaster in Nuuri's hand. But Doveril had already launched himself forward as if to tackle her. The energy bolt went wild, passing over the Morilaru's shoulder and dissipating itself harmlessly in the atmosphere. Before Nuuri had a chance to fire again, Doveril was upon her, hurling her to the ground, his hand grasping for the blaster she still clutched.

Catton scowled. The girl had disobeyed him! He flipped up the jetsled's exit hatch and ran toward the struggling pair as they grappled on the frozen field.

Nuiiri was screaming hysterically, blanketing the audio channel with her outpouring of hatred. But Doveril's hand grasped the wrist that controlled the blaster, and she could not fire. Catton was still twenty yards away from them when Doveril pounced on the blaster, ripping it from the girl's hand, and leaped back, dragging Nuuri in front of him as a shield.

"Put down your gun, Earthman, or I'll kill the girl," Doveril said evenly.

They faced each other over a twenty yard gap, with Nuuri between them. Catton felt naked and unprotected. If Doveril chose to fire, he could kill the Earthman easily.

But Doveril was backing away, toward the ship. Catton saw the Morilaru's lips moving, but Doveril was talking on another audio channel. Nuuri shouted, "I can hear him, Catton! He's ordering the crew to ready the ship for blastoff! Kill him, Catton! Kill him!"

Catton tensed. Doveril said, "You'll kill her too, Earthman."

"I don't want to kill anybody. I want to stop that ship from blasting off."

Doveril laughed mockingly. "Of course you do. But I'm afraid that's impossible."

Catton weighed the chances. Doveril was no more than forty feet from the ship's open airlock. The Vyorni who had loaded the cargo were standing in a row at the edge of the field, showing no interest in what was taking place.

Doveril was close to the airlock now. Suddenly Nuuri squirmed in his grasp, twisted round, pummelled with both gloved hands on his helmet as if trying to break it. Momentarily confused, Doveril shoved her away from him.

Catton fired, but the shot went wild. A microsecond later Doveril's blaster spouted energy too. But Nuuri, launching herself at Doveril in a frenzied attack, caught Doveril's beam and was hurled to one side by the energy bolt. Catton fired again quickly. The second bolt caught Doveril at the waist and ripped open his breathing-suit, cutting a flaming hole through the middle of his body. The Morilaru screamed.

Catton ran forward and knelt over Nuuri. The bolt had ripped her suit open at the shoulder. She was still alive. "Did you ...kill ...him?" she asked feebly.

"Yes."

"Good. Thanks, Earthman." She started to close her eyes. He grabbed her. "Nuuri! The hypnojewel secret—tell me!"

She giggled hysterically. "They're made on Skorg, Earthman. I ...took you a little out of your way, didn't I? Too bad."

She was dead. The airlock of the waiting ship slammed shut. The warning gong that was the clear-the-field signal sounded. He ran from the field. The ship was blasting off.

Unconcerned Vyorni were standing idly by in the spaceport's administration building. Catton gestured with drawn blaster to a Skorg. "Do you speak Vyorni?"

"Yes."

"Take me to the control center."

At blaster-point, the Skorg did not stop to argue. He led Catton down a corridor to a gravlift, then up to the top of the building. They burst into a central monitoring tower. Three Vyorni peered quizzically at Catton as he entered.

He glanced at the viewsereen that monitored the field. The ship outside had retracted its atmosphere fins, and landing jacks. In a moment it would be blasting off. Catton snapped to the Skorg, "Tell them that they mustn't let that gray ship blast off. That they must withdraw clearance and immobilize its controls."

A simple radiolock was all that would be needed to freeze the ship. The Skorg obediently translated Catton's order and drew a blunt, brief reply from the Vyorni. "They refuse to do it," the Skorg said. "They won't get involved in other beings' private quarrels."

"But this isn't private! Do you know what's aboard that ship? If—" Catton scowled. He waved the blaster fiercely at the emotionless Vyorni. "Tell him I'll kill them if they don't freeze that ship," he said to the Skorg.

"They won't listen to you," the Skorg said.

The Skorg seemed to be right. The Vyorni did not fear his blaster. And now it was too late to do anything. On the field, the ship was rising, incinerating the bodies of Nuuri and Doveril in its rocket-blast. An instant later the ship lurched upward and out of sight—bearing its deadly cargo of matter duplicators intended for Earth.

CHAPTER SIXTEEN

By the time, two hours later, that Catton had finished ransacking Doveril's quarters at the residence compound, night had fallen. Catton did not trust himself to make the two hundred mile journey safely during the night. He slept over in the dead man's bed, and left early the following morning.

There was no inquiry, no question raised by the Vyorni. Oxygen-breathers could evidently kill each other with impunity on Vyorn without arousing curiosity.

Catton was not happy over the way his pursuit of Doveril had ended. Nuuri, who might have been useful again, was dead; and Doveril, whom Catton had hoped to capture alive, was dead as well. Hardly a molecule of their bodies had survived the holocaust of the rockets. Nuuri had tricked him; she had not wanted to help him capture her faithless Doveril, merely to get herself to wherever Doveril was and exact her vengeance. Catton wondered about her last statement—that the hypnojewels were made on Skorg. Another of her lies? A deathbed fantasy? Or was it the truth, and had she deliberately led him away from Skorg to hunt down Doveril?

Worst of all, the cargo ship had escaped. Documents he found in Doveril's room told him that the ship contained a cargo of one thousand matter duplicators, built on Vyorn. No doubt it was simple to build the duplicators; all you needed were two pilot models, and the rest could be made by self-duplication. They were being shipped to Morilar, and from there to Earth. The trip to Morilar would take the freighter almost a month, which meant that Catton would arrive there about the same time as the cargo ship. And then—

And then would come the moment of crisis. Catton knew he had to intercept that ship before it left for Earth. Once it became lost in the infinite expanse of nullspace, there would be small chance of tracking it. The matter duplicators would get safely through to Earth. And one day, between one dawn and the next, a thousand crates would drift down through Earth's atmosphere, a thousand matter duplicators would land.

Perhaps half would be destroyed on landing—would fall into oceans, or crash on inaccessible mountain peaks. But if only a hundred—fifty—twenty, got into the hands of men shrewd enough to realize the value of the device and greedy enough not to care about its dangers, Beryaal's plot would have succeeded.

Catton knew he was entirely on his own now. There would be no help from the Interworld Commission of Crime, where Beryaal ruled supreme. Relaying a warning to Earth was risky; it might be intercepted, since subradio beams were easily detected, and in any event he did not want word of the plot indiscriminately spread about the galaxy.

He rode back alone through the windswept wastelands. The Skorg he had rented the jetsled from made an oblique remark about his lady companion not returning with him; Catton merely glared as he received back his deposit. The Vyorn-Hennim shuttle departed early the following morning, with Catton aboard. Six hours later, he was on Hennim; later the same night he blasted off for Dirlak on an ancient transport ship.

The trip back to Skorg seemed to take forever. From Dirlak to Tharrimar, from Tharrimar, finally, to Skorg. Catton touched down on Skorg on the eighteenth day after leaving Vyorn; the return trip had been shorter than the voyage out. The vessel bearing the matter duplicators was still more than a week away from Morilar, according to the flight plans in Doveril's papers.

Catton went immediately to Estil Seeman's hotel. The Earthgirl seemed surprised to see him. She kept the door half closed, as if concealing someone within.

"Oh—you're back."

"Yes. Can I come in?"

"I'd—rather you didn't. I—have company—"

Catton ignored her and pushed the door open. There was a slim Morilaru in the far corner, just beginning to draw a knife. Catton pressed forward, slapped the knife out of the Morilaru's hand, and knocked the man tumbling to the floor. Then his eyes widened in recognition.

"You—you're Gonnimor Cleeren, Doveril's friend!"

The Morilaru nodded. Catton said, "You were tortured to death by Beryaal. He said so!"

The Morilaru shrugged. Catton grabbed him by one pipe-stem arm and yanked him up. To Estil he said, "What's this doing here?"

"He—he saw me at the restaurant," the girl said in confusion. "He was Doveril's friend, and he wanted to talk to me." The Morilaru quivered with fright. Catton said, "Beryaal secretly released you, didn't he?"

Gonnimor Cleeren made no answer. Catton was too tired for toying with the alien. He slapped him, hard, twice in quick succession. "Yes," Cleeren mumbled. "He let me go after the arrest."

"And why are you on Skorg now? What do you want here?"

The alien was silent once again. "Lock the door," Catton said to Estil. "And turn your back."

"What are you going to do to him?"

"Never mind," he snapped. The girl obeyed him. Catton seized the terrified Morilaru by the throat and said quietly, "I'm going to give you sixty seconds to start telling me all you know about Beryaal and hypnojewels. Then I'm going to put out your eyes with my thumbs."

"Barbarian!"

"That's right," Catton said easily. "Too much is at stake to waste time now. Talk whenever you're ready." He eyed his watch. The alien remained silent for thirty seconds, forty, fifty. Catton put his fingers to the Morilaru's eyes and gently exerted pressure.

"No! No!" Cleeren screamed.

"All right. Talk, then."

"What do you want to know?"

"Where are the hypnojewels made?"

"Here on Skorg," Cleeren whimpered. "There's a factory outside Skorgaar. On the outside it seems to be making toys. The police leave it alone."

"How are the jewels made?"

"They're assembled by machinery. It's a complicated process—tremendous heat, great pressure. I don't understand it."

"And who heads the outfit?"

Cleeren was silent again. Catton raised his thumbs and the alien said, "No! Don't! It's—Beryaal and eMerikh. They run the whole hypnojewel show. And they suppress any evidence that might unmask them, since they're on the Crime Commission too."

"Very neat," Catton commented. It tied in with what he had been told by Nuuri. "Beryaal has it all dovetailed nicely. I suppose he used the profits from the hypnojewels to pay the Vyorni for the matter-duplicators."

"No," Cleeren offered. "He paid the Vyorni with hypnojewels themselves."

"What?"

"Hypnojewels can't be duplicated on a matter duplicator; there's something about the submolecular structure that makes it impossible. They're unique that way. And the Vyorni covet hypnojewels—they use them for entertainment and decoration, since the jewels don't affect them very seriously."

Catton nodded. He knew all he needed to know, now. It tied up into a neat whole. Beryaal and eMerikh running both the hypnojewel racket and the investigating committee; hypnojewels going to Vyorn to pay for the duplicators; a cargo on its way with menace for Earth.

He felt drenched with sweat. For one ghastly moment it had seemed that Cleeren intended to call his bluff. It wouldn't have been fun, gouging out the alien's eyes.

He said to Estil, "All right. You can turn around now. I'm not going to hurt him."

The girl was pale. "D-did you find Doveril on Vyorn?"

Catton nodded. "He's dead. There was a gunfight and I killed him."

"Dead?" she repeated distantly.

"You don't feel sorry about it, do you?"

"I—I loved him once," she said. She looked troubled. Catton shook his head.

"Never mind Doveril now. Start packing. I'm going to drop our friend here off at the local jail, and then you and I are going to go to Skorgaar spaceport. We're leaving for Morilar on the first ship out tonight."

CHAPTER SEVENTEEN

The trip took eight days. According to Catton's figuring, the cargo ship from Vyorn would reach Morilar a day after he would. Delicate timing would be necessary.

The girl was terrified of the reception she would get at home. Catton reassured her. "Your father can be manipulated—you know that yourself. We'll tell him you were abducted and that the note you left was dictated by Doveril. He'll believe you."

On the eighth day the ship entered landing orbit around Morilar. At the spaceport Catton phoned the Embassy and arranged for a car to pick them up, not telling anyone that the girl was with him. Reaching the Embassy, he led her quickly to the Ambassador's office, and made her wait in the hall, away from the beam of the scanning field.

The Ambassador looked like his own ghost. His huge frame had shed perhaps thirty pounds. His face was pale, his skin sagging loosely into pouches where the fat had dissolved away, his eyes weary and sad. He had taken Estil's disappearance badly.

"I thought we were never going to see you again," Seeman said. "After that terrible spaceship disaster—for weeks we thought you'd been killed. And then word came that you had escaped after all—"

"Does Earth know I'm alive?"

"Of course. We sent a message when your ship was reported missing, and another when you turned up safe."

"Have I missed anything important in the last three months?"

The Ambassador shrugged. "Not much. Things have remained about the same since you left."

Catton smiled. "Not entirely. I've got a surprise for you, Ambassador Seeman. Will you excuse me for a moment?" He ducked out of the office. Estil was waiting in the hall with a pinched, nervous look on her face. "Go inside," Catton told her. "He isn't expecting you, so be prepared to shock him."

"You didn't tell him anything?"

"Just that I had a surprise for him. Nothing more. Remember: Doveril *kidnapped* you. He made you write that note. Got it?"

"Aren't you coming in with me?"

Catton shook his head. "I don't belong in there. And I don't want to be around when the weeping and wailing starts. I don't like to watch a man the size of your father cry."

The girl smiled shyly at him. She stood hesitating at the edge of the green scanner-field that registered on the screen inside the Ambassador's office. Catton gave her a blunt shove into the field. Then, quickly, he turned and strode away, up the stairs to his own room on the fifth floor.

It was late in the afternoon. Tomorrow, probably around noon, the cargo ship would be docking at the spaceport outside Dyelleran. The ship wouldn't remain in port long—no longer than necessary for Beryaal or one of his agents to verify the nature of the cargo and send it on its way to Earth.

Catton saw he was in an ambiguous position. As a member of the Interworld Commission on Crime, he had a legal right to inspect the cargo of any ship entering or leaving Morilar. But Beryaal, as chairman of the Commission, could overrule him. Most likely Beryaal would take precautions to keep any spaceport officials from snooping into that ship's cargo.

Catton reached for the phone, punched out the number of Dyelleran Spaceport, and asked to speak to the supervisor of customs inspection. Ten minutes and three sub-supervisors later, the lean face of an elderly Morilaru appeared on the screen.

"Yes?"

"Lloyd Catton speaking—of the Interworld Commission on Crime. Can you give me a list of the cargo ships due to arrive at Dyelleran tomorrow?"

"All of them?"

"I'm interested in a particular one that's probably coming in with an unregistered planet of departure. Or else it's registered as coming from Vyorn."

"Vyorn? Not very likely. Hold it—I'll check."

The screen blanked for a moment. Then the customs official reappeared. "No, no ships coming in from Vyorn tomorrow, sir. There isn't much traffic between Vyorn and Morilar, you see."

"I know," Catton said impatiently. "Are any ships landing with unregistered planets of departure?"

The official ran his eye down a list outside the field of the visual pickup. "Ah—yes. One ship, due in at eight minutes past noon. Doesn't give planet of departure, simply says it's from the Rullimon Cluster. Might be your ship from Vyorn, sir—Vyorn's in that Cluster."

Catton nodded. By law, an incoming ship did not have to register its planet of departure prior to customs inspection; it merely had to indicate the galaxy from which it came. He would have to chance it. This ship was probably the one.

"I'll be at the spaceport tomorrow to conduct a personal inspection of that ship's cargo," Catton said. "I don't want any of your men going aboard till I've looked the ship over."

"Yes, sir."

"And if I'm late, impound the ship and hold its crew for questioning. I suspect it's running contraband. I'll have further instructions for you tomorrow."

Catton left the Embassy early the next morning and had himself driven to the spaceport in an official car. The morning papers were splashed with the story of Estil Seeman's return. Her overjoyed father had released the kidnap story, but with few accompanying details. Details, thought Catton, might expose the holes in the story.

Shortly before noon Catton reached the spaceport. The ship from Vyorn would arrive in a few minutes. He went immediately to the office of Erwal Kriuin, Supervisor of Customs Inspection at the big spaceport. Kriuin looked a little surprised to see him. "Oh—Commissioner Catton. I didn't think you'd be coming out here."

"Why not? I told you yesterday I'd be here at noon to inspect that incoming cargo."

"Yes, of course, but I thought the later instructions from Commissioner Beryaal cancelled that arrangement, and—"

"*What* later instructions from Beryaal?"

The Morilaru looked bewildered. "Right after you called, he phoned me to find out about the same ship. I told him you had already made plans to inspect it, and when I said that he said never mind, that he was going to take care of the job himself. And since he's chairman of the Commission, I thought that you wouldn't be coming out here today, and—"

Catton nodded, cutting off the voluble flow. "There's been a mixup, I see. Is Beryaal here yet?"

"Yes, sir. He's on the field waiting for the ship to land."

"Which will be when?"

Kriuin glanced at a wall clock. "Six minutes, Commissioner Catton."

"Is Beryaal alone?"

"He has a group of men with him, sir. But he ordered me to keep my inspectors away from the ship until he was finished looking at it."

Catton's face darkened. No doubt the group with Beryaal was the special crew that would take the cargo of matter duplicators on to Earth. Beryaal's plan seemed simple enough: he would check the cargo to make sure all was well, supervise the changing of crews, and send the ship off again with his blessing. No mere customs inspector would dare to protest once Pouin Beryaal himself had okayed a cargo for transit.

A showdown with Beryaal was inevitable. The wily Morilaru had so thoroughly embedded himself in positions of trust that defeating him might be close to impossible. But Catton had to try. For Earth's sake.

"Get me a hand camera," Catton ordered suddenly.

Kriuin burrowed into a closet and produced one of the pistol-sized closed-circuit video cameras used in customs work. When a customs inspector went aboard a ship, he carried one of the little cameras, which he trained on any item of interest in the cargo hold. It not only broadcast the image to a special screen in the customs office, where other officials could take note of it, but also piped the image into a video taper which made a permanent record of the inspection for use in later inquiry.

Casually Catton opened the camera and detached the micro-miniaturized phosphor-coated "eye" that was the core of the instrument. He slipped the "eye" into his jacket pocket.

Kriuin said tactfully, "You understand, sir, that the instrument will not function unless the perceptor tube place—"

"Of course I realize that," Catton said irritably. He did not *want* the camera to function. He wanted to avoid creating any permanent record of the scene that would take place inside the cargo ship—but he intended that Beryaal and his men would think that such a record was being made.

A few minutes later, field warning signals began to wail. The ship was landing. An area was cleared on the field and the dull-gray ship that Catton had last seen rising from the spaceport on Vyorn now descended on a fiery tail of jet exhaust. It came to rest in the middle of its clearing. The decontaminating squad came scurrying out to swab down the landing area.

After five minutes the ship's hatch opened and the crew of eight came down the catwalk, one after another, while nine other figures walked out onto the field. Catton recognized the figure in the lead. It was the immensely tall, dominating figure of Pouin Beryaal.

Catton fretted a few impatient minutes more. Then, as Customs Supervisor Kriuin goggled in utter confusion, Catton carefully checked the charge units of his blaster, smiled at the customs official, and left the office. He trotted downstairs and out to the main approach to the field.

A Morilaru guard stared inquisitively at him. Catton flashed his Crime Commission credentials. "I'm inspecting that ship."

"Of course, sir." The guard stepped complacently aside.

The five-hundred-yard walk to the ship seemed endless. At last Catton reached the entry hatch. He climbed up, hand over hand, and hauled himself into the open lip of the freighter. Beryaal's crewmen, standing around uncertainly, frowned at Catton as he came aboard.

"What is it, Earthman?" asked a big, rough-looking Morilaru.

"I'm inspecting the cargo. Anyone want to see my credentials?"

"Inspection won't be necessary, Catton," said a familiar voice. Pouin Beryaal strode out of the shadows at the rear of the cabin. The Morilaru's brooding eyes glared daggers at Catton. "I'm handling inspection in here myself, Catton. I thought I left word at the customs office that you didn't have to bother coming aboard."

Catton smiled to mask his inner tension. "I thought I'd help you look around, Beryaal."

"I don't need any help."

The Earthman let the hand-camera become visible, projecting from his clenched left fist. He flashed it around, then centered it on Beryaal. "Surely," Catton said quietly, "you don't have any objection to letting me examine the cargo—just for the record?"

Facial muscles bunched and knotted in Beryaal's cheeks. The big Morilaru seemed to sizzle inwardly. Thanks to the camera, Beryaal was in an awkward position. If everything were being monitored and taped in the customs office, then Beryaal could not in good faith deny Catton the right to examine the cargo without subjecting himself to embarrassing inquiries later. And once Catton succeeded in filming the cargo, everything was lost.

Beryaal growled, "This is a special cargo. Put your camera away and we'll inspect it together."

"Why can't I use the camera?"

"Because this is a matter of Commission security. If you videocast this back to the customs office, it'll be whispered all over the port in ten minutes. I insist on security."

Now it was Catton's turn to sweat. Beryaal had a valid point there. But if Catton surrendered the camera, and Beryaal signalled the crew to jump him—

He had to risk it. He made an ostentatious show of clicking the camera off and putting it in his pocket.

"Come," Beryaal said. "I'll take you down to the cargo hold."

They rode down in the creaking elevator together. As it reached bottom Beryaal muttered, "You inquisitive idiot, do you think I'm going to let you get out of this ship alive?"

"Threatening a fellow Commissioner?" Catton said with false innocence. "Why, whatever for, Beryaal?"

Beryaal let his torch glint on the rows upon rows of crates stacked in the hold. Hundreds of crates, each holding a matter duplicator. Catton heard the elevator creaking behind them, on its way back up. Probably Beryaal had already given the ambush signal. The crewmen would descend, attacking him in the darkness of the cargo hold.

Beryaal chuckled. "You think there are hypnojewels in these crates, eh, Catton?"

"Not at all," the Earthman said levelly, "I wouldn't be risking my life over some hypnojewels, and you know it. You've got a thousand matter duplicators aboard this ship. Your henchman Doveril went to Vyorn and paid for them with hypnojewels—just before I killed him."

Beryaal gasped. "What—you know?"

"Yes. I know." The elevator creaked again, descending, bringing with it Beryaal's hand-picked crew. Had Beryaal trusted them with the secret, Catton wondered? That was the all-important information he needed.

The Earthman stooped, picked up the nearest crate, and ripped its seal open. Beryaal tried to interfere, but he was too late. Catton yanked off the top of the crate. Within, cushioned in layer on layer of shock-absorbent plastic, was a small, exquisitely machined device. Catton felt a chill as he looked on a matter duplicator for the first time.

"Get him," Beryaal murmured.

The Earthman straightened instantly and yanked the hand-camera from his pocket. The crewmen, armed with heavy cargo-pins, were about to charge.

"Hold it," Catton snapped. "This thing in my hand is a camera. It's sending a film back to the customs office outside. And if you touch me, it'll be valid evidence of who my murderers are."

"Don't believe him," Beryaal said coldly. "I order you to attack!"

But the crewmen continued to hang back. Catton grasped at their moment of indecision. "He's just trying to get you in trouble," the Earthman said. "He wants you to jump me with the camera going. But he doesn't care about you. You know what kind of cargo you're carrying?" He seized the matter duplicator and held it up. "You know what this is? It's a matter duplicator! You're supposed to dump them on Earth. But it's death to deal in duplicators—death on any world! And that's the stuff your boss is paying you to carry!"

Beryaal uttered a strangled cry of rage. He lashed out, knocking the camera from Catton's hand. The crewmen milled about in confusion. Evidently Beryaal had handed them some cock-and-bull story about the cargo; they had had no real idea they were carrying anything as risky as matter duplicators.

Catton went for his blaster, but Beryaal leaped, knocking the blaster skittering back behind a heap of crates. The Morilaru was panting with anger and frustration. His long spidery arms reached out to encircle Catton, to hug him tight.

The Morilani was four inches taller than Catton, but he was thin and fleshless, weighing no more than the Earthman and perhaps less. Catton's fists pummelled desperately into Beryaal's body midsection. Beryaal gasped, gave ground. His claw-tipped fingers reached for Catton's eyes. The Earthman writhed out of the way in time, charged forward, smashed Beryaal heavily back against the bulkhead.

Beryaal screamed for help. But the crewmen simply stared at the contestants without moving. Catton's fists hammered Beryaal's thin body. The Earthman reached up, seized Beryaal's throat, tightened. He crashed the Morilaru hard against the bulkhead again. Shoulder-spikes splintered. Beryaal howled.

Suddenly he broke loose. He darted into the midst of the crewmen and snatched up a fire-hatchet. He swung it down in an immense arc; Catton sidestepped, clubbed down with his fist on the back of Beryaal's head. The Morilaru dropped. Catton seized the hatchet just as Beryaal struggled to his feet and charged.

Catton swung the blade in a short chopping curve. Beryaal ran full tilt into it. Purple gouts of blood spurted from the Morilaru's chest. Beryaal plunged face-down into the pile of crates and lay there.

Catton sucked in breath and said, "Which one of you is the navigator of this ship?"

"I am," answered a lean, muscular Morilaru.

"Good. You wait here." To the others Catton said, "The rest of you get out of the ship and report to the spaceport police." Catton picked up the fallen camera, activated it by inserting the "eye," and flashed it on the crewmen. "I'm sending these men outside. Have them picked up and held," he said to the listening customs officials.

He clicked the camera off. The men sullenly herded into the elevator, rode upward to the hatch, and filed out of the ship.

Catton said to the terrified navigator, "You know how to compute an automatic-wave orbit?"

"Of course."

"Good. Get into the control room and compute an orbit that will take this ship right into the sun."

"What?"

"You heard me. Don't worry—neither of us will be aboard when the ship blasts off."

Catton shepherded the man into the control room and watched him as he set up the sunward orbit. Catton made the man run a visual check on the orbitscope. It phased out perfectly, showing a trajectory that curved in one grand sweep into Morilar's sun. "Good. Now radio the control tower for blastoff clearance," Catton commanded.

This was, he knew, the best way to resolve the situation. Destroying the evidence was justifiable when the evidence consisted of matter duplicators. The entire mission, after all, had been unofficial. And this way, at least, the duplicators would be destroyed. The deadly cargo would fall neither into Terran nor alien hands, and that was just as well. A commercial society could not endure the existence of matter duplicators.

Clearance came. "Come on," Catton ordered. "Activate the autopilot and let's get out of here."

They trotted across the field to safety while the seconds ticked away. He still had a little work to do, he thought. The detained crewmen would have to undergo a mnemonic erasure. And he would have to say goodbye to Estil and her father.

Then he could return to Earth and file his report. Present danger averted—but enemies still existed. No formal complaint would be lodged by Earth. The crisis had been solved unofficially. But with Beryaal no longer obstructing justice, it would be possible to seize subtly the illicit hypnojewel factory on Skorg; the Skorg government could not afford the galactic ill will it would risk by refusing to crack down. And, just as subtly, an espionage net would tighten around Vyorn, to prevent any further exports of matter duplicators or other dangerous contrivances. But Earth would have to remain on guard against the Beryaals and eMerikhs who plotted her downfall. Which meant plenty of future employment for Catton.

A booming roar split the silence behind him. Catton turned, shading his eyes against the fury of the rocket blast. The cargo ship rose from the field, hovered a moment, then soared upward, carrying its freight and its one dead passenger on a smooth arc toward the blazing yellow sun of Morilar. Catton smiled to himself. The mission was over.

THE END

One of Our Asteroids is Missing

CHAPTER ONE

The asteroid was just a rock, a big rock floating free in the long night of space. It had a purplish glitter to it. John Storm was seeing it against the distant backdrop of cheerless Mars. Tiredly, Storm punched out landing coordinates.

I'll go down and have a look, he thought.

There was no point passing this one up. Even though he had been out here in the asteroid belt for a year and a half, seeking and not finding, he knew it was foolish to pass up any uncharted, unclaimed asteroid. Perhaps this one would be the ore source he wanted. Perhaps.

The last one hadn't. Nor the one before that. Nor any of the others. But perhaps—

Perhaps.

He jabbed at the keys of the ship's computer. It wasn't much of a computer, wasn't much of a ship, but he couldn't afford to be choosy. At the turn of the century the Hawthorn 113 had been the finest thing in small spacecraft. But the century had turned eighteen years ago, Hawthorn had its model 127 on the market now, and Storm knew he was lucky not to get blown to bits every time he coaxed some blast from the rattletrap rocket's elderly tubes.

The asteroid glittered in his viewplate. Storm smiled grimly at it, and scratched his cheek where the stubble itched, and wondered for a moment if he'd ever get to take a bath again. Then he tapped the *Function* key, and relays clicked somewhere in the shiny nose of his ship, and impulses spurted back toward the reaction chamber, and the old Hawthorn shuddered and bucked and dipped asteroid-ward, down and forward by spacelubberly ways of thinking.

As his little ship matched orbits with the floating hunk of rock, John Storm clambered into his spacesuit and readied himself for landing. Names went through his mind like a litany. *Cesium, tantalum, lithium. Praseodymium* and *neodymium. Cesium, tantalum, lithium. Praseo.*

Light metals. Reactive metals. Rare earths. An oddball bunch of ragtag elements. A few generations ago they'd been as useless as uranium was in 1875. But not any longer. They were the elements that kept the space industry going. The cesium ion-engine, powering fifty million spacecraft, for instance. How much cesium was there on Earth? Not enough to meet that hungry demand. Tantalum and niobium, for computer elements. Where did you get five hundred pounds of niobium on a day's notice? You couldn't, that's all. Gallium for semiconductors? Rubidium? Lanthanum?

The whole vast complex of Earth's electronics industry was crying out for those obscure elements. But where could they be found? Canada's great treasurehouse of reactive metals had been mined heavily since the middle of the 20th Century. Those deposits up in Manitoba couldn't last forever, not at the present rate of consumption. There was cesium in Africa, beryllium in South America, but who knew when some cockeyed revolution would cut off the supply?

Earth needed those metals. A fortune waited for the man who found a new source.

But where? Under the Antarctic ice-shield, maybe, only Earth wasn't that desperate yet. The other place to look was space. The asteroid belt in particular.

And so a new band of '49ers went to space. They weren't looking for gold, of course. No one gave a damn about gold any more, except the jewellers and their customers. The big money was in metals with strange names.

Gallium and tantalum and cesium and lanthanum—

Hopeful prospectors went to space. John Storm was one of them.

Everybody said he was crazy to go, of course.

He was twenty-four, which made him eight years older than the 21st Century, and he had a graduate degree from Appalachia Polytech, as a mining engineer. There were plenty of jobs waiting for him. Good jobs.

Donovan, the personnel man from Universal Mining, was the first to tell him he was crazy to go. Donovan had interviewed Storm on the Appalachia campus in June of 2016, waving job offers around. He was a short, florid man with fantastic eyebrows, thin lips and a grim-set jaw, but he was kindly at heart.

"Start in August," he told Storm. "We need engineers at our installation in Tierra del Fuego. It's $16,000 base pay, plus maintenance allotments."

"Will you hold the job for me for two years?"

"Why?"

"I'm going to go prospecting," Storm told him. "If I don't get anywhere in two years, I'll come back and go to work for you. But first I want to go."

"Don't be crazy," Donovan told him bluntly. "You don't want to be a sourdough, Storm. We've got this nice neat job all ready for you."

"Will it wait two years?"

"Why throw away two years of advancement? Man with your talents, he can be making twenty grand in two years. Stock options and all the rest. Why—"

"If I find what I'm looking for, twenty grand will seem like pennies," Storm said doggedly.

Donovan's eyebrows fluttered like flags in the wind. His jowls shook in bewilderment. "You know how many guys are out there poking around the asteroids now? I don't mean corporation expeditions, I mean solos? Hundreds! You know how many find anything?"

"I mean to try."

"Half of them get killed out there, Storm. You don't want to get killed. You've got a girl, don't you?"

"What about her?"

"Marry her. You're how old? Twenty-four? What are you waiting for? We'll give you a good house to live in. Settle down, draw your paycheck, have kids. Leave the asteroids to the dopes."

Storm laughed. "Settle down in Tierra del Fuego, huh? Why not on Mars?"

"You ought to see our installation down there," Donovan said. "We've got the whole place climate-rigged. You wouldn't know you were in Patagonia. It's paradise down there. Outdoor swimming ten months a year. You take my advice, let us send you down there for a look. Just a look, and we'll pay your way back and forth. Smell the air. The perfume of the flowers. You'll love it down there. And there's plenty of room for advancement. Someone like you, with your drive, your brains, you'll be moving up all the time."

It was all very poetic, Storm thought, and all very tempting. But not for him. Not yet. First he had to look to the stars, and then he could accept the split-level home in Tierra del Fuego, the stock options, and all the rest.

"Will you hold the job for me for two years?" he asked.

"You must be out of your head," Donovan said.

Storm's friends thought so too, though they were less blunt about it. They had been all through college and graduate school with him, and they knew the career situation as well as he did. When the Universal Mining Cartel offered you a job, you took it. You didn't go helling around in the asteroids first.

"Prospecting is for crackpots," his friend Ned Lyons told him. "You know what the odds are!"

"I'm going to try it. If that makes me a crackpot, so be it."

"Be reasonable, Johnny. They're giving you a job, Liz is ready to marry you, only a lunatic would go to the asteroids, and you—"

"I'm a lunatic," Storm said. "Okay?" He leaned forward, tensely curving his thick, strong fingers. There was golden hair sprouting like fine wire on the backs of his hands. He was a big, blonde man, thick-shouldered and powerful. He liked to think he had Viking blood in him, and he was probably right. "Look," Storm said, "if I go with Universal and stick with them I can make lots of money, right? A senior mining engineer gets about forty grand, and that's not bad, is it?"

"Damned right it isn't."

"Okay. Suppose I go to the asteroids and hook onto a million dollars' worth of cesium? Invest that million at four percent and I've got the same forty grand—and my freedom. I don't have to live in Patagonia, and I don't have to jump when UMC tells me to jump. I can do independent research, write books, just loaf if I like."

"It's a gamble, Johnny."

"It's a damned big gamble. But it's worth it. Two years of my life against independence."

Of course, it was two years of someone else's life, too. There was Liz to consider, and Storm *had* considered her. They had been over it a hundred times, a thousand times, and he had probed her viewpoint until he was sure she meant it. She wanted him to go, and she would wait. Two years.

"I won't guarantee what I'll do after the two years," she told him gravely, and she could be *very* grave when she wanted to be, hazel eyes solemn as the tomb. "But I'll wait the two years. That's a promise."

"You're sure you want to?"

She smiled. "I want *you*," she said. "But I know I can't have you unless I let you go there first. Otherwise, every time you looked up at the stars—no. No. I wouldn't be able to spend the rest of my life knowing I had kept you back. Women are always trying to keep their men back, settling for the sure thing and the easy life. I won't. Go. I wish I could go with you."

"I wish you could too. But it's something I'll have to do alone."

"I know. Only ...Johnny—"

"Liz?"

"Find your treasure fast, will you? Find it right away and come home?"

"I'll see what I can do," he promised softly.

He hadn't been able to do very well. His time was nearly up, now. Part of the bargain he had made with himself was that he would stay two years to the day, no more. He didn't want to join the ranks of the aimless drifters who wandered the spaceways forever, always in search of the big strike. The sane man has to know when to give up.

Storm didn't like the idea of giving up. Somewhere out here, he knew, there was commercial-grade ore. Once there had been a planet between Mars and Jupiter, and some unimaginable catastrophe in the inconceivable past had blown that planet to flinders, and there was every reason to think that the fragments of that world—the asteroids—were rich in light metals. There had already been some remarkable strikes to prove it.

Storm's luck hadn't been very good. It was a year before he found anything worth spitting at, and even that was only a scratchy handful of lepidolite, lithium ore. Not in a commercial grade, not in a commercial quantity.

On he went, from one forlorn drifting rock to another, burrowing here, scrabbling there. Some asteroids were pure granite or basalt, chunks of mountains in orbit around each other, while others held traces of something worthwhile. Only traces. Then came the time he came across something remotely promising, a tiny asteroid that held swirls of lepidolite and pollucite and spodumene and half a dozen other interesting ores. Not enough to repay the cost of shipping to Earth, but enough to give him hope of finding something more to his needs.

Some rough computations told him the approximate part of the asteroid belt where he thought other asteroids of the same general makeup might be found. He headed there, nosing from one to the next.

Now this one. Eight miles in diameter, glinting purplish in reflected light from Mars. Storm left his tiny ship in a parking orbit, a hundred feet up, and descended by flexible titanium rope. The ship seemed to hover directly overhead, though actually it was still moving, following the asteroid's own orbital rotation exactly and so maintaining the same relative position.

Storm dropped the last five feet to the surface of the asteroid. On an asteroid so small, it wasn't a good idea actually to land your ship. The shock of blastoff would kick the asteroid a little way out of its orbit, and lead to complications that were best avoided.

He looked around. The skyline, such that it was, was jagged and unfriendly. Low hills, but sharp-edged. The stars gleamed brightly beyond the horizon. With no atmosphere, there was no twinkle, of course, and each star was like a hard jewel riveted in the firmament.

Storm began to roam, to gather his ore-samples. He was skilled enough in his trade to be capable of intuitive guesses, and wise enough not to trust them. Even so, an irrepressible feeling of excitement grew in him this time. He had felt the same sort of excitement the first time he had gathered ore samples on an asteroid, but that had only been a wild, irrational, and doomed, hope that he would be first time lucky. Now, after nearly two years of steady disappointment, the sensation of imminent success came alive in him again.

He nearly ran back to the ladder with his samples. Running, on an asteroid practically without gravity, might have been risky. It wouldn't have taken much of a push to jolt him out into space, where he could flounder forever without getting back to his ship or solid ground.

With controlled strides, he got to the ladder, and stamped his foot hard. The equal and opposite reaction sent him shooting up, feather-light, even lighter. When he was twenty feet off the ground, he reached out, grinning, and snared a loop of his ladder, and clambered quickly the rest of the way into the hatch of his ship.

He pulled off his helmet, but didn't bother with the rest of his spacesuit just then. Into the analysis hopper went the ore samples.

The verdict came soon enough.

There was ore here. Marketable ore.

The way it looked, he had a whole damned planet full of marketable ore.

Jackpot!

CHAPTER TWO

Storm was a little puzzled by the letdown, but not really surprised at all. Two years of steady disappointments had ground down his spirits, so that now, with unbelievable success his for the grasping, he had no real way to react to it. He was tired, and two years of loneliness had drained away his emotions, so all he could do was grin faintly and be mildly pleased that he would not be going home empty-handed.

I'm a millionaire, he told himself. But the idea failed to sink in.

I won my gamble, I can laugh in Donovan's fat face now.

No reaction. No tingle down the spine, no wild laughter, no whoops of glee. He found himself taking it as a matter-of-factly as though he had found a lost dime, not an asteroid chock-full of valuable minerals.

Storm shrugged and told himself that the reaction would come later. He could jubilate afterward. Right now there was work to do, and plenty of it.

He allowed himself a frugal meal—there wasn't much left on board, anyway—and then went down the ladder again, to run some tests. He needed data on the asteroid's mass and density, on its chemical makeup, on a lot of things. Oh, most of it could come later, he knew, but he wanted to find out at least approximately what he had.

Eight hours later, he knew, more or less. And the immensity of it dazed him even more. It was simply too big a find to react to emotionally at all.

The asteroid, it seemed, was a solid chunk of reactive ores. There was lepidolite here, chock-full of lithium and run through with gallium as well. There was beryl ore. There was cesium-bearing pollucite. There were half a dozen other valuable ores, formed in who knew what caldron untold billions of years before. Storm had been on field trips to Manitoba, of course, had seen the astonishing conglomeration of ores in places like Bernic Lake, the dazzling jumble of exotic metals stirred helter-skelter through the earth. Well, this was Bernic Lake all over again, he thought, uprooted and sent spinning through space!

There was no point wasting time estimating the cash value of all this. Millions? Billions? Who could tell? He was rich, that was all he knew. Or would be, as soon as he could file his claim to the incredible rock.

And that was the next order of business: filing the claim.

Mars was ninety million miles away. That was almost as great a distance as the gap between Earth and the Sun, but at the moment Mars was the closest heavenly body to John Storm. It was another seventy million miles on to Earth, at the moment, though the figures changed constantly as Mars, Earth, and this nameless asteroid continued to whirl along their respective orbits.

Mars would be John Storm's first stop. He had the orbits on his side, since Mars and the asteroid would be approaching one another all the time he was en route, while Earth would be heading the other way. When he was ready to leave Mars for Earth, Earth would be coming round the other side of her orbit, which would save him some time there. Hopping from planet to planet is a little more complex than taking a jet from New York to San Francisco. New York and San Francisco, at least, stay put.

Storm checked out the location and orbit of the asteroid, "his" asteroid, now, and reeled in his ladder and punched out fresh coordinates for Mars. There was no blaze of light as he blasted out of his parking orbit, just the invisible cloud of ions from the cesium engine. It was pleasant to think that every time a spaceship blasted off, the universe's supply of cesium diminished ever so slightly, hiking the value of the ore that he had just discovered.

Acceleration built up. Storm was in a hurry now, and he had the computer plot a maximum-velocity course. The gravity-drag bashed him back into his acceleration couch like a giant fist, but he didn't mind, because the faster a start he got, the quicker he would get to Mars, and that meant the quicker he'd get home. Home to Liz.

He was tempted to relay a message to her now. All he had to do was beam it ahead to Mars, and the communication satellite there would catch it and flick it on to Earth. "Coming home with the bacon," he could say. "Everything 100% successful!"

These days it cost $50 to beam a message from Mars to Earth. With his dwindling funds, he had been able to send word to Liz only four or five times a year, the same mixture of discouragement and affection each time. It would cost an extra $25 to relay the message from the asteroid belt to Mars.

Thriftily, he decided against it. He'd be on Mars soon enough. Liz had waited this long for news; another few days wouldn't be critical.

Then he grinned. "What the hell am I being thrifty about?" he said out loud. "I'm a multi-millionaire now!"

He began to switch the communication beam on. Then a new thought occurred: suppose someone monitored the call? Someone who knew he was a prospector, who would correctly interpret his message as word of a strike in the asteroids? He might be inviting trouble that way. Who knew what would happen? Claim-jumping, piracy—this was a pretty raw frontier, after all, 21st Century or not.

This time Storm laughed. The relay system was completely automatic. He didn't need to worry about snoopers. He would make the call, he decided, and to hell with the expense, to the deuce with suspicious little fears.

He flicked on the beam.

"To Miss Lizabeth Chase, 11735 Coolidge Lane, Greater New York 113, Appalachia, Western Hemisphere, Earth:

"Bringing home the bacon, baby. Get ready for a celebration.

"Johnny.

"End of message."

He listened to the playback, nodded, touched the *Transmit* button. Off went the message toward the Mars communication satellite. It would take about four minutes to get there, Storm knew. Allow some time for a backlog of transmissions, and he could figure that within an hour the message would be on tape at one of the communication satellites orbiting Earth. Liz would have it tomorrow.

The speed of light, John Storm thought, was a wonderful thing.

He was travelling at a somewhat slower speed, unfortunately. But he'd get there, too, not quite as fast as the message. He was on his way.

Mars gleamed reddish-brown in the very black sky. The little ship surged forward, and Storm waited, and slowly the importance of his find seeped into his mind and he accepted it and began quietly to laugh with glee.

"I want to register a mining claim," Storm said.

"Use the machine," the clerk told him, and pointed.

Storm nodded and made his way to the end of the hall. On Mars, there was no room for dead weight. One clerical worker and a bunch of machines handled the work that a hundred human beings would have done on Earth.

He confronted the machine. It wanted a filing fee, first of all. Storm put a two-dollar piece in the slot, and the machine hummed and a green light flashed and a lucite panel came sliding forward. Under the panel was a printed form. Glowing instructions told Storm to use the stylus to file his claim. *Please Print*, he was advised.

Storm printed. He took more care than on any other document he could remember filling out, and in his twenty-six years he had filled out plenty. He put down his name, and his various identification numbers, and the nature of his claim, and the catalog number of his asteroid, and its orbit designation, and about fifty other things.

There, he thought.

He studied the filled-in form, nodded in approval, and punched a button. A yellow light flashed, the panel retracted, and an instant later a stamped copy of his claim form came rattling out on a tray. Storm jerked it free.

The asteroid wasn't his, yet. By the Space Act of 1997, it was possible for individuals to claim mining rights on natural orbiting bodies of less than planetary mass, with various provisos. The claiming individual had to begin mining operations within six months, or lose his claim; that was to prevent people from running around randomly claiming everything in sight. There were limitations on the number of claims any one individual (or corporation) could make. And, since space was deemed to be the property of the human race in general, it was necessary to agree to pay a whopping royalty to the United Nations in return for a grant of mining privileges.

What he had just done was file a preliminary claim. By tight-beam relay, the claim would be forwarded to the master computer on Earth. If all went well, a formal mining grant would be forthcoming in a month or two. His claim would be checked out, first, and a certain amount of red tape was inevitable. But at least he had seen to it that no one else could claim the billion-dollar asteroid.

Unless, he thought, someone had already claimed it. It was listed on his charts as unclaimed, but the charts were never up to date. For all he knew, someone else had been there two weeks ahead of him, and his claim was already being processed.

It wasn't anything Storm liked to think about. He brushed the idea from his mind, carefully put his copy of the claim form away, and left the Hall of Records.

Marsville still had a raw, unfinished look. Almost fifty years had passed since the first expedition of humans had set foot on Mars, and the colony itself was twenty years old. It sprawled haphazardly under a series of interlinked geodesic domes, and the air, while thin, tasted almost like Earth's to one who had not breathed Earth air for a while. Most of Marsville was built of corrugated tin shacks. Architecture would have to wait a while longer.

Storm's first call, after the all-important business of staking his claim, was Marsville Spaceport.

"When's the next liner for Earth?" he asked.

"Three days."

"Martian days?"

"You bet," was the unsmiling answer. "We got no other kind of days around here, pal."

"Got room for another passenger?"

"I suppose we might. Cash on the line, though. You can't get home on credit."

"Don't worry," Storm told him. "I bought my ticket before I left Earth. Here."

He presented the wrinkled document. The colonist looked at him coldly but with respect.

"Smart one, eh? Not one out of ten buys himself a round-trip ticket."

"I did," Storm said quietly.

"Prospector?"

"Yes."

"Lost your shirt, eh?"

Storm shrugged. "It wasn't so bad."

The colonist chuckled. "I see them come, and I see them go. Young ones and not so young. A bunch of damn fools. No offense meant, y'understand."

"Of course not," Storm said. "Why'd *you* come to Mars?"

Storm was favored with a yellow-toothed grin. "It was a place to go, something to do. Ten thousand people up here and seven billion down there. I figured I had a better chance here. Not to get rich. I didn't come here to get rich, and I didn't. Just to live."

"You like it here?"

"I bought a one-way ticket, and I'm not sorry." The cold eyes centered on Storm's. "I guess you want to sell your ship, eh?"

"I guess I do."

"Fellow over there, he'll give you the best deal. Tell him Jerry Burke sent you. He won't rob you."

Storm pocketed his validated ticket and crossed over to see the dealer in used ships. It didn't pay to try to pilot a one-man or two-man ship from Earth to Mars or back again. It was a whole lot cheaper to take a commercial space-liner out to Mars, buy an old heap of a used two-manner, and sell it again after exploring the asteroid belt.

Half an hour of haggling and Storm had sold his ship. All in all, he was pleased with the deal. He had paid twenty thousand for it, and sold it for fifteen. That was only two and a half thousand a year for the use of the ship, not bad at all. And a tax deduction, too, for the depreciation. He smiled at that. In the bracket he was going to be in, tax deductions would be important!

But now he was stuck in Marsville for three days—three *Martian* days, the colonist had told him with a kind of provincial arrogance. Each Martian hour was only a minute and a half longer than an Earth hour, but oh, how fussy they were about their extra 37 minutes a day!

He took a look around town. He saw the shacks, and the hopefully marked-out places where the civic buildings would rise, and the tool dumps and all the rest. It was only ten years since women had been allowed to settle here, making Marsville a true colony. The first Mars-baby was six years old—the first one that had survived babyhood, anyway.

Six *Earth* years, of course. Storm smiled at that. The Martian year was 1.88 Earth years long, so of course the first Mars-baby was not yet four years old, Mars-fashion. Well, he couldn't object. It was their planet, after all.

There were no real native Martians. Nothing lived in the wind-swept red deserts except stunted, scrubby little plants and a few animals somewhat less impressive than mice. The "Martians" were the Earth-born colonists. Storm wondered what Mars would be like a couple of generations from now, when it began to diverge from the mother world. It would be interesting to watch, he thought.

But right now Mars held no fascination for him at all. He was itching to get home. There was no help for it, though. Here he was, marooned on Mars, and there he stayed, three solid Martian days, until the big Earthbound liner was ready to leave.

It could have been worse, he figured. The liner made only one round trip a month. He had showed up almost at the best possible time.

Almost. And finally, with a roar and a blaze, the ship broke free of Mars' feeble grasp, and carried John Storm and a hundred other passengers back to the mother world.

CHAPTER THREE

The Hall of Records in Greater New York was a good deal more imposing than its counterpart on Mars. It was a towering skyscraper on the banks of the Hudson, the tallest building in the suburb of Nyack. John Storm had lost no time getting there. The spaceport was another hundred miles to the north, just beyond the last outlying fringes of the city. Storm had phoned Liz to let her know he was home, and they had agreed to meet at the Hall of Records.

"Is it true?" she had kept asking. "Did you really find something out there?"

"I really did," he said. "Look, it's too big to tell you about this way. Come meet me, and I'll give you the whole story."

She hadn't arrived yet. Storm waited none too patiently on an endless line on the thirtieth floor of the Hall of Records, moving up a painful notch at a time. His muscles were no longer adjusted to Earth gravity, and he felt his body sagging against the unaccustomed pull. The space liner had had artificial Earth grav, and when he stepped aboard it felt at first as though there were magnets on the soles of his shoes.

He reached the front of the line, finally. There were no machines here, not with seven billion Earthmen needing jobs. A thin, bespectacled, harried-looking face peered from behind the wire cage at Storm.

"Validation of mining claim," Storm said. He slipped the copy of the form he had filled out on Mars through the wicket. "Would you check that, please?"

"Certainly, sir." Vague, gray noises. A pallid hand took the form, laid it face down on a glowing scanner plate. Storm tapped his fingertips on the counter. This was the moment he had been losing sleep over for days. His application was being scanned, somewhere in the depths of the vast computer that handled mining claims. Suppose his claim was rejected, for some reason or other? Suppose someone else had filed a prior claim on the asteroid? Suppose—

The clerk was frowning. A strip of tape came clicking out of the machine. Storm could not read the words on it.

"I'm sorry, sir," the clerk was saying. "There's no record of any such claim having been made on Mars."

The quiet, impersonal words hit Storm like a sledgehammer in the teeth.

"*What?* What did you say?"

"No record of this claim being filed on Mars."

"That's impossible!" Storm blurted. "Look, here's the duplicate? It's been stamped, hasn't it? That means the claim was recorded and transmitted to Earth!"

"I'm sorry, sir. The computer says it hasn't."

"Hasn't been transmitted?"

"Hasn't been filed, sir. I'm very sorry. Next, please?"

"Hold it!" Storm bellowed, and heard people muttering angrily behind him on line. His hands trembled and his face grew red. He had been prepared for almost any eventuality, but not something like this. "You mean to tell me that the claim filed got lost on way to Earth?"

"No, sir. Claims never get lost. The transmittal process is automatic and failure-proof. If the claim was filed at all on Mars, there'll be a record of it in the files here. No record, no claim. I'm very sorry, sir. Would you please move along, now?"

"But what about this copy I've got here? It's got a claim number on it! Can't you check and—"

"I *have* checked, sir." The wan figure behind the counter looked at Storm reproachfully, almost apologetically, and tapped a bell. It tinkled gently. Storm turned, half expecting to be collared by guards and roughly shown the gate. Instead, a slick, supervisory-looking woman appeared. She seemed young, thirty at the outside, but Storm saw the brittle, thorny glint in her eye and knew she was going to mean just more trouble for him.

"Yes?" she asked. "Is there any difficulty?"

"There sure is," Storm said. "I'm trying to check on this mining claim. The fellow here buzzed the computer, and got told no claim was ever filed."

"But you filed one?"

"Of course I did! Here's the slip," Storm said. He felt the forces of bureaucracy gathering round him, and there was a tightness at his throat. "There's been some kind of error in the computer, that's all. Or maybe the chap there punched the wrong button. Here. Take a look."

She glanced at Storm's document and flashed a smile as warm as a glacier's core. "Of course, Mr. ...ah ...Storm. If you'll come with me, we'll investigate. We can't settle the matter right out here in the hall, you know."

"Where are we going?"

"Only to my office, Mr. Storm. Just across the hall."

"I'm supposed to meet someone here. A young woman. I told her I'd be—"

"It'll take only a moment or two, Mr. Storm. Please. Come with me."

Feeling very much as though they were humoring him, as though they regarded him as some kind of crank or perhaps a criminal, Storm followed her. Her office was small, austerely furnished, depressing.

She waved him into a seat in front of her desk. Storm began to feel he was applying for a loan at a bank, facing a particularly flinty vice-president. The placard on her desk told him that she was Miss Vyzinski. Was Miss Vyzinski in charge of the crackpot detail, he wondered?

She studied his claim sheet for a moment. "It looks perfectly genuine," she said.

"It ought to. It is."

"Well, we'll soon have some idea. Suppose we begin by running a recheck."

"Suppose we do," Storm said grimly.

Behind her desk was a machine very much like the one the clerk had used. Motionless, hardly even breathing, Storm watched her place his claim sheet over the glowing scanner plate. A long moment ticked by, and then a ribbon of tape extruded itself from the machine. This time Storm was able to read what it said. It said 324.

"What does that mean?" Storm asked.

Miss Vyzinski looked at him sternly. "It means, I'm afraid, that no such claim has been recorded."

"But—"

"One moment," she said. "I'll run some further checks. The first thing to do is see if your claim has somehow been misfiled. It's a one-in-a-billion possibility, but, even so—"

"It's worth checking," Storm said, dry-throated.

She punched something out on a keyboard, and put the claim sheet on the scanner again. The machine emitted a vague humming sound. While they waited, she said, as though to soothe him, "It once happened that a claim less than six months old went to the storage drum. That's where the older claims go. There's at least a finite chance that yours—"

Another strip of tape emerged from the machine. Miss Vyzinski studied it.

"No?" Storm asked.

"No. Your claim's not in current, and it's not in dead storage, and it's not in pending. That means it's not anywhere, Mr. Storm."

"But ...how—?"

"Let's attack it from another angle," she said crisply.

"There's a claim number on this paper, right? Very well. Let's run a check and see what's entered for this claim number, shall we? I can get a facsim."

"Go ahead," Storm said hollowly. He looked down at the carpeted floor. Miss Vyzinski began efficiently to push buttons and tap keys, and Storm waited, trying to keep calm in the face of this nonsense.

It took three or four minutes, this time. Storm wondered if Liz had arrived by now. She might be outside in the main hall, looking for him. Well, she had waited so long that another few minutes wouldn't matter. He had to get this mess cleared up before he left Miss Vyzinski's office.

A yellow facsim sheet came popping out of the slot. Storm had to restrain himself from lunging across the desk and seizing it. Miss Vyzinski's manicured fingers tugged it free.

"It's my claim, isn't it?" Storm said.

She was glancing from Storm's paper to the new one, and frowning furiously now. "No," she said in an odd voice. "No. It isn't."

"No?"

"Here. Look for yourself!"

She passed the two sheets over to him. Storm studied them in rising bewilderment. They were identical in every way, the same form even to the imprinted identifying number, six digits and four letters, in the upper left hand corner. Both had been filed from the office on Mars, on the same day. Even the time-stamp was the same, down to the last tenth of a second.

The only thing wrong was that the claim on record wasn't his. The sheet had been filled out in a different hand-writing, by someone named Richard F. McDermott, and he had filed a claim on an asteroid within Mars' orbit, nowhere near Storm's.

"I don't get it," Storm said. "Are you trying to tell me that two different people filed two different claims on the same machine at the same time?"

"I'm not trying to tell you anything, Mr. Storm. I'm simply showing you what the computer has on file. If you press me to interpret the evidence, I'd have to say that you're attempting some kind of game. What you've got here looks like a perfectly valid claim form, only it can't possibly be one. It's some kind of clever imitation, I'd say. But I certainly don't understand what you hoped to gain by presenting it, since this sheet itself is worthless unless there's an original claim on file, and quite clearly there is not."

Storm stared at her in silence for a long moment. He felt as though he were strangling in red tape. He filled his lungs with air, but the sensation of congestion remained.

"All right," he said finally. "I don't understand any of this, but let's just skip it. Forget the whole thing. I'll pretend that I never filed my claim at all, which is what you're trying to tell me. Okay?"

"Very well. But—"

He cut her off. "Now, It's start all over again. I've been prospecting out in space and I've found something I want to claim. Since the machinery got fouled up the first time, I'll file a brand new claim. Is that permissible?"

"Of course."

"I'd like to file it in your presence, if I may. So that I'll have a witness this time, in case the computer loses the record again."

Her grin was frosty. "I assure you everything will go smoothly this time. If you'd really like to file a new claim, please come with me."

She led him to an adjoining office. There was a different sort of machine in there, the twin of the one he claimed to have used on Mars. She stood by while Storm laboriously copied onto a new form everything he had written on the first one.

When he had finished, she pressed the actuating button for him. "In just a moment," she said, "your claim will be recorded, and you'll get your duplicate copy. I'll countersign it, just to be certain. After that, it'll simply be a matter of time before your claim can be processed, and—"

She stopped. His claim sheet had come popping out of the machine and stamped across it in big red characters were the numbers 217 and the letters XX.

"What now?" he asked.

She looked at him in an indescribably peculiar way. "Mr. Storm, when was the last time you were on Earth?"

"About two years ago. Why?"

"Are you sure you copied your identifying numbers properly onto the claim sheet?"

"Of course I'm sure."

"Would you let me see your identity cards?"

"Suppose you tell me what this is all—"

"Your identity cards. Please."

There was no refusing the schoolmarmish command. Numbly, Storm surrendered his documents. She compared them with the things he had written on the claim.

"Yes," she said. "Yes, the numbers are the same. But—"

"But what?"

"Your claim was returned in Category 217-XX. Which means that there's no record of you in the computer."

"No record of me?" he repeated blankly.

"That's right," she said, watching him more closely than ever. "No one named John Storm who matches these particular identity numbers. Mr. Storm, if that's your name, I can't imagine what sort of prank you think you're pulling, but we don't have time for jokes here. To come in with a set of fraudulent documents, to turn the place topsy-turvy having us check the files for a pseudonym's phantom claim."

"Give me my papers!" Storm said in a strangled voice.

He grabbed them from her. Her eyes flared. "Where are you going, Mr. Storm? We'll have to check on these papers! Such clever forgeries will have to be—"

He strode quickly toward the door. The choking sensation grew almost overpowering. He couldn't remain in her stifling presence another instant.

Storm emerged in the crowded main hall. Half dazed, he came to a halt, stared around like an elephant at bay.

"Johnny! Johnny, there you are at last!"

It was Liz. She saw him, and came running toward him, her shoes clattering on the stone floor, her face aglow, her eyes shining with tears of reunion.

"Johnny!"

Storm didn't budge. She came running up, her arms wide as though to embrace him. But when she was still a few yards away she stopped and looked up at him.

"Johnny, what's the matter?" she said. "Your face ...you look so strange."

"I don't exist," he said in a hoarse, stupefied voice. "They just told me I don't exist!"

CHAPTER FOUR

It took her a couple of minutes to get him calmed down, and a couple of minutes more before he could communicate to her the nature of the trouble. She looked at him blankly, uncomprehendingly.

"No record of you, Johnny?"

"That's what the witch in there keeps telling me."

"But that's impossible!"

"Try to tell her that," Storm said.

"Let's go in to see her."

Storm nodded. He smiled at Liz, touched her hand briefly. Her fingers were cold. She looked thinner than he remembered her, and older, though not very old. He took his hand from hers. He was starting not to believe in the fact of his own existence himself now, and he shrank back from the contact with her.

Miss Vyzinski was waiting.

"So you've come back," she said triumphantly.

Storm nodded. "Let's get to the bottom of this thing."

Liz said, "I'll vouch for him. His name's John Storm, and I've known him for years. He—"

"The computer doesn't seem to have any record of him," Miss Vyzinski said. "At least, not under that name, not under those numbers."

"But it is my name," Storm said doggedly. "I know it. And those are my identity numbers. Look, the computer records can slip up once in a while. The scanners aren't infallible."

"We like to think they are," Miss Vyzinski said. "But we'll check. We'll see, Mr. Storm."

She closed her office door and made some calls, and the bureaucrats began to gather. In a few minutes there were half a dozen worried, baffled-looking officials in the room, discussing the case in a low murmur.

Storm watched tensely. He was as baffled as they were, but much more worried. A man without an official existence cannot fight to defend a mining claim. A man without an official existence is like a ghost. Can a ghost get a check cashed? Can a ghost rent an apartment? Can a ghost take a job?

With Earth crowded and getting more crowded every second, the only way to keep track of people was by computer. Everyone had a number, assigned at birth, and everyone acquired other numbers as he went along. You were the aggregate of your numbers. Idiots and cretins had numbers. Convicts had numbers. Babies who died in birth had numbers. Everyone had numbers.

Everyone but John Storm.

He was outside the system. Alone among Earth's swarming billions, he had no number. It made no sense, and small wonder the bureaucrats looked pale and worried, for the stability of their entire system was threatened by the existence of this one anomalous individual.

A round-faced, melancholy-looking man in late middle age confronted Storm and said, "My name is Dawes. I'm the regional supervisor. May I see your documents, please?"

Storm handed them over. Another conference began. He watched, impassively, a muscle flicking in his cheek.

Liz whispered, "Johnny, what did you find out there?"

"An asteroid full of goodies. Eight miles in diameter, and the whole blasted thing commercial-grade ore."

"Wonderful!"

"Not if I can't claim it," he said darkly.

Dawes came over. "According to these papers," he said, "you were born on 6 May 1992. Is that right?"

"Right."

"We're running a check on births for the whole year 1992. For good measure we're checking '91 and '93."

"Save your time. I was born in '92."

Dawes shrugged. "We're also checking the records of your education. We're checking your residential history. We're checking your tax file. If nothing checks—"

"*What* if nothing checks?" Storm asked tightly.

"I don't know," Dawes said. "I simply don't know, Mr. Storm. I don't know at all."

They had their answer in a dozen minutes.

Nothing checked.

So far as the computer banks knew, he had never been born, had never gone to school, had never occupied a residential unit, had never been tallied in a census, had never paid a cent in tax to any revenue agency. He had never been inside a hospital, never been vaccinated, never voted.

"*You* explain it," Storm said.

Dawes sputtered and fussed. "There are two possible explanations," he said limply. "One is improbable and the other is inconceivable. The improbable one is that the computer somehow dropped a stitch and accidentally erased your entire record. The inconceivable one is that you never *had* a record—that you're some sort of being from another world, some creature of fantasy trying to bluff his way into official existence on Earth."

Storm laughed coldly. "You're overlooking the most likely explanation of all, Mr. Dawes."

"Which is?"

"That my records have been tampered with. That someone managed to obliterate me entirely."

"That's impossible! The records are tamper-proof!"

"Are they? Then what happened to mine?"

Dawes began to look greenish. "Mr. Storm, I fail to see why anyone should want to tamper with—"

"Look," Storm said, "I went out to the asteroids and I made a valuable find. Now I come home to sew up my claim and I find the claim's been erased from the computer, and so have I. I'm entitled to suspect something fishy. I *know* I'm not a being from another planet, for God's sake. I'm a human being and until yesterday I could prove it."

"And you think someone is trying to cut you out of this claim, Mr. Storm?"

"It's the only possible answer."

"Is it widely known that you were successful in space?"

Storm shook his head. "I didn't tell a soul. I sent a message to Miss Chase here, but it wasn't very specific. And it went by automatic beam, anyway. But someone might have found out. Someone on Mars, where I filed my claim. I don't know. All I know is I'm a rich man if I can get my claim validated."

"I understand, Mr. Storm. But—"

"Look here, I want to file that claim so that it sticks, Dawes. We can worry about my identity records later. The claim is vital."

"I'm sorry. Only a person with official existence can file a claim, Mr. Storm. So far as the computer is concerned, you don't exist. It can't accept any document concerning you."

"But the asteroid—"

"I'm terribly sorry. It's getting late, don't you see? If you'll come back tomorrow, we'll try to get to the bottom of this. We'll have the East Coast supervisors here and we'll all try to work things out."

"And if someone else claims my asteroid overnight?"

"There's nothing I can do for you tonight, Mr. Storm. Nothing. Absolutely nothing."

A ghost has a hard time of it in Greater New York, John Storm found out that night. He had only five dollars in actual currency on him, and the rest in travellers' checks. But part of the check-cashing process is a split-second computer call to validate signature and number. Storm didn't even try to cash his checks. He borrowed ten dollars from Liz, and hoped it would see him through until he was real again.

There was no place he could stay for the night, either. Not legally. There was no room at the inn for a man without a number.

"I wish I could bring you home, darling," Liz told him. "But Helene would be awfully startled. My roommate. We've only got one little room to begin with, and—"

"I'll manage. Let's hunt up one of my pals from school. Ned Lyons, or someone. I'll sleep on the floor if I have to."

They found a cafeteria and had a dismal little snack, and then began combing the phone directories. Storm found nobody he knew listed. *Of course,* he thought. *They're all of in Tierra del Fuego working for Universal Mining.*

Two years had distributed his classmates all over the world, it seemed. Storm felt more forlorn than ever. It was a lucky thing Liz had still been around to greet him, he thought. Otherwise he'd have been completely alone. He could cope with a couple of years of total solitude in the asteroid belt, but not in Greater New York, where you were ever so much more thoroughly *alone* when you were alone.

Liz said, "I'll find a place for you to stay."

"Where?"

"There's this fellow Helene sees. He'll put you up. I know he will."

Two phone calls and it was arranged. Storm had a roof for his head, at least. That was some small comfort.

"Where can we go to eat?" Liz asked. "Some place fancy. To celebrate your return."

"I don't feel much like celebrating."

"Cheer up! We'll get this stupid business cleared up in the morning. And then you'll claim your asteroid, and you'll be rich and famous, and all this trouble will seem like a lot of nonsense. Where is the asteroid? Show me!"

He looked up. City glow and city haze blotted out the stars. Squinting, Storm searched for the red dot of Mars, but failed to find it. "I don't know," he said wearily. He flung a hand at the stars. "Somewhere out there. Somewhere. It's just a little hunk of rock."

"*Your* hunk of rock, Johnny."

"I can't be sure of that, even."

She looked at him sharply. "Johnny, are you *sure* you didn't tell anyone what you found?"

"Sure I'm sure." He took her hand in his, squeezed it lightly, and managed a faint smile. Tension racked him, and the smile was a costly effort of will. They were after him, he thought, and he didn't even know who they were. They had blotted out his claim. They had obliterated his records. They were going to steal his asteroid. *They*—

Storm shook his head and tried to brush the irrational thoughts away. Like scruffling things with claws, they came crawling back into his brain. He took a deep breath.

"Let's just walk," he said. "I haven't seen a city in two years. We'll walk, and then we'll eat somewhere, and then we'll take in a show. Or something."

"Whatever you'd like to do," Liz said. "It's *your* homecoming, after all."

They walked, first. It was good to be walking down a city street again, good to be seeing lights and activity and people, the overhead glow of a commuter-copter and the sour drone of a Europe-bound strato-rocket. It was good to feel the honest tug of Earth's gravity again, and the warmth of Liz at his side, and good to be able to breathe real air out under the open sky. The noise of the city, the filth, the crowdedness—all these were good to have again, after the silent emptiness up there.

But the bitterness and the tension kept returning to puncture his tranquility. All about him were people, millions, billions of people, and all of them, the humblest, the dirtiest, the ugliest of the lot had a number, had official reality.

But not John Storm.

He was maimed by the loss of his identity the way another person would be maimed by the loss of his limbs. Without identity numbers, he could not file or press his claim to the asteroid. So long as the asteroid remained up for grabs, his whole future was uncertain.

He resented the element of irrationality that had entered his life. It was one thing to gamble on making a lucky spin of the dice; he had taken that gamble, the dice had fallen his way, and luck had been his in the asteroids. But then to come home and find that the rules of the game have surreptitiously been changed by an unseen hand, that the table is gone and the dice are now round, that his luck has arbitrarily been cancelled out—no, it made no sense, it was too much to accept.

"Johnny?"

"Yes?"

"Stop thinking about it!"

"I wish I could."

"Look up. Up at the stars. It's up there, Johnny. Your asteroid."

"I don't see anything but smoke and haze," he said.

"It's there, and it's still yours."

"No," Storm said. "They're taking it away from me. And I don't even know who they are!"

Liz began to say something, halted, started again. "There's a restaurant," she said. "I'm starved!"

"So am I," Storm lied. "Let's eat."

They ate. It was a so-called "Martian" restaurant, and Liz told him that this sort of place had become very popular in the last year. The decor was imitation Mars, with murals of the red deserts. And the menu included a couple of "genuine Martian specialties." There was a sketch of Marsville on the menu cover, but it was a Marsville of some ideal future.

Storm didn't tell Liz about the tin shacks of Marsville, or about the slop that passed for food on that rugged planet. He let the illusion remain unbroken, and ate his food with as much enjoyment as he could muster, and paid the inflated check, and they left.

Liz dragged him off to a solly show next, a tri-dim that had opened only the week before. They stood in line for twenty minutes to get into the theater. The show was a comedy of some sort, Storm gathered. But he watched the realistic three-dimensional figures capering around the stage as though from a million miles away. He was totally detached, and the plot made no sense to him, and the jokes rang hollowly.

Maybe they're right, he thought. *Maybe I am some kind of creature from another world. I'm sure not part of this one right now.*

He saw Liz home, near midnight. Helene was there, and Helene's friend, who turned out to be some sort of chemist for a large drug corporation. The three of them made a futile attempt to draw Storm into a conversation about his experiences in the asteroid belt, but he was sullen and uncommunicative, and they soon let the talk peter out.

"He's tired," Liz explained. "He just landed from Mars today, you know. And he's had a long day."

They accepted that, and Storm left with Helene's friend, who was going to put him up on a day-bed.

Liz said, "Meet me here in the morning. I'll go up to Nyack with you. For moral support."

Storm smiled thinly. He knew he'd need whatever support he could get. He had a big job ahead of him, tomorrow. He had to prove he was real.

CHAPTER FIVE

The Grand Panjandrums of the Records Office had assembled in full force to deal with the perplexing case of John Storm. Storm noted with some pleasure that Miss Vyzinski was not among them. She was strictly lower echelon. This was a matter for Dawes and his bosses to decide.

Storm summoned his flagging energies. He was bone-tired. He hadn't had much sleep on the day-bed, and the crushing commuter ride virtually from one end of Greater New York to the other had left him drained. He squared his shoulders and stared them down and said, "Well? What's your verdict? Do I exist or don't I?"

Dawes crinkled his lips testily. "We don't question your existence, Mr. Storm. Obviously you exist. What troubles us is the absence of your records."

"Unprecedented," someone thin and angular muttered farther down the conference table.

"Intolerably confusing," said someone chubby and pink-faced.

Dawes said, "There is a prescribed procedure for entering in the records someone who has not previously been recorded. As, for example, the people on that Pacific island a few years back, you may remember. But to re-enter someone who is so positive he was once listed—"

"I have my papers," Storm said. "Are you going to tell me they're all forgeries?"

Pink-faced and chubby said, "We've given your documents laboratory tests. They're genuine, all right. Or else the cleverest fakes that ever were faked."

Storm drew a deep breath. "Give me the benefit of the doubt. Admit that they're real."

Thin and angular said, "But in that case, why don't they have correlatives in the computer files?"

With great patience Storm said, "Could it possibly be that my records were carefully and intentionally erased from the master file?"

"Such a thing is unheard of!" Thin and angular protested.

"It seems to me we may be hearing of it now," Storm said. "It isn't impossible, is it? Clerks can be bribed. It isn't hard to delete something from a computer's files. Entries aren't etched with acid. Data can be released. It's just a matter of punching the erasure keys, and—"

The bureaucrats exchanged glances. Storm began to realize that these people were frightened. A great yawning hole had appeared in the airtight structure of their system, a hole wide enough to chuck a computer through, and they couldn't understand what had happened. Storm wasn't the only one who hadn't slept soundly last night.

Somebody was saying, "We'll have to devise some new procedure for re-entering him."

"But the documents—"

"Real. Unquestionably real."

"And the claim?" Storm said. "My mining claim? Suppose someone else has filed a claim on the same asteroid while all this haggling has been going on?"

"That'll have to be investigated," Dawes told him.

"So you're willing to believe I was telling the truth?" Storm asked, a little dazzled by the prospect of cutting through the tangle.

Dawes shrugged. "There's clearly been something irregular done here. In some cases other people have been shifted into your position, but not consistently. The job wasn't perfect. For example, the records of your university show a graduating class of 1132, but we could only find 1131 names, and yours was missing."

"You see?" Storm cried triumphantly. "That's what I was telling you! There was bribery involved!"

"Let's not say too much, Dawes," came a warning word from pink-and-chubby. Storm got the impression that pink-and-chubby was a good deal less affable than he looked. "We should be able to work something out for Mr. Storm."

Something was worked out for Mr. Storm.

It took half the day. Storm cooled his heels in an anteroom, making fitful conversation with Liz, staring at newsfax sheets without really reading them, and pacing the corridors. At length an emissary appeared. It was good old Miss Vyzinski; the troublesome matter had obviously worked itself back down to the lower echelons from the administrative levels.

"We're issuing you a new identity card," Miss Vyzinski told him crisply. "You'll have the same numbers as before, but the asterisks will indicate a re-issue. We intend to do everything in our power to discover how such an error could have taken place."

"And my mining claim," Storm said. "What about that?"

"Well, I'm afraid you'll have to file it all over again, as soon as we've processed your re-entry. It shouldn't take more than another hour to complete the processing, and then you can enter your claim once again."

"But it's more than a month since I originally filed it," Storm said. "What if someone else has claimed it since my first filing? Who's got title?"

Miss Vyzinski looked disturbed. "That would be a matter for decision on a higher level, if—"

"All right. All right. I'm sorry I asked."

Miss Vyzinski disappeared within. Storm turned to Liz, who smiled at him.

"How can you be so cheerful?" he asked. "Here I am, fighting for my very identity, and—"

"They're giving you your identity back, aren't they?"

"They're doing it grudgingly. They would have been much happier if I had dropped dead over night."

"That isn't so," Liz said with mock solemnity. "They would have had to bury you, and deduct you from the population records. But how could they deduct someone who wasn't on the records to begin with? They'd have had a worse headache if—"

"I suppose," Storm said. "Meanwhile *I'm* the one with the headache. Why has all this happened? Why couldn't I have just come back home and found that my claim had been validated? I didn't need all this. It's hard enough to go roaming the asteroids in a rickety tin bucket, without coming home to this kind of nonsense."

"The nonsense will all be over soon," Liz said soothingly. "You'll have your numbers again, darling, and you'll have your claim, and everything will be all right."

Storm subsided. He was vaguely aware that she was speaking to him as one might to a child, but he decided he deserved it. He was badly overwound, tight as a drum. Fatigue and strain and tension were doing this to him. But she was right: it would all be cleared up soon. And, being realistic about it, the odds were that nobody had stumbled across his asteroid. There was an infinity of asteroids up there, and it would take decades to explore them all.

On the other hand, though, who had pulled this monkey business with his records? It hadn't simply been a joke. Someone was dead level interested in obliterating his identity, and that could very well have some connection with his mining claim. It wasn't a pleasant thought. He sat back, and impatiently riffled through the newsfax, and looked at the stock market quotations with great show of fascination, though he had never owned a share of anything in his life, and waited, and fidgeted, and waited some more, and at last Miss Vyzinski appeared with a sheaf of new-minted documents in her hand and a gleaming professional smile on her face.

"Congratulations," he said out loud to himself. "You're a person again, Johnny."

They sped back toward the heart of the city. Storm said little. He had been through the mill, and felt the effects. Every nerve in his body cried out for relief. But there would be no real relief, he knew, until the mining claim was safely nailed down for keeps.

Was it worth it, he wondered?

Had it been worth two years of hell, worth mortgaging himself to the hilt, worth this latest confusion? Here he was, shadowboxing with unseen antagonists, and he still wasn't sure whether or not what he had found was his.

How much simpler it would have been, he thought, to say yes to Donovan, to take the job and forget about pie in the sky. He and Liz would have been married now, perhaps there'd be a baby on the way, he'd have money in the bank. Instead, he was deep in debt, tired beyond all endurance, and not at all certain of anything.

But then he thought of his asteroid, and the freedom it promised. His own laboratory somewhere, and endless leisure, and complete independence from pressures, commercial and otherwise. Nobody would transfer him from continent to continent like a hapless pawn. Nobody would demand obedient responses to foolish assignments. He'd be his own master in every way.

If. If. If—

He and Liz rode upward out of the tube, and emerged on street level. "I'll go over to Bud's and pick up my things," Storm said. "Then I'll rent a room, now that I'm official again." He laughed. "You know something? We couldn't even have been married without those papers! It's against the law to marry a non-person, I imagine."

Liz looked at him slyly. "Oh? Are we getting married?"

"It seemed like a good idea to me."

"It seemed like one to me, too," Liz said. "Two years ago."

"How about now?"

"I've got to think about it," she said. "I've got to evaluate the situation. After all, a person can change a lot in two years. How do I know I still love you?"

"Pretend you do."

"That wouldn't be right, would it?" She began to giggle. "Oh, you big silly, I've been waiting so long! But we can apply for the license today."

"No," Storm said. "I've had enough bureaucracy for one day. I'd crack up completely if I had to fill out any more forms. We'll apply tomorrow. We can—*hey!*"

He whirled suddenly. A car had come rimming around the corner, a black, snubnosed limousine on manual drive. Some fuzzy intuition sent Storm into a frenzy of activity as the car angled toward their side of the street.

"Johnny, what—"

He grabbed Liz and hurled her against the door of the nearest building. The air-field broke and she went tumbling inside, sprawling down out of sight. A moment later Storm himself leaped through the doorway, felt the faint tingle of ozone in his nostrils as he broke the field of electrified air that comprised the door, and dropped to the floor. Rolling over, he went skittering down flat.

The whole operation had taken no more than two and a half seconds. The occupants of the black limousine had been busy during those same two and a half seconds. A frosted window came rolling down, and the ugly snout of a high velocity automatic came thrusting forth.

Bullets spattered against the wall of the building, skewering the space where Liz and Storm had been standing only a fraction of a minute before. The stream of bullets raked the doorway of the building at midsection-level, and then passed on to the other side of the building.

Someone screamed. Storm stared at the hot slugs hitting the lobby floor. People were rushing to and fro, voicing their panic. Storm glanced around for Liz, and saw her, dazed but unhurt, sitting up and rubbing her elbow where she had bruised it in her fall.

Uneasily, Storm got to his feet. There was the cold trickle of sweat running down his sides under his tunic, and he realized that he was starting to tremble. The delayed reaction was hitting him now. On watery legs he walked gingerly toward the door and peered out.

The death-car was gone. The assassins were completely out of sight by now. Shakily, Storm eyed the row of chips the bullets had dislodged in the building wall. Policemen were appearing, now. A crowd was gathering.

"What's been going on?" an officer asked, speaking to no one in particular.

"Bullets!" someone cried.

"A car ...a gun—"

"They were shooting at us!"

Storm ignored the hubbub. He stared grimly off into the distance as though trying to see the retreating cars of his would-be killers.

He was aware of Liz at his side. She looked pale, wide-eyed with fear.

"Johnny, they weren't after you!"

"Yes."

"It was some accident, wasn't it? Some kind of gangland execution, and they thought you were someone else?"

"No," he said, and his voice sounded metallic in his own ears. "They were after me."

"Who?"

"God only knows. But they were trying to get me. They found out that just obliterating me from the records wouldn't work. So they tried some more permanent way to get me out of their hair."

He looked down at her. She was biting her lip, trying to hold back the tears.

"Why ...why would anyone want to kill you, Johnny? What have you done? What have you done?"

"I found an asteroid," he said. "It's worth a lot of money. But not *that* much. Not so much that anybody needs to go killing me about it. I don't understand, Liz."

The policemen were going through the crowd, interrogating everyone. When it was Storm's turn, he simply shrugged and said, "A car pulled up and they started to shoot. That's all. We ducked until it was over."

"You didn't see any faces?"

"All I saw was a gun coming out of that car window," Storm said: "I didn't stick around to watch the details."

He didn't bother to explain to the policemen that the car had probably been after him, that the gun had been aimed specifically at him. He didn't request police protection. He didn't do anything that would bring him back into the web of red tape once again.

He had reached his decision, and it didn't involve the local authorities.

"What are you going to do, Johnny?" Liz asked anxiously.

"Something you won't like, I'm afraid."

"What?"

"Go back to Mars."

"Mars? *Why*, Johnny?"

Storm shrugged. "I filed my claim on Mars. I've got to nail that claim down beyond doubt, and the place to do it is Mars. I'm going to get into the record office there and find out who sold what to whom, and why. Mars is the only place I can get answers to all my questions."

"Don't go, Johnny!"

"Stay here and get killed, then? Or simply lose my claim and stay alive?"

"It isn't worth it," Liz said.

"It is, and I've got to go."

"Then take me with you!"

"Don't talk nonsense," he snapped at her, and instantly regretted his harsh tone. "Space is a lousy place for a woman. I wouldn't want the responsibility of your safety up there. It would only multiply our risks by a factor of ...oh, maybe fifty or a hundred. No, Liz."

"So you'll just leave me again? Go off for another two years?"

"Liz, please—" He groped for words to get through to her, couldn't find any, and bit down savagely on his lip. His nerves were frayed almost to the breaking point, now. Liz wanted him here on Earth, Liz wanted to marry him and settle down in that damned little split-level in Patagonia, and she wasn't going to smile benignly while he went haring off to space again.

But he had to go. The answers lay on Mars.

Her tear-flecked eyes glared at his for a long moment. Then she said, "You're going, aren't you?"

"I don't have any choice."

"Suppose you get killed up there?"

He pointed to the neat row of holes in the building wall. "It doesn't look so safe down here on Earth, does it?"

"Okay," she said. "Go. Go to Mars and find out whatever it is you have to find out. Only this time I don't guarantee to be waiting for you when you get back. *If* you get back."

"Liz!"

But she was gone. He watched her neat, retreating figure for a few moments, and then she vanished round the corner. Storm eyed the bullet-holes again. He shook his head, and walked away, keeping his eyes sharp for another black limousine.

CHAPTER SIX

A day later, he was aboard a liner bound for Mars.

It was the same ship he had come in on, the *Martian Empress*, making a quick turnabout to take full advantage of favorable orbital conditions. A couple of days for refueling and checkout, and the *Empress* was ready to go, and so was John Storm.

About half the crew was the same as on the Mars-Earth voyage. A couple of them recognized Storm.

"Commuting?" they asked him.

He smiled cheerlessly. "I liked the trip so much I thought I'd take it again," he said.

He was in anything but a jolly frame of mind. Passage to Mars was a luxury item, and he was already in hock for two or three years of anticipated earnings. He had had to take another loan to buy the tickets, and if something went wrong with his mining claim he'd be in debt for the rest of his life. Of course, if he could only be sure the asteroid was really his, he wouldn't need to worry about paltry five-figure debts. But he had no certainties of anything.

He figured he was lucky simply to be alive and on board the ship. Whoever had knocked his records out of the computer file and had sent the bungling hoodlums to gun him down obviously had a far-flung organization, and there was no reason why they couldn't have made a second attempt to kill him.

They hadn't. Of course, he had taken every precaution, such that he could take. Even so, he doubted that he had really avoided them very well. Had they decided to let him live? Did they want him to get to Mars, where they could take care of him with greater ease? Were they just curious about his activities, and letting him live to see what he did next?

Storm didn't know. Life had suddenly become unimaginably complicated for him, and he was aware that he had become a pawn in some power grab that he did not comprehend at all. But he was aboard the liner, and on his way to Mars, and unless they planned to blow up the liner en route, he'd get to Mars intact.

It was too bad, he thought, that Liz hadn't come to see him off. He hoped she'd calm down later. She was a sensible girl at heart, he knew. It was just that she'd been overwrought, and why not? Being shot at could overwring anybody.

He peered moodily out the porthole. Mars glittered like a copper coin in the sky. Giant Jupiter was invisible, somewhere on the other side of the solar system just now, but there was Saturn, obligingly tilted axiswise to give him a fine tourist's view of the spectacular rings.

Storm didn't look for Earth. He would have had to cross the ship to get a look, and at the moment he had had enough of Earth. He stared at Mars for a while, imagining that he could actually make out the tiny moons. It was, he knew, impossible to see them except from extremely close range, but his fatigued mind saw two specks whirling round the red planet, and he told himself they were Deimos and Phobos, and smiled at his own foolishness, and realized that it was so long since he had last smiled that his face muscles hardly knew how to go about it.

The clerk in the Hall of Records at Marsville blinked at him myopically and said, "You back so fast?"

"Any harm in it?"

"Just wondering if I'd see you again. You filed that asteroid claim a while back, huh?"

Tension formed a constricting band across Storm's chest. "That's why I'm back," he said. "I want to ask some questions about that claim."

The pale blue eyes were suddenly cold as space itself. "What kind of questions, mister?"

Storm leaned forward. There was nobody in the room but the clerk and Storm and the recording machines. Storm said, "When I got to Earth I looked up my claim. It wasn't in the records there."

"Sheesh! That ain't possible!"

"That's what they said. They looked up my claim number and said somebody name of McDermott had filed a claim with that number. No record of mine."

"Sheesh!"

"Yeah," Storm said. "Sheesh. You mind running through the records and letting me see if my claim's recorded here?"

"Well, now, I can't do that, mister."

"Oh?"

"Nobody gets to see the records without permission from the registrar."

"Where do I find him?"

"Well, you don't, really. You just sort of wait. He's out doing a little prospecting himself, round about Syrtis Major. Figures on being back, toward the end of the month, I'd say. He's the man can help you."

Storm scowled. "Nobody else?"

"Well, maybe the Acting Registrar might okay it—"

It was like pulling teeth. "Where do I find *him*?" Storm asked, struggling to control his temper.

"He's right here, mister. He's me."

"You could have told me that ten minutes ago!"

"Didn't ask."

"I'm asking now. I want permission to examine the claims records in this office."

The man smiled. There was mischief in the blue eyes now. "Sorry," he said. "Permission denied."

"What?"

"That's right. I can't have no strangers poking through the records here. You want to talk to the Registrar, that's your business, but he'll tell you the same thing. Want to move along, now? Got work to do. Claims to process."

Storm stared at the little man, and felt himself about to erupt. He had been getting the grand runaround from the high and mighty and the low and downtrodden, and he had had about enough.

Did the man want a bribe?

Storm said, "Listen, I've got fifty bucks here that's yours if—"

"Skip it. I can be bought, but not that cheap."

The bland words touched the spark. Storm moved without really realizing what he was doing. His big hands shot out and wrapped themselves around the skinny neck.

"Hey ...choking—"

"Dammit, I'm not taking any more!" Storm gritted. His fingers knotted tight. His arms trembled with rage, and he shook the little man violently. "We're all alone in here," Storm said. "I can shake your damned head off and nobody would know."

"Pl ...please!"

"Will you help me?"

"Y-yes!"

"You mean it?"

"Y-yes!"

Storm gave him one last shake for good measure, and let go. The little clerk backed away, fingering his throat.

"Sheesh, mister," he whispered hoarsely. "You coulda choked me, you know that? Sheesh!"

Storm didn't reply. He was trembling at his own outburst. There was tremendous strength in him, but he had always kept that strength under control, for fear of hurting someone. It would have been no trouble at all to snap the little man's neck. Storm's flesh crawled. The last time he had laid violent hands on anybody he had been ten years old.

The clerk said, "Come on. I'll show you the files. Just make it quick, though. Anybody asks you, did you see the files, you better not tell 'em I showed you."

"Hurry it up," Storm said. "Trot them out!"

The little man nodded. Still fondling his throat, he turned to one of the machines and began punching out coordinates. A screen came to glowing life.

"What month you want?" the clerk asked.

Storm told him. He read off the claim number on his duplicate sheet, to help him out.

The microreel continued to turn, and claim after claim appeared on the screen. Storm examined each one in turn, as the numbers descended toward his own.

"Okay," Storm said. "Slow up. We're getting close to my number now."

The speed at which the record reel turned diminished. Each claim now remained on the screen a full five seconds. Tension mounted inside Storm as the numbers came within ten of his, five, three, one—

"This one must be yours," the clerk said. "I'll stop the reel, okay?"

A magnified claim sheet appeared on the screen. Storm looked at it, and felt sickness in the pit of his stomach, felt reality dropping away from him again.

The claim was the same one Miss Vyzinski had showed him in the Records Office on Earth. It bore the same number as his, the same time-stamp. But it had been made out by Richard F. McDermott for an entirely different asteroid.

"That's not the one," Storm said.

"But it's the number you gave me."

"It's not the claim I filed, and you know it!" The little man was quivering, and his face was stippled with red splotches of shame or guilt or fear. "That claim's been substituted for mine!"

"Listen, mister, you asked me to show you the records, and I showed them. I can't help it if they don't look like you expected them to look."

Storm said, "I filed a claim. My name's John Storm, not McDermott. I've got a duplicate of that claim right here. You were in this office the day I filed it. After I left here, somebody yanked that claim and substituted a phony. I wonder who that somebody could be."

"You looking at me, mister?"

"Why do you say that?" Storm spat. "Start turning the reel again. Maybe my claim got misfiled somewhere."

Storm had the clerk roll the files back a month before the date of his claim. Nothing turned up. Grumbling every minute, the little man reeled them forward again. Storm watched, his eyes narrow and frowning, his lips firm. There was a coppery taste in his mouth, the taste of rage. It was just as he had feared. They—whoever *They* were—had begun at the source, had eradicated his claim at the point of filing.

Did that mean someone else had claimed the asteroid?

"You seen enough, mister?"

"Keep turning," Storm said. "Shut up and keep turning."

Storm watched the screen, not really knowing what he expected to find, and then something familiar whisked past his eyes, and he gasped, and snapped, "Hold it. Go back one notch, will you?"

"Listen, mister—"

"Go back or I'll pull your head off, dammit!" Storm roared.

The little man was quaking like a leaf, now. He pushed the stud and the screen flickered and the reel moved, and a magnified claim appeared on it.

Storm eyed it, and chills raced along his spine as he saw that the claim was for an asteroid with the same number as his, the same orbital coordinates, the same everything. The asteroid—his asteroid—had been claimed about six days after the filing of his own claim. One Clyde Ellins was down as the claimant.

So at last he knew. It was out in the open, now. He had a rival for the asteroid, not a prior claim but a subsequent one, and his title was clouded by the absence of any record of his claim. Someone had been pulling strings behind his back; he no longer had any reason to doubt that he was the victim of fraud, not simple innocent error.

The clerk was livid with fear. Storm glowered at him and said, "Who's this Ellins?"

"A ...a prospector, I guess."

"You know him?"

"Not really."

"Where is he from? Is he still on Mars?"

"I couldn't rightly tell you, mister."

Storm advanced toward the cowering little man, and let his huge hands dangle menacingly at his sides, the fingers clenching and unclenching. "You better rightly tell me," Storm said. "If you want to get out of here alive. How much did Ellins pay you to substitute his claim for mine?"

"Mister, I—"

"Out with it!"

"You got the wrong idea. He—"

Storm's massive hands reached for the slender throat. But the little man had had enough choking for a while, it seemed. He flung up his hands and said, "No! Don't! I'll tell you what you want!"

Storm waited. "So?"

Thin lips worked incoherently for a moment. "He ...he gave me a thousand dollars," the clerk said hoarsely. "To throw out your claim and slip the phony in."

"When?"

"About a week after you made the claim. He come right in here with the cash in his pocket, and set the whole deal up."

"And who is he, this Ellins?"

"You mean you don't know?"

"If I knew I wouldn't be wasting time asking you," Storm snapped. "Who is he?"

"Ellins? He's the local UMC man, that's who." The clerk risked a snickering laugh. "Let me tell you, you're up against the big boys. The really big boys, mister."

Storm felt a moment of something close to panic. UMC was trying to beat him out of his claim? UMC was the Universal Mining Cartel, the same outfit that had offered him a job in Patagonia, two years ago. It was a hydra-headed, multi-continent organization, one of the new business units that had come into being after the repeal of anti-trust legislation in the United States thirty years back.

The Cartel was vast and all-powerful. If anybody could get into the master computer files to obliterate somebody's records, UMC could do it. If anybody could finger a man for assassination, and come within an ace of doing it, it was UMC. If anybody could grab a free-lance's mining claim and get away with it, it was UMC.

But why, Storm wondered?

His asteroid, valuable though it was, was only a drop in the bucket of the Cartel's overall wealth. Why should they go to all this trouble to grab it? UMC wasn't that hard up for raw materials that they had to pull stuff like this.

Storm said, "Where's Ellins now? Still on Mars?"

The clerk shrugged. "He was here a few days ago. Outfitting a new expedition, I think. Haven't seen him around all week, though."

"Are you telling me the truth?"

The little man cowered. "Yes! Yes! Sheesh, are you gonna slam me again?"

Storm shook his head. "No," he said emptily. "It isn't worth it." He paced round the record room for a moment, wondering what to do now. UMC had foxed him out of his claim, and there didn't seem to be any way around it. He couldn't prove he had ever had a claim on the asteroid. If he tried to trot the little clerk forward as proof that skulduggery had taken place, UMC would see to it that the man's throat was cut before he could testify. Storm realized dully that there was no legal way he could fight UMC's billions.

They had him.

There was nothing much he could do except give up his claim, return to Earth, and—oh, this hurt!—meekly accept a job with another branch of the same UMC that had just done him out of his wealth.

No, Storm thought. *I'll fight! I'll fight with all I have!*

The office door opened. Storm whirled, half expecting to find UMC men bearing down on him. But the figure in the doorway was simply that of a prospector. He was a man a few years older than Storm, with a slouch-shouldered, weather-beaten look about him. As he came down the long room, he threw a faint grin at the clerk, and smiled at Storm in a friendly way. He seemed unaware that there had been any sort of tension in the room before his arrival.

He looked at the clerk and said, "Hi, Jimmy. Who's your friend?"

"Prospector named Storm," the clerk said. He rubbed his throat again, perhaps to hide the bruises that were beginning to show there.

The newcomer turned to Storm and put out a calloused hand. "Name's Fletcher," he said easily. "Sam Fletcher. Been working the asteroids seven years, now, and I finally got me some luck. How's that, Jimmy? I struck it rich at last. Let's have a claim sheet."

Storm said, "Whereabouts you hit it?"

"Belt Sub-seven," Fletcher said. "Found me an asteroid full of lithium. Just a little chunk, mind you. But it's real stuff. I'll clear maybe a hundred thou on it."

"I was in Sub-seven a while back," Storm said tightly.

"Find anything?"

"Yes," Storm said. "But there's some trouble on my claim, it seems. I'm trying to get it straightened out."

Fletcher looked up and laughed. "Trouble, huh? Well, I sure hope it wasn't your claim I saw them fooling around with yesterday."

"What do you mean?"

"Just a sec," Fletcher said. "Let me get this thing filled out and I'll tell you about it."

Storm waited tensely while Fletcher painstakingly wrote out the claim form. At length, the prospector looked up. "On my way back from Sub-seven," he said, "I passed this asteroid, this little one. Eight, ten miles across, maybe. And there was this big UMC ship there. They're hitching rocket tubes to the asteroid. I think they figure on moving it into another orbit."

"UMC? You're sure about that?"

"Well, I didn't stick around to have tea with 'em. But I saw the insignia on the ship, anyway. They're jumping somebody's claim, I guess. You'd think those guys had enough money already, without pulling a stunt like this."

Storm glanced across at the claims clerk. The little man shrugged and looked away. Clenching his fists, Storm said, "Have you sold your ship yet, Fletcher?"

"Yep. Why, you interested?"

Storm nodded. "I need a ship in a hurry."

"You wouldn't have wanted mine. I just about limped home in it. You go down to the spaceport, see the man there, he'll fix up something for you. Hey, you in that much of a hurry?"

Storm didn't answer. He was already on his way out of the room.

CHAPTER SEVEN

On his way over to the spaceport, Storm tried to fit together the pieces of the story as he had learned it so far. What he knew added up to trouble, and the trouble kept getting bigger every minute.

He had a rival for his asteroid. Obviously.

The rival was the sprawling Universal Mining Cartel. That in itself was practically enough to make him want to throw in the towel now, because nobody had ever defeated UMC in any sort of dispute.

UMC wanted his asteroid badly. So badly that the whole business became suspicious, in fact. By and large, UMC didn't need to descend to petty theft, and to do a free-lance prospector out of an asteroid claim amounted to petty theft by UMC's financial standards. It couldn't possibly be worth it for them to go to all this complicated schemery just to steal a few hundred million dollars' worth of commercial ore.

Item: they had bribed the claims keeper on Mars.

Item: they had somehow obliterated Storm's records from the master computer on Earth, which must have cost them a pretty penny.

Item: they were even now, according to Fletcher, hitching up a rocket installation that would blast Storm's asteroid into a different orbit.

That was the worst blow of all, Storm thought. As matters stood now, he had at least some title to the asteroid, even though it was thoroughly clouded. There was his duplicate copy of the original claim, which would have to be argued away in court. There was the undeniable fact that his records had somehow been wiped from the computer. He could make out a case that the asteroid was his. Chances were a thousand to one against his being able to best UMC in a court fight, but at least he had some sort of case.

He wouldn't even have a fragment of a case if UMC moved his asteroid. Mining claims in space were dependent wholly on orbital location. The absolute position of asteroids, and of all other heavenly bodies, for that matter, keeps changing every instant. But the orbits, the paths of travel, remain constant.

So the only way of tagging an asteroid is by orbit. But orbits are not immutable. An orbit can be changed, simply by applying a deflecting force.

The orbit of a thousand-pound space satellite can be altered simply by firing a small jet. The orbit of the Earth itself can be altered too, given enough muscle-power.

And as for a tiny asteroid only eight miles in diameter—

It didn't take much, really. One good swift kick from a bank of rockets would do it. Stir up a thrust of a few thousand tons and permanent changes in the asteroid's orbit could be effected. Keep the thrust going for a while, and you could push the asteroid anywhere you wanted—clear out to Pluto, if you felt like footing the fuel bill.

Of course, it was expensive. Hitching that much thrust up to an asteroid wasn't done for dimes. You had to make sure you were putting your installation in a part of the asteroid strong enough to take the kick, or otherwise you might just smash your asteroid to pebbles. So there had to be some engineering work ahead of time, and probably some structural .reinforcements. Then, too, the rockets cost money, because you needed pretty big ones for the job. And there was labor, too, at the usual high rates for space work.

Moving an asteroid into a new orbit might cost as much as ten or twenty million dollars, or perhaps more, if you wanted to ice things by carrying the asteroid far from its original orbit. Say, forty million for the job. A lot of money for John Storm to spend, but only pennies by the standards of an outfit like UMC.

Even if the job cost a hundred million, or five hundred million, UMC could swing it, Storm knew. They would move his asteroid into some different orbit, "discover" it, and file a brand-new claim, unencumbered by Storm's rival title. He could squawk to Doomsday without establishing any claim to the asteroid, once it was moved. True, there was now at least one witness to the moving job, but he could be bought off. Everybody, Storm thought coldly, could be bought off. UMC could bribe half the population of Earth if they felt they had to.

But why?

The whole thing baffled him. Why go to such lengths to secure a single small asteroid? The cartel would be lucky to break even, after they finally had secured their claim. Unless, Storm realized, there was something *else* on the asteroid, something that he had overlooked, something that could justify all the expense and the furious extra-legal maneuvers that the cartel was undertaking.

He knew that he had to go out to the asteroid at once.

The dealer in used spaceships was doing business at his accustomed place at Marsville Spaceport. He was a thick-set, jowly man in his early fifties, with the permanent bronze tan of someone who has spent decades on Mars, where the sun's rays, feeble as they are, strike through the thin atmosphere with blazing intensity.

He eyed Storm with a puzzled frown and said, "I've seen you before."

Storm nodded. "I sold you my ship last month. You gave me fifteen thousand. It was a Hawthorne 113."

"I remember."

"I'm back," Storm said. "And I'm in the market for another ship. I'll take the 113, if you've still got it."

"Sold it," the dealer said. "Not much in stock now. There's a 122, if you want. Cost you sixty grand, but it's a beauty of a ship."

"Something a little cheaper."

"Got a McIntyre B-8 at twenty-seven, if you like. Needs a core job, but otherwise sound. Like to have a look?"

Storm said, "I've got three thousand cash."

"You can't get a nose-cone for three thou, buddy."

"I've got something else for collateral," Storm went on. He produced his claim sheet. "I've got a claim on an asteroid in Sub-seven. Chock full of goodies. But for technical reasons I've got to make a quick trip out there and re-inspect it. If I don't move fast, I'm likely to lose the claim. But if I hold the claim I'm a millionaire."

"So?"

"Sell me a ship. I'll give you the three thousand down and a mortgage on the rest of the ship. You name the interest rate. You can have a lien on my asteroid besides. I'll sign all the papers you want. Just let me have the ship."

The dealer eyed Storm speculatively. "You must think I'm crazy, friend. I sell you a ship, and you go off to the asteroids and maybe crack it up, and I'm stuck with a lien on a claim that maybe isn't any good? What kind of sense do you think that makes?"

Storm began to sweat. "I was out in space for two years without an accident."

"So the law of averages is against you, then."

"Look," Storm said, "Name your own terms. I'm a desperate man."

The fat man shook his head. "What good are terms? You could sign a paper agreeing to pay me ten million bucks, soon as you get back from the asteroids with your claim sewed up. Only the claim isn't sewed up, you never come back, and I've got a lien against a vacuum. Uh-uh. No deal. Cash down or nothing. I got a family."

"Is there anyone on this lousy planet who's willing to take a risk?" Storm asked.

"Sure," the fat man said. "See Charlie Byrd, at Town Hall. He's the Mayor. He's a gambling man. You talk to him, see what he says. Then come back here."

Charlie Byrd was lean and hawk-faced, without an ounce of fat anywhere on him. Storm had to search half over Marsville for him, and finally found him, supervising a drain-building project at the extreme east end of the colony. He towered over Storm; he was close to seven feet tall, Storm figured, though he couldn't have weighed much more than a hundred sixty pounds. He was about sixty, Storm guessed.

Storm said, "Mr. Byrd, I've got a proposition for you."

"Always ready to listen, son."

With sweat rolling down his cheeks, Storm lined the deal out for the tall man. Byrd listened to him, without saying a word. It was impossible to read the expression on the sharp-beaked, fleshless face. Perhaps it was amusement, perhaps boredom, perhaps irritation, perhaps contempt. Storm had never seen such an enigmatic face before.

When he had finished, Byrd said simply, "Let's see that claim sheet of yours."

Storm handed it over. Byrd studied it for a moment and handed it back.

"It looks okay," Byrd said. It seemed to Storm as though Byrd had put a wee stress on the verb: "It *looks* okay." All he had to do, Storm thought bleakly, was to call the Records Office and check on the claim, and discover that it was not officially recorded, and that would be the end of it. Storm would have to walk to his asteroid, if he wanted to get there at all.

A long moment passed, as perhaps Byrd considered whether or not to check on the claim, and it occurred to Storm that Byrd did suspect it, and was deciding whether or not to take the chance anyway.

Finally Byrd said, "You need about twenty thousand, is that right?"

"Yes."

"How do you feel about usury, son? Are you against it on philosophical grounds?"

"Right now I just want the money," Storm said.

"Well, all right. I'll loan you twenty thousand. The rate of interest is fifteen percent per annum or fraction thereof. When you pay me back, you give me $23,000, any time within the next year. Okay?"

"Anything you say," Storm agreed.

"Now, as to collateral. You'll sign over the ship, of course. That goes without saying. But there's also some extra risk in it for me. You'll sign a paper agreeing to pay me back out of future mining royalties on this or any other claim you may make. The first $20,000 that comes out of your claim is mine, in case you default on the loan, plus interest. Agreed?"

"Agreed."

Byrd smiled for the first time. "You know something, son? We're both a couple of damned fools. You're an idiot for agreeing to be soaked like this. And I'm a worse idiot for lending you money on a claim that most likely won't pan out. But we got ourselves a deal. Give me half an hour and I'll get it all drawn up."

Storm nodded. "The quicker the better," he said.

The ship he got was a Hawthorne 117, a one-man ship, even tinier than the one he had gone out in the first time. It was a compact little gleaming bullet, not much more than twenty feet long. There was enough room in it for a man, and the blast tubes, and the fuel racks, and hardly anything else.

Storm didn't care. He wasn't looking for a luxury liner, just now.

The mortgage was duly made out, and title to the ship was transferred to him. It struck him that he was getting off cheaply, that 15% interest was more than reasonable considering the risks Charlie Byrd was running in making the loan. The thought occurred to him that it was more like philanthropy than usury, despite what looked like a high interest rate, and he quietly blessed the hawk-faced man.

Of course, Charlie Byrd didn't really know how dismal Storm's prospects were. Byrd thought there was a claim in existence. He wasn't aware that UMC workmen were busily jumping that claim right now, and that Storm was about to poke his nose into trouble.

Storm checked out the controls of his ship, running the tedious tests that were required by law. One after another, the green safety lights buzzed their responses. It wasn't too hard to operate a little ship like this: a little tougher than driving an automobile, but not much. An automobile's computer brain did about 98% of the work. The spaceship's computer would take care of only some 95% of the responsibility. Even so, the pilot's area of control was not very broad.

Storm studied his charts. During all the weeks since he had made his big find, his asteroid had been moving across space toward Mars at a rapid clip, and the distance he would have to cover was very much less than it had been on the first trip. It was still something more than an overnight jaunt, but not much of a journey by space standards. A little 117 like this carried enough fuel to get it out to Jupiter and back, provided you made the trip in slow orbit and didn't have a very hefty appetite. Hopping into the asteroid belt was no trick at all.

Storm activated his communication channels.

"Request blastoff clearance," he said crisply.

"Tower here," came a bored female voice. "When are you blasting, 117?"

"Whenever you give the word. Immediately or sooner, if possible."

"There's a Brewster AV-11 blasting downrange," came the tower voice. "Give him three minutes' clearance and you can go."

"Right."

Storm waited. He had never known that three minutes could last so long. They were Martian minutes, of course, fractionally longer than those of Earth, but that tiny difference alone couldn't account for their endlessness.

The time ticked away. Storm stared through his narrow port. Red Martian sand, scarred by frequent jet-blasts, stretched out ahead of him. Behind him, invisible now, lay the gleaming geodesic dome of Marsville. He wondered if he'd ever see Mars again, let alone Earth. Out there on the asteroids, if the UMC men ever got hold of him, it would be no great problem to dispose of him for keeps. All they had to do was open his faceplate, let his atmosphere whoosh out, and point him on an orbit toward the Sun. They'd have no further problems with rival claims, then. They wouldn't even need to bother going through with the business of shifting the asteroid.

And poor old Charlie Byrd would be out twenty thousand dollars, Storm thought.

For an instant he wondered whether it might be smarter to give up, to forget his dreams of glory and go back to Earth. One man couldn't fight a cartel. He had sixty years of estimated life-span ahead of him, he had Liz waiting—maybe—and he had a good job for the asking. Why look for trouble?

"You have clearance, 117," came the brassy voice from the control tower. "Blast within twenty seconds."

Storm shrugged away all defeatist thoughts. He was on his way, and there was no turning back now.

He punched keys. Somewhere in his little ship, computer elements flashed in their bath of liquid helium, and completed the job of activating the ship. Storm hunched back against his acceleration couch, and waited for the big fist to smash into him.

The moment of lift-off came.

Storm relaxed, letting the mounting g's flatten him, and the tiny ship rose unsteadily on a tongue of flame, hovered for an instant, and arced up at an increasing pace. Storm closed his eyes. The die was cast, now. All he needed to do was sit tight, and the ship would carry him to his asteroid, and from there he'd just have to play it by ear.

Mars became a dwindling red dot in the rear periscope. He watched it for a while, and then lost interest in what lay behind him. It was what was ahead that counted.

CHAPTER EIGHT

Seeing the asteroid again was almost like coming home.

They hadn't meddled with its orbit yet. Storm came upon the precious little rock just where his ship's computer said it would be. He cut in the manual controls, and brought the ship down. Instead of matching orbits at first, he put himself in a moving orbit around the asteroid, and peered at it from a distance of a hundred miles.

He didn't have to worry about being detected. Spaceships don't make any noise, not out in space where nothing carries sound waves. And his tiny ship was no more visible from the asteroid at a hundred miles than a gnat would have been.

It wasn't hard to see the activity going on down on the asteroid. With his scanners on fine, he could plainly make out the work area. A crew was busy on the side of the asteroid facing Jupiter, and even at a hundred miles up Storm could make out pretty clearly what they were doing.

They were putting in a rocket installation.

There was a big ship in parking orbit around the asteroid, and it was emblazoned boldly enough with the UMC monogram. On the surface of the asteroid itself, Storm saw what looked like ants, and knew that they were work-trucks and crawlers, unloaded from the mother ship.

He circled the asteroid in his orbit a couple of dozen times, scanning the whole surface of the asteroid to make sure the intruders were gathered all in one place. Although he still had no strategy for coping with them, he knew he had to remain unnoticed as long as possible.

There was no sense in making a direct challenge. A fool might march up to the UMC men and order them off, but Storm was no fool. He knew how quickly and quietly they would dispose of him if he tried anything like that. He was armed with a gun, but they probably outnumbered him fifty or sixty to his one, and he suspected they had guns, too.

About the best he could hope for was to get a series of three-dee camera shots showing the men at work. It wouldn't be much, but the pictures would help bolster his contention that UMC had whisked the asteroid out of his possession by sheer craftiness. He didn't think he'd get far in court against UMC's battery of lawyers, but at least he'd make the giant cartel look silly as it tried to explain why they were building a rocket installation on an asteroid they had already claimed.

He knew what would happen. They would wiggle out of it somehow, and the asteroid would be theirs. Then, all smiles and blandness, they'd come around to him and say, "Would you like to work for us, Mr. Storm? That job offer is still open." And he'd disappear forever into the maw of the UMC organization, all dreams of fortune exploded.

Storm scowled. He studied his keyboard for a moment, and began to pick out the programming instructions for his computer. What he wanted was a landing orbit that would set him down, neatly and quietly, on the side of the asteroid opposite the UMC camp. Eight miles of diameter wasn't much, by planetary standards, but it wasn't hard to lose twenty feet of spaceship on an asteroid that big.

The ship descended.

It spun inward, twisting through the blackness, slicing down in contracting spirals toward the surface of the asteroid. As before, Storm did not actually bring his ship down to the surface of the asteroid. A parking orbit was good enough. The ship dropped, and the canny little mind of the computer worked out the mathematics, matching the orbital rotation of the asteroid to the velocity of the ship, down to the last fraction, the final decimal.

The little ship entered orbit.

Storm dropped his ladder.

He clambered down. It was good to be back, he thought. But it would be better if he knew that the asteroid was really his, as by rights it should be.

He glanced up at his ship, and smiled. Then he looked toward the nearby horizon, and thought of what was taking place just beyond the jagged mountains that rimmed the tiny world, and his smile vanished.

He started to work out a strategy.

It was a fair distance, he knew, to the UMC camp: ten or twelve miles, practically halfway around the twenty-four-mile circumference of the asteroid. Under these low-gravity conditions, every step he took would be as though with seven-league boots, and he could cover the distance without any particular strain. Before he went, though, he had to figure out some way of handling the situation. He couldn't just barge in.

He looked around.

He had landed near the edge of a miniature plain, bordered at the far side by the jagged mountains that ran around the equator of the asteroid, and bordered at this side by low rocky hills. The pale green light of the distant sun gave the hills a barren, forlorn appearance. Out here, the sun was so weak that he could make out a few of the stars even by daylight. Over on the other side of the asteroid, he knew, it was night, and the stars would be gleaming brilliantly, with Mars and perhaps even Earth lending color to the display.

He nearly overlooked the mouth of the cave, when he first saw it. Storm had been roaming the plain purposelessly for ten minutes, and when he saw the cave-mouth at first it seemed to be only a dark shadow against the side of the hills. But as he stared at it, the asteroid continued in its orbital motion, and the shadows shifted, and the dark round area remained where it was.

Storm went to have a closer look.

He strode across the plain, covering ten and fifteen feet at a bound. Almost at once he had covered the few hundred feet, and he saw that it was, indeed, the mouth of a cave he had noticed. It was about ten feet in diameter, an almost mathematically perfect circle carved into the side of the cliff. He approached it and peered within.

All was black in there.

Something about the cave puzzled him. It was too regular, too mathematical. Caves were usually carved by water, and there was no water on this asteroid. Of course, a stream could have run here once, hundreds of millions of years ago, in the days when this asteroid was still part of the planet that once had orbited between Mars and Jupiter. But you generally found caves in soft, water-soluble rocks like limestone. You didn't find them in tough igneous stuff like this cliff.

So the cave wasn't a natural formation. But in that case—

What the hell was it?

Storm forgot, for the moment, the problem of the UMC rocket installation. There was a mystery here, and he needed the answer to it before he could go any further. Switching on his helmet-light, he stepped hesitantly into the utter blackness of the cave.

The floor was smooth beneath his feet. Storm was startled to see that the walls of the cavern, above and below him, were almost glassy, as though they had been carved out by the blast of a controlled thermonuclear explosion. Somehow, a tunnel of marble-smooth regularity had been slashed into this cliff.

Storm followed it inward, counting off his paces.

When he was twelve paces into the cliff, the tunnel began to veer away at a right angle. It made a complete ninety-degree turn, which took it along a parallel with the outside face of the cliff. Storm's frown deepened as he followed the tunnel another eight paces and saw it swing around again, making a second ninety-degree swerve.

Now it headed straight into the cliff again. Storm's helmet-light gave him only five yards' illumination, and beyond that the darkness quickly shaded in to conceal anything that lay beyond. He counted off fifteen, eighteen, twenty-one paces, and then saw the tunnel was making yet another turn. The walls of the tunnel gleamed in his light.

He rounded the turn.

What he saw was so unexpected that he halted, dazzled and gasping, and for a long moment his mind failed to accept the sight.

It simply did not register. A span of perhaps three full seconds went by before the vision got through to his mind as anything he could comprehend.

The tunnel had widened abruptly into a spherical chamber about fifteen feet in diameter, which began right around the bend from the path Storm had been following. A kind of curtain covered what lay beyond—not a tangible, material curtain, but something more like a thin fog, glowing a lambent greenish-yellow, giving off a bright radiance that made Storm's helmet-light completely superfluous.

And beyond the glowing curtain—

Storm's eyes, adjusting to the sudden brightness, peered through the swirling patterns of the intangible wall of color, and gradually the cloud cleared a little, to reveal the things within.

Machinery, first of all.

The walls of the chamber were lined with machinery. Gleaming cabinets held who knew what complex instruments. Bank upon bank of delicate shining metal shielding rose to right and to left, dizzyingly complex with tubing and pipes and dials and meters, a nightmare of mechanisms. The machinery rose perhaps ten feet high, two or three feet deep, along the curving walls of the chamber.

But there was something else in the chamber too.

It was floating (*floating?* Storm thought incredulously) about ten feet above the floor of the chamber. It was an object perhaps three feet long, shrouded in a denser fog of the greenish-yellow stuff that made up the curtain of the chamber. Narrowing his eyes, Storm struggled to penetrate that inner fog.

He could not clearly see what lay within. It was a creature of some sort, he decided. He could make out, or thought he could, the shapes of limbs, like pipestems, and something that might have been a head, and other things that could have been ropy coiled tentacles.

It was, he realized dazedly, some sort of alien being, some creature from the depths of space. It had to be. There was no other explanation. None of the worlds Mankind had explored had yielded any form of life of this complexity. Mercury was utterly barren; Venus had only insects; Mars had nothing higher than rodents. Jupiter, Saturn, and Uranus had been explored only by robot vehicles, because no human being could hope to land on those giant planets and withstand the crushing grip of their gravities, and the robot explorers of the big worlds had found no signs of life at all. As for the outer worlds, Neptune and Pluto, they were too cold to support any kind of comprehensible life.

And yet here, in a tunnel into a cliff of an asteroid eight miles in diameter—

Here, suspended in some kind of cocoon ten feet above the ground, wrapped in a bewildering nest that seemed to have neither substance nor form—

Here, surrounded by bedazzling machines and instruments that no Earthly mind had ever created—

Here, high above the floor, rested some kind of alien creature, some representative of what Storm guessed was an incredibly advanced creature. A visitor from the stars, Storm wondered? A stranded wayfarer?

Storm stared at the glowing dark core of the chamber, at the place where the shrouded alien hovered in mid-air suspension. As Storm peered in awe and terror into the jewelled heart of the green cloud, it seemed to him that the fog was clearing, thinning.

Illusion, he wondered?

No. It was really happening. Imperceptibly, moment by moment, the curtain was growing more scant. He could see the machinery clearly, now, though it was no more understandable for that. And the dark figure high above the floor seemed more discernible now too. The inner cloud was not parting as rapidly as the outer, but it too was giving way slowly.

Storm half-saw the creature, now, as though through the waters of a stagnant lake. Yes, there were limbs, small ones, and yes, tentacles too, dangling like limp snakes from the shoulders of the creature. And a skull, swollen and distorted, and ...were those things eyes? Those gleaming, multi-faceted diamonds glittering in the broad forehead?

Beyond doubt, it was a living creature suspended up there. And just as certainly it was a creature spawned on no world of the solar system.

The cloud ceased to grow thin. The alien had obviously revealed all that he was going to reveal. The outer curtain was faint as smoke now, but the inner cocoon surrounding the creature was still close and thick, so that Storm got only a partial view. He remained at the entrance to the chamber, not daring to approach further. The outer reaches of the curtain were a foot away from him.

His head throbbed with wonder and excitement. And then something new touched him, and he quivered convulsively, stepping back a stride in fright.

It had been like ...like—he struggled for some way to explain it—like a hand reaching into his skull, slipping down behind the bone wall of his forehead to stroke the ridged gray furrows of his brain!

He thought he was going to be sick, and being sick inside a space-suit can be a harrowing experience. Storm fought for his self-control. Panic gripped him, and he wanted to turn and run, to flee from the chamber and the strange being it contained, to escape to the open plain before—

Again!

Again the invisible hand reached out to stroke his brain! Storm shuddered, trembled. Reaching out one gloved hand, he braced himself against the smooth glassy wall of the tunnel to keep from falling.

Run, he told himself. *Turn yourself around and get the hell out of here!*

But he stayed where he was. His first wild fears were giving way to curiosity, now. Storm stood straight again, and peered into the swirling cloudy mists, staring up at the thing above him.

A third time there was the feeling of something trying to enter his brain. The contact had an almost physical tangibility to it. He felt as though something slimy were being dragged across his brain, something that felt like a wet fish. But yet it was not altogether unpleasant.

And he sensed something else, something emotional, an undercurrent of ...what? Yearning? Pleading? A current of loneliness?

It's trying to communicate with me, he thought.

Yes, that was the only explanation. The thing was reaching out, sending waves of mental force at him, probing his brain, trying desperately to make contact with him. Storm wondered if it could be achieved.

Go ahead! he thought. *I'm listening!*

He had never believed in telepathy, psychic communion, extrasensory perception, or anything else of the sort. But this was no question of theory, of belief or disbelief. This was something that was happening, unrolling from moment to moment, and Storm could only follow along the path of events from one instant to the next.

He had no idea of how to go about making him receptive to the mind of a creature from another galaxy. All he could do was stand where he was, feeling the alien being probing at his mind.

The moments of probing were coming more rapidly, now. The first two had been nearly a minute apart. The third had followed, about half a minute after the second. But now they were coming every few seconds, quick, eager jabs. There was something almost panicky about them, Storm thought. As though the alien had a message of the greatest importance to communicate to him.

Go ahead! he thought. *I'm listening!*

Another probe came, more intense than any of the others, a hard thrust to the core of his mind. Storm felt ear-splitting agony, but he remained upright, and despite his fear he tried to remain sympathetic. He had the feeling that contact was only moments away, that one more jab would do it, would establish some kind of linkage between their minds.

The jab didn't come.

Instead, the creature withdrew, and Storm stood there blinking, suddenly bereft of his uncertain contact with the alien being.

The next moment, before Storm had fully recovered from the shock of being abandoned by the being, gloved hands grasped his arms from behind, and a helmet was thrust against his, and a voice said roughly, "Don't move or you won't live to regret it."

CHAPTER NINE

Storm's first impulse was to turn and fight. But that, he saw immediately, was as good as committing suicide.

He switched his helmet radio on, and heard the voice saying, "I've got a gun in your back. Turn around slowly with your hands up or I'll blow a hole in your suit."

"I'm turning," Storm said.

He took a last look at the chamber ahead of him. The strange cloud-curtain had thickened again, growing even more impenetrable than when Storm had first stumbled around the bend in the tunnel. Now only dim shapes could be seen in the chamber, glittering yellowness where the banks of alien instruments rose, and darkness midway up, where the alien himself remained suspended.

Storm turned.

The man directly in front of him wore a copper-colored spacesuit bearing the UMC monogram. There were three other cartel men behind him, and all four were carrying guns. Through the panels of their helmets, Storm could see cold, merciless faces. Not stupid faces, not the faces of hoodlums, but the faces of grimly determined men.

"Let's go," the one in the lead said. "Walk past me and start walking down the tunnel. Walk at a steady pace, and slow down if I tell you to slow down. If you don't obey, I'll have to kill you. Move!"

Storm glanced back over his shoulder at the enigma behind the swirling greenish-yellow cloud. But no response came, no clearing of the cloud, no mental probe, no contact at all. Dark turquoise streaks slashed across the curtain, as though displaying the anger or frustration of the being within.

Hands high, Storm began to walk.

He retraced his steps. Twenty-one paces to the next turn, then eight paces, then twelve paces more, and he was at the mouth of the tunnel. He stepped out. Two more UMC men were waiting for him there, with guns drawn.

A glance at the plain told him what had happened. Two UMC crawlers were parked near his ship. Whether on a routine surveying tour, or in search of a detected intruder, they had come across the asteroid's equator and had come upon his ship. As Storm looked, he saw a suited UMC man emerge from the cabin of the ship and crawl down the ladder.

All the UMC men were out of the cave, now. The one who seemed to be in charge said, "You're coming with us. Just walk quietly toward those crawlers."

Storm obeyed. His mind was half-paralyzed by the rapidity of events. To come across some inconceivable kind of creature in a cave on a dead asteroid, to have his mind probed by alien thought-waves, then to be captured without a fight by the very enemies he had come here to surprise—things were happening much too fast, all of a sudden.

They hustled Storm into the nearer of the two crawlers. One man sat on each side of him, with guns ready. Not that he could have made much trouble for them, he thought. He had left his weapon in the ship, and they had probably confiscated it by this time. But perhaps they didn't realize he was unarmed.

The crawler was a versatile vehicle adapted for moving through any imaginable climatic circumstances. Torpedo-shaped, a dozen feet long, it rose on pivot-mounted legs, six in all. A transparent plastic shield formed a dome over the crawler. The vehicle lurched forward, skittering across the empty plain toward the mountain range that separated this hemisphere of the asteroid from the other.

Storm, unable to do anything but sit still, remained motionless. The fact that he had been captured by UMC hardly registered yet. His mind still glowed with the unearthly experience he had had at the end of the tunnel.

The UMC installation on the asteroid was more impressive than Storm had suspected when surveying it from a hundred miles up. They had chosen a plateau about five hundred yards square, nestling between two jagged hills, and had blown three big permoplast domes. One dome seemed to be serving as headquarters; the second looked like a tool dump. The third, at the far side of the plateau, appeared to house the rocket installation, whose launch-pads lay just alongside it.

The UMC men led Storm, none too gently, into the main dome. As he was getting his helmet open, a short, almost reckless man in a serge jersey strode up to him and peered in his face.

"Here he is, Mr. Ellins," said one of Storm's captors. "The one who landed the ship. We found him in the cave."

"The *cave*, you idiots? Couldn't you have gotten to him faster?" Ellins snapped coldly.

"Sorry, Mr. Ellins. We did our best."

"Next time do a little better, will you?"

Storm stared down at the man who had come to represent for him the personification of all the forces that were working against him. So this was Ellins? He looked tough, Storm thought. He wasn't a neat, slick, smooth-talking executive type at all. There was steel in his eyes and in the bear-trap set of his jaw. His lips were thin and bloodless, his face square and hard, his body compact, ruggedly muscular.

Ellins glared at him and said, "What the hell are you doing here, anyway?"

"I was going to ask you the same thing," Storm said. "I've got a right to be here. You don't."

"This asteroid belongs to UMC," Ellins said thinly. "I'm the UMC man in this part of space. I belong here. You're a trespasser on our claim."

"It's my claim," Storm said. "You know that as well as I do, Ellins. I was here a week ahead of you and got there first with a legitimate claim."

"What's your name?" Ellins asked.

"John Storm."

One corner of Ellins' mouth turned up in a bleak smile. He folded his arms, tapped his fingers against his elbows. "Storm," he repeated. "John Storm. Sorry, Storm. I never heard of you in my life."

"Maybe not. But somebody in your outfit did. Somebody pulled my claim out of the records and replaced it with a UMC claim. Somebody named Clyde Ellins filed that second claim. That *illegal* claim."

Ellins spat. "The claim's legal. What do you think UMC is, a pirate organization?"

"Don't make me answer that."

"There's a claim on file on Mars," Ellins said, "and one recorded on Earth too. It shows that this was an unclaimed asteroid until a UMC prospecting party landed here. We've had the claim searched and the title's clear. The asteroid is ours, Storm, and you're a trespasser, and you ought to know what happens to claim-jumpers out here."

"Sure I know," Storm said evenly. "Do you?"

Ellins didn't smile this time. "You're annoying me, Storm. I warn you, I can punish you heavily. You came down by stealth on an occupied asteroid. Luckily we had mass-detectors here, and we spotted your landing. You were obviously on some sneaking mission of mischief."

"I was coming to inspect my claim," Storm said doggedly.

"You have no claim!"

"You know I do, Ellins! Maybe you've phonied up all the records, but I still have a duplicate of my original claim. I've got witnesses on Earth who know my computer file was deliberately erased. I've got someone on Mars who'll testify that he saw UMC workmen building a rocket installation here. Why build rockets on an asteroid, unless you want to shift its orbit to jump a claim?"

Ellins said smoothly, "The rockets will take the asteroid closer to Earth for more efficient mining."

"Hogwash! You're just trying to run it into a different orbit to clear your claim!" Storm shook his head. "You won't get away with it, Ellins. I've got enough evidence to stir up a real stink. Maybe I'll lose the asteroid anyway—nobody beats UMC in court—but at least I'll get a hearing for myself. I'll see to it that UMC gets smeared in every newsfax sheet in the solar system!"

"Listen, if you—"

Storm cut him off. "I know how UMC worries about its public image. There are plenty of people on Earth who still aren't happy about the cartel system, and all UMC needs is to be caught pushing some free-lance prospector around. Oh, UMC will survive it, I guess. But what's going to happen to the guy who let UMC in for the trouble? What will UMC do to a local representative who couldn't cover his tracks well enough to avoid some bad publicity?"

There was a long moment of silence. Storm saw that his thrust had reached a vulnerable spot in Ellins. The way to strike terror into a company man was to put him in a position where his actions could be construed as hurting the corporate image. For the first time, Ellins looked troubled.

He shrugged, exhaled annoyedly, scowled at Storm. Storm face him calmly, with the calm of a man who knows he had almost nothing left to lose, and perhaps a great deal to gain.

At length Ellins said, "What do you want, Storm?"

"My asteroid."

"Don't be an idiot. We've found the asteroid and we've claimed it. It's ours, and any claim you made would be just a nuisance claim. We'd squash you like a mosquito."

"Sometimes people get stung themselves while they're squashing mosquitoes," Storm pointed out.

"All right," Ellins said. "I asked you, and I'll ask you again: what do you want?"

"I thought I told you."

"I thought I answered you," Ellins retorted. "You can't have the asteroid. What will you settle for?"

"Does that mean you're trying to buy me off?" Storm asked in surprise.

"Call it that if you like."

"No sale," Storm said.

"Don't be a bigger lunatic than you have to be," Ellins said. A look of craftiness came into his eyes. Craft didn't look appropriate in those flat, menacing, reptilian eyes. He said in a soft voice, "I'm not admitting you have any valid claim to this asteroid whatsoever, Storm. But I'm interested in protecting the reputation of my company. Rather than get into a long legal hassel which we're sure to win but which will cost us a pile of dough, I'll offer you a fee to drop your claim right here and now."

"I said I wasn't interested."

"I'll offer you a million dollars," Ellins said crisply. "We can have the deal set up in an hour. I'll beam Mars for the authorization and UMC will deposit a certified check to your account in any bank you name, in return for your signature on a document that declares—"

"No sale," Storm repeated.

"You damned blockhead, why not? Isn't a million good enough for you? You can invest it and have an income for life. You can retire when you're still a kid."

"I'm not selling out. Why should I sell you a billion dollars' worth of commercial-grade ore for a million dollars, Ellins?"

Ellins was sweating heavily now. "Take two million, then. Don't be a fool."

"Not two million either."

"Five?" Ellins said hoarsely.

"No, and not fifty." Storm smiled. "I'll listen to you if you raise the bid a little more, though. Let's say, half a billion dollars. That's what I call real money. I'd be willing to turn the asteroid over to you without prejudice, for that. Maybe I'd do a little better if I held my rights and mined it myself, but I'd settle for half a billion."

"Funny man," Ellins said bitterly. "My final offer is five million. It's an outrageously high price, and I'll get roasted for paying it, but I want to get rid of you. You can take it or leave it."

"Suppose I leave it?" Storm asked.

Ellins glanced sharply up at him, his eyes no longer crafty at all, but simply mean and beady. "Then we'd have to play rough with you, Storm. We can't afford to let you go back to Earth and start howling about how UMC swindled you. We'd just simply have to play rough."

"How rough?"

"About as rough as it can get," Ellins said. "If you don't agree to sell out, you'll have an accident. We'll take you back over to where your ship is, and we'll arrange it so your face-plate pops open. A little fluke with the servo controls, that's all. One of those one-in-a-million things. Then we put you in your ship and plot a nice orbit for you. Say, a hyperbolic orbit clear out of the solar system. Or maybe a straight line into the sun. Getting rid of bodies is easy, out here. Lots of room, hardly anybody to see."

Storm had no doubt the UMC man meant it. For a long, crackling moment the two of them eyed each other in silence. Then

Storm said, "That's not much of a choice, is it? Either I sell out for beans, or you murder me?"

"Five million isn't beans."

"Compared with the value of this asteroid, it is. The ore alone is worth two hundred times that. And then there's the thing in the cave."

Sudden fury blazed in Ellins' eyes. "You forget what you saw in the cave, you hear? You just wipe that out of your mind! Any deal we make, it's going to include buying your silence about that cave."

"What is that thing in there, Ellins?"

"I don't want to talk about it. Just stay off the subject. The subject is your alleged mining claim. Will you sell us a waiver of your claim, or do we have to arrange an accident for you?"

"I need to think it over," Storm said. "Can you give me some time?"

"Sure," Ellins replied magnanimously. "Take all the time you like. A month, two months—just so long as you stay here where we can watch you. Think it out all the way, Storm. Don't jump to any rash decisions." Ellins shook his fist at him in anger, then turned away, his face knotted contemptuously. "Tie him up," Ellins muttered. "Put him where he can't get loose and make trouble. We got work to do. We can't stand around moving our jaws all year."

CHAPTER TEN

The UMC men tied Storm up with silent efficiency, and made sure he wouldn't be going anywhere when they got through with him. They used copper baling wire, thin and bright, and he was lucky that he was wearing a spacesuit because the way they trussed him the wire would have cut to the bone if it had touched bare flesh.

They strapped his wrists together behind his back, and tied his ankles, and for good measure threw in a binding length linking his wrist-bonds to his ankle-bonds. They left him huddled against the wall of the dome, body doubled up and arched backward in a bow. They left him helmetless, so that even if by some miracle he got free of his bonds he would be unable to leave the dome and return to his ship.

With Storm safely under wraps, the UMC men got back to their main business—building the rocket installation.

Storm watched sourly. They were well along in their work, he saw. Another few days, perhaps, and the job would be done, or possibly it would take a bit longer, but not much. The rocket banks would be in place, and Ellins would touch a switch and the rocket engines would roar, and the asteroid would be wrenched from the orbit it had followed for maybe three hundred million years, and they would move it across space to some uncluttered part of the heavens, and that would be the end of Storm's hopes of claiming it.

He pondered the choice Ellins had given him.

On the surface, it didn't look like any sort of real choice. On the one hand, an offer of five million dollars. On the other, death.

Who would take more than a fraction of a second to make up his mind between two alternatives like those?

But it was more complicated than that, Storm knew. He couldn't be certain that Ellins really meant to go through with his threat. Before any murder took place, there would be another war of nerves, of bluff and counterbluff, between him and Ellins. Would Ellins be so eager to kill him if Storm claimed that in a safe-deposit box on Earth there was a full account of the whole story, marked "To be opened if I do not return by January 1, 2019?"

Would Ellins believe him, though?

And, Storm asked himself in annoyance, why hadn't he taken that little precaution? Why had he rushed off alone without arranging in some way for his story to be told in case he met with an "accident" out here?

No matter. An imaginary safe-deposit box would be as good as a real one, if only he could get Ellins to believe it existed. So there was at least a remote chance he could scare Ellins out of the murder idea, if he worked at it convincingly enough. Ellins was worried about UMC's reputation, because he was worried about his own status in the cartel. He wouldn't want to get the company denounced not only for claim-jumping but for murder as well. So maybe—

But if I sell out, Storm told himself, *that's the end of it. I've got no further recourse. I've got my five million bucks, and they've got their signed waiver of claim, and any yelling I do after that will be laughed off as crank stuff.*

The choice was anything but clear-cut, then. So long as he was still alive, he had at least a remote chance of regaining his legitimate rights to the asteroid—provided he didn't sign those rights away in blind fear.

Stick to your guns, he warned himself. *Ellins may not be as tough as he tried to sound.*

There was no sense rushing ahead, selling out for a pittance. And five million dollars *was* a pittance, considering what he knew this asteroid to be worth. No, Storm thought, the thing to do was take a tight grip, hang on to the last moment, try to call Ellins' bluff. If it really did come down to a choice between signing a waiver and getting murdered, well, he'd take the obvious choice. But he suspected that if he held on, his stubbornness might win him some sort of concession from Ellins.

Maybe.

It was the slimmest of chances, but worth trying.

There was also the matter, Storm thought, of the alien being in the cave. Obviously Ellin and his cohorts knew that the creature was there. Had they made contact with the strange being? Was there some kind of communication between the alien and the UMC men?

An interesting possibility emerged. Suppose, Storm thought, UMC wanted the asteroid not for its mineral content but for the creature in the cave. Was that possible, he wondered? The asteroid was rich in ores, but UMC had no real need to do all this undercover stuff simply to secure another ore source. But suppose they had some special use for the alien or for the weird machinery in the extra-terrestrial being's cave.

Yes, Storm thought. That might explain UMC's strange eagerness to do him out of the asteroid. But so much of the story was missing that he could not figure out any specific motives. He could only make guesses.

He shrugged such speculations out of his mind, and turned his attention to his bonds. They had done a superb job of packaging him, he saw. By pivoting his body and twisting his spine about as far as it would go, he could get a good look at the way they had tied up his wrists. They had bound him as though he were an escape artist.

He wasn't. He didn't have the foggiest idea of how to get free. He couldn't reach his wrists either with his feet or with his teeth, nor did straining against the wire do anything but tighten the bonds. As for the wire round his ankles, there was no way of removing that either.

Hopeless even to think about it.

Storm lay still. He felt cramped, tense. It was only a few minutes since they had dumped him here, but already he could feel his muscles stiffening up in this unnatural position. In another couple of hours, he would probably be so gnarled he'd be unable to walk even if his bonds miraculously dropped off. He wiggled his shoulders uneasily, tried to stretch his legs. His knees and elbows were beginning to throb. There was the first twinge of pain at his armpits. His fingers and toes were starting to go numb. No one was paying the slightest attention to him. The UMC men were going about their chores, leaving him to writhe and twist as best he could.

Storm scowled at them. *Just let me get hold of you, Ellins,* he thought. *Let me get my hands on you once, and—*

He recoiled in sudden surprise.

What was that?

A sensation in his brain, he realized. It was something like what he had felt before, only the texture was different now. In the cave, there had been a feeling of sliminess when the alien's mental probes had tried to enter his mind. Now, it was more like a feather being brushed against his brain.

Had he imagined it?

Or was the alien trying to reach him again, trying to make contact across the ten or twelve miles that separated them now?

Storm waited tensely, and an endless moment passed, and he began to think it had only been an illusion, a phantom of his tired mind. But then ...yes, there it was again! Unmistakably.

It was as though a feather were being drawn over the exposed lobes of his brain, as though his skull had been sliced away to bare the ugly, pulsing thing beneath and leave it open for wandering thought-waves.

There was a third probe, and it seemed more intense this time, but still feathery. His scalp began to itch fiercely. He wondered why the probes were different in texture now, and decided tentatively that it must be some function of the distance, that what he had felt as sliminess at close range felt different out here.

Other than the texture, it was the same as before, the same hopeful, yearning gesture, the same feeling that something was reaching eagerly toward him.

Go on, Storm thought. *I'm listening!*

He forced himself to relax. He let his aching body go as limp as the constricting wires would allow, and closed his eyes, and allowed his face to sag into an idiotic droop. He tried to lower all barriers of tension that might be blocking the consummation of the contact.

He waited.

It was a long while before the alien tried again. Two, three, four minutes went by. Perhaps the creature was gathering strength for one mammoth effort, Storm decided. Or maybe the alien was—

The thrust came.

Relaxed and unwary, Storm was taken off guard, and the assault penetrated to the deepest recesses of his brain. It felt exactly as though a powerful man standing directly above him had grasped a spike with both hands and had driven it through the top of Storm's skull.

A blaze of nerve-searing agony blasted through Storm's entire body. He let out a wild howl of pain, and his body twisted convulsively, half-rising from the ground, every joint straining as if jolted with electricity. Sweat bathed him, and he sank back, whimpering with pain, trembling, dazed and stunned by the onslaught.

A silent voice said hesitantly, somewhere within him, *I ...I am sorry ...to have hurt you.*

Storm blinked. "Where are you?" he asked, through the red haze of pain.

Still in my chamber, came the silent reply. *But now ...now there is contact!*

Storm said, "You mean our minds—"

Are joined. Superficially. Yes. I apologize for the pain. It was not easy to make contact with a mind so different from my own.

Storm did not answer. The pain was ebbing, now. He could still feel the contact, but it was no longer like a spike thrust into his skull. More like an adhesive plaster fastened to his forehead, now. There was an awareness of something not him attached to him, but no pain. He had a sensation as of gentle fingers stroking his brain, soothing him, calming him, and he relaxed.

Then he was aware of figures standing over him: Ellins, and one of his workmen. They had heard his howl of pain, evidently, and had come running over to see what was the matter.

"You call us?" Ellins rasped.

Storm shook his head. "No. No, I didn't say anything," he said huskily.

"Funny. I could have sworn—"

"You must be imagining things, Ellins."

The UMC man knelt and peered at him. "Hey, are you sick or something?"

"Do I look sick?"

"You're drenched with sweat. Your face is pale. You look like a ghost, Storm. A sick ghost."

Storm managed a grin. "Not yet, Ellins. But don't worry. I'll haunt you when the time comes."

Ellins stood up, and kicked coldly at the pebbles in front of Storm. "You make up your mind yet, Storm?"

"I'm still thinking about it."

"Keep on thinking, then. Hey, you're *sure* you aren't sick? You look like hell, Storm."

"Suddenly you're so concerned for my welfare, are you?" Storm chuckled. "Okay. You can get me an aspirin, if you're worried about me. And a shot of Scotch, while you're at it, pal."

Ellins spun on his heel and walked away without a word. Storm closed his eyes, tried to recover some of his strength. He wondered what he looked like just now. Probably pretty frayed, if even Ellins had noticed it. Making contact with an alien mind was apparently a severe physical strain, Storm thought. He felt as though he had just run a five-mile race.

Quietly he said, "Are you still there?"

Yes. I was waiting for them to go away.

"Who are you?"

I will tell you everything. I need your help.

"That's pretty funny," Storm said. "My help. I can't even help myself. How can I help you?"

There is a way, came that calm, patient, voiceless voice. *But not yet. It will take a while. I will explain, when the proper time comes.*

"The proper time better not be far off," Storm murmured. "I don't think they're going to give me very much more time to decide."

We will find a way to delay them, was the telepathic answer. *You are not yet strong enough to help me. The shock of first contact has weakened you. You will need time to recover your full strength.*

"Whatever you say," Storm replied. There was something dreamlike and unreal about lying here bound in baling wire listening to a voice within his brain. If he had not seen the thing in the cave, if he did not know that Ellins had seen it too, he might have begun to suspect his own sanity.

The alien was silent for a long while. Storm lay still, watching the workmen just beyond the dome.

Things began to happen within Storm.

They were odd things. First, the pain of his uncomfortable position lessened. His body seemed to be adjusting to the cramped, awkward posture, and his knees and elbows no longer protested, his spine no longer felt as though it were going to snap any moment.

It happened subtly. Storm was not aware of any lessening of his pain. The pain simply dwindled and then it was gone, without gradations.

Next, other symptoms of discomfort ebbed. He still had a lingering headache, but it vanished now, leaving only the most vestigial trace of the alien's forcible joining of their minds. He felt weak and hungry, but the lassitude that had gripped him in the past hour began to depart. He could imagine the alien doing things as if by remote control, touching up the physical tone of his mind-partner the way a sculptor would use his sensitive hands to smooth the roughness out of a half-finished clay model.

Storm felt new vigor, new vitality grow in him from one moment to the next.

The process was still going on when the alien said, calm as always, *May I tell you who I am, and how I came to be here on this little world?*

CHAPTER ELEVEN

Storm assented, and a swirl of strange images came flooding into his mind.

It was a chaos. However the alien saw his own story, he did not visualize it in a linear sequence. He did not imagine it as one event followed by another, like ducklings tagging along behind their mother.

What came swarming into Storm's dazzled brain was a jumble of events, a random, sequenceless mixture of happenings, a group of floating incidents that lacked any causal relationship with each other.

"I ...don't understand." Storm said.

Wait. I am trying to find a means of telling you. I must organize the events in a way that you will comprehend.

Storm closed his eyes. He wanted to roar, to bellow, to scream. It was not the alien's fault, certainly. But so totally different was the alien's way of looking at the time-sequence that Storm was driven panicky by the flood of images. He trembled, and shrank back into himself, and silently begged that he be spared the narration if it had to be as incoherent and as terrifyingly bewildering as this.

I am so sorry, came the humble mental voice. *I am making a greater effort. It will be but another moment, I promise you, and then all will be well.*

Storm fought the panic away. He wondered what sort of being this was, capable of grasping a story from beginning to end simultaneously, able to examine a dozen or a hundred or a thousand separate incidents in the same cloudburst of imagery.

The flood of images subsided.

The confusion began to diminish. Storm felt the alien assembling, reconstructing, arranging his tale.

Now we will begin again, the creature in the cavern declared, and began to transmit his story a second time.

It was more vivid than any solidofilm could possibly have been. Sometimes, in the better three-dee sollies, Storm had almost had the illusion of reality. But this was no illusion. The alien was actually reliving what had happened, and Storm, his mind joined in strange union to that of the creature from the stars, found himself participating.

Storm saw the broad sweep of the heavens, the glittering jewels of a million stars spread against the black velvet backdrop of space. But nothing looked familiar. Certain of the constellations seemed relatively constant when viewed from Earth or from the nearby planets, but the vision of space that blossomed in Storm's mind bore no relevance to any star-chart he had ever seen. There were constellations, yes, but they were alien configurations.

Storm knew, without benefit of any verbalized promptings from the alien, that what he was seeing was space as it had looked untold millennia ago, and space as it appeared in the far galaxies. Earth was nowhere to be seen. Somewhere high in the blackness was a small spiral nebula, a faint, indistinct, unimportant cluster of stars, and Storm was numbedly aware that within this aggregation of stellar bodies was the sun known as Sol, and the nine planets that circled it.

He was in a ship of some sort ...or, rather, the alien was re-experiencing the thought of being in a ship, and Storm was sharing that relived sensation. The ship was not extraordinarily different in form from the spaceships Storm knew. It was roughly cylindrical, with an outer skin of some hard, gleaming, bluish metal. Storm found it perplexing and unsettling to be seeing the ship both from without and within at once, but he let the strangeness of the double vision go unremarked, and gradually he accepted it as a normal way of perceiving things.

The ship did not seem to be of any great size. Storm could judge that by comparing its dimensions with that of the figure he had seen in the cave. That figure had been about three feet long, and using it as a yardstick he could estimate that the ship was no more than a hundred fifty feet long, its corridors seven feet high and perhaps five feet in width.

In the cavern, the figure of the alien had been shrouded and hidden from his sight. In the vision Storm now experienced, he had a clear view of the alien, and of others like him.

There were about twenty of them on board the ship. Storm found them bizarre, yet not repellent. Since he was seeing through the eyes and mind of the alien creature, it was impossible for him to feel disgust or shock or fright at the sight of the occupants of the star-ship.

They stood upright, all of them just about three feet tall. Two stubby legs, ending in round sucker-pads, supported them. They had four tiny arms, looking deformed and shrunken, and two opposing pairs of ropy, coiling tentacles with prehensile tips. Their heads were large in proportion to their bodies, and their eyes, many-faceted and gleaming, were the most strange aspect of them—solemn, immense eyes taking up half their faces.

They wore no clothes. So far as Storm's unpracticed eye could tell, there were no distinctions of sex among them—they all looked alike, in fact—yet he was subliminally aware that in reality the aliens fell into several sharply different groups. One group, numbering almost half the total on board, was male, or male-equivalent. A second group, seven or eight in all, were female-equivalent. The other few aliens were of neither sex, yet somehow important in the reproduction of the species. Storm accepted these distinctions without understanding them at all, but there was no way of stopping the flow of images to ask for an explanation, any more than a dream could be halted for a footnote.

The ship was traveling. It had left its own home world an enormous span of years before. There was no way for the alien to communicate the actual length of that span, for, Storm sensed, the aliens did not perceive time in a linear way, and could not put the duration of the voyage into Storm's terms in any other way than "very long."

So it was a very long voyage. The ship had been away from home a very long time, and a still greater span of time was due to elapse before it would return. Storm watched, baffled and yet enthralled, enjoying his double inner and outer view of the ship as, a slim gleaming needle, it darted across the heavens on its endless journey.

It was hard to tell *why* the journey was being made. For scientific research? Sightseeing, tourism, travel-for-its-own-sake? Military surveying? Storm did not know. He could not sort an intelligible motive out of the impressionistic welter of reasons the alien presented. The best Storm could conclude was that the motivating force behind the journey was beyond his comprehension, no more his to understand than the motivations behind the contours of a Beethoven symphony, a Picasso canvas. The journey was like a work of art. Storm did not press for elucidation. He knew none would be forthcoming.

The vessel was moving at incredible velocities. Storm was granted a view of the ship's power plant, but what he saw made no sense to him—gleaming machinery that did not seem to move or glow or function in any way—and he suspected that even if he were a propulsion engineer instead of a mining engineer he would not have understood a thing. The ship moved, covering light-years in a moment, and the force that drove it was beyond an Earthman's comprehension.

The alien gave Storm a capsule view of some of the ship's ports of call.

There was a planet of a bluish sun, a jungle-world where worms of titanic size oozed through steaming mud, where towering creatures with shimmering scales thundered over the fallen hulks of trees a thousand feet high. There was a world without land, a water-world whose cool seas abounded with life, where sleek brown mammals with fins and flippers streaked through the depths, debating points of abstract philosophy as they swam. There was a desert world, a world that made Mars look like Eden in contrast, a wind-swept, waterless world whose blazing white sun nearly filled the cloudless sky, a world where small stunted beings scrabbled out a precarious living and sped the hours with tales of a greatness long since departed from their race.

There was a world much like Earth, too, a quiet, beautiful world of green leaves and blue seas. The air was fresh as new wine, and the animals of this world were gentle as lambs, and winter never came, and the soft golden sunshine seemed reluctant to fade from the sky. But the world was not the Earth Storm knew, for its happy people were green-skinned and tailed, and at night two glittering moons chased each other through the strangely starless skies.

There was a world that was no longer a world, for sizzling lava pits rose where cities once had been, and clicking clouds of radioactivity drifted in the hazy atmosphere. There was another world that looked like a nightmare of the Earth that was, a world without trees, without rivers and streams, a world of fifty or a hundred billion people crammed into box-like cubicles that covered every inch of land area.

World followed world in dizzying array. Storm followed the tour, breathless, his mind reeling under the display of unfamiliar images. Eyes closed, he dreamed of the long night of space, and of the multitude of planets out there in the darkness, a million light-years beyond Pluto.

The journey continued.

Miraculously, time was compressed for Storm. He came to know the people aboard the ship, and he thought of them now as *people*, not as "aliens" or as "creatures." He knew which one was *his*, the one who was telling him all this, and he knew some of the others too, saw them as contrasting personalities. He saw a little of their hopes and fears and dreams. And, though much of what he saw was utterly incomprehensible, there were certain responses that he understood as well as he understood his own. Certain things were universal. The response to beauty was a constant, though the idea of beauty itself was not. The need to love and be loved was a constant, if not the shape of desire. The feeling of brotherhood, of kinship, of shared endeavor—all these things came through to Storm, and he perceived them readily enough.

The journey continued.

In the telescoping of time, millions of years passed in a handful of seconds for Storm. The ship was now approaching that part of the universe Storm knew as *home*.

The star cluster that had looked so insignificant before now took on presence and majesty as the slim ship needled into its midst. The heavens were blazing with glory. Somewhere in that arc of radiance, Storm knew, was the sun of Earth—a small sun, a yellow sun, a not very important sun in all this fiery splendor.

The ship moved through the new galaxy, stopping at this world and at that. The galaxy swarmed with planets and with life. Giant red stars and searing blue ones, shrunken white dwarfs and drab little yellow and green ones—the star cluster abounded in stars, and each star had its worlds, and on many of those worlds there was life.

And still the journey continued.

Storm sensed the approach of familiar territory. Yes, there was Earth's sun now, looking like a pinpoint of yellow light as the aliens viewed it from the frozen wastelands of Pluto. Inward they came, dodging from one planet to the next, slicing across orbits as it pleased them. Barren Uranus, and vast Neptune, and vaster, triple-ringed Saturn, and mighty Jupiter—the expedition landed on each world. Storm wondered at the calm way the aliens came down on planets Earthmen did not dare to tread. The crushing gravity of the three giant planets did not seem to trouble them at all. Some device, some strange instrument from their stock of baffling miracle-working things, protected them against gravity's pull.

Inward, still. Inward toward the small worlds where life could be detected.

Storm saw Mars, red but green-dappled, looking younger and fresher and far more alive than he had ever seen it. Were there seas on Mars? Yes! And life ...cities ...intelligent creatures!

He knew that the journey he was experiencing had taken place millions of years before, and the knowledge chilled him. Yet he was able to set at least a hazy limit on the voyage's duration, because there was no planet between Mars and Jupiter. The explosion that had wrecked that world had already taken place. The asteroids pebbled the sky.

Storm longed for a view of Earth as it had been in the days when Mars had seas. He wondered what he would see there? Snorting dinosaurs locked in mortal combat? Flapping sea-creatures hesitantly crawling to land? Or scurrying mammals hiding timidly in the strange underbrush?

He never found out. He could see Earth, blue-green and inviting, hovering nearby in space. But the expedition did not reach it. The catastrophe struck while the ship was still crossing the orbit of the asteroid belt, heading inward toward sea-green Mars.

The alien told the tale without passion, without weeping. Something had gone wrong. The miraculous mechanisms that powered the ship rebelled. Not even the super-science of the beings from the far stars could halt the runaway destruction.

The ship exploded.

Storm quivered and shook as the image formed itself in his mind. He saw the hideous black gash developing along the gleaming blue hull of the ship, and it was as though his own body were splitting open. He cried out, tried to halt what was happening, but there was no halting it.

The ship split like a seed-pod that had ripened. And it hurled its strange seed outward to the untender mercies of space.

Storm watched in horror as five small figures spurted from the interior of the wrecked ship, their bodies congealing instantly, their blood freezing in their veins. Like dolls they spun in orbit, limbs spreadeagled, around the shattered vessel.

Another convulsion. Four more of the star creatures tumbled into space. Two of them had tried to protect themselves, had donned the masks they wore when visiting strange worlds, but they had not had enough time, and they died too. The ship's atmosphere was gone, now. The chill of space penetrated everywhere, and even those who had remained on board died now.

All but one.

He had moved with instinctive reaction, donning his protective garb at the first quiver from the ship's engine, and he alone survived the moment of destruction. Dazed, stunned, he clung to a bulkhead while explosion after explosion rocked the ship, while the sweet atmosphere he knew vanished into the void.

The fury seemed to end. The ship was quiet again.

Sadly, the star-being explored the ruins of the ship aboard which he had voyaged so long. He saw his comrades dead, twisted and distorted, their bodies hideous to behold. He looked through the ruined ports, saw the other corpses orbiting the dead ship. He realized, finally, after he had combed the gutted hull from end to end, that he was alone. His mind had already brought him that information, since no one answered his frantic mental calls, but he had not believed it, could not believe it until he had seen them all dead.

He worked quickly, with the energy of complete despair. One of the lifeboats had escaped destruction. Speedily, he stocked it with everything that remained undamaged aboard the ship. He loaded the little craft with instruments whose function Storm could not even begin to guess at, and prepared to take his leave, the long voyage at its unexpected end.

Before he could quit the ship, one final explosion racked it. He was within the lifeboat already, and when the explosion came it hurled him hard against the walls, and he lay there a long time. A trickle of blood seeping from his lips, his limbs broken in half a dozen places.

There was silence again.

Feebly, he activated the controls. The mother ship, he realized, had been blown to fragments. There was nothing left of it, or of the corpses of his comrades. He had been lucky to survive that final blast, though he was only barely alive himself.

Where to go?

While stocking the lifeboat, he had thought of heading for Mars, which looked inviting enough from a distance. But that was out of the question, now. The lifeboat, twisted and half-wrecked, could never make it across a gulf of more than a hundred million miles, a gulf that was widening with every passing instant.

Where, then?

Not far away, an asteroid orbited. It was nothing more than a chunk of rock, barren and forbidding, without atmosphere, without water. But it was the only landfall within reach. The star-being's decision had been made for it.

He forced his broken body to obey. Activating the life-boat, he guided it down, brought it to a landing in a plain on the tiny asteroid. There he rested, for a staggeringly long while, letting his body knit once again before venturing from the ship.

A driving need to survive impelled him to feats that should have been impossible for him. Using tools from the life-boat, he carved a dwelling for himself, blasting it out of the living rock—a tunnel, and a chamber. He hauled his salvaged equipment inside. He set up a force-field to screen himself from the savagery of his environment, and within the force-field generated an atmosphere for himself.

Then he rested.

Recuperation was a slow process. He cast himself into a sleep beyond sleep, and for thousands of years he slept, while his body rebuilt its strength. Even at best, he had never been physically strong, and he had sustained crippling injuries in the explosion.

His body knit together. It would never be truly whole again, but at least he could move without too much pain. He was still too weak to leave the cave, and thousands of years passed before he ventured outside.

He was alone.

That was the hardest fact to accept. His was not a race that enjoyed solitude. There was always contact with others, always the comforting feeling of another mind nearby, and now there was a silence that held terrors. No member of his race was within a million light-years. Not even the super-minds of his species could span such a gulf.

He was alone, cut off from all contact with his own kind.

Of course, he had certain resources. His memory was perfect and permanent, and he could relive happier days with complete clarity and an illusion of reality. He spun away hundreds of millenia that way. But ultimately it became a hollow pastime, and he ceased it.

He was alone and no natural cause could kill him.

A prisoner for all eternity!

His only hope was to build a beacon that would reach his home world and bring a rescue party. But it was not an easy task. He had no real knowledge of such things, and he had to rack his mind, plumb his memories. Millions of years crept by as he worked on the beacon. He cannibalized his useless lifeboat for it, so that not a shred of the boat remained.

The years passed. The seas of Mars grew dry, and bitter winds swept the red planet, driving all life away. On Earth, a two-legged mammal came to supremacy, invented civilization for itself, built pitiful little empires. And still the castaway of the stars toiled on in lonely exile.

He built the beacon, finally. He tested it, and it seemed to work, and he sent a message off to his home world. But he knew there was little hope of a quick rescue. His thoughts travelled at a speed that could not be measured, but his beacon wave was limited by the speed of light, and had half the heavens to cross before it reached a listening ear.

The castaway went on waiting. Even the patience of an immortal can fray, but he lived through the dark moments of loneliness. Suspended in the force-field of his cave, snug in his nest, he slept, and rested, and husbanded his strength, and dreamed away the millenia.

Then came an intruder.

The alien sensed the presence of another being on the asteroid. Tentatively, timidly after so long an isolation, the star-creature sent out a faint probe, but drew back in uncertainty. It was, he knew, one of the creatures from the blue-green planet, one of the two-legged ones. The castaway hesitated and finally decided not to make contact at all. He would wait for his own people. It was safest that way.

Almost at once, the intruder went away. But a short time later, other intruders came. Their mental vibrations jarred the alien; these were harsh, crude, greedy people, whereas the first visitor had seemed to have a kind of honesty and integrity about him. The star-wanderer had no intention of making contact with these newcomers.

But they made contact with him.

They stumbled on his cave by accident, and explored it with trepidation, and came upon the glowing curtain, and saw the creature that lay beyond it, surrounded by the salvaged instruments from the ship that had perished millions, of years before. They stared, and murmured in awe, and began to scheme to turn their discovery to their own use. And the alien, cringing with distaste, was helpless.

Here the vision ended. Here the dream shattered, and Storm, his eyes dazzled with the light of distant suns, blinked in confusion as the story halted.

CHAPTER TWELVE

Storm said, "What do they plan to do with you?"

Kill me, I suppose.

"But why?"

I am a threat to them, they think. First they will torture me, to get from me the secrets of my instruments. And then they will kill me.

"What do they know about your instruments?" Storm asked.

Very little, really, the alien responded. *But they are shrewd beings. They have guessed that there is power in them—the power to rule the solar system.*

"Only if you show them how to use them!"

They have their ways of extracting knowledge, the alien said gently.

Storm stared at the distant figures of Ellins and his workers. His mind went back over the things the star-being had just said, and over the miraculous voyage that still glowed in his memory.

Yes, Storm thought. There was great power in those gleaming banks of machinery. He could only guess at the nature of the instruments. The power to carve tunnels out of solid rock? Yes, certainly. Anti-gravity machines? Probably. Atmosphere-manufacturers? Food-manufacturers? Power-sources that would draw energy from the structural bones of the universe itself?

It was a cave of miracles, no doubt of it.

Storm thought of such things falling into the hands of UMC, and was sickened. It was unlawful, it was blasphemous, that such power should be concentrated in the possession of one group of men.

It cannot be prevented, the alien said. *Unless you help me defeat them.*

"Won't you tell me how I can help?"

Later, the alien said. There was a note of sadness in the star-creature's voice. *We must both find the strength to do it, you and I. Never in all our history has a member of my race knowingly taken an intelligent life. But there are certain emergencies that transcend even the most ancient of codes. This is one of them.*

Storm did not answer. He was chilled by this new vision the alien had presented, the vision of the tools of the star-creatures in the hands of the controllers of UMC.

It was not a vision of evil. The Universal Mining Cartel was an impersonal entity, beyond evil and beyond good as well. Individual members of the cartel might be evil, as they chose, but not the cartel itself.

What Storm saw was a vision, not of evil, but of concentrated power. Armed with the technology of an ancient super-race, UMC could put itself beyond the control of any political organization. It would become, even more than it was already, a super-state, a government in its own right. It would automatically become the richest, most invulnerable state that had ever existed.

Could UMC's technicians solve the secrets of the alien's cave?

Storm did not doubt that they could. Oh, it would take time, a generation or two of tinkering, but eventually the gleaming instruments would yield up their mysteries, and a billion years of evolution would be vaulted in a single leap, to the greater glory of UMC.

And if UMC could make the alien cooperate, could torture him into revealing those secrets, it would happen so much the faster.

Would the alien be able to resist?

Storm doubted it. The star-being had great mental powers, obviously. But physically he was weak, weak as a baby. His was not a strong race to begin with, and this was a crippled, accident-broken individual, his strength sapped by a loneliness of millions of years, a loneliness beyond all human comprehension. And these gentle creatures were not trained in self-defense. They were incapable of violence. The castaway might find himself helpless before UMC's greed.

"We've got to stop them," Storm muttered.

Yes. That is why I risked making contact with you. I sensed you were different. I gambled that you would help me against them.

"I'll do whatever I can," Storm declared. "But I don't see how—"

Be patient. You will understand all, in time.

Storm wondered what they could do to keep the treasures of the cavern from falling into UMC's hands. The alien was without physical strength; and while he, Storm, was strong, he was weaponless and outnumbered and strapped with baling wire too. How could they fight back?

It looked hopeless.

It was abundantly clear, now, why the cartel had gone to such extraordinary lengths to get the asteroid away from him. Not for the cesium and lithium and gallium it contained, certainly. UMC did not play dirty for such small stakes. If the UMC prospectors had landed here, and found that a rival claim was already in effect, they would almost certainly have abided by that claim and made no attempt to jump it.

But the presence of the alien, and the things stored in the alien's cave, altered all the ground rules.

The asteroid now was worth billions to UMC, worth any sort of skulduggery to get. What did it matter if they compromised their corporate image in obtaining it, with such wonders as the prize?

The alien said, *We will defeat them.*

"How? How?"

Patience. Build your strength. Our time will come.

The alien said no more. Storm was still aware of the contact in his mind, but he heard no further words from the star-rover. He knew the alien was there, though. He could feel the imperceptible changes taking place within him. He felt stronger, not physically but in some indefinable sense. For all his depression and pessimism, there was yet a sensation of tremendous well-being. His body throbbed with new vigor and fresh vitality. He felt younger, like a boy of eighteen, rippling with the first strengths of new manhood.

But still his wrists were trussed, still his ankles were bound. He was no closer to being free than he had been two hours before. And, he knew, he was a great deal closer to death.

Some time afterward, Ellins and his work crew re-entered the dome, their labors finished for the time being. Several "days" and "nights" had passed on the asteroid, which spun on its axis every few hours, presenting now this face, now that to the distant, pale sun. Storm had had nothing to eat for more hours than he cared to think about, and he felt a trifle lightheaded. But, oddly, not really hungry. Some magic of the star-creature was responsible for that, he decided.

Ellins stripped off his space-suit and strode over to the corner of the dome where Storm lay. He glanced down, his eyes unfriendlier than ever.

"Still thinking it over?" Ellins asked.

"You aren't going to give me a rush act, are you?" Storm retorted.

"Who's rushing? I just want to know how you're coming along."

"I'm still here."

"Comfortable?"

"It could be worse," Storm said.

"It could be a lot worse," Ellins agreed. "And it's going to be, very soon now. You know, I'm getting tired of having you around, Storm."

"Just say the word and I'll get into my ship and clear off, Ellins."

"Funny man. There's only one way you'll get into that ship of yours, and that's as a corpse."

"You don't sound friendly."

Storm's calmness seemed to bother the UMC man. He hunkered down in an awkward squat, so that his face was on a level with Storm's, and said in a low, angry voice, "Come on, now! Stop fooling around. For the last time, will you take the five million and renounce your claim?"

"No."

"I said, for the last time."

"Go to hell."

"Not me, Storm. You. Right now. If you're a praying man, you better do some praying."

Storm managed a mirthless smile. "You ought to know one thing, Ellins. If I don't get back to Mars on schedule, there's a bank vault that's going to be opened. And in that vault is the whole story of what happened to my claim, including the name of the man who bribed the record-keeper. And that's you, Ellins."

A muscle flicked momentarily in Ellins' cheek. But he did not look at all demolished by Storm's revelation. Storm had played his trump, and it did not seem to be taking any tricks.

Ellins said easily, "I figured you'd do a thing like that. Well, it's all right with me. UMC will protect me against any inquiry."

"You sound awfully confident."

"I am. What I found on this asteroid will make the UMC brass very warmly inclined toward me, Storm."

"You mean the alien?"

"I mean what I mean," Ellins said. "We'll ride out any fuss that your little bank vault document might stir up. We'll squash it the way we cut you out of the computer records You aren't fooling around with small fry, Storm."

"You aren't going to get away with it."

Ellins laughed and straightened up. "I think we will, okay? Now—and this really is the last time—will you sign a waiver or do we shove you out the airlock? Yes or no, Storm. Yes or no.

Storm considered.

He had run out of bluffs. He couldn't stall any longer. The alien had promised in some nebulous way to strike out at the UMC men, but could he take that promise seriously? Where was the alien now? Storm wasn't even sure he felt the contact any more. He hadn't heard a word from the star being in a half hour or more.

If he signed that waiver, he was finished. Ellins would transmit it to Mars instantly, and no matter what the alien planned to do, it wouldn't affect the fact that Storm had conveyed title to the asteroid to UMC.

But if they threw him out of the airlock, he was finished in a much more permanent way.

Ellins was offering wealth, not staggering wealth, but more than he stood to earn in all his life. Taking the wealth, though, meant selling the asteriod, selling not only a billion dollars' worth of rare ores, but selling the alien too. Storm hesitated at doing that.

Where was the alien, though? Why was he silent?

"Speak up, Storm," Ellins prodded.

One final time, Storm weighed the alternatives. He couldn't sign the waiver. He couldn't. The instant it was done, his recourse was gone.

The only thing to do, he decided, was to choose the other alternative, and hope that the alien could work whatever miracle he promised.

In a wavering voice Storm said, "I'm not going to sell you anything, Ellins."

"You know what that means."

"I know."

Ellins shrugged in relief. "Okay. That settles that. Get the wire off him, boys. When he walks the plank he'll do it on his own two feet."

They snipped the wire away. Ellins watched closely, warning them not to leave any snip-marks in Storm's spacesuit. "This has to look like an accident," Ellins said.

Storm watched, his face rigid, as Ellins picked up Storm's space helmet and studied the face-plate for a moment. He found the servo controls, pondered them, made a tiny adjustment. The face-plate swung open and stayed there.

"How unfortunate," Ellins said with a cold smile. "The mechanism seems to have sprung. I understand that can be a real catastrophe, when your face-plate pops open and there's nothing but high vacuum around you." Ellins laughed. "Hold him tight, will you? He's a big ox. I'd hate to have him get loose."

Two of them held him, while a third kept a gun jammed into his kidneys. Ellins approached, holding the helmet. Storm didn't try to break free. At best, he could land a solid kick in Ellins' midsection, but a moment later there would be a hole eight inches wide running through his body, and that didn't strike him as very appealing.

Storm allowed Ellins to put the helmet back on. The face-plate dangled open.

"Okay. Let go of him," Ellins said. "Just keep the gun in his back. Storm, you can start walking toward the airlock. If you decide you'd rather sign the waiver, all you have to do is say so. Some time in the next sixty seconds, that is. After that I'm afraid it won't do you much good to change your mind."

Stoney-faced, wordless, Storm began to cross the dome toward the lock. It wasn't going to be a pleasant death, he knew, although it would be a fairly quick one. He could picture it clearly enough. The permoplast wall of the air lock would slide shut behind him, and the wall in front would open, and he would step from the protection of the dome into the nothingness of the asteroid outside.

Such air as there was in his spacesuit would go whooshing out into the void in an instant. The air in his body would try to escape too, pressing outward at fifteen pounds per square inch, and there would be no countervailing suit-pressure to press inward.

He tried not to think of what would happen. He wondered how many seconds he would have to endure the pain before death came, and his shattered body could be loaded into a crawler and taken across the asteroid to his ship. Both body and ship would be sent orbiting toward the sun, and there would be no evidence of the crime once that furnace devoured it.

The lock was only a few steps away. Storm thought of Liz, back on Earth so many millions of miles away. He thought of that split-level in Patagonia. He thought of how comfortable he could be with five million dollars in the bank.

Then he thought of what the future of mankind would be like if UMC grabbed the alien's treasures for its own profit.

"Where are you?" he asked softly, hoping the alien was listening.

No reply came.

The airlock's inner door slid open. "Get inside," Ellins ordered.

Where are you? Storm thought frantically.

He started to enter the lock.

Suddenly the silence broke, and Storm felt the contact re-establish itself, and heard the welcome silent voice saying, *I am almost ready. Another few seconds—can you delay them? Just another moment. That is all I need!*

CHAPTER THIRTEEN

Storm halted at the brink of the airlock and turned to look into Ellins' gleaming, expectant eyes.

"Go on in," Ellins snapped.

"I've changed my mind;" Storm told him. "I'll sign your paper. I'll take the money."

Ellins laughed harshly. "I knew you would. No man's fool enough to turn down a deal like that." Ellins barked orders over one shoulder. "Whitey, get me that paper! Gus, set up radio contact with Mars!"

Storm waited near the airlock panel.

Are you ready? he asked the alien.

Just one more moment—

Ellins was holding a slip of paper in his hand, reading it over carefully and nodding. "Yes, that should do it," he murmured. "In consideration for five million dollars paid in hand—"

Storm heard the alien say, *My people are conditioned against taking intelligent life. It violates our every precept. But you have no such qualms.*

"Especially not in self defense," Storm said quietly, out loud.

Ellins looked up. "You say something, Storm?"

"You must be hearing things," Storm laughed.

The alien went on, *What we will try now is very dangerous. It may kill both of us. Are you willing to risk it?*

"Yes," Storm whispered, thinking of the gleaming machines of the cave.

The alien said, *We must join our minds. I will use you as a mental focus, and through you I will attempt to strike down these men. I will use your strength. The death-blow will be from your mind, and not from mine. Only in that way can I function.*

Ellins said, "All right, Storm. Here. Sign this and I'll beam it to Mars to be recorded. We'll have a certified check for you right away. Signed, sealed, and delivered. Then you can get the hell out of here and go count your money without bothering us, okay?"

"Let's see what I'm supposed to sign," Storm said.

"Read it carefully," Ellins said with a cynical grin. "I wouldn't want you to think you were being swindled, or anything. Once you sign, brother, that's it."

Storm scanned the paper. It was simple enough: a conveyance of title, crudely worded but comprehensive enough. It would probably stand up in court, he thought.

The alien said, *I am ready now. You must let me enter your mind to the deepest, now. It will be more painful than before, but it cannot be helped. I need your full cooperation. I cannot enter unless you throw your mind willingly open to me now.*

"Does it read okay to you?" Ellins asked.

"What?"

"I said, does it read okay?"

"Oh. Yeah. Yeah."

"Then sign it, and stop wasting time."

"All right," Storm said vaguely. "Just a minute, will you? I'm trying to think of something."

"Do your thinking some other time," Ellins said. "I want to get this finished up."

"He's stalling, chief," one of the other UMC men said. "Why don't he sign?"

"Just a second, will you?" Storm said. "Another second won't matter!"

He could feel the alien probing at his mind again, the same feathery touch as before. How did you go about opening your mind? Storm wondered. What did you do? What barriers did you drop? If you had no control over your own thought processes, how could you admit another mind voluntarily?

The alien's probing grew more urgent.

What if he doesn't make contact? Storm asked himself.

Please, came the silent voice. *You are not concentrating. Clear your mind. Make it a blank. Admit me!*

Storm replied, *I'm trying. You're part way in now anyway, aren't you? Can't you manage it the rest of the way?*

The alien did not respond verbally. But Storm felt the pressure intensify. He was glad, now, for the extra strength that the star-creature had endowed him with. He knew he could not have withstood such a probe earlier.

Storm was dimly aware that Ellins was saying something to him, but he did not pay attention. His mind was riveted on the problem of attaining union with the alien. Another probe came, and another, and yet another, more intense than any that had gone before.

Yes, Storm thought! *Yes! Yes! I'm open! I'm waiting!*

He closed his eyes, blotting out the puzzled, uneasy faces of the UMC men, and threw back his head, and let all thought drain from his mind. He waited, receptive, open, offering no hindrance.

The alien thrust.

Found the barrier.

Burst through it.

Storm tottered, nearly dropped to his knees as the impact hit him.

"Looks like he's having a stroke, chief," one of Ellins' men said. "What's going on?"

Storm hardly heard the words. They held no meaning for him. His face worked in agony. He could feel the alien's very being flooding into him, could feel the union of the star-creature's mind and his own. It rocked the Earthman to his core. There was pain, stunning pain, and he felt that his skull would burst and the pulpy ruins of his brain explode outward, or that his mind would burn out. It was not simply a spike being driven into his skull now; it was a direct jolt of high-voltage power, searing him endlessly.

But it was happening. The merging. The union. The joining. Storm could feel it happening, and despite the pain he welcomed the ancient being joyfully, throwing his mind wide, admitting the star-creature fully.

And then—

Oneness!

It lasted only the merest fraction of a moment.

Storm never knew just how brief the union was. For him, it could have lasted a millisecond or a million years, there was no way of telling which.

He stood erect, swaying a little, his mind blurring under the impact of finding out what it was like to be hundreds of millions of years old.

He knew.

He saw the alien's home world, through the alien's eye, and his heart cried out at the beauty of that far-off planet. A greenish-gold sun filled the sky, and through groves of strange trees and shrubs walked the alien's people, smiling, peaceful, their minds intertwined in delicate congress. It was a vision of harmony, a city beyond all human dreams, a greatness humanity could not hope to attain for millions of years. Storm stared in wonder-struck awe at the city's glassy towers, at the feather-light bridges of spun sunshine that linked the mighty buildings, at the gleaming ships in the skies. It was a vision of a world where living creatures had become as gods.

Storm knew what it was like to have been born on that world, to be a member of its harmonious society, to have a station and a place and a purpose, to love and be loved.

Storm also knew what it meant to leave that world, and voyage on an eternal journey through space.

He had experienced that journey once, but if it had seemed vividly real to him before, it was almost frighteningly so now. He was caught up in the cross-current of emotions aboard the ship, the web of love that linked everyone on it. He shared with them the thrill of planetfall, the delights of arriving at a new and strange and beautiful world, the bitter-sweet sadness of leaving again and moving onward.

Now he learned what it was like for immortals to die. He learned, too, what it was like for a member of this race to survive the death of his comrades.

For the first time, John Storm really understood what loneliness meant, what exile meant.

In that blinding fraction of a second he relived millennia of isolation in a cave on a barren chunk of rock. He felt the pain of the crippled alien, and the numb awareness that he was cut off from all his kind. He shared the task of building the beacon that hopefully would bring a rescue team some time in the distant future.

All this passed through Storm's mind in that single tiny fragment of an instant. No longer was the alien telling him things. He *was* the alien, and the alien was John Storm.

A sense of godlike strength swept through Storm. The universe was his for the taking. He could reach out and sense everything. He was aware of the miserable gray souls of Ellins and his men, surrounding him. More than that, he could extend his mind across millions of miles.

He reached out.

Mars was first. Storm's enhanced mind embraced the ten thousand souls of Marsville. He felt the busy ambitions there, the envy and the covetousness, and also the hard work, the drive to build a city in barren desert. It was as though he held everyone on Mars in his own arms.

But he could reach past Mars. He could reach all the way to Earth.

His mind recoiled, at first, as he brushed against those swarming seven billions. But the alien's strength buoyed him up, and he was able to fulfill his purpose. He descended into the crowded warrens of Earth, in search of a particular person, and he found her, all in that same fraction of a second.

Liz.

He touched her mind, and felt the warmth of it, and beamed his own love, and felt her response of love, sensed her eagerness for his return. Storm saw her frown, puzzled at the contact in her mind. She turned her face starwards, and he read her wishes, absorbed her longing for his return, and knew that she was still waiting, still loved him.

Come, said the voice in his mind, and there was no longer any way of telling whether the voice was the alien's or that of his own thoughts, for now they were one. *There is work for us to do.*

Yes, came the shared reply. *And we are ready.*

It was so terribly, terribly easy.

The same way that he had reached out to Earth for a moment's contact with Liz, Storm reached out for the minds of the UMC men who surrounded him.

He encountered Ellins' mind first, and probed it with his double strength. There was resistance, but not enough to matter. Storm easily thrust aside the barriers Ellins had erected, and forced his way in.

It was like entering a pit of worms.

Storm did not long linger. He had no desire to remain and inspect Ellins' mind. The quicker this was done, the better, Storm felt.

He did it.

It was the equivalent of twisting a water tap. One moment the water flowed, and then the tap was turned, and the flow ceased. That was what Storm did. A little twist, a mental twist, and the dense, sickening flow of Ellins' thought ceased, and Storm withdrew.

The others presented even less of a challenge. They lacked the fiber Ellins had, and offered no resistance. One by one, Storm entered them and—

...turned them off.

It was done.

Storm felt an inner quiver, a sigh, a mental tear. Sudden regret welled through him, self-revulsion at the act of violence that had just been performed.

I have killed, came the inner thought, and it was the alien's thought alone.

We have killed, Storm corrected.

Yes, the alien agreed. *We have killed!*

Storm felt the linkage beginning to slip. With the task accomplished, the alien was withdrawing, and they were reestablishing separate identities.

No, Storm cried in panic. *No! Don't leave me! Stay!*

I must, came the quiet reply.

Storm fought against being deserted, but his strength was ebbing now, and the alien had his way. In a moment more, the alien had withdrawn from Storm's mind.

He was alone again.

The shock of separation stunned him. He stood upright for a moment, shivering, sobbing in sudden isolation as contact with the alien broke. Then Storm's strength failed him, and he fell headlong, dropping like a tree.

CHAPTER FOURTEEN

The return to consciousness was almost unbearably agonizing.

Storm woke, and opened his eyes uncertainly. There was a hammering in his head. His eyes ached as though he had just been through a thirty-g acceleration. He felt dazed, stunned, his brain all but burned out by the intensity of what he had experienced.

He rose to his knees, and crouched there a moment like an animal, gathering the strength to raise his head. A long moment passed, and then he looked around.

He saw the UMC men.

They looked peaceful enough. Their passing had been quick and merciful. Ellins was sprawled only a few feet from Storm, and the others were strewn like dolls in a wide circle around them. Storm felt a qualm of pity. These men were strangers to him, and though they had been ready to kill him for purely abstract reasons of corporate greed, Storm was saddened that he had needed to kill them for his own survival.

And for the survival of someone else, too.

Where was the alien's voice? Storm felt no contact at all. The solitude was crushing. In that single moment of union, he had shared his existence with the being from the stars as no two human beings had ever shared it. It had been a kind of marriage, Storm reflected in wonder, though he knew that the alien had been neither of the "male" sort of his race, nor of the "female," but of that mysterious intermediate sort. A kind of marriage. And a swift divorce.

"Are you all right?" Storm asked, his voice sounding forced and hollow to himself.

No answer from the alien.

The effort, perhaps, of what they had just done, had strained the alien, Storm decided. Perhaps he—it?—was resting.

Storm got to his feet. He was still weak, but the strength was returning rapidly to him. He crossed to Ellins, looked down at him, saw that he and all the others were really dead. Storm picked up the document he had been asked to sign, the waiver of his claim, and crushed it and jammed it into his spacesuit. He found his gimmicked helmet, and studied the controls for a moment, readjusted it to undo what Ellins had done to it, and donned it.

He looked around in satisfaction. The authorities were going to be mystified by this, he thought. He would report that he had gone out to the asteroid to investigate a story that UMC was trying to jump his claim. That he had found a UMC base already established there, but that everyone in it was mysteriously dead. Let the coroners puzzle over it. What would their verdicts read? Heart failure? Cerebral hemorrhage? Death from causes unknown?

Storm didn't care. The asteroid was his again. UMC would not dare to fight his claim, after being caught red-handed installing orbit-changing rockets. They would quietly shush the matter up, Ellins' fraudulent claim would vanish from the records, and Storm's original claim would be reinstated.

All that was fine. But now he had to see after the alien.

He stepped through the airlock, safely helmeted, this time, and jumped into one of the UMC crawlers. A few minutes later, he was on the asteroid's other hemisphere, roaming the plain in search of the alien's tunnel.

It took him a little while to find it. It was night, on the other side of the asteroid, and the only illumination came from the stars, and from the faint beam of Storm's helmet. He discovered the cave, and entered it, making his way down the winding tunnel.

There was no contact with the alien, none at all. Storm was frightened, now.

He came to the final bend in the tunnel, and rounded it, and gasped.

The greenish-yellow cloud-curtain that had screened the star-being's chamber was all but gone. Only a few faint lemon-colored wisps blocked Storm's view of the interior of the chamber. Nor was the alien floating high above the chamber floor any longer. He lay in a huddled heap.

And the machinery—the glittering, fantastic instruments from a distant world—

Ashes!

Ruins!

Storm gaped at the sight. Everything destroyed, all the wonderful treasures shattered and incinerated.

"Are you all right?" Storm asked.

The alien's voice came, feebly, haltingly, *I wish ...to thank you ...for your ...help.*

"What happened here?" Storm demanded. "Why is everything in ruins?"

I destroyed it, came the answer.

"Why? Why?"

They must not be used by your race, the alien told him. *You are not ready ...far from ready. These things could have ruined your civilization. They are things no young race can have. They must be developed, not taken from others.*

"But you could have seen to it that they didn't fall into the wrong hands," Storm said.

You do not ...understand. Any hands would have been ...the wrong hands—any human hands.

Storm saw what the alien was too tactful to tell him directly. Only a fool or a madman gives a loaded gun to a child, and this creature was neither. Earth's wisest minds, in the alien's view, were still only the minds of children. So the glittering instruments had had to perish, lest the next time the alien were less lucky in preventing their capture.

"And you?" Storm said. "You sound so weak!"

I am dying, the alien responded. *The effort of doing what we did—I knew it would kill one of us. I am happy it was not you.*

"No!" Storm shouted. "Don't die! Maybe your people will rescue you soon!"

Not for many years. And I am not sad at dying. At last to rest ...no longer to be alone. I am so tired, so tired—

Storm stared. For an instant, he felt a touch of the warmth of contact that he had known earlier, but it faded. The surge of mental energy needed to merge with Storm's mind and wipe out the threat Ellins posed had drained the alien's life-force, and he was dying.

Helplessly, Storm watched the being ebb away.

There was a sudden sensation of coldness, of air rushing down a corridor, and Storm knew that death had come, that a life older than the dinosaur age had ended. Storm turned away. He no longer could comprehend anything of this. For a flickering instant, he had *been* the alien, he had understood what it meant to live forever. But the moment of union was past, and the things Storm had experienced in the alien's mind now seemed like fading dreams.

He was alone on the asteroid of death.

Slowly, Storm turned, and made his way through the tunnel again. His ship was waiting, where he had left it. He clambered up the ladder, entered, explored his gear until he found what he wanted: a small explosive charge, the kind used in making mining surveys.

He returned to the cave, and set the charge, and ran into the clear again, and waited. There was no sound, of course. Storm counted off sixty seconds in his mind, and knew that the charge had erupted by now. He entered the cave once again, but this time he could penetrate only to the second bend. Beyond that, the roof of the tunnel had collapsed in the explosion, and the alien and his chamber and the charred ruins of his wonderful instruments were buried forever.

Storm entered his ship. He sat at the controls for a long while, motionless, dazed, like a man emerging from a dream so vivid that it still captivated his waking mind. Then, shaking his head to clear it, he straightened up, and began to set the computer for blastoff.

The asteroid was his.

He needed only to return to Mars and claim it. No one need ever know of the creature in the cavern. That would be Storm's secret, and no one would ever pry it from him—not ever.

Liz said, "I've often wondered what it's like to be a multi-millionaire's wife."

Storm grinned. They stepped out on the terrace of their hotel, and looked out at the tropical glory below them. The sea was heartrendingly beautiful, the deepest blue they had ever seen, as it came rolling up against the crescent of the beach.

"Now you know," he said. "What's it like?"

"It's just like being the wife of a pauper," she said. "Except more comfortable. Otherwise it's exactly the same ...provided the man is you."

"Provided," Storm said. He slipped his arm around her. They had been man and wife for three days. They would have two weeks together, and then he would have to leave her briefly to return to his asteroid, and supervise the start of mining activities there. After that there would be no more separations.

Liz looked up at him. "There's one strange thing I've been meaning to tell you. Don't say it's silly, though."

"What is it?"

"One night, when you were away up there—I felt you were *calling* to me, Johnny. It was the weirdest thing. You seemed to be reaching out, to be touching me with your mind, and I knew it was you, and I told you I loved you, and I asked you to come home quick, and you said you would."

Storm chuckled and said, "It must have been a dream."

"But it was so *real*, Johnny!"

He smiled, but made no answer, and thought of a curious little creature huddling in a cave on a tiny worldlet. Sadness stole over him.

And another thought, a thought that had been recurring almost obsessively in the past few weeks. For thousands of years, the alien had broadcast a beacon beam. Those beamed impulses were streaking across space, and some day they would be picked up by monitoring stations of the alien race.

They would send out a rescue party, of course. They would cross the gulf of space, in search of their lost comrade. Perhaps it would be in the near future, or perhaps not for thousands of years. Storm wondered what would happen to Earth when these unimaginably advanced creatures came to visit.

Here we are, thinking we're kings of the universe, lords of creation. And then they come, gentle and friendly, but as far beyond us as we are beyond toads and snails.

He shrugged the thought away. It was not his problem to face. Time would supply the answers.

Meanwhile, the asteroid was his, and Liz was his, and the future was his. One other thing was his: the dazzling memory of that tremendous moment when he linked minds with the creature from the stars, and saw that gleaming city in all its splendor.

"A hundred dollars for your thoughts," Liz said.

He blinked in surprise. "Why such a high price? Inflation?"

"I'm just trying to think like a multi-millionaire's wife," she said. "Do you mind?"

Storm laughed. "Not at all. But my thoughts aren't worth that much. I was just ...daydreaming," he said.

"Tell me about your daydream?"

"I can't," he said softly. "It's ...it's just a silly dream. It doesn't matter. How about a swim?"

"Love one," she said.

He smiled at her, and drove the dream from his mind, and they ran hand in hand down to the cool, swirling water, laughing as they ran.

THE END

ACE COVER GALLERY

The following images are covers to other Robert Silverberg Ace Doubles.

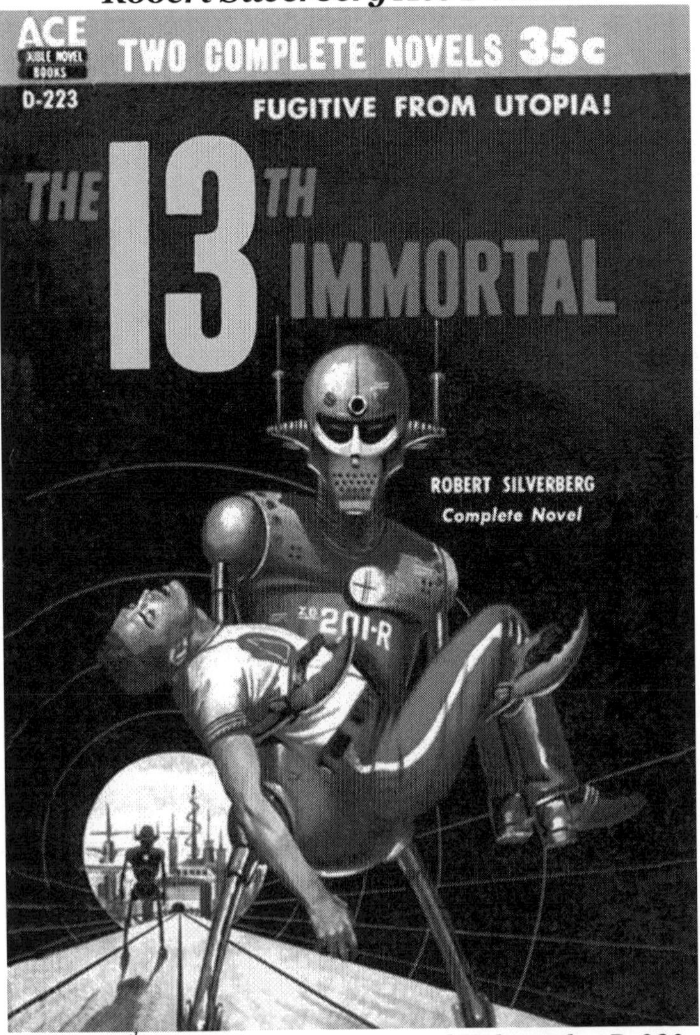

"The 13th Immortal," Cover by Ed Valigursky, D-223

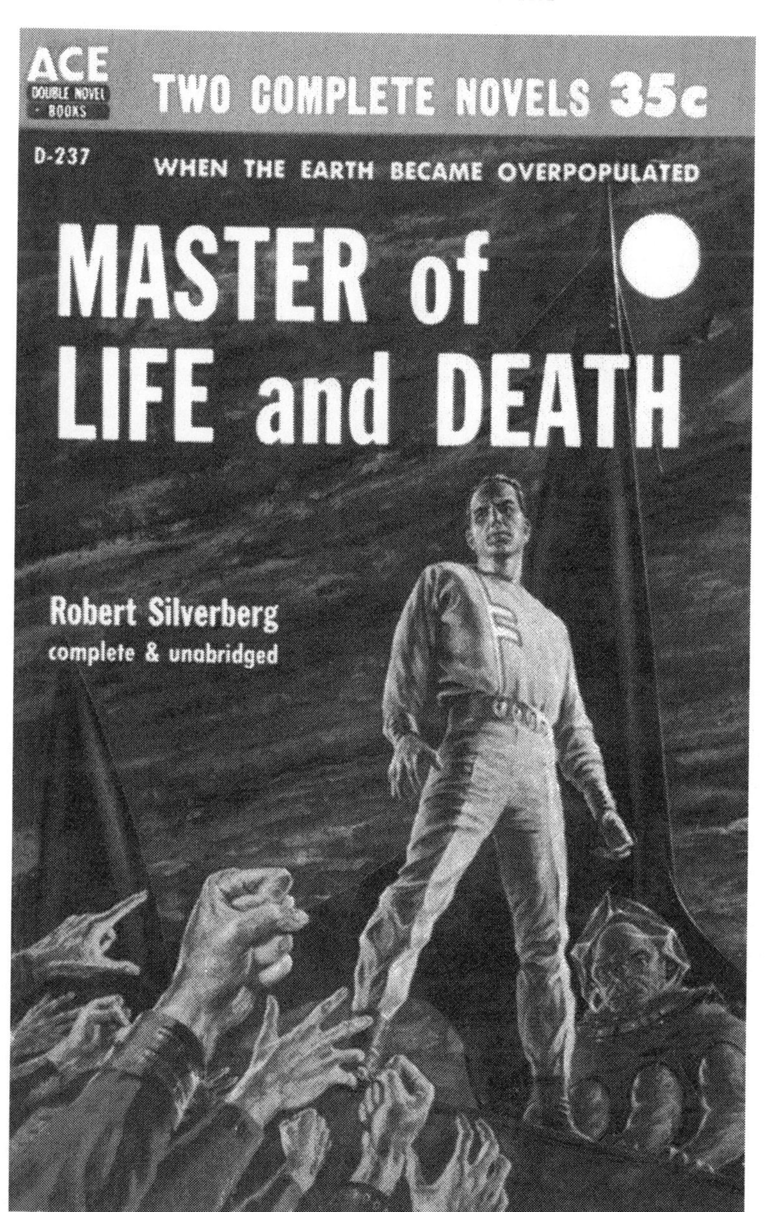

"Master of Life and Death," Cover by Ed Emshwiller, D-237

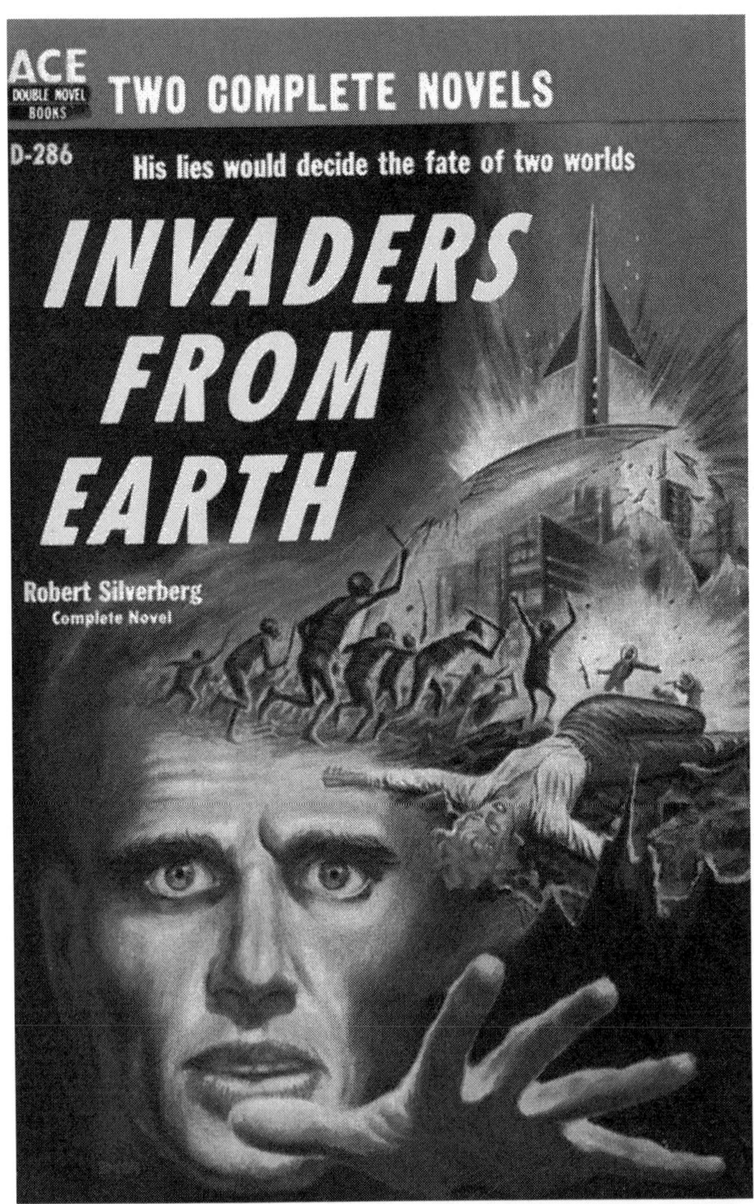

"Invaders from Earth," Cover by Ed Emshwiller, D-286

"Collision Course," Cover by Ed Valigursky, F-123

"The Seed of Earth," Ace Double F-145, which was paired with the Silverberg "Next Stop the Stars" story collection

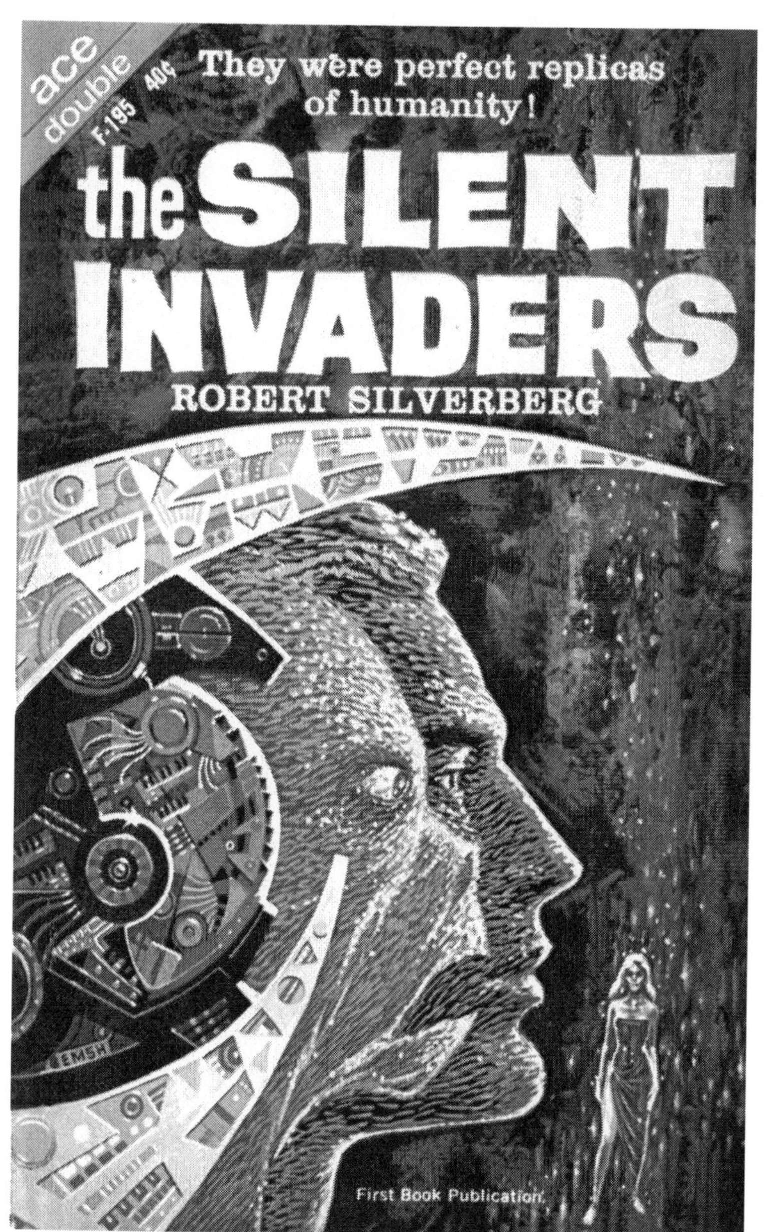

"The Silent Invaders," Cover by Ed Emshwiller, F-195

Death's Planet

Planet Seven on Star System A was a hideous place, a world where sudden, violent death was the rule—not an exception. Nature was harsh, ruthless, and cruel on that awful world.

I found out about World Seven of Star System A quick, and the hard way. I pulled short straw and came down out of the Exploration Team's ship first. There was just about time for me to take three or four hesitant steps on the purplish grass when something came bounding out of the thick jungle and knocked me end over nose.

I got to my feet dizzy and started to grope for my blaster. This time I got a good view of the whatever-it-was. It was the size of a man, roughly, except that about a third of it was head, one-sixth stomach, and half a pair of huge coiled kangaroo-like legs. I caught the flash of white teeth the length of my fingers, of staring red eyes and scaly yellow skin. Then the kangaroo legs tensed, released, and the thing bashed into my chest and knocked me sprawling a second time.

I didn't have a suit on, so I couldn't radio for help. They were probably watching me, up in the ship, waiting for a clear chance to fire. I found myself facing a headful of spike-like teeth. Some getaway, I thought. Escape from a murder rap on Velliran only to be gobbled up alive in this unexplored system.

But just as those teeth seemed ready to bury themselves in my neck, the weight began to lift. Some other friendly beast had come forth from the Jungle. I was being granted a reprieve.

This new one was a lulu. It was tall and thin, maybe fifteen feet high and a foot wide. It looked like a walking telescope, green all over, with two tremendously long dangling arms, a pair of tiny legs tucked away underneath it, and a petal-like arrangement at the very top. One of the dangling arms had grabbed the thing that was sitting on me, and was now hoisting it in the air.

I got to my feet again and stepped back into the shadow of the ship, and watched. The beast with the teeth was kicking and squirming, but the telescope thing had a good grip on it and wasn't letting go. I saw the animal rise higher and higher, until the spindly arm held it over the petal arrangement on top. Then the arm let go.

The petals spread wide to receive the animal.

There was a lump, live and kicking, in the telescope thing's throat. Then, slowly, horribly, that lump started to sink stomachward. I shuddered.

The telescope creature folded its long arms around its middle, hugged itself in a little dance of contentment and joy, and waddled back into the jungle. A second later, I was surrounded by my shipmates.

"We've been welcomed," I said.

DEATH came quick and fast and ugly on World Seven of Star System A. But it came just as fast on the allegedly civilized world of Velliran, and when it came you had to look out or it would sweep you in along with the intended victim.

That's what happened to me.

I'm from Earth, originally; I wasn't born on any of the outworlds, but right on Homeworld herself. Not that that meant anything. With umpty-ump billion people scrabbling for a living on Earth, I made like everybody else and took off for the outworlds, where, I thought, I could live comfortably and well and breathe fresh air.

I went to Velliran. Velliran's a world in the Pollux system; it's big but not too dense, and so the all-important grav ratio is 1:1 with Earth. I settled on Velliran and I lived there eight years, and I probably would still be there except for the events that led me to World Seven of Star System A.

Velliran is populated chiefly by native life—small, finely-formed blue-skinned humanoids whose ancestry goes back into the dim years of the universe. They speak softly to each other in a strange, liquid language, and they keep pretty much to themselves, not mingling with the Earthmen who have built cities on their world. They have a keen sense of the ethical, and I'm told their religion is one of the galaxy's noblest. I don't know. I never had much to do with them.

I was operating a yangskin syndicate on Velliran, and bringing in a tidy profit. I employed six Terran hunters who ventured into the interior to hunt the strange eight-legged yangs, and I employed three skinners and four curers and two packers. At its best it was a medium-big syndicate, and I was bringing in some 20,000 credits a year profit, with more orders tumbling in day by day as the women of Earth found it more and more fashionable to deck their shoulders with the soft, clinging black-and-white skins.

I was on the way to the bank one morning with the week's loot in my pocket. It was a bright, clear morning, the sky having the fantastic transparent look that makes Velliran so lovely. I remember thinking about how glad I was just to be here. The streets weren't crowded; a couple of slim, soft-eyed little natives were walking up ahead, and a few Terrans.

Exactly what came next I wasn't sure. It felt like I'd been clubbed over the head and struck with lightning simultaneously, except that when it was all over I was still standing right where I was, and the street was just as quiet.

Only now I was holding a jeweled knife tight in my right hand. It was dripping bright red. *Blood red*—but not Earthman red. Oh, no. The only people who had blood as flame-red as that were the native Vellirani.

There was one of them at my feet, looking peaceful even in death. But he hadn't died peacefully at all. His blue body had been ripped open with a knife. With the knife I now was staring stupidly at.

THEY reeled me into court a little while later—naturally, a Corpsman came strolling along while I gaped at the murder-weapon I held—and the trial took about six minutes. The judge was a stranger to me, which was too bad.

He squinted down from the bench and said, "Defendant Crawford, you have slain a Vellirani in broad daylight. Do you have any explanation for this crime?"

I blinked. "None."

What else could I say? I couldn't argue with the bloody knife in my hand.

The judge said, "The crime lies outside the jurisdiction of Terran court on Velliran. But, of course, this does not mean you will go unpunished."

I stared at him. "I didn't do it. It couldn't have been me."

"The Vellirani have ways of justice of their own. To them do we commend you."

And they turned me loose.

I stood outside the courtroom a few minutes, looking up at the transparent sky and wondering how it was that your life could crumble to hell inside half an hour. The deposit was still in my pocket. Two thousand credits, backed by pretty Terran platinum. They weren't going to get to the bank, now. I was going to need them. And there wasn't much time.

Someone had put the frame to me, but there was no point trying to convince anyone of my innocence. The Vellirani would never understand the concept of falsely blaming another for a crime he hadn't committed. To them, I had killed their countryman, and I had to die. That was the way Vellirani justice worked. And, I knew, their methods of execution were unpleasant.

There was a man I could see, though. His name was Geoffrey Hallan, and he was an Expediter. He made things easy for people.

He was a small, squint-eyed man with a sharp nose and a pale face. He said, "You really didn't kill the alien?"

"Honest. Unless I had a sudden kill-fit and now I can't remember it."

He shrugged. "Well, it doesn't matter whether you killed him or not, does it? As far as the Vellirani are concerned, *someone* has to die for the crime, and it might as well be you as anyone else."

"Exactly." I took out my bank deposit, flicked the bills with my fingers, and slapped them down on my desk. "Here's two thousand, Hallan. Can you get me off Velliran by nightfall?"

HE took the bills, riffled through them speculatively, studied the serial numbers, rubbed his thumbs over the portrait in the middle. At length he said, "Maybe."

"Maybe?"

"There's an Exploratory Corps ship in town, due to leave tonight. Their ecologist died in space, and they asked me to find them a new one. I contacted the Corps headquarters and had them ship a replacement out here. His name is Paul Markham, and he's here in the city."

"So?"

"Suppose," he said, "I got *you* aboard that ship instead of Markham."

"Me? I'm no ecologist! I don't know anything about—"

Hallan smiled bleakly. "You don't have to. All you need to do is get aboard that ship. They're bound for unexplored territory in the Andromeda region, and if you can bluff your way until you're in hyperspace, you've got it made. They won't turn back on your account. If there's any trouble, I'll make up some story or other. When they return, you go to some other planet and change your name. The galaxy's big; the Vellirani won't bother you."

"What about this Markham?"

"Him? He'll just miss the boat, that's all. There are plenty of ways of delaying a man past blastoff time."

THE three moons of Velliran were high overhead, casting their orange light, when I arrived at the spaceport. I had spent the day at Kalian's, arranging things. He would hold all my property and my bank account for me, and when I returned from my exploratory jaunt he would forward them to me on my new world. I didn't trust him too much, but under the circumstances I was happy to get away from Velliran alive, let alone with any property.

He drove me down to the spaceport at 19:45, and the ship was there—tall, slim, glittering faintly in the moonlight. He escorted me to the ship's elevator.

"Okay. You should make it clear from here, Crawford—ah, *Markham.* Take it smooth, and I'll watch for the word from you."

"Thanks, Hallan. Thanks."

I stepped into the elevator and rode up into the ship. Eight or nine men were waiting for me.

"I'm Markham," I said. "The new ecologist."

A tall man in blue-and-gold uniform said, "Welcome aboard. I'm Captain Hendrin. These are the men you'll work with."

He introduced me rapidly around: there was a biologist, a medic, an anthropologist, a botanist, a chemist, and so on—all the usual manpower of an exploratory mission. Captain Hendrin said, "We're bound for the Andromeda system, as you may have heard. It's going to be the standard six-month jaunt. We're beginning in Star System A, and the orders are to name and survey as many worlds as we can within our time period."

I grinned, trying to make it look scientific. "Glad to be aboard, Captain."

Gradually I settled into shipboard routine, bluffing mightily as I went. Actually, it wasn't too hard. The Exploratory Corps has been dealt with pretty frequently in adventure fiction, and from the novels I'd read I had a fair knowledge of shipboard routine and the like. Of course, I didn't know a thing about ecology, but from my readings in the ship's tape-library, I slowly acquired a working knowledge of my subject.

All that mattered was that I had gotten off Velliran alive. I didn't know who had framed me or why, nor did I think at the time that I'd ever find out, but all that was behind me. I had been put in a situation where it was get offworld or else, and no time to argue about the rights and wrongs and moral undertones of the thing.

It was a three-week journey—the first two days in standard ion drive, then, when we were clear of the Pollux system, the conversion and wrenching screech into hyperdrive. Three weeks in the nothingness of warp, as the ship gulped up space.

Then we were out of our galaxy altogether, and into the Andromeda cluster. It hung all around, bright strange starry dots against the black field of space. In the first few minutes after we emerged from warp, I peered out the viewplate, looking at the immensity of stars.

I was thinking that the universe was appallingly big. Here we were, exploring a galaxy the size of our own—and, on and on through the endless night, there lay galaxy after galaxy, millions of them, each with its thousand billion stars or so. Man could send out Exploratory Teams from here to the end of time and probably not have a chance to touch down on each world of space as much as once.

The autopilot homed in on the arbitrarily named System A, a group of eleven worlds revolving around a bright young yellow main sequence sun. We'd spend our next six months in System A, and probably not even do that job thoroughly. Near-infinite worlds, near-infinite life forms—

I realized I had been developing a pretty provincial attitude, in my previous life as a prosperous yangskin-exporter on Velliran.

The universe was a big place. I was only now getting to appreciate that.

The eleven worlds of Star System A hung outside our viewplate like spinning bright-colored globes. Two of the planets were ringed; one spun so close to the sun that it could not possibly have any form of life; two more, double worlds, revolved about each other in a strange orbit that would require detailed investigation.

But Captain Hendrin selected World Seven of Star System A as our first port of call. We swung into a landing orbit, and as the ship spiraled down, the chemical team studied the atmosphere and reported that it would be breathable.

We landed. The tests were checked and double-checked. It was clear that we could go out without spacesuits. Custom now dictated a lottery; we drew, and I got the short straw.

Captain Hendrin chuckled. "I suppose it's fitting that our ecologist should be the first one out on World Seven. You'll be the first to see the fauna."

I stepped through the lock and out. I was the first to see the fauna, all right. But the fauna saw me, too—and they moved faster than I did.

MY nine shipmates were standing around me, looking worried.

"You all right?" Hendrin asked.

"Pretty good. That beast with the teeth took me by surprise. I guess I'd have been down the old alimentary canal by now if the other one hadn't come along."

I flicked some sweat from my forehead and stared at the dark forest. The air was thick, hot, hard to breathe; a sort of sweltering moistness about it made it unpleasant. Far within the thicket of sharp green leaves, I heard a cry: a harsh, croaking, desperate cry.

A death-cry.

"This is a rough, primitive world," said Lazenby. He was the biologist. "It's a young world. Life is cheap here."

Hendrin nodded. "We'd better operate in teams on any explorations," the Captain said. "And go about heavily armed. Wide-beam blasters for everyone. There's no telling what strange beasts are lurking in there."

I was still shaking a little. That sudden encounter with the toothed creature hadn't done my nervous system any good. I said, "Maybe we'd better leave this world, Captain. It's too dangerous for us. We ought to go on to some of the other planets in this system."

Hendrin wheeled around to face me, and I saw all the joviality drain from his face. The *real* Hendrin pocked forth for the first time since I had come aboard. His face was the face of an ascetic; of a man dedicated to his job, ready to perform it no matter what the cost. I felt chilled.

"Markham," he said, "You haven't been with us long, so I can forgive you for that remark. But coming from a member of the Exploratory Corps, and from an ecologist as well, your words shock me. Once an Exploratory Corps ship lands on a planet, it stays there until its job is done. I've operated that way for thirteen years, and I'll keep on operating that way." His voice crackled like a whip. He turned to the other men of the team. "Is there anyone else who feels like leaving now?"

No one spoke.

I nibbled my lip unhappily. Part of me wanted to tell Hendrin that I was no ecologist, no Exploratory Corps man at all, just a fugitive yangskin-exporter who was fleeing a phony murder rap and had used his ship as a handy way out. But I saw that would never do at all. Hendrin was too dedicated to his lofty principles to let me stay at large if he knew the truth. From the expression on his face, I knew he was the sort who would bring me for the duration of the voyage and return me to Velliran when it was all over.

Geoffrey Hallan probably had known that. Well, Hallan was just out for a buck, like the rest of us. I was going to have to keep up the pretense of being an ecologist until Hendrin decided he'd explored World Seven of System A fully enough. It wasn't going to be easy.

Another death-cry sounded in the forest.

"I'm sorry. Captain," I said, making my voice appear humble. "The experience of being suddenly attached—my nerves—"

"Okay Markham," he said. His voice was gruff but sympathetic. "I understand. But no more talking of leaving here until our job is done!"

I forced a grin. "Right, Captain!"

But as I heard the sounds of rending and killing coming from that wild, steaming jungle all around us, I wondered whether I would have been safer back on Velliran.

WE began formal full-scale exploration of World Seven an hour later, after a quick briefing aboard ship.

By this time I had soaked up enough of standard exploration procedure to be fairly confident of passing as a genuine Corps man, provided no one studied me too closely. I knew the general routine.

The purpose of the Exploratory Corps was to size up each of the worlds of the universe, of which there were billions, and to file a full report with Central Control back on Earth. Central Control, the vast computer that made existence in a galaxy of a hundred billion people possible, would digest and tape the reports.

We were supposed to bring back, primarily, a yes-no statement on the world's value as a potential Terran colony; a comprehensive report on the planet's natural wealth, its minerals and soil fertility and livestock; a comment on the presence of intelligent life on the world. All this data went into the great hopper of Central Control, and the Exploratory Corps moved ever onward into unexplored regions of space.

My job as ecologist was to study the relationships between animals and their environment on World Seven, and prepare a report indicating how these relationships could be put to use in the event of Earth colonization of the planet: which animals controlled the breeding of which other animals, how the extermination of certain forms of plant life would affect the distribution of life, etc. In a way, it was an easy job; in another way, it was an overpoweringly hard one—because it required me to get out there and explore that jungle.

Which was one thing I had little desire to do. Murray, the cartographer, had it easy: he spent his hours aloft, in the tiny copter the ship carried, mapping out the world. Unless there were monsters of the air, he'd be in no danger.

But me? I was going to have to get a first-hand look at life on World Seven.

I was teamed with Lazenby, the biologist. He was a slim, stoop-shouldered man in his middle forties, mild-mannered, quiet. Just the sort who would spend his life roving from world to world, collecting algae and protozoa. I had been hoping to be matched with Bartlett, the anthropologist—a big, square-built, blocky man who would be of some value in case of trouble. But Bartlett was paired with Dorvin, the chemist, and I drew little Lazenby.

We rode down the ship's elevator together, out of the ship and to the ground. This time, before venturing into the little clearing that surrounded the ship, I looked around in all directions. I wasn't taking chances.

The coast was clear, though. "Come on," I said to Lazenby. "No trouble in sight."

We were armed with stubby blasters, but we were weighted down with note-taking apparatus too, and Lazenby carried a couple dozen collecting bottles slung in a harness around his waist.

The jungle was heavy with moisture: not rain but dew, precipitated straight from the air and beading out on anything and everything, leaves, stones, ground, us. I glanced at my watch. We had arranged to cover as much ground as we could in an hour's time, and then return to the ship.

I kept my ears tuned. I knew this forest was full of strange and probably dangerous creatures, and I wanted to be ready for them.

It didn't take long.

We had been walking for perhaps five minutes when I heard rustling up ahead. I glanced at Lazenby. He was kneeling over a tiny pond, scooping up samples of its water for later bacterial analysis. I said, "Better look sharp. Something's coming."

"Where? I don't hear anything."

"Listen up ahead."

The sound of thrashing vines and splintering saplings came to us—and then, thundering toward us like a runaway express, came an animal. I caught Lazenby's arm and dragged him into the shade of a thick, gnarled tree.

THE creature was perhaps twenty feet long, glossy brown in color. It had four legs that terminated in splaying toes, a long, thin neck, an equally long tail at the other end. It weighed perhaps ten tons, and it was moving fast.

It had no head.

At the end of that neck was a jagged slash, and then nothing but welling gouts of blood that pulsed forth with each convulsion of the animal's heart, and squirted out over the trees. The beast was dead, but it was so slow-witted it hadn't realized it.

"We ought to follow it," Lazenby said. "It's bound to drop soon. I'd like to examine it close-up."

I shook my head. "Uh-uh. That boy may be dead, but I'll bet the thing that did it to him will be along any minute now. Let's wait."

I was right.

The animal that appeared moved with almost sickening grace: it slid through the forest as if it were on wheels, gliding along effortlessly. It was ten feet high, standing upright on two tapering legs with two more up beneath its throat. A mouth full of razors yawned at us, and dripped blood. It sped past us and pounced on the headless beast we had seen first, which had stumbled and fallen in the underbrush ahead.

I watched, chilled, as the killer dug its two tiny forepaws deep into the still-quivering flesh of the other, and brought its teeth down for the first bite. I couldn't stand the sight. Before I knew what I was doing, I had the firing stud of my blaster yanked back, and gave the killer full beam.

He sizzled and fried for a second or two before he knew what hit him. Then he reared up from the dead or dying body, came at me, and actually travelled three or four feet before he fell. I finished ashing him and lowered my blaster. I realized I had been shouting incoherently all through it.

Within moments half a thousand tiny creatures had come from nowhere—out of the trees, out from under rocks, up from the pond. They began to feed on the two hulking corpses. The smell of death pervaded the place.

I turned and saw Lazenby staring at me in utter horror. For the first time in minutes, I regained self-control.

"I've never seen anything like that," he said, in a hushed voice.

"The killer? Vicious bastard, wasn't he?"

"No," Lazenby said. He looked pale and uneasy. "I mean *you*. The sadistic joy with which you killed the animal! The cries of hate! Markham, it was horrible!"

"Look here, Lazenby—that animal was a killer. I had to blast him."

"Why?"

That stopped me. I didn't have any answer.

He said, "It had already killed its prey. It hadn't attacked you at all. Your job was to record the feeding process, not to interfere with that damned blaster of yours. But you did."

"I lost my head. Something just broke open inside me and I had to fire. Silly of me," I said.

"Silly? It was downright criminal! For an ecologist to destroy life wantonly when he could've been observing the process of—"

That was when the tree wrapped its arms around Lazenby and lifted him off the ground.

"Lazenby!"

He was pinioned by a thick green tendril that had wrapped itself three or four times around his waist. His face was gray ashen; he was ten feet off the ground, and rising. I saw the treetop writhing in anticipation; there was something uncomfortably like a mouth up there.

Carnivorous trees?

"For the love of God, get me out of here!" Lazenby was pleading. I drew my blaster and tried to aim it, but he was kicking and squirming wildly, trying to fight the inexorable lift of that tendril.

"Hold still," I shouted. "I don't want to hit you."

I fired above his head, at the tendril, and missed. I caught a limb of the tree instead. The tree shook convulsively. I fired again, and this time I nailed the tendril squarely.

The tree screamed.

It was a bellowed howl of pain and rage that wrung itself up out of the thick trunk and sounded all over the forest. Lazenby came tumbling down, bouncing from branch to branch. I caught him and broke his fall. The seared-off tendril still clung to his middle, and his face was pale green.

I unwrapped the tendril and flung it to one side. He got up, shakily.

"Thanks," he said hoarsely.

I looked up at the tree, which had resumed its stationery position now. It looked totally innocent. Scowling, I looked at the ground at my feet, as if I expected it to open a fanged mouth and swallow me.

"Let's go back to the ship," I said. "We can explore some other time."

BACK in the safety of the ship, I was able to let my tight-strung nerves slacken a little.

Hendrin had been aboard ship, dictating log notes, and he came forward to demand why we had returned so soon. I told him.

"Carnivorous trees?" he repeated. "We'll have to send Grover out for a look at those." Grover was the botanist of the group. "Did you get films of the attack, Markham?"

"I was too busy getting Lazenby out of that tree," I said. "I couldn't think about films."

Hendrin frowned. "Saving Lazenby was important, of course. But you should have taken films. And I hope you don't expect to take the rest of the day off, do you?"

"We're a little shaken up, sir," Lazenby began diffidently. "Some time to rest before we go back out—"

"All right," Hendrin said. "Take half an hour. But don't waste any more time than that. I don't want the schedule chopped up."

We left the Captain, heading for the ship's lounge to have a drink or two before returning to the job outside. "He really means business, doesn't he?" I said.

Lazenby grunted. "It's the right way to run an Exploratory Team. You get the job done, that way."

We had a couple of drinks each, and I saw the color come back into Lazenby's face. He wasn't as ruffled by his narrow escape as I might have expected him to be; he took it more in the line of an occupational hazard, which it was—something that might happen in the course of everyday work.

He turned to me and said, "There was something I was meaning to ask you before that tree got me."

"Shoot."

He paused for a second, then said, squinting up his eyes, "Who are you, Markham? *Really*, I mean."

I put my drink down. "Huh?"

"Don't play innocent." There was a sudden strength behind the watery eyes. "I know damned well you're not Paul Markham of the Exploration Corps. Suppose you tell me just who you *are.*"

"Lazenby, has that tree-thing driven you nuts? Of course I'm Markham!"

I'm afraid I wasn't a very good liar. The little biologist smiled wryly. "You're no more of a trained ecologist than I am a circus strongman, *Markham.* You might as well admit it. The real Markham had been in the Corps five years. I don't know him, but I know damned well you aren't any ecologist with five years' field training. The way you blasted down that killer animal before—"

I looked at him coldly. He had me nicely pinpointed. "Suppose I'm not Markham. What of it?"

"Nothing. You saved my life, whoever you are, and I don't intend to turn you in. But it's unusual, to say the least, to have an impostor in an Exploration Team. For my own curiosity, I'd like to know why."

I look a deep breath. "My name is Ree Carpenter. I'm a native of Earth, and I lived on Velliran for eight years. Somebody framed me while your ship was down to pick up the real Markham, and I had to get off planet in a hurry. This was the quickest way."

"And what happened to Markham? The *real* one?"

I shrugged. "A friend of mine was supposed to arrange that he show up late at the spaceport. I don't think they did anything to him."

Lazenby smiled and said, "How much of this am I supposed to believe?"

"As much or as little as you want," I said. "It all happens to be true. I was framed for murder—they accused me of having killed a Vellirani native. It wasn't so. But the evidence made it look that way, and on Velliran, that's enough. So I'm here, on this hellworld."

He was looking at me strangely. "You were accused of killing a Vellirani native?"

"Damned right! I don't know how it was done, but I found myself holding a bloody blade, with a dead Vellirani lying in the street at my toes. I didn't kill him."

Lazenby smiled. "I'm sure you didn't. That reminds me of a very funny story. Remind me to tell it to you some time."

HE wouldn't elaborate on that, though I tried to pry it out of him. After a while we decided we had rested enough, and went back outside for another survey of the forest.

Lazenby was very helpful. As we advanced warily, inch by inch, through the sweating jungle, he made occasional comments that were designed to help me in compiling my report, pointed out things that I, as a presumably skilled ecologist, should have noticed, and was generally of assistance. We didn't encounter any other carnivorous trees, or anything else that was really dangerous. But every minute I spent in the jungle of World Seven, I liked the planet less.

There was something *sick* about it—something broodingly rotten. Every manifestation of life shared that characteristic.

"Look here," Lazenby said. He pointed down, at a pool of water perhaps three feet across. There were tiny creatures swimming in it.

"So? A puddle with tadpoles in it."

"Take a look at the tadpoles," he said.

I knelt while he stood guard and peered into that puddle. The "tadpoles" were small dark things about an inch long—with bright little teeth, jagged and sharp. They moved fast, those "tadpoles." And they were busy.

A snakelike creature about twenty inches long lay beneath the muddy water, wriggling slowly—while the tadpoles energetically picked away pieces of its flesh. The snake evidently had taken a shortcut through the puddle, or perhaps he had wanted a bath. But the tadpoles had been lying in wait.

"It's the same everywhere on this planet," I said. "The animals are killers. The plants are killers."

Lazenby nodded. "Life is short and tough, here. You have to be fast to survive, and you need a good pair of teeth."

"It's a vicious world," I said.

"No. Nature isn't vicious, or ugly, or any of the other moralistic tags you're probably getting ready to toss up. That's just life you see down there. And on World Seven life is a tough proposition."

"It's a tough proposition anywhere," I said. "But here it's more obvious."

"Exactly."

I looked down at the hungry little beasts in the puddle and shuddered, "I'm a lousy excuse for a scientist," I said. "I can't be cool and detached in a place like this. Not where even the trees try to eat you. I'd like to get the hell off this planet. There's something filthy about it."

He only smiled. "You don't have the true scientific mind. You aren't detached."

"I won't have to bluff being a scientist for long," I said. "Just till Hendrin decides he's ready to return to civilization. If I'm still alive by then," I said, looking at the quivering fronds of a huge fern nearby. "If this planet doesn't get us all first."

AS it happened, not every member of the team seemed to share Lazenby's calm, precise, scientific attitude. That became clear that evening, when we were gathered back aboard the ship to compare notes on the day's work.

Murray, the cartographer, said, "This is the nastiest world I've ever seen."

I snickered. "You see it from a thousand feet up. Go take a walk through the jungle if you want to find out how nasty it can be."

"I did," he said. "I brought the copter down to let Chung, here, study some geological formation. We weren't on the ground ten minutes when a brawl started. Some big blue and red beast the size of a hill came toward us looking mean. But before he got anywhere, three jag-toothed flying creatures came swooping down like dive-bombers on him. Sliced his neck open and had themselves a feast."

"I didn't get to see the formation I was interested in, either," Chung, the geologist who had flown with Murray, said. "We decided not to wait."

"It's the same everywhere," said Grover, the botanist. "I went out to examine that devilish carnivorous tree that nearly swallowed Lazenby."

"Did it perform for you?" Lazenby asked.

"Damned right it did! I had no sooner got there than it lashed out with a tendril and swooped up a hulking deer-like creature. I filmed the whole thing. It wasn't pretty."

Fernandez, the medic, a swarthy heavyset giant, looked up from his brooding silence in the corner and said, "This is no world for a ten-man team. We ought to go on to the next place, and let Earth send a fully armed expedition out here if they're interested. We're risking our lives every time we step outside the ship."

"Yeah," said Bartlett, the brawny antropologist. "We already know this planet isn't suitable for colonization—at least not for another hundred million years or so. Why are we sticking around?"

"Why don't you ask Captain Hendrin that?" Lazenby suggested quietly. He was loyal to Hendrin, I knew. "He seems very interested in giving this world detailed study. And I am too; it's quite a remarkable primitive tropical planet."

Bartlett's eyes blazed. "Remarkable! Remarkable, when every beast in that jungle's waiting to feed on you? I'd like to get moving—to a safe planet."

"What's that, Bartlett?" said a cold voice at the door.

We all turned. It was Captain Hendrin, standing at the entrance, one hand clamping the edge of the bulkhead. "Would you care to repeat that in my presence, Bartlett?"

The husky anthropologist was pale, but he looked squarely at Hendrin and said, "I was expressing the opinion, sir, that possibly we had achieved all we could achieve on this planet and should move on, since it's obviously an unsafe world."

"Oh. I see," Hendrin said in a dead, flat voice. "You didn't hear the little speech I made to Markham when he advanced the same idea, earlier?"

"I heard it. I think it's suicide to stay here. Captain."

"Who else feels this way?" Hendrin demanded. He glared around the cabin. "Chung? Grover? Lazenby?"

"I'm not so happy here," Fernandez admitted quietly. But none of the rest of us spoke up. At length Hendrin said, "You seem to be in the minority, Bartlett. We'll stay here and do it the way the Corps always does it. This planet will need at least a month's intensive work."

Bartlett smothered down his anger. It required a visible effort.

"Let's have no more talk of leaving," Hendrin said. "Is that understood?"

IT was. But it wasn't understood or accepted gracefully, I could see. After Hendrin left, Bartlett and Fernandez had a conversation of low whispers in one corner of the room, and after a while, they called Grover over. I didn't know what was going on, but I could guess they were planning some way of getting Hendrin to change his mind.

In a way, I was a little disillusioned. Only Hendrin and Lazenby, of all these men, was a Corpsman in the sense I was accustomed to from reading the adventure stories. The rest of them were ordinary people like me—scientifically trained, but not particularly anxious to martyr themselves in the name of scientific investigation. This was a bitch of a world; they recognized the fact, and they wanted out, just the same as I did.

That night, the forest howled and hooted at us from sundown to sunup. I spent a good chunk of the night staring out the viewplate at the waiting jungle outside. World Seven had two moons, but they weren't attractive golden spheres like the three of Velliran; they were jagged little rocks that cast a pale white light, old and baleful. In their glimmer, I saw strange wolf-like animals range themselves around the ship and bay their anger, and slinking cat-beasts that slipped among them and fought in the World Seven; the others didn't last long at all.

The next two days saw the pattern spread out and intensify. I learned more about World Seven, and the more I learned the more anxious I was to get offworld fast—and most of my shipmates seemed to feel the same way.

Lazenby and I turned up sights on our rambles through the forest that sickened me—and once even bent the slim biologist's scientific poise. That was the little incident where we came upon a bloated black-and-gray striped mammal lying on its side in a swamp—*her* side, I should say, because the creature was plainly a female.

She looked something like a wart hog, something like a Minervan *brolla,* and something indescribable. She was perhaps eight feet long, and had recently given birth. A little cluster of offspring, small enough to be cute if they weren't so hideous, jostled and pushed at each other in order to suckle.

Seven of the little ones managed to get in on the food supply. Two more were left out in the cold—and, when the seven had fed, mama calmly lifted her massive head and snapped up the two weaklings in a mouthful apiece.

I looked at Lazenby. He hadn't enjoyed that.

"Survival of the fittest," I said acidly. "Mother Nature in action."

He glanced at me for a second, then back at the chop-licking beast in the swamp. "I've never seen a world like this," he said curtly, and began to scribble notes.

That was what World Seven was like. We slogged through the mud and slime and heat, and the more I saw of it the less happy I was about the eventual report I'd be expected to file. The planet was an ecologist's nightmare, an interlocking series of biological dependencies that seemed to have no end. Even with Lazenby's help, I'd never be able to bluff my way through and fool Hendrin.

Somehow we avoided the carnivorous trees and the various toothy killers long enough to make a fairly complete survey of our sector. Work was proceeding on other fronts, too. Murray was preparing his aerial maps, and Chung, flying with him, had given the geology of the planet a thoroughgoing job. Since there was no intelligent life here, anthropologist Bartlett could not function in his specialty, so he teamed with Dorwin the chemist and served as lab assistant. The report was shaping up.

Then Evans, who doubled as radioman and assistant chemist, came back from his hike carrying what was left of botanist Grover.

I didn't get a good look at Grover. I only got half a look, and that was enough. Fernandez, who's a medic and who doesn't get bothered by such sights easily, grabbed up a plastic tarpaulin and wrapped it around the body in a double hurry.

Captain Hendrin appeared, looking grimmer than usual, and glanced around.

"What happened to Grover?"

"He—fell, Captain," Evans said. The radioman licked his lips nervously. "He saw a plant he wanted to examine, and took a couple of steps off the beaten road. Then he yelled and slipped out of sight. It was some sort of trap—it looked like solid ground, but it wasn't. It—I don't know what it was. Whether it was a plant or an animal or what. He screamed a couple of times. I saw something yellow frothing around, and thin little tentacles waving.

He held out his hands. They were red, raw, blistered. "I reached in and yanked him out. Some of the stuff spilled on my hands. It was like acid, sir. Like acid."

Hendrin was silent for a moment. Then he said, "Bartlett, Murray—get a grave dug outside the ship. And make it deep, this planet may have a few ghouls along with its other forms of life."

They shambled off to do the job. We were all pretty stunned at Grover's death—not so much the fact that a man had died, as the *way* he had died. He'd been eaten alive by—what? A pool of protozoa? Who knew?

He was the first human victim of World Seven. The planet's deadly spell was extending to us, now.

Grover's death cast a shadow over the rest of that day. No one went out of the ship after sundown; the moons had risen, and their cold light glittered on the crude grave outside. We spent our time filing reports, transcribing notes, doing anything at all to keep our minds busy.

LATER that night, Fernandez came over to where I sat in the ship's study, and tapped me gently on the shoulder. I looked up, startled.

"Markham?"

"What is it?"

"Can you come to my cabin for a minute? I want to talk to you."

I didn't object. I followed the hulking medic up the narrow companionway to his private cabin and we went inside. He clicked the lock closed.

"What's this all about, Fernandez?"

He held up one beefy hand. "Patience, friend. All in good time." Going to his closet, he drew forth a drink flask containing an unmistakably sparkling liquid, and handed it to me, grinning. "Have a drink first."

The stuff was Vellirani whiskey, one of the finest beverages known to the universe. I had missed it. "Where'd you get this?" I asked, as I punctured the drink flask seal and took a sip. "Is it allowed on board?"

"Medicinal purposes," Fernandez said blandly. "A little privilege of my position. Have another drink."

I had another, and two or three more. Then I said, "You didn't invite me here to drink your liquor. What's on your mind, Doc?"

"Hendrin."

"Eh?"

"Grover's death this afternoon could have been avoided—if we'd left this planet yesterday. I don't know how you feel about this, Markham. You're new to the crew. The rest of us have been together a long time, and Grover's death hurt. Hurt hard. You want me to stop talking, or should we go on?"

"Go on," I said.

"Okay. You may or may not know the clause in the Corps charter that refers to replacement of superior officer when he no longer is capable of commanding ship."

"I'm familiar with it." I saw now what Fernandez was driving at. "I'm with you so far," I said. "Keep talking."

"Some of us—Bartlett, Murray, myself, mainly—have come to the conclusion that remaining here is not in the best interest of the group's common safety. We're not equipped for a world like this, and it's suicide to keep wandering around on foot in that jungle. This ought to be a three-ship team, with land-crawlers and heavy artillery. You were the first one of us to be attacked by native wildlife. You know what it's like.

"In my position as medic, I can issue an opinion that Hendrin is temporarily insane. It'll stand up anywhere in the galaxy. We'll remove him from command, put him down below where he can't interfere, and get off World Seven. But I won't issue the opinion unless I have a majority behind me. That's why I have to know where you stand, Markham."

I frowned. "You're proposing mutiny, in other words?"

"No. Legal removal of a temporarily insane commander is not mutiny. And it'll mean the deaths of all of us if we stay here the full period. Well, Markham? Are you with us?"

Grinning, I said, "What do you think? I like to stay alive just as much as the next man."

I HAD a few more drinks and left Fernandez' cabin, and so far as I knew the mutiny remained in abeyance for the next day or two. Perhaps Fernandez was waiting until he had a unanimous backing behind him; I didn't know. So far as I knew four of the eight crewmen were in favor of deposing Hendrin—Fernandez, Murray, Bartlett, and myself. Only one—Lazenby—seemed to prefer remaining on World Seven to complete the observation. The other three, Chung, Evans, and Dorwin, had made no definite statement, at least not to me, but I was fairly certain where their sympathies lay. None of them was the deep-down dedicated type that would vote to remain on a suicide world like this one.

But nothing happened, during the next day. I saw little of Captain Hendrin, and what little I did see I didn't like: he was dour, grim, and stern, as if he expected what was brewing and was determined to squash it the moment it started.

For some reason, the field pairings were switched around the next day. It seemed that Chung wanted to investigate the geology of our region more closely, and had requested that he be teamed with someone who had been working in the area. I was paired with him; Lazenby was shifted over to work with Bartlett, and Murray did his stint in the copter with Dorwin. With the death of Grover, the balance of the teams was disrupted; we had always had four-two-man teams out and two men guarding the ship, but now the breakdown was three two-man outfits and three men back at ship.

Chung and I set out on a parallel track to fine-comb the area, and Lazenby and Bartlett roamed out somewhere near us. The forest was so thick there was no way of seeing anyone nearby.

Chung devoted most of his time to rocks and ridges, while I, feeling a little lost without Lazenby, bluffed my way through an ecology tour. Luckily, Chung didn't say much, and I wasn't forced to reveal just how ignorant of my specialty I really was.

We were gone about half an hour when I heard a very human yell echo from the left.

Chung was bent over, studying a quartz outcropping. I said, "You hear that?"

"Sorry, no. Some animal?"

"Animal hell! That sounded like Lazenby, and I'll bet he's in trouble!"

As if to punctuate my mark with an exclamation point, another yell came from the adjoining glade.

"Come on," I said. "Let's see what's going on."

WE cut our way blindly through the infuriatingly thick overhang of vines, slashing madly in the direction of the noise. I yelled, "Lazenby! Bartlett! Is there any trouble?"

After a moment Bartlett's voice, quite close, said, "No, no trouble at all."

I hesitated—but then I saw Bartlett dimly veiled by close-packed fern fronds, and decided to see what was up anyway. I stepped through the ferns, followed by Chung.

Bartlett stood there, looking down at the ground. At Lazenby.

The little biologist was lying sprawled grotesquely on his stomach, rigid, corpselike. I felt chilled. That Lazenby, who of all of us had the most vivid interest in searching the forest for its secrets, should meet death this way—

"What happened?" I asked.

Bartlett was very pale. The anthropologist said, "I didn't know. Something sprang at him from the tree up there, and he fell over. I couldn't see what it was."

There was a moment of silence. Then I went white as the "corpse" wriggled, painfully flopped over, and stared at us. I could see the knife wound in his chest.

"That's a lie," Lazenby said in a half-whisper. "It wasn't any animal. Bartlett knifed me…the way he did the Vellirani native…because I was going to tell you…"

He slumped, caught at his middle, tensed. His face was a mask of agony. I looked up from him to Bartlett, and now I saw the bloody knife clutched in the anthropologist's powerful hand.

"You had to be nearby?" Bartlett asked bitterly. "You had to get here before he died? You had to hear everything?"

I saw Chung backing away, frightened. "What is this, Bartlett?" I asked in a voice I didn't recognize.

"I killed him. Sure, I killed him. Like I killed a blueskin on Velliran."

"Why?"

"I didn't mean to. Never meant to. The native wouldn't answer questions; threatened to report me for unethical practices. Lazenby...gave me a drug. I used it on you. It stepped your time-perception; I killed the native, put the knife in your hand, left you standing there."

My mouth sagged open. I heard the chittering of the million insects on the forest floor. "You—"

"Me. It didn't have to be you. It could have been anyone; it just happened to be you that came along. And then I saw you join the crew as Markham. Why did it have to be *you?"*

So Bartlett had killed the Vellirani, and planted the weapon on a total stranger—me. Only I had followed him to World Seven. That was the "funny story" Lazenby had enigmatically promised to tell me, someday...and now, never would.

I stared at Bartlett across Lazenby's stiffening body. And then Bartlett leaped.

The knife went high, but my hands were quick. I slapped his wrist, deflecting the aim outward, and clamped my other hand down before he could compensate. I twisted; tire knife fell.

"Get help, Chung! He's out of his mind!" I managed to yell. Bartlett, weaponless, pummeled me back against a tree. I caught a freezing glimpse of some forest creature crawling out to feed on Lazenby's body. I blocked Bartlett's fists as well as I could, landed a cross to the chin, followed up my advantage with a heavy smash to his stomach.

He reeled back, stunned. I hit him again. I wanted to knock him out, to bring him back to the ship, and eventually back to Velliran to clear my name. But it wasn't going to be that way.

He staggered, off balance. I landed another blow and he took three awkward wide falling steps backward—

And the ground gave way.

He sank down with a little terrified gasp, and I saw something yellow and slimy in the ground, and fifty shiny transparent tentacles twine up and wrap around him. Within seconds he was below the surface, and out of sight. The yellow liquid swirled satedly, and then the trap began to close over again.

I stood staring at it, feeling sick. The trap was simple: the fluid at the surface congealed, forming a sticky, fragile surface to which leaves would adhere, creating a seemingly innocent patch of ground that gave way when a foot touched it. And then…it fed.

I shuddered and turned away. Chasing a small striped feeder from Lazenby's body, I shouldered the corpse and sadly made my way back to the ship to announce that World Seven had claimed two more human victims.

AS I drew near the ship, I heard a strange sound: the high sucking whine of a blaster being fired. I moved faster, despite the burden on my back.

Then I stepped into the clearing, and saw the ship. Chung lay dead some twenty yards from the ship's elevator, a blaster-hole where his chest should be. A little closer to the ship was Dorwin, his face a crust of ash. The sound of shouting, struggles came from the ship.

Somehow my mind found time to tally the score as I ran toward the ship. Five members of the team were dead; I, the sixth, was out here. That left Hendrin, inside, holding off Fernandez, Evans, and Murray. *Damn* this world anyway, I thought.

I looked up. The hatch opened, and someone tumbled down. Murray. A second later Fernandez' head poked out. "Markham! Where's Bartlett?"

"Dead. What's going on?"

"We sprang the mutiny on Hendrin, but he's holed up in the front now with a blaster. Just Evans and me left inside. You have a gun?"

"Yes," I said.

"Come on up here. But be careful."

I heard a blaster-shot, and Evans came staggering out to fall almost at my feet. That made seven corpses for World Seven, I thought. Nice and neat.

I edged my way toward the fore cabin. The sound of struggle reached me: a fistfight, k seemed like. But I wasn't going to risk anything foolishly. I clung to the cold metal skin of the wall, and went forward step by step.

Then I saw them in the cabin—Hendrin and Fernandez, looking like two wild men, slugging it out with bare fists. Hendrin's blaster lay discarded, on the floor; out of charge most likely. Fernandez turned his head a second and yelled, "Markham! He's unarmed! Help me!"

Hendrin's captain's uniform hung in tatters. I crept around behind him, snaked an arm around his throat, and yanked back. I bolstered my blaster and pinioned him with my other arm.

"Hold still, Captain," I said warningly. "I've got a blaster here."

Hendrin held still. But suddenly, before I knew what was happening, Fernandez grabbed the blaster from my hip and felled Hendrin with a single shot. I let the Captain's body drop, jumped forward, and clamped Fernandez' wrist.

But I didn't need to. The gun dropped of its own accord, and Fernandez stood there, a giant of a man, brooding foolishly like a small boy over Hendrin's body.

I picked up the gun. "Why'd you kill him? He was under control. Why'd you kill him, Fernandez?"

He looked into my face, and I saw sheer horror in his eyes. "I don't know'," he said quietly. "I...was out of my head. It's all over now." He was shaking convulsively. He found a seat and took it, head in his hands.

"They're all dead," I said. "Every last one but you and me. Some expedition."

Fernandez was sobbing. It hurts to see a man his size sob. He said, "I'm supposed to be a healer, a curer...and I killed him. I didn't need to. I just killed him."

"You couldn't help it. There was killing in the air. This World could drive anybody crazy."

We worked for four hours straight, and when we got through seven more graves were ranged alongside Grover's. The jungle trumpeted defiant noises at us as we worked.

When it was done, Fernandez looked up at me, an ironic smile on his heavy face. "Well, it's done with now. We know all we need to know about World Seven of Star System A. We can go back now. I'll pilot the ship. But—"

"But what?"

"We're forgetting one thing…according to regulations, the last thing an Exploration Team's supposed to do before it winds up a tour is to name the planet. We haven't done that."

I looked at the jungle—the pestilent steaming hothouse of a jungle—and down at the eight graves. "That's easy," I said. "We'll call it *Death's Planet.*"

THE END

The Assassin

Bigelow had a grand idea; he would travel more than a hundred years through time to Ford's Theater, see the President, and warn him about his own impending death...

THE TIME WAS DRAWING near, Walter Bigelow thought. Just a few more adjustments and his great ambition would be fulfilled.

He stepped back from the Time Distorter and studied the complex network of wires and tubes with an expert's practiced eye. TWENTY YEARS, he thought. Twenty years of working and scrimping, of pouring money into the machine that stood before him on the workbench. Twenty years, to save Abraham Lincoln's life.

And now he was almost ready.

Bigelow had conceived his grand idea when still young, newly out of college. He had stumbled across a volume of history and had read of Abraham Lincoln and his struggle to save the Union.

Bigelow was a tall, spare, rawboned man standing better than six feet four—and with a shock he discovered that he bore an amazing resemblance to a young portrait of the Great Emancipator. That was when his identification with Lincoln began.

He read every Lincoln biography he could find, steeped himself in log-cabin legends and the texts of the Lincoln-Douglas debates. And, gradually, he became consumed with bitterness because an assassin's hand had struck Lincoln down at the height of his triumph.

"Damned shame, great man like that," he mumbled into his beer one night in a bar. ""What's that?" a sallow man at his left asked. "Someone die?"

"Yes," Bigelow said. "I'm talking about Lincoln. Damned shame."

The other chuckled. "Better get yourself a new newspaper, pal. Lincoln's been dead for a century. Still mourning?"

Bigelow turned, his gaunt face alive with anger. "Yes! Yes—why shouldn't I mourn? A great man like Lincoln—"

"Sure, sure," the other said placatingly. "I'll buy that. He was a great president, chum—but he's been dead for a hundred years. One hundred. You can't bring him back to life, you know."

"Maybe I can," Bigelow said suddenly—and the great idea was born.

It took eight years of physics and math before Bigelow had developed a workable time-travel theory. Seven more years passed before the first working model stood complete.

He tested it by stepping within its field, allowing himself to be cast back ten years. A few well-placed bets, and he had enough cash to continue. Ten years was not enough. Lincoln had been assassinated in 1865—Friday, April 14, 1865. Bigelow needed a machine that could move at least one hundred twenty years into the past.

It took time. Five more years.

He reached out, adjusted a capacitor, pinched off an unnecessary length of copper wire. It was ready. After twenty years, he was ready at last.

BIGELOW TOOK THE MORNING bus to Washington, D.C. The Time Distorter would not affect space, and it was much more efficient to make the journey from Chicago to Washington in 1979 by monobus in a little over an hour, than in 1865 by mule cart or some other such conveyance, possibly taking a day. Now that he was so close to success, he was too impatient to allow any such delay as that.

The Time Distorter was cradled in a small black box on his lap; he spent the hour of the bus ride listening to its gentle humming and ticking, letting the sound soothe him and ease his nervousness.

There was really no need to be nervous, he thought. Even if he failed in his first attempt at blocking Lincoln's assassination, he had an infinity of time to keep trying again.

He could return to his own time and make the jump again, over and over. There were a hundred different ways he could use to prevent Lincoln from entering the fatal theater on the night of April 14. A sudden phone call—no, there were no telephones yet.

A message of some kind. He could burn down the theater the morning of the play. He could find John Wilkes Booth and kill him before he could make his fateful speech of defiance and fire the fatal bullet. He could—

Well, it didn't matter. He was going to succeed the first time. Lincoln was a man of sense; he wouldn't willingly go to his death having been warned.

A warm glow of pleasure spread over Bigelow as he dreamed of the consequences of his act. Lincoln alive, going on to complete his second term, President until 1869. The weak, ineffectual Andrew Johnson would remain Vice-President, where he belonged. The South would be rebuilt sanely and welcomed back into the Union; there would be no era of carpetbaggers, no series of governmental scandals, and no dreary Reconstruction era.

"Washington!"

Moving almost in a dream, Bigelow left the bus and stepped out into the crowded capitol streets. It was a warm summer day; soon, he thought, it would be a coolish April evening, back in 1865…

He headed for the poor part of town, away from the fine white buildings and gleaming domes. Huddling in a dark alley on the south side, he undid the fastenings of the box that covered the Time Distorter.

He glanced around, saw that no one was near. Then, swiftly, he depressed the lever. THE WORLD SWIRLED around him, vanished. Then, suddenly, it took shape again.

He was in an open field now; the morning air was cool but pleasant, and in the distance he could see a few of the buildings that made the nation's capitol famous. There was no Lincoln Memorial, of course, and the bright needle of Washington's Monument did not thrust upward into the sky. But the familiar Capitol dome looked much as it always had, and he could make out the White House further away.

Bigelow refastened the cover of the Distorter and tucked the box under his arm. It clicked quietly, reminding him over and over again of the fact that he was in the year 1865—the morning of the day John Wilkes Booth put a bullet through the brain of Abraham Lincoln.

Time passed slowly for Bigelow. He made his way toward the center of town and spent the day in downtown Washington, hungrily drinking in the gossip. Abe Lincoln's name was on everyone's tongue.

The dread War had ended just five days before with Lee's surrender at Appomattox. Lincoln was in his hour of triumph. It was Friday. The people were still discussing the speech he had made the Tuesday before.

"He said he's going to make an announcement," someone said. "Abe's going to tell the Southerners what kind of program he's going to put into effect for them."

"Wonder what's on his mind?" someone else asked. "No matter what it is, I'll bet he makes the South like what he says."

He had never delivered that speech, Bigelow thought. And the South had been doomed to a generation of hardship and exploitation by the victorious North that had left unhealing scars.

The day passed. President Lincoln was to attend the Ford Theatre that night, to see a production of a play called "Our American Cousin."

Bigelow knew what the history books said. Lincoln had had an apprehensive dream the night before: he was sailing on a ship of a peculiar build, being borne on it with great speed toward a dark and undefined shore. Like Caesar on the Ides of March, he had been warned—and, like Caesar, he would go unheeding to his death.

But Bigelow would see that that never happened.

History recorded that Lincoln attended the performance, that he seemed to be enjoying the play. And that shortly after ten that evening, a wild-eyed man would enter Lincoln's box, fire once, and leap to the stage, shouting, "Sic semper tyrannis!"

The man would be the crazed actor John Wilkes Booth. He would snag a spur in the drapery as he dropped to the stage, and would break his leg—but nevertheless he would vanish into the wings, make his way through the theater he knew so well, mount a horse waiting at the stage door. Some days later he would be dead.

As for President Lincoln, he would slump forward in his box. The audience would be too stunned to move for a moment—but there was nothing that could be done. Lincoln would die the next morning without recovering consciousness.

"Now he belongs to the ages," Secretary of State Stanton would say.

No! Bigelow thought. It would not happen. It would not happen…

EVENING APPROACHED. Bigelow, crouching in an alley across the street from the theater, watched the carriages arriving for the performance that night. Feeling oddly out of place in his twentieth-century clothing, he watched the finely dressed ladies and gentlemen descending from their coaches. Everyone in Washington knew the President would be at the theater that night, and they were determined to look their best.

Bigelow waited. Finally, a handsome carriage appeared, and several others made way for it. He tensed, knowing who was within.

A woman of regal bearing descended first—Mary Todd Lincoln, the President's wife. And then Lincoln appeared.

For some reason, the President paused at the street-corner and looked around. His eyes came to rest on the dark alley where Bigelow crouched invisibly, and Bigelow stared at the face he knew almost as well as his own: the graying beard, the tired, old, wrinkled face, the weary eyes of Abe Lincoln. Then he rose and began to run. "Mr. President! Mr. President!"

He realized he must have been an outlandish figure, dashing across the street in his strange costume with the Time Distorter clutched under one arm. He drew close to Lincoln.

"Sir, don't go to the theater tonight! If you do—"

A hand suddenly wrapped itself ell around his mouth. President Lincoln smiled pityingly and turned away, walking on down the street toward the theater. Other hands seized Bigelow, dragged him away. Blue-clad arms. Union soldiers. The President's bodyguard.

"You don't understand!" Bigelow yelled. He bit at the hand that held him, and got a fierce kick in return. "Let go of me! Let go!"

Ford's Theater

There were four of them, earnest looking as they went about their duties. They held Bigelow, pummeled him angrily. One of them reached down for the Distorter.

In terror, Bigelow saw that his attempt to save Lincoln had been a complete failure, that he would have to return to his own time and try all over again. He attempted to switch on the Distorter, but before he could open the cover, rough hands had pulled it from him.

"Give me that!" He fought frantically, but they held him. One of the men in blue uniforms took the Distorter, looked at it curiously, finally held it up to his ear.

His eyes widened. "It's ticking! It's a bomb!"

"No!" Bigelow shouted, and then watched in utter horror as the soldier, holding the Distorter at arm's length, ran across the street and hurled the supposed bomb as far up the alley as he could possibly throw it.

There was no explosion—only the sound of delicate machinery shattering.

Bigelow watched numbly as the four men seized his arms again.

"Throw a bomb, will you? Come on, fellow—we'll show you what happens to guys who want to assassinate President Lincoln!"

Further down the street, the gaunt figure of Abe Lincoln was just entering the theater. No one gave Bigelow a chance to explain.

THE END

If you've enjoyed this book, you will not want to miss these terrific titles...

ARMCHAIR SCI-FI & HORROR DOUBLE NOVELS, $12.95 each

D-211 **PLANET OF EXILE** by Edmond Hamilton
BRAIN TWISTER by Randall Garrett & Laurence M. Janifer

D-212 **LORELEI OF THE RED MIST** by L. Brackett & Ray Bradbury
GOLD IN THE SKY by Alan E. Nourse

D-213 **NEXT DOOR TO THE SUN** by Stanton A. Coblentz
MARTIAN NIGHTMARE by Bryce Walton

D-214 **THE OSILANS** by Arthur J. Burks
THE METAL MONSTER by E. K. Jarvis

D-215 **LIFE EVERLASTING** by David H. Keller, M. D.
FOREVER WE DIE by Milton Lesser

D-216 **SECRET OF THE FLAMING RING** by Rog Phillips
THE SECRET MARTIANS by Jack Sharkey

D-217 **THE CRUCTARS ARE COMING** by Paul Lawrence Payne
MADE TO ORDER by Frank Belknap Long

D-218 **SEVEN FROM THE STARS** by Marion Zimmer Bradley
THE GIRL WHO READ MINDS by Robert Moore Williams

D-219 **DAWN TO DUSK** by Eando Binder
THE BEAST-MEN OF CERES by Aladra Septama

D-220 **THE TERRIBLE PUPPETS** by Paul W. Fairman
THE COSMIC GEOIDS by John Taine

ARMCHAIR MASTERS OF SCIENCE FICTION SERIES, $16.95 each

M-11 **MASTERS OF SCIENCE FICTION, Vol. Eleven**
Robert Silverberg: The Ace Years, Part One

M-12 **MASTERS OF SCIENCE FICTION, Vol. Twelve**
Robert Silverberg: The Ace Years, Part Two

ARMCHAIR MYSTERY-CRIME DOUBLE NOVELS, $12.95 each

B-41 **LAUGHTER CAME SCREAMING** by Henry Kane
THE EXTORTIONERS by Ovid Demaris

B-42 **THEY ALL RAN AWAY** by Edward Ronns
BACKFIRE by Floyd Mahannah

B-43 **BLOOD OF MY BROTHER** by Stephen Marlowe
THE GUILTY BYSTANDER by Mike Brett

B-44 **MURDER WITHOUT TEARS** by Leonard Lupton
NO WAY OUT by Milton K. Ozaki

If you've enjoyed this book, you will not want to miss these terrific titles...

ARMCHAIR SCI-FI & HORROR DOUBLE NOVELS, $12.95 each

D-21 **EMPIRE OF EVIL** by Robert Arnette
THE SIGN OF THE TIGER by Alan E. Nourse & J. A. Meyer

D-22 **OPERATION SQUARE PEG** by Frank Belknap Long
ENCHANTRESS OF VENUS by Leigh Brackett

D-23 **THE LIFE WATCH** by Lester del Rey
CREATURES OF THE ABYSS by Murray Leinster

D-24 **LEGION OF LAZARUS** by Edmond Hamilton
STAR HUNTER by Andre Norton

D-25 **EMPIRE OF WOMEN** by John Fletcher
ONE OF OUR CITIES IS MISSING by Irving Cox

D-26 **THE WRONG SIDE OF PARADISE** by Raymond F. Jones
THE INVOLUNTARY IMMORTALS by Rog Phillips

D-27 **EARTH QUARTER** by Damon Knight
ENVOY TO NEW WORLDS by Keith Laumer

D-28 **SLAVES TO THE METAL HORDE** by Milton Lesser
HUNTERS OUT OF TIME by Joseph E. Kelleam

D-29 **RX JUPITER SAVE US** by Ward Moore
BEWARE THE USURPERS by Geoff St. Reynard

D-30 **SECRET OF THE SERPENT** by Don Wilcox
CRUSADE ACROSS THE VOID by Dwight V. Swain

ARMCHAIR SCIENCE FICTION CLASSICS, $12.95 each

C-7 **THE SHAVER MYSTERY, Book One**
by Richard S. Shaver

C-8 **THE SHAVER MYSTERY, Book Two**
by Richard S. Shaver

C-9 **MURDER IN SPACE** by David V. Reed
by David V. Reed

ARMCHAIR MASTERS OF SCIENCE FICTION SERIES, $16.95 each

M-3 **MASTERS OF SCIENCE FICTION, Vol. Three**
Robert Sheckley, "The Perfect Woman" and other tales

M-4 **MASTERS OF SCIENCE FICTION, Vol. Four**
Mack Reynolds, "Stowaway" and other tales

If you've enjoyed this book, you will not want to miss these terrific titles...

ARMCHAIR SCI-FI & HORROR DOUBLE NOVELS, $12.95 each

D-11 **PERIL OF THE STARMEN** by Kris Neville
THE STRANGE INVASION by Murray Leinster

D-12 **THE STAR LORD** by Boyd Ellanby
CAPTIVES OF THE FLAME by Samuel R. Delany

D-13 **MEN OF THE MORNING STAR** by Edmond Hamilton
PLANET FOR PLUNDER by Hal Clement and Sam Merwin, Jr.

D-14 **ICE CITY OF THE GORGON** by Chester S. Geier and Richard Shaver
WHEN THE WORLD TOTTERED by Lester del Rey

D-15 **WORLDS WITHOUT END** by Clifford D. Simak
THE LAVENDER VINE OF DEATH by Don Wilcox

D-16 **SHADOW ON THE MOON** by Joe Gibson
ARMAGEDDON EARTH by Geoff St. Reynard

D-17 **THE GIRL WHO LOVED DEATH** by Paul W. Fairman
SLAVE PLANET by Laurence M. Janifer

D-18 **SECOND CHANCE** by J. F. Bone
MISSION TO A DISTANT STAR by Frank Belknap Long

D-19 **THE SYNDIC** by C. M. Kornbluth
FLIGHT TO FOREVER by Poul Anderson

D-20 **SOMEWHERE I'LL FIND YOU** by Milton Lesser
THE TIME ARMADA by Fox B. Holden

ARMCHAIR SCIENCE FICTION CLASSICS, $12.95 each

C-4 **CORPUS EARTHLING**
by Louis Charbonneau

C-5 **THE TIME DISSOLVER**
by Jerry Sohl

C-6 **WEST OF THE SUN**
by Edgar Pangborn

ARMCHAIR SCI-FI & HORROR GEMS SERIES, $12.95 each

G-1 **SCIENCE FICTION GEMS, Vol. One**
Isaac Asimov and others

G-2 **HORROR GEMS, Vol. One**
Carl Jacobi and others

If you've enjoyed this book, you will not want to miss these terrific titles...

ARMCHAIR SCI-FI & HORROR DOUBLE NOVELS, **$12.95 each**

D-1 **THE GALAXY RAIDERS** by William P. McGivern
SPACE STATION #1 by Frank Belknap Long

D-2 **THE PROGRAMMED PEOPLE** by Jack Sharkey
SLAVES OF THE CRYSTAL BRAIN by William Carter Sawtelle

D-3 **YOU'RE ALL ALONE** by Fritz Leiber
THE LIQUID MAN by Bernard C. Gilford

D-4 **CITADEL OF THE STAR LORDS** by Edmond Hamilton
VOYAGE TO ETERNITY by Milton Lesser

D-5 **IRON MEN OF VENUS** by Don Wilcox
THE MAN WITH ABSOLUTE MOTION by Noel Loomis

D-6 **WHO SOWS THE WIND...** by Rog Phillips
THE PUZZLE PLANET by Robert A. W. Lowndes

D-7 **PLANET OF DREAD** by Murray Leinster
TWICE UPON A TIME by Charles L. Fontenay

D-8 **THE TERROR OUT OF SPACE** by Dwight V. Swain
QUEST OF THE GOLDEN APE by Ivar Jorgensen and Adam Chase

D-9 **SECRET OF MARRACOTT DEEP** by Henry Slesar
PAWN OF THE BLACK FLEET by Mark Clifton.

D-10 **BEYOND THE RINGS OF SATURN** by Robert Moore Williams
A MAN OBSESSED by Alan E. Nourse

ARMCHAIR SCIENCE FICTION CLASSICS, **$12.95 each**

C-1 **THE GREEN MAN**
by Harold M. Sherman

C-2 **A TRACE OF MEMORY**
By Keith Laumer

C-3 **INTO PLUTONIAN DEPTHS**
by Stanton A. Coblentz

ARMCHAIR MASTERS OF SCIENCE FICTION SERIES, **$16.95 each**

M-1 **MASTERS OF SCIENCE FICTION, Vol. One**
Bryce Walton—"Dark of the Moon" and other tales

M-2 **MASTERS OF SCIENCE FICTION, Vol. Two**
Jerome Bixby—"One Way Street" and other tales

If you've enjoyed this book, you will not want to miss these terrific titles...

ARMCHAIR SCI-FI & HORROR DOUBLE NOVELS, $12.95 each

D-31 **A HOAX IN TIME** by Keith Laumer
INSIDE EARTH by Poul Anderson

D-32 **TERROR STATION** by Dwight V. Swain
THE WEAPON FROM ETERNITY by Dwight V. Swain

D-33 **THE SHIP FROM INFINITY** by Edmond Hamilton
TAKEOFF by C. M. Kornbluth

D-34 **THE METAL DOOM** by David H. Keller
TWELVE TIMES ZERO by Howard Browne

D-35 **HUNTERS OUT OF SPACE** by Joseph Kelleam
INVASION FROM THE DEEP by Paul W. Fairman,

D-36 **THE BEES OF DEATH** by Robert Moore Williams
A PLAGUE OF PYTHONS by Frederik Pohl

D-37 **THE LORDS OF QUARMALL** by Fritz Leiber and Harry Fischer
BEACON TO ELSEWHERE by James H. Schmitz

D-38 **BEYOND PLUTO** by John S. Campbell
ARTERY OF FIRE by Thomas N. Scortia

D-39 **SPECIAL DELIVERY** by Kris Neville
NO TIME FOR TOFFEE by Charles F. Meyers

D-40 **RECALLED TO LIFE** by Robert Silverberg
JUNGLE IN THE SKY by Milton Lesser

ARMCHAIR SCIENCE FICTION CLASSICS, $12.95 each

C-10 **MARS IS MY DESTINATION**
by Frank Belknap Long

C-11 **SPACE PLAGUE**
by George O. Smith

C-12 **SO SHALL YE REAP**
by Rog Phillips

ARMCHAIR SCI-FI & HORROR GEMS SERIES, $12.95 each

G-3 **SCIENCE FICTION GEMS, Vol. Two**
James Blish and others

G-4 **HORROR GEMS, Vol. Two**
Joseph Payne Brennan and others

Made in the USA
Middletown, DE
21 January 2023